OMEGA
THE 11TH PERCENT
BOOK SEVEN

T. H. MORRIS

Simply put, this book is dedicated to everyone who has stuck by me, every step of the way. You know who you are. So many people faded away, fell by the wayside, and ultimately disappeared. But you select few remained by me, stalwart and steadfast, for every hardship, snag, and speed bump. I love you all with everything in me and do not have the capacity to illustrate the enormity of my gratitude. Thank you all hundredfold.

COUNTDOWN TO OMEGA

Ω

1
NIGHT REUNIONS

Glenn Hansen had been chronically homeless for more years than even he could count by now. He had, for the past several months, found refuge on a park bench off Wallace Avenue. He loved it there. The park itself was open from dawn until half past eight at night. During that time, his unsightly, disheveled appearance was problematic for the joggers, walkers, photographers, and whoever else dared to intrude on his own personal kingdom. And this was indeed his kingdom. The trees were his palace. The public bathroom was his relaxing chambers. And the central bench had the dual role of his bed and throne.

He tolerated the spectators and tourists at his palace during these hours, though. Because he barely saw them. The daytime was when he went to "work". If he exhibited enough cleverness and was careful, most days brought about some form of success or pleasure. Sometimes people were especially stingy, and his routine had to be sharp as a knife and done to perfection. Other days, charity was like the tide; he just had to find the right place and time and wait for it to come in. He would bring back the spoils of every victory each evening, when his "kingdom" was quiet, and his throne waited. He could get a good night's sleep, and look forward to the next morning, which always brought about new challenges.

And this night was no different.

In his travels, Glenn had rummaged a pair of pants, scrounged enough scraps for a nice couple meals, and had even guilt-tripped a couple into sparing him ten dollars. Luck was in his favor like that sometimes.

He returned to the park pretty late that night; the watch he'd scrounged months ago never kept good time. If he had to guess, it was probably a quarter to nine in the evening. His kingdom was his own once more.

He was truly thankful that the other vagrants didn't hang out here. They avoided the place like the plague because the occasional police officer would come around every so often to enforce closing time. They were imbeciles. The cops were easy enough to elude. One just couldn't be stupid enough to come into the park by the front entrance. The woods around the park weren't deep, but they were dense enough to avoid lazy police officers whose sweeps were only halfhearted at best.

He had just emerged from his route through the woods, having cunningly hidden his new stash of goods in a secret location. His mound of cardboard that served as his pillow was under his arm, and he was already putting his mind towards the next day's adventures as he neared his central bench—

And discovered that it was already occupied.

A thin trickle of fury ran through his body. What in hell was this shit? He'd picked this place for the *lack* of after-hours company. Now someone was on his bench.

This had been a good day. He had had fun.

And now it was marred by the presence of this trespasser.

He approached them, trying to keep his annoyance at bay. All he had to do was get close enough. This time of night, a questionable figure such as himself was bound to scare off anybody.

He was ten feet away. The person hadn't moved. Five feet, the same. Three feet ... this just had to be the moment when they would get up and hurry off.

But it still didn't happen. The person hadn't even flinched.

"Ahem."

Silence.

Now Glenn was pissed off. This bastard needed to go! He needed to sleep! There was a busy day ahead!

"Um, this park is closed," he said clearly, adding just a bit of gruffness to his tone, which he hoped would aid in scaring the person off already.

But, to his surprise, the occupant still hadn't moved. They did, however, speak for the first time.

"If that is the case, then why are you here?"

Glenn's droopy eyes widened. It was a woman! What was she doing out here alone at this time of night? "Uh, little lady, you have no business here at this hour," he said, just a little alarmed. "You are very lucky right now—for all you knew, I could have been some miscreant predator—"

"At this point, I don't give a shit," murmured the woman. "I couldn't give less of one if I tried."

There was sadness in the woman's voice. Glenn rolled his eyes. He did not need this right now. He had to sleep! He wasn't interested in what was wrong with her. Either she'd been wronged, had a falling out with parents, experienced a job loss, or had gotten knocked up. He hadn't had a job himself since he didn't even know when, and *he* wasn't crying.

But if it meant that he could get her off his bench so that he could sleep ...

"What's bothering you?" he questioned reluctantly.

"There was a death," answered the woman in a miserable tone.

Glenn deflated. Oh. This lady had experienced somebody dying, and she must have been particularly bad off to brave a dark park after hours. That could have been why she was on the bench in the first place. She'd probably wound up here after aimless wandering and decided to rest her weary feet.

Now he actually felt a little ruffled. A little uncomfortable.

He had half a mind to give her his newly acquired ten dollars.

Half a mind.

"Who?" he decided to ask. "Who died?"

The woman mumbled, but it was too low for Glenn to hear. "Sorry?"

The woman muttered something again, but it was still barely audible. Glenn had to move in closer, so that he was mere inches away from the depressed woman.

"You're gonna have to forgive me, lady, but I still didn't hear you. Now, who died?"

The woman finally lifted her head to face him. "I said, *you.*"

So quickly that it could have been imagined, she slit a razor blade across his throat.

Glenn cried out, feeling his eyes bulge as he instantly grabbed his neck. It almost seemed as though he thought that by covering the wound, he could keep his life and blood within. But the woman rose swiftly to her feet, grabbed the back of his neck to prevent him from collapsing too soon, and shoved a small bottle near the deep laceration she'd made. She made a noise of derision as he gurgled and choked.

"Will you fuckin' die already?" she demanded as Glenn kept up his struggle, though it was much feebler by this point. "I don't have all night!"

With a final anguished gasp, Glenn struggled no more.

The woman continued to collect his blood in the bottle for a little while longer, until the amount was substantial. Then she shoved the limp body away from herself.

She gave the area around the deadfall a quick scan. Satisfied that her actions hadn't had an audience, she turned and began to walk down the path that led away from the bench. After fifteen deliberate steps, she abruptly turned left and began walking in the grass. Ten steps later, she turned right. If someone had seen her, they might have thought that she did this every single day. But that wasn't the case.

Before today, this woman hadn't ever been in this park.

All the while she walked, she'd been casting off the drab, flat, dark clothing that made up her disguise, revealing her true outfit of a burgundy halter top and skin-tight black jeans. A nonchalant, lazy yank at the wig on her head, and the listless brown hair gave way to long, strawberry blonde locks.

There was no more character now. The woman was once again her true self.

She stopped at a seemingly insignificant spot of land, tapped her throat with two fingers, and uttered, *"Per mortem, vitam."*

Suddenly, the previously near-empty park was much more active. People stepped out of thin air, holding twigs in their hands, and in other locations, crows bulleted down from the night sky, shapeshifting in the air and landing on their feet with grace that illustrated they'd done it hundreds of times before.

Even though all this activity occurred all around the woman, she barely paid attention to any of it. She seemed quite bored as she lit a Camel cigarette.

One of the figures who'd just mutated from avian form approached her, moving at a curious saunter.

"This is the place?" He didn't even bother to hide his skepticism.

The woman drew from her cigarette. "Yes."

The man raised an eyebrow, still skeptical. "In a very public park?"

"Where would you rather it be, Sam?" the woman demanded. "In the middle of Neiman Marcus?"

There were a few snickers, but Sam's eyes narrowed.

"I have a valid reason to be iffy about you, Hale. Let's face it...your claim to fame ain't been, well, fame-worthy as of late. I ain't the only one who thinks so. Is it true that an Ungifted librarian broke through your C.P.V.?"

The question elicited some more snickers. Jessica Hale lowered her cigarette and smiled sweetly.

"Sam?" Her tone was as sweet as her smile. "Come here."

Just that quickly, there was a subtle change in her voice. Sam, who'd been laughing before, suddenly desisted. His eyes widened as he approached where Jessica stood.

"Take this cigarette," she said in that same deliberate voice, "and bring the filter end to the side of your face."

With a look of fury, Sam took it from her and did as she ordered. There was a hiss of air, and he growled in pain. Jessica then kneed him in the groin and head-butted him full on in the face. He fell to the ground, clutching his shattered nose. Jessica then gave the onlookers a scathing glance.

"He just said that he's not the only one who thinks I've lost my touch. Who else has been talking about me as opposed to talking *to* me?"

Sam was on his feet in seconds, bloodied and minutely singed, but not incapacitated. "You bitch—"

"That is enough."

The wintry voice sliced cleanly through the tension, silencing everyone present. They only had eyes for the tall man who had just appeared in their midst, having neither dropped a twig nor reformed from an animal shape.

His pale face stood out against the evening, but the dark eyes contrasted starkly with the brightness of the moon. In the time since he had returned from the grave, his hair had grown out and a beard had begun to form. Although it was a summer evening and not the slightest bit cool, he wore a bluish-black trench coat.

Creyton's mere presence would have brought about silence, but his voice made the fact that much more certain.

"You are a lady, Inimicus," he murmured to Jessica. "Show some class."

Jessica lowered her head. "Yes, Transcendent."

"And Samuel," Creyton slowly turned to face him, "if it is dissension that you desire, by all means, begone from here and go join the unworthy. Or set up shop with Laban Cooper. Of course, you'd never make it that far, but if it's what you want—"

"No, Transcendent!" cried Sam, who looked appalled and terrified at both options. "I was only saying that Hale over here ain't really been up to snuff—"

"That's your assessment?" interrupted Creyton. "Do you speak for all your fellows? You believe that you can watch over the Deadfallen disciples? If you could, then I wouldn't be here, would I?"

"No, Transcendent." Sam's eyes bulged when he realized what he said. "I mean—I mean, well, I didn't mean that! It's just—"

"Shut up and stand there." Creyton turned back to Jessica. "Is this the place, Inimicus?"

"Yes, Transcendent." Jessica shot a filthy glance at Sam. "Nature is simple enough to control. It just took a bit of ethereality to function as a sort of jammer. Rivers was a fool to think that his auditory trick couldn't be countered."

"Well, think about his daddy," muttered someone among the Deadfallen disciples. "Seems like the apple fell right next to the tree on that one!"

There was a smattering of agreement. Creyton paid it no mind. His eyes remained on Jessica.

"Are you sure that it's enough in the bottle?"

"I am," said Jessica readily. "It's weak, and from an Ungifted bum. But even that is far more than he deserves."

"Very well." Creyton stepped back. "Proceed. Jerome, help her."

Another Deadfallen disciple stepped forward, holding some sort of short sword. He cut a deep, jagged groove in the earth at Jessica's feet. When he was done, he nodded and backed away. Jessica knelt and poured the blood she'd just collected along the groove.

"Listen, conform, accede," murmured the former spy as she poured the blood, that subtle thing in her voice again. "You are at my will, like the spirits chained and subjugated in this blood. Listen ..."

After several seconds, the trail of blood glowed and then turned very dark, taking on the composition of sludge. It was as though something vital had freed itself from the red mass and continued to permeate the ground. Seconds afterward the groove began to expand. What was once Jerome's jagged line became even more misshapen and elongated as the earth around it boiled and broke. Then a filthy, rank figure sprang from the earth, open-mouthed and emitting harsh, ragged gasps. Dirt fell in large clumps from his hair and clothing, but he gave it no notice as he doubled over in agony.

"The silver," he moaned. "Please ..."

"Broreamir." Creyton's indifference practically dripped from his tone. "Handle it."

The tall, dreadlocked disciple approached the bent figure

with disgust, grabbed the silver needle-like objects protruding from his chest, and yanked them free. With that one action, the figure stood without struggle and looked at Broreamir and Jessica and all the others around him. Every single face was a study in hatred.

The figure ran a filthy hand over his equally filthy face, now recognizing many of the faces around him. He realized the gravity of the situation. He slowly turned and looked into the face of the man he clearly had never expected to see again.

"T—Transcendent," he whispered, his very being alight with terror. "I—I—"

"You what?" A nearby disciple spat on the ground. "Went into business for yourself? Just disregarded all of us by taking the Transcendent's plan and—"

He immediately ceased when he caught sight of Creyton's quelling look. Creyton then turned back to the quaking individual, who at that moment finally managed a coherent sentence.

"Are you here to kill me?"

Creyton took a deliberate breath. "If I wanted to kill you, 49er, then you would be dead."

He walked to the vampire. The 49er was easily 6'9" and outstripped Creyton by several inches. Yet with his every step towards him, the 49er flinched a little more. Cowered a bit more.

"As it so happens, and it is very lucky for you, I once again have use for you. Things need doing, and we could use the set of hands."

The 49er's breathing became slightly less shallow. He stood a bit straighter. "I understand, Transcendent." The subservience in his tone was almost tangible. "Would you be so kind as to tell me what the date is?"

"It's the Season of Omega," replied Creyton. "That's all you need to know."

The vampire's eyes widened. "The Season of...? Then I haven't missed it?"

"Obviously not." Jessica's sneer was only disrupted by her pull from her second cigarette.

"But then ... the Six ..."

"Has come to fruition and is now past," finished Creyton. "Jonathan Grannison is no more."

The 49er allowed himself a smile of delight, which faded in seconds. "How much time have I missed exactly?"

Creyton lifted his eyes to the ceiling of stars. "Enough for my rage to cool enough to see that you might still be useful."

The 49er noted the statement. The small amount of security that had built up inside him took a hit with those words. "Do you need me to reorganize the Haunts, Transcendent? I have no doubt that they've been running amok in my absence—"

"No, they have not," dismissed Creyton. "I've found a much more efficient disciple to corral the Haunts in your absence."

Broreamir, who stood a few feet behind Jessica, gave the 49er a two-fingered salute. The 49er swallowed his envy, knowing full well the thin ice on which he stood mandated no objections to the current status quo.

"Understood, Transcendent. What is it that you want me to do?"

Creyton pocketed his hands. "The current state of things has illustrated a shift to the position they should have been all along. It is laughably ironic, but in an attempt to show strength, Jonathan weakened the entire cause."

"That so?" asked the 49er. "How?"

"When my War Haunt tore his essence to tatters, Jonathan declared Jonah Rowe the Overseer of the Grannison-Morris estate." Creyton's words caused snorts and choking sounds from the crowd. "As a result of his decision, Titus Rivers III incited an insurrection. It is my understanding that a brutal skirmish broke out between Rivers' allies and those of Rowe. Then the two of them engaged in an equally brutal exhibition. The end result? Rivers and his friends abandoned the estate, but not before he gave a rousing monologue that swayed even more people to abandon Rowe right along with him. He played heavily on their fear, uncertainty, and lack of faith in Rowe's ability to lead. That is amusing in itself, because Rowe has yet to fully embrace the role. Right now, he has the unenviable position of a laughingstock playing at power."

The 49er appeared to let that information sink in. The momentary flash of rage that he felt for Trip Rivers and Jonah Rowe faded. He had to arrange his own fate before he could go off sealing the fates of others.

"There is one more thing that you need to know," Creyton went on. "Laban Cooper is currently at large. On the run from both the Curaie and myself. For his sake, he had better hope that the Curaie find him first...at least before they crumble, anyway. Because if I am the one to find him first, he will be lucky to *just* get murdered."

The 49er repressed a shudder. He remembered with perfect clarity how Laban Cooper turned himself into the Curaie and went to The Plane with No Name to escape Creyton's vengeance for his ambition and ulterior motives. There was undoubtedly a moment of jealousy of Laban; being on the run seemed much more appealing than being surrounded by not only the Deadfallen disciples he'd betrayed, but Creyton himself.

Much to the lifeblood looter's relief, Creyton turned his attention to other matters.

"That is all the catching up that you will need. Now that we are all accounted for, the council can begin. Broreamir?"

Broreamir squared his shoulders. "The Curaie feel the ground shrinking under their feet. The Networkers have no days off, and their work has suffered accordingly. Engagah may have been stone-faced at Jonathan's memorial, but the Protector Guide's vanquishing rattled her greatly. The Old Regime views us as a disease that they have taken too long to cure."

"Hmm," mused Charlotte Daynard. "Never been regarded as a disease."

"Don't get comfortable with the label, as it is absurd." There was anger in Creyton's words. "The Curaie are the disease. *We* are the cure." He switched his attention to Jessica. "Inimicus?"

Jessica nodded and took one final pull off her cigarette, her fourth since the beginning of all of this, before she spoke. "Gabriel Kaine is having an even harder time than Rowe, and that's with leadership in his blood. He would love to pool resources with Rowe, but between the disorganization and distrust within his own ranks, he is better off keeping his ass in Florida."

"Spare me your opinions, Inimicus," said Creyton.

"Right, Transcendent," said Jessica hastily. "Apologies. Anyway, the estate has all but become an island. Hope for anything is dwindling, and they are one step away from scattering."

"Stephen?" Creyton turned his attention to a tall, unshaven, awkward-looking bespectacled man.

"Nearly there, Transcendent." Stephen's voice had hint of triumph. "I can have one ready for every Deadfallen disciple in about two weeks, give or take—"

"You have five days," Creyton told him.

Stephen blinked. It looked very comical behind those

glasses, but there was no humor to be felt in the situation. "Pardon me, Transcendent?"

"You heard."

"But, five days ... that's impossible!"

Without warning, Creyton swung his crow-tipped staff at Stephen's head. It flew clean off; the severed body part flew into the darkness, landing with a thud somewhere in the distance. Stephen's body remained erect for a few seconds before it crumpled to the ground. Everyone started at Creyton with fear and alarm. But Creyton's cold eyes stared angrily at the heaped corpse.

"We are Eleventh Percenters." Despite whispering it, everyone caught Creyton's words. "Nothing is impossible."

A black man with an eye patch stepped forward, though not by much. Clearly, he wanted to remain out of range of Creyton's staff. "I can have it done in five days' time, Transcendent. You can count on me."

Creyton's eyes still stared lasers through Stephen's body. "Then get it done, Sean."

"Yes, Transcendent." Sean nodded and returned to his original place.

Creyton then turned his attention to a woman not far from Sean. "It is a pleasure to see you able-bodied and whole, India."

The star-white haired woman smiled. "The skills that you taught me weren't for naught, Transcendent. I am very glad to be here. Being in your presence is the highest honor of my life."

"There is something I require of you." Creyton didn't even acknowledge the groveling.

"Anything, Transcendent."

"It will require you to return to the Plane with No Name," Creyton told her.

India's eyes widened. Then she glanced to the bloody tip of

his staff. "Of...of course, Transcendent." Her voice was quiet. Controlled. "That's not going to be a problem."

"Very good." Creyton smiled as though he were pleased. Or perhaps he was content in the knowledge that India knew the consequences of anything less than her agreement to do it. "You will receive further instructions in due course."

It was at that moment that he returned to addressing the group at large. Before doing so, he removed a black handkerchief and cleaned the blood from the tip of the staff.

"Omega has been mine to control ever since Rowe revealed his eternal weakness."

At those words, Jessica lowered her eyes. Several disciples away, Charlotte Daynard looked at her with narrowed eyes. Creyton paid no attention to either woman.

"Omega can be a long and glorious enterprise," he went on. "And I intend for that to be so. But it will be more enjoyable without the presence of Jonah Rowe."

Creyton regarded all his disciples. They looked back at him with equal parts curiosity and anticipation.

"It has been said that Jonah Rowe, as the Light Blue Aura, is the beacon of hope. The rallying point of all of my opponents. The one who has it within his power to restore the balance. In short, he is supposedly my equal."

Those words got looks of revulsion, disagreement, and outrage.

"But just imagine it, my disciples," whispered Creyton. "Imagine the effect it would have on the collective psyche of the ethereal world if their wonderful beacon was gone?"

Creyton knelt and surveyed a patch of green grass near Stephen's body.

"The imbeciles, the barely gifted, and the great unwashed. They never change. They never lose their tendency to rebel or resist the things that are best for them when they have inspiration. As long as they have their hope—their faith—they will behave irrationally. Even in the face of oblivion."

Creyton rose, and the bunch of green grass rose with him, still green and whole-looking, despite the fact that it was no longer attached to the ground.

"But I have the remedy for that, my friends. Hope and faith are substances that are fragile ... perhaps moreso than glass. And when they are crushed ..."

The patch of grass hovering in front of Creyton suddenly withered and died.

"How wonderful will it be"—Creyton had all of his disciples hanging on to his every word by this point—"to dispose of victims utterly devoid of hope and faith? To have prey who are at their absolute lowest, who have finally accepted that resistance is useless? Can you imagine that?"

The Deadfallen disciples were practically salivating. There was a malicious sparkle in every eye. Creyton grinned.

"That beautiful dream will cease to be a dream very soon, my disciples." His words were a promise. "This is where you come in, 49er. I have a task for you, Charlotte, Jason, and Walden to perform. Your enterprise with mental linkages will be of great benefit. You will bring Jonah Rowe to me, alive. I will lower the final curtain myself."

The other Deadfallen disciples still made it clear that they had no trust for the 49er. But the vampire nodded eagerly.

"It will be an honor, Transcendent."

"Very well," said Creyton. "Now go clean yourself up. Welcome back to the family. This council is adjourned."

Everyone turned to leave via twig portals or shape-shifted back into crows.

"Oh, and 49er?"

The 49er turned. Creyton waved his staff, and what looked like a black shockwave flew in its wake, knocking the 49er to the ground. Creyton pounced on him and began to pummel and batter the vampire with black gleaming fists, snarling curses and jeers the entire time. When the 49er was completely dazed and bloodied, Creyton ripped a vial from his pocket and poured a silver liquid on the 49er's face. The flesh hit with the liquid instantly began to burn, almost to the bone. The 49er howled in pain, and Creyton grabbed him by his soiled shirt.

"Those burns won't heal," he growled. "Now listen and understand, you treacherous filth. If you ever double-cross me again, I'll castrate you and put that substance tha currently burning your face in the wounds. Then it will lace the stake that I drive through your heart. Do you understand me?"

The 49er's face was burned and bloodied. Creyton had given him such a vicious beating that he could barely move. "Y-y ... yes, Transcendent."

Creyton released the 49er's shirt and rose. "Now, get out of my sight before I re-evaluate your usefulness."

2

SCATTERED STATES OF MIND

July 7th, 8:02 A.M.

Reena sat, idly sketching. She didn't say it often, but it had always been amazing to her that even as her mind wandered, it still seemed to achieve synchronicity with her hands.

Very soon after she'd begun, the pages in her pad were covered with cloud sequences, animals to which she felt a kinship, pedestrians she'd seen ... things as random as the thoughts that swirled about her mind.

"Reena?"

Reena turned and smiled without hesitation. Even though the source of the voice was hooded and rather in shadow, there was no threat whatsoever. It was Kendall Rayne, her fiancée. She'd just gotten out of the shower and had been on her way to the bedroom when she caught sight of Reena at the kitchen table, with multiple drawings spread out in front of her.

"Everything is just fine, Kendall. It's no secret that I'm the artsy-fartsy one."

Kendall rolled her eyes and walked Reena's way. The

morning had just begun to bathe her kitchen in sunlight, which illuminated a drawing of a cat's face. She slowly grasped Reena's hand, to coax her into ceasing. "You may be able to read essence, Reena, but I don't have to have powers to gauge you. I've been with you long enough to know that, yes, you are indeed the 'artsy-fartsy' one. But you paint regularly. You only sketch when you're really stressed out."

Reena paused, and then relented. "Guilty as charged," she muttered, though she smiled a second later. She dropped the pencil and sighed. Kendall didn't release her hand.

"So, what's the problem?" she urged.

Reena straightened her posture in the chair. "Kendall, I don't know how we are all going to make it through this. And I hate not knowing. Can't stand it. I'm the smartest one, or so they say—"

"And they're right," interrupted Kendall.

Reena allowed herself a smile for that, then she continued. "But this entire situation is something that can go ten kinds of wrong. And with all of this shit … with Creyton … no amount of Plan Bs will help us if anything goes wrong."

Kendall's face showed concern for several moments. Reena had to admit that she was grateful for that. Sometimes Kendall might have been a stickler concerning her students, but she allowed Reena her moments to have her feelings when she spoke on her ethereal life. They never spoke about it much, anyway; there was an unwritten code between them that said that Reena didn't go into too much detail about the current state of the ethereal world. The less Kendall knew, the safer she was. Still didn't mean that she wasn't at least partially in the loop. "Have you spoken to Jonah and Terrence?" was her next question.

"Of course I have. But at the moment, they have their own minds to rein in. We all do, I suppose."

"Uh-huh," murmured Kendall. "That's fair. But are they doing any better than you are right now?"

Reena stood and wandered over to the sink, staring out the window at nothing in particular. "They all look up to me, Kendall. Even Jonah, for whatever reason. He has more than enough on his plate as the Light Blue Aura. I just want to be of use ... hold up my end. In recent weeks, Terrence has started to call me *Miss Action*. It's tacky, but the more I hear it, the more it fits me. But I don't know how any of this will turn out for us. Any of us. That scares me. Yeah, I admit it."

Kendall joined Reena at the sink, kissing the back of her neck as she did so. She then wrapped her arms around Reena's waist. "Reena, I will not pretend to understand all that's happening, but I do know this much. Whatever role throws itself your way, you will adapt to it and thrive in it, just like you always do. If all the things that Jonah and Terrence say are true, you've been doing that long before we met. The only thing that matters is that they believe in you. And everyone trusts you. Your best friends ... your *brothers* ... trust you. And I trust you too, wholeheartedly."

Reena gave her a small smile. Yes, fear was still on her mind. But Kendall's words aided her nerves. She was intelligent enough to know that fear of the unknown was inevitable but sitting here, allowing fear and worry to consume her, didn't stop the fact that Omega was coming. Perhaps if she kept her wits about her, she'd have some type of edge. "You've always had such a way with word. I am abundantly thankful for that."

"You flatter me." Kendall grinned. "And, speaking of Miss Action," she gave Reena an appraising look, "you up for some this morning?"

Reena snorted. "Is this a question?"

Kendall grinned once more. "I was headed to the bedroom anyway—"

"Who needs a bed?" scoffed Reena. "That's too damn far."

Kendall gave her a sinful smirk before they clashed in a kiss right there by the kitchen sink, with Reena relieving Kendall of her bathrobe within seconds.

July 7^{*th*}*, 9:15 AM*

"You alright, son?"

Arn Decessio saw Terrence lying idly on a weight bench in the backyard and must have assumed that he hurt something. Terrence shook his head at his father's concern.

"Yeah, Dad." He pulled a smile on his face. "I'm good. Just thinking."

Mr. Decessio gave him a look of understanding, but returned inside, choosing not to pry. Terrence rose and followed suit.

He smelled breakfast in the kitchen, mightily delicious smells, but he walked on by, headed to his bedroom.

He looked at all the pictures that were bunched up on the dresser. Him and his brother Bobby, him and Alvin, the complete group of the brothers, Raymond, Sterling, Alvin, Bobby, and himself. Pictures of fishing trips with Mr. and Mrs. Decessio. The picture taken in the family's kitchen the night he'd cooked his first meal for the whole family. There was also a picture of him with his famous adopted brother, the football legend Lloyd Aldercy. It had been a great surprise and blessing to have reconciled with him. All good things, all good times.

Then his eyes moved to the other pictures there. The ones from the estate. With Reena. The sister he'd acquired through tough times and surviving some serious shit shows. They were all images of family. Unity. Illustrations of awesomeness, as he had said from time to time. But just the combination of pictures made him grimace.

Every single person in the pictures had achieved something amazing. His father's meticulous record-keeping and retention of details while he was in the S.P.G. was revered to this day, and that was before he opened a successful garage. His mother was the backbone and glue of the entire family ... no small feat since she was surrounded by so many male egos. Raymond was a self-defense instructor for both Tenths and Elevenths, and his work had always been lauded. Even the Networkers employed some of his techniques. Sterling was a mentor. Alvin was such a *present* individual, capable of being mindful of surroundings and details while also being just detached enough to remain objective and clear-headed. And then Bobby, who, just like his brother Lloyd, was a football czar. Blessed with good genes, natural strength that he cultivated further every day, and a mind tailor-made for the sport, he was about to finish college and was a legend in the making. Not to mention that he had the greatest girlfriend on earth.

Then there was his "brother" Jonah Rowe. The Light Blue Aura, who could touch just about anything and make it flourish. At times, he had even managed to do heroic things without a spiritual endowment.

And Reena, smarter than everyone he knew, equally as badass, and seemed to have the perfect blend of book sense and common sense.

And there was himself. Terrence.

What had he done?

Everyone had a niche. The thing they brought to the table. Eleventh Percenters were all artistic in some form or fashion, in just about every field. Terrence hadn't found his niche yet. Other than having good genes that prevented him from ever gaining weight, there was nothing remarkable about him. He was an awesome cook and could buff floors pretty well. And he was a damn great auto mechanic, thanks to Arn Decessio's tutelage.

Big whoop to all of those.

Omega was coming. Because of that fact, culinary talent, mechanical work, and janitorial skills weren't the stuff that would assist him, or anyone else, in survival. He needed some real skill, some profound talent. What did he bring to the table? Cooking? Cleaning? The ability to fix a car, and muscle someone around from time to time?

None of those traits sounded very endearing at the moment.

The steel knuckles that were his weapon of choice sat in front of him, near all the pictures. He just stared at them and sighed.

In all the action movies, the nameless, aimless people were the ones taken out first. *Not* the comic relief. The nameless strong guy. And in this particular movie, Jonah was the chosen one. Reena was the smart one.

And he, Terrence Wade Aldercy, was the nameless one.

He pulled himself up and went back to the kitchen. Perhaps he'd have better thoughts on a less empty stomach.

July 7th, 12:28 P.M.

Jonah slowed his car to the mandated twenty-mile speed limit as he passed the long sun-beaten sign that didn't evoke very many positive memories: **RADNER CITY LIMITS Pop. 219**.

He regarded that sign for a few seconds. Two-hundred nineteen people. It had been two-hundred-and-one when he'd moved away. That meant that either eighteen kids had been born, or eighteen people decided that small-town living was what they desired in life.

He didn't know and didn't care.

Jonah had never liked Radner. The place was worse than

dog years; one year here was like one decade everywhere else. He could still remember going to the store to get sweets and overhearing people talking passionately about matters that everyone else had long since forgotten. And his schoolmates? Oh, they thought they knew everything about how the world worked. And Jonah believed that that was true for the longest time. It took moving away from this lump-on-a-hill for him to realize that those fools didn't have a clue.

He looked around here and there as he rolled, and snorted when he saw that Donovan Burke, who was the biggest bully and asshole on earth back in high school but got away with it because he was the star linebacker from whom many people expected big things, was now the assistant manager at a bait-and-tackle shop. Jonah hadn't even known. Nasty fall from grace, that. But Jonah didn't mind. One had to savor life's little blessings.

But he filed that away. While the effects of karma were always refreshing, they didn't really matter at the moment.

He slowed to a stop at a vacant lot. It was the site where his former home used to be.

His and Nana's.

It had fallen into disrepair after Nana had passed into Spirit, and Jonah wanted nothing more to do with the place after that. None of his other relatives had cared, either...not that they cared before...and it was his understanding that after it had been vandalized a few times, the other family members made the decision to bulldoze it. It didn't matter much to him, though it did haunt him a little on occasion.

Jonah accelerated and drove on. For what reason had he stopped there? That hadn't even been his destination.

Luckily (or not), his destination was only about five minutes away. He hadn't been there for years, but in recent weeks, he suddenly felt the need. So here he was.

The Radner Memorial Cemetery.

He walked slowly, consciously, through the rows, well aware of where he was headed. He avoided Spectral Sight at all costs due to an extreme need for no distractions. He couldn't help but wonder how he remembered the route with complete clarity, despite the fact that he hadn't been there in years.

Somewhere in the distance, birds chirped rhythmically, and random traffic passed. But those sounds seemed otherworldly somehow. Detached. The silence, deafening and uncorrupted, was the only thing that prevailed here.

He nodded absently at the caretaker as he walked a few more steps, and finally stopped, taking a moment to drink in the scene that was branded into his memory for the rest of his physical life:

Doreen Lucille Beech-Rowe
June 3, 1913 – November 10, 2005
Beloved Mother, Grandmother, and Friend

Almost reverently, Jonah knelt and stared at the spread of grass, beneath which laid the human shell of the most wonderful woman he had ever known. It had been so long ago, and so much had changed since that rainy night that had derailed his entire being. But no matter how much time had passed, he still felt abandoned and alone sometimes. That night, all those years ago, he had been jarred out of a loving routine that had needed no deviation. None.

Yet it still happened. Damn it all.

"Hey, Nana." He looked at the familiar marble that was now slightly worn and faded by sunlight and the elements. "I brought your favorite."

He carefully arranged the impatiens around the stone and rose.

"You were one who always said that flowers were God's greatest gift," said Jonah as he backed away to look at his work.

He wished with everything in him that he could speak to her again. He wished that he could get that all-encompassing hug, the sweet words, and the neat assurances. The simple things that he had taken for granted when he had them and had missed more than anything now that they were gone.

"Nana, I made you a lot of promises when that ambulance took you away." He sighed. "I can't say that I've made good on most of them. I've often wondered if you are proud of the man I've become. I've tried to do the right things, tried to live right. Tried to make the smartest decisions. I've tried very hard to follow your example. But then I realized that I have my own opinions ... my own mind ..."

He closed his eyes. He was his own person, with his own life. Yet he still felt like he'd betrayed his grandmother by taking a different path.

"Nana, I'm the Blue Aura. The Light Blue Aura, the best hope, at the forefront of Omega. A big hero, supposedly. Basically, a million things have happened in my life that I didn't want"—he caught himself—"and many things that I didn't mind at all."

He slipped his hands into his pockets. The left pocket contained his batons in their dormant form. The right contained the Vitasphera, which had been passed to him the night Jonathan was vanquished. He kept it out of sight, because its pitch-black composition always put him in a negative state of mind.

"I wonder if you knew anything about any of it, Nana," he went on. "If you knew about the Eleventh Percent. If you knew that I was an Eleventh Percenter, or at the very least, knew that I was strange."

He felt his eyes begin to burn. Why wasn't she here? She

always had an answer. Always. He remembered that night when he was eighteen, when he was supposed to be of age. It didn't matter. When he knew that Nana was gone, he was terrified about being alone in the world. The blade of grief that was embedded in his heart remained as sharp as ever, although he'd learned to live with it. He simply resigned himself to the fact that it'd probably never go away. He changed tack again.

"I met this woman." He impatiently wiped his eyes. "You probably would have liked her. But you would have hated her sister, who's a murderer and well ... crazy. You probably wouldn't like her boyfriend, either, come to think of it. I also met this other woman, but there weren't any strings attached there, it was just sex—Christ, why am I telling you about that, Nana?"

He resumed his silence. He didn't know how to stay on subject. It wasn't easy conversing with a headstone. This damned headstone. The symbol that illustrated the unfairness of Nana being gone. All this time had passed, and it still wasn't fair.

"In case you haven't figured it out, Nana, I wish you were still here. Maybe I could make sense of all these things happening to me if you were. But..." He stopped yet again. After all these years, the conversation still wasn't any easier.

"Say hi to Mr. Steverson for me, Nana. And Jonathan?" Jonah's voice caught once more. "Nana, I know that we can't see the spirits of people that we were close to in life, but if you happen to be around me, if there were some kind of way for that to happen, please ..."

Silence. Still as deafening as it was when he'd first arrived.

He turned his back on the headstone. It was time to go. He had to get away from here. Give himself some time to compose himself before he saw everyone again.

Fifteen paces away, Jonah turned around, closed his eyes,

took a deep breath, and willed the curtain to rise and the actors to perform. When he opened his eyes, there were the bluish-white sheens that shimmered around the headstones, which indicated spirits and spiritesses that still walked Earthplane.

There were dozens of them.

But his grandmother's headstone wasn't one of them. The marble remained resolutely white and weather-beaten.

Jonah had expected that. Jonathan had told him when they first met that his grandmother was on the Other Side. Besides, he wouldn't have been able to have seen her, anyway.

He knew those things already. All of them.

That knowledge still did nothing to remedy the pain and disappointment he felt as he turned to depart.

3
THE NIGHTMARE SCENARIO

Jonah had worked up an appetite, which wasn't a surprise because he'd had no lunch. He just couldn't focus on eating earlier; his stomach was too full of shaky resolutions to have any room for food.

And he'd actually remained in his car for a while, doing nothing. He had to get his emotions under control. He'd seen far too many movies where people hit the road while they were a bundle of emotions and got into grisly car accidents as a result. Jonah had enough threats to his physical life to be concerned with inattentiveness on the highway.

Despite that, he'd be damned if he was going to eat anywhere in Radner. Everybody knew everybody. If he got accosted, he would have to have a zillion conversations, playing catch-up on subjects that he didn't give a shit about. Couple that with the fact that he might have run into one of his stupid relatives. Even though Jonah had dropped weight and had a perpetual five o'clock shadow, he was certain that he'd be recognized by every single person that he didn't want to see.

So, after an hour or so in his car, still deep in thought but functional, he got out of Radner and back on I-40.

He saw restaurant signs after about a half an hour on the road, but he kept on driving. Thirty minutes away wasn't far enough. Not from Radner.

After another twenty minutes or so, he saw more outlets for food. But fifty minutes was hardly better than thirty minutes with Radner. It was almost as though there was a radius that spread from that damn place, which put one at risk of seeing someone they knew if they didn't properly escape it.

When Jonah finally felt comfortable enough to stop, he'd been on the road about ninety minutes.

He'd seen a sign for a diner in a small town named Ruby River. He remembered seeing it on the map when he was a kid. It might have been small but, as was the case with over half the towns in North Carolina, Ruby River wasn't as small as Radner. with its two-hundred-plus hangers-on. Ruby River had twenty-seven hundred people, and was considered a tiny town? Please. If Jonah had said it once, he'd said it a thousand times. People did not know what small was.

He stopped at the Ruby River diner and looked it over. It was a neat little place, bigger than he'd expected, with a (what else?) ruby-tinged paint job. Because of Reena, he always checked the rating. The place had an A. So far, so good.

Jonah stepped inside the door with the vaguest feeling that he'd forgotten something. Before he could focus on that thought, however, he was distracted by the meal of the day: chicken-fried steak, rice with homestyle gravy, and iced tea with unlimited refills, all for $4.65.

"Wow," he whispered to himself. That was some really heavy food, particularly on an empty stomach. But that price was beyond great. He shrugged, figuring that he would be alright so long as he didn't eat like a hog, and he could always work it off later.

He sat in the far corner, with no desire to be near the door. There was an unforgiving gust of heat every time somebody opened the damn thing. Within a few minutes, a maternal-looking woman with pulled-back brown hair came up to him, pen and pad ready.

"What'll it be, sweetie?" she asked with a smile.

Jonah returned the smile and pointed to the board near the door. "Meal of the day and, um ..." he glanced at her nametag, "I'd like some ice water with that sweet tea, Lavonda. I haven't ever been here before, and I don't know if you have sweet tea, or *sweet tea.*"

"I'll bring you the water, sweetie." Lavonda chortled. "Because I can already tell you that here, we have the latter."

She left him. Jonah felt his mind improve. Lavonda had such a warm demeanor that it put him at ease almost immediately. He almost wanted to tip her before she'd done anything. He already liked and respected her. That was something that people learned quickly when they were around Jonathan, who had always stressed that it was vitally important to respect everyone's position, because everyone had some valuable purpose that they brought to the table.

Jonah closed his eyes for a moment. He ought to be happy for Jonathan, because he was on the Other Side, together with his soulmate Francine. And when he thought about it, he actually was happy for him. But the Protector Guide's absence still felt wrong. Still felt unnatural. It felt like the pillar that had always bore most of the load had been yanked away from the estate, and everything had been shaky ever since. So many people had abandoned the estate ... left them all high and dry. Liz repeatedly implored Jonah not to think of it that way, but a part of him still did. It just made more sense to band together rather than tuck tail and run.

His head was down as he contemplated all of this, eyes on his hands. The bell continued to ding every once in a while, indicating new patrons. He could swear that one of the groups sounded rather large. In his head, he was mildly envious of them and their normal lives. On the other hand, he was glad that he got here when he did. Everyone came for the meal of the day. He didn't have to worry about being eighth or ninth in line.

"Here you go, sweetie!" Lavonda slid a hearty, piping hot platter underneath Jonah's nose. "And I got your sweet tea and water, like you asked!"

Jonah thanked her and began to eat. Man, if it wasn't one of the most delicious things he'd ever tasted. He sipped his tea, and his eyes bulged. The fact that every tooth that had just been washed with that sweet tea didn't suddenly have a cavity was a blessing. He diluted it with some of the water and tried it again. Much better.

Despite the deliciousness of the food, Jonah was still mindful of his previously empty stomach. He took his time with the food and sipped from his drink at regular intervals. After a while, he was sated, and his stomach didn't feel bad at all. He could never tell Reena that she gave such good advice on eating. He'd never hear the end of it.

He was about to ask for the check when Lavonda approached him again, polite curiosity in her features.

"Let me clear that for you, darling. You must be really hungry!"

Jonah frowned. He couldn't eat another bite! "Um, Lavonda ...?"

But she had already walked away with the dirty dishes. He didn't have long to wait, however, as Lavonda was back with a new plate which contained the largest hamburger Jonah had ever laid eyes on.

"Lavonda," Jonah regarding the burger with distaste only because he was full, "there must be some mistake. What is this?"

"It's the Ruby Classic!" answered Lavonda with pride. "Quarter-pound burger with homemade slaw and chili! And you needn't worry; it's cooked well done, so the meat's dead. Very dead."

Jonah looked at her. Dead meat ... that was unsettling for some reason. But there was nothing sinister or strange in Lavonda's grin. Okay, so it wasn't her. "Lavonda, who put in this order?"

"Your friend by the door. I don't want to point. But it's the man in the duster. You know him, right?"

Jonah glanced at the door. And his gut suddenly lined with lead.

The man near the door sat in a booth. There was an untouched cup of coffee in front of him. It was a severe-looking guy with unruly stubble and hard blue eyes, which were fixated on Jonah with an almost hungry gaze. Seriously, the guy looked seconds away from salivating.

Jonah had seen him before. At that godforsaken house a while back. He was one of the many Deadfallen disciples who'd chased him as he ran for his physical life after Creyton achieved Praeterletum.

Jonah had only just processed this information when Lavonda sighed and shook her head.

"I asked him whether he was hot in that duster," she whispered to Jonah, "but he said that he was wearing it because of our A/C. I didn't think it was that cold in here."

"You're right, Lavonda." Jonah manufactured a smile. "This isn't a mistake after all ... the burger, I mean. I'm sure it will be as delicious as the chicken-fried steak. Thank you, ma'am."

With another warm smile, Lavonda returned to her other tables. Jonah's eyes returned to the Deadfallen disciple. The man did a barely noticeable dart of his eyes, which indicated to Jonah that they were not alone.

Jonah looked several tables away. Sure enough, there was another disciple there, who also wore a duster and a bandanna around his spiky blonde and black hair. Unlike the wooden-faced guy, this man actually snorted as he darted his eyes to the other exit. Jonah looked that way and could have sworn out loud.

Charlotte Daynard was right next to that door. She looked him square in the face. How had he not seen her?

Then he remembered. He'd had his head down while deep in thought as he waited for his plate. He was certain the Dead-fallen disciples had ways to not be noticed while he ate. Then again, the food had been so good that he hadn't bothered doing much looking around. And now they positioned around him, Paul Bunyan at one exit, Bandanna in the corner, and Char-lotte Daynard at the other exit. Jonah was badly placed. He couldn't even get to the bathroom without the three of them seeing it.

With a pang of irritation, Jonah realized what he had forgotten. He hadn't gone into Spectral Sight to check the spirit count of the area before he walked into the diner. If Deadfallen disciples were around, the spirit count would be low or non-existent. If he had known that, he'd have kept on rolling to the next county!

Very discreetly, Charlotte cleared her throat so as to bring Jonah's attention back to her. She closed her eyes, took a deep intake of breath, and then opened her eyes and performed a cutthroat signal.

Jonah's own throat tightened at the maneuver. So, there was no need to go into Spectral Sight. There was nothing to see. They must have usurped every spirit and spiritess around the area. Swell.

Jonah was so caught up in thoughts about those poor spirits that he almost missed the fact that Charlotte wanted to catch his eye again. She opened her jacket, and revealed a crescent-shaped blade, its handle stamped with the head of a crow. One prod of her index finger darkened the steel.

They were spiritually endowed. He was not. So, unless he thought of something, he really *was* dead meat.

Just then, what sounded like a pained howl made everyone jump and look around for the source. By the looks on Charlotte's, Mountain Man's, and Bandanna's faces, that noise was not part of the plan.

A man stormed through the door near Mountain Man. He was clad in a disheveled flannel shirt and ragged jeans. Dirty, stringy hair obscured his face. He lumbered straight for Jonah.

"You didn't think I'd find you, Thomas?" the man shouted at him. "You thought you were untouchable or some shit, boy?"

Several of the older people looked appalled at the swear word, but Jonah paid that no mind. Because at that moment, his mind went from *"What now?"* to *"Thomas? Who the hell is Thomas?"*

"Um, you've got the wrong guy, dude. My name isn't Thomas—"

"Don't gimme that shit!" bellowed the disheveled man. "I told you I wasn't going away! You tried to run all the way to Ruby River to get away from your responsibility? Oh, *hell* to the naw!"

Jonah had no idea what this guy was talking about, but he needed to figure it out, and quickly. He had enough problems at the moment. He glanced at the Deadfallen disciples. They didn't know what to make of this guy, either. Charlotte, in particular, kept looking between Jonah and the dirty man with puzzlement.

Lavonda, who was obviously somewhat braver than her fellow colleagues, stepped toward the man. "Look here, sir, this here diner is a peaceful establishment. I think it's high time for you to leave—"

"Why?" the man snapped at Lavonda. "Because I'm dirty? Because I look like I look? That is the true scum right there!" He pointed a filthy finger at Jonah. "Sitting there as bold as I don't know what! He made a slut out of my sister! Knocked her up!"

Now several faces snapped Jonah's way, looking accusatory and judgmental. Jonah rose from the booth before he was even fully aware that his legs were at work, moving him. Confusion and anger grew side by side within him.

"I haven't done anything of the kind! And since you didn't seem to hear me the first time, my name is not Thomas, it's J—"

"Stop the lyin', Thomas!" interrupted the man. "You promised my sister the moon! Now, she's wobblin' all over the place big as a house, and you ain't been nowhere in sight! You got all this money to buy fancy meals and leave ladies nice tips, but you ain't give Essie one thin dime!"

While Jonah was momentarily distracted by the name Essie (it sounded like a damn cow), Lavonda got between them. She thrust something forcibly into Jonah's hand.

"Take it," she snapped. "And both of you get out."

Jonah realized that it was the tip he'd put down for Lavonda. He hadn't even paid for his food yet! He'd put the tip down first!

"But ma'am—!" he began in anguish, but she shook her head.

"I don't want your tip, boy." A scathing look now contorted

Lavonda's previously friendly face. "Why don't you give it to that poor girl you wronged? Now, both of you get out of here before I call the sheriff!"

"Yeah, you little shit." the dirty guy and grabbed Jonah's shirt. "Get outside so I can beat some child-support out of you!"

Flabbergasted, humiliated, and angry, Jonah noticed that they'd passed by Charlotte. He clearly saw that she was seething but didn't want to be noticed. But the next thing he knew, he was outside, where the anger once again muscled out everything else.

"Look, you filthy bastard," Jonah readied himself for a fight. "I've already told you that my name's not Thomas—"

"Get in the car, Jonah." The man no longer sounded angry, but tense. "We need to get out of here."

Jonah's eyes bulged. *Huh?* "You just called me Jonah! Who are—?"

Impatiently, the man shifted his filthy hair, and Jonah's eyes widened.

"*Raymond?* But—"

"In the car, Jonah," repeated Raymond. "I bought us five minutes. Three if they're smart. Which they are, unfortunately. Now come on!"

In a daze, Jonah got into the passenger seat of Raymond's car. Raymond waited until they were both in the car to remove that god-awful wig. They were on the road in seconds.

"Why did you make me look like an asshole back there, Ray?"

"Had to." Raymond looked genuinely apologetic. "That's exactly why I cut you off when you were about to shout out your name in that diner. Someone might have tried to look you up or something."

"Ray, I'm grateful that you got me out of there, but that was truly the best story you could think of? That whole Thomas thing?"

"Thomas was the first name that came to mind," shrugged Raymond. "And I figured that in a cozy town like this one, nothing would be more scandalous than an unwed mother and a sorry-ass father. What better way to get you away from those Deadfallen disciples?"

Jonah's anger evaporated at that. It wasn't like there was any truth to those accusations, anyway. Now, on to the important questions.

"Let me save you some breath." It was as though Raymond read Jonah's mind. "Creyton expected you to visit your grandmother's grave. According to Dad and Patience, he prides himself on the notion that he knows everything about you. So, he stationed some Deadfallen disciples around the area."

"What? Dude, I was an hour and a half outside of Radner!"

"These are the sticks, Jonah," Raymond reminded him. "Distance doesn't mean shit out here, especially to Creyton and his ass-kissers."

Jonah growled. He thought he'd heard a tiny note of criticism in Raymond's voice, as though he viewed him as too predictable. But at least he didn't come right out and criticize him for it. But this wasn't the time for aggravation. File it away. On to the next thing. "So, how did you know where I'd be?"

"Terrence. He said that you were going to Radner to pay your respects. When I used the *Astralimes* to that cemetery, you'd already left. So, I used the *Astralimes* back to the car, and started driving. I knew that you, of all people, would be leery of using ethereal travel nowadays, at least alone. I had hoped to see you, either on the road or stopped off somewhere. I saw when you took that exit to go to Ruby River, but I lost you at the light once we were off the highway. It took a little while to find you again, but then I saw your car at the diner. I went into

Spectral Sight but saw no spirits or spiritesses. Was that your doing? Did you tell them to run?"

Jonah heaved a sigh. "How did you know you'd have to be in disguise?" he asked, choosing to ignore the question. "Was that outfit ready-made?"

"No, not really. I helped Ma clean out the basement and had a bunch of my old crap in the trunk as a result. The wig was something I wore in a short film one of my buddies made in college. I was on my way to donate some of it when Dad said that one of his contacts warned him that there might be an attempt to get at you like this. That was the exact same time that Terrence said that you were in Radner to visit your grandmother's grave. I was the one who could get here the fastest, so I came."

"Back up a second." Jonah noticed something weird in Raymond's story. "You can't have driven from Rome to Radner to come looking for me. You'd still be on the road right now. But you just said that you used the *Astralimes* to try and find me in the cemetery, but then used them back to this car. Did you steal this car from someone in Radner?"

"It's only temporary." Raymond was now about twenty over the speed limit. "Your well-being trumps a car theft. I'll try very hard to get it back to them."

"Wait a second!" Jonah just realized something. "*My* car's still back there!"

"Your car can be retrieved, Jonah. I'll tell Dad to get Patience or somebody to handle it, don't you worry. Your car's location is the least of your problems right now. Believe that."

Jonah fell silent after that. Evidently, visiting his grandmother's grave was a miscalculated risk. Especially if Creyton expected him to do it. But something in his mind was defiant, unapologetic about it. Jonathan always said that your opponent had already won if you deviated from the normal course of events in your life because of them. It was one of the reasons why he still had feelings of anger and disappointment towards the people who left the estate. And Trip? Oh, buddy ... it would probably be better for everyone if they never spoke to, or saw, each other again.

"Thanks, man." It was hard for Jonah to force himself back to center. "I appreciate it."

"Don't thank me, Jonah. We aren't done just yet."

Jonah frowned. "What are you talking about?"

Raymond sighed. "Remember when I said that it was Terrence who told where you were headed, and how I used the *Astralimes* and all that? And how Dad said one of his contacts said there might be an attempt like this?"

"The last part isn't a surprise, I guess." Jonah sighed to himself. "Creyton has been after me from minute one. I have to deal with that every day."

"Look in the side mirror," commanded Raymond. "And then tell me about what you have dealt with every day."

Jonah did so, confused. Then he saw them.

Three crows, in formation like fighter jets, followed them in the sky.

"Son of a bitch."

"Yep, pretty much," said Raymond. "That's what I meant when I was talking about buying us time. Before that happened."

"What the hell are they doing?"

"I don't know much about it, Jonah, but Dad filled me in, sort of. His contact said that it's something called a Nightmare Scenario."

"A what?"

"Basically, it's a trap," Raymond explained. "They've sprung it to get you. It's my understanding that Creyton put it in play when he figured out you were going to Radner, and that you'd likely be alone."

"What is the Nightmare Scenario? I dont understand."

"According to Dad, it's set up like a nightmare." Raymond kept glancing into his own side mirror. "Each one is set up to get you. But if you luck yourself out of one, if you escape one trap, you fall into another one, or something like that. I'm guessing Charlotte and those two in the diner were like the first attempt—"

"Don't say it like that." Jonah voice was suddenly sharp and cold.

Raymond gave him a puzzled expression, which instantly made Jonah feel shame.

"Sorry," he muttered, looking back out of the window to see the pursuing crows. "I didn't mean to blow up at you, man. It's just when you said it like that, it reminded me of the Six. Not something I want in my mind right now."

Raymond's face showed understanding. "Gotcha."

"So, if this is a trap," said Jonah, eager to change the subject and also focus on the task at hand, "their ... Nightmare thing or whatever, that would mean they blew their chance. Does that mean that they aren't actually chasing us right now?"

"No, not exactly. They're trying to herd us to the next bag of tricks."

Now, Jonah felt numb. In that moment, he experienced a sharp reminder of a time right before he found out that he was an Eleventh Percenter, that night when the minions Howard and Walt told him that they'd found him because thinking of his grandmother had fired up some type of mental link, or something. Now, after he'd visited her grave, they'd "figured out" his location.

Raymond said that Creyton liked to think that he knew

everything about Jonah. Bullshit. He had simply remembered Jonah's weakest point.

"What can be done to get out of this and safely back to the estate?" he grumbled

"Patience and Daniel quarterbacked this the second we found out Creyton might try something. Since Creyton has a plan in place that deals with predictability, they said the best thing to do to combat it is to be unpredictable. They threw a plan together against the short time frame. Dad was in on it, too. One of his friends was supposed to alert him. And that's what happened. Today."

Jonah stared at him. There was a plan? "How long has this been in place?"

"Damn if I know. After Dad got the message, he told me to find you. That's why I asked Terrence where you were."

Jonah took a deep breath. "With all due respect, Raymond, why did they send you to Radner? They could have easily sent Terrence or Reena."

"Driving skills." There was a note of pride in Raymond's voice. "Sterling, Ma, all of them claim that I can drive like a Hollywood stuntman."

"Holly—*whoa!*"

Raymond took an abrupt turn off-road and drove down a dirt path. It wasn't the smoothest one in the world. Far from it.

"W-Where are w-we g-g-going?" sputtered Jonah as they jostled along the poorly packed earth.

Raymond didn't answer. Laboriously, Jonah looked out of the window again. He didn't see the trio of crows. Raymond had lost them on the path when they reached the trees. Seconds later, he stopped and killed the engine.

"Wasn't trying to ignore you," he said. "I needed to focus. Now, get out with me."

Jonah got out of the car, trying to focus his hearing to hear those crows. Unfortunately, the woods were full of many sounds. He had no time to process that before he and Raymond were hit by a gust of wind. A man stepped in front of them.

He looked to be around Mr. Decessio's age, with salt and pepper hair pulled back in a ponytail. His eyes were gray like Jonathan's, but nowhere near as piercing. And at the moment, he didn't look like he was in the mood for chit-chat.

"Charles, three disciples were in the sky," said Raymond without hesitation, "they are likely on the ground now. If there are any more of them, I didn't see—"

"There were an additional five," interrupted Charles, who dispensed with a torn vest. "They were chasing me because I muddled the second trap they had for the boy here. I killed one of them, but that didn't do a damn thing to help my situation because I only pissed off the remaining ones. They'll be here soon enough, probably with the three you saw flying."

Jonah just looked at the man, who regarded him in an odd sort of way. He met the gaze with a confused one of his own, because he still didn't fully understand what the hell was going on.

"Rowe, my name's Barisford Charles. I'd love to go into detail...do the pleasantries and all that...but we don't have the time. Raymond, have you given him at least given him the skeleton of what's happening?"

"Skeleton?" Raymond almost laughed. "I think poor Jonah barely got a femur and a skull."

"If that!" Jonah wrung his hands. "I don't even know what we're doing! Look, I'm not trying to be critical of anyone, but Raymond said that this was planned in advance. This right here feels very thrown together!"

"That was by design." Charles said it like it was obvious to all. "The only thing we had planned in advance was that we would need to improvise, having no idea when or where.

Creyton had your return mapped out. At the current time, randomness is our only weapon. I'll take it from here, Raymond. Take care of yourself."

"Always." Raymond pat Jonah's arm. "See you at the estate, Jonah. We can speak and be able to sit and breathe at that time!"

"Raymond, wait!"

But Raymond had already stepped into nothingness and was gone, abandoning the car that he promised to return. This situation must have be *really* fucked up. Charles snapped his fingers to get Jonah's attention.

"Listen clearly, boy. And I pray that you're as good at retention as I've heard, because I pick my words carefully, and I hate repeating myself. You and I are using the *Astralimes* to Elizabeth City—"

"What? Why are we going there? Why can't we just go to Rome? Straight to the estate?"

"Didn't I just say that Creyton had your return trip mapped out? They are expecting a straight shot! Creyton has stationed Deadfallen disciples in specific spots, and he has trained them to recognize specific patterns on the pathways, particularly the ones that are made when someone takes a straight shot for the Grannison-Morris estate via the *Astralimes*. You'll be snatched and bagged within seconds. So, we have to do randomly picked spots. Now, as I was saying, we're going to Elizabeth City. There, we will meet up with Patience. He'll drive you maybe a mile outside of the city limits, and then you'll be using the ethereal travel somewhere else. Patience knows, so don't ask me."

Jonah's already minimal faith in this haphazard plan diminished further with each step. For all he knew, the Deadfallen disciples were already well on their way to adapting to this so-called unpredictability. "Charles," he said in a steady tone, "before we go any further, I need a spiritual endowment."

"There is no way." Charles didn't even hesitate. "You can't establish rapport with a spirit or spiritess quickly enough, not on our time schedule. Assuming any are even around with those bastards around."

"I need to be able to—"

Charles raised a hand for silence. His head swung to the left, listening to something that Jonah couldn't hear. Then branches began to shake, and four crows descended a tree, dipping Charles' and Jonah's way. The crows began to shape-shift in midair, and they landed gracefully right in front of them.

Jonah cursed. Four!

Charles removed a short retractable staff from his pocket, which grew to four-and-a-half feet long. It then gleamed a neat copper color, which had to be his aura. Unimpressed, the tallest of the disciples moved in front of the others. He produced a length of steel, which gleamed black the second his fingers wrapped around it.

"I was hoping we'd find you, Charles. You killed Evan not too long ago ... I wanted to be the one to return the favor."

Jonah tensed, hating the vulnerability that he felt. Charles positioned himself in front of him.

"I'm right here, Ricky." Then he threw a command over his shoulder at Jonah. "Change of plan, boy! *You're* going to Elizabeth City!"

"What!" Jonah removed his batons. "I'm not doing that, man! Let me help!"

"Go now!" snarled Charles. "If you get hurt or killed, then what the hell are we doing this for?"

"Wait a second," said another disciple, "that's Rowe back there! Kill this bum and grab him!"

"Damn it all!" snapped Charles. "Run, boy! You can't use the *Astralimes* from here; they'll be on us too quickly!"

Charles waved his staff in a wide arc, and dirt and dead leaves flew up into the Deadfallen disciples' path.

"Go!" Charles shouted again.

Jonah roared in frustration, but tore off into the woods, Charles right behind him. They hadn't made it ten feet when they heard the disciples behind him. Jonah supposed that he should count his blessings that they actually gave chase on their feet as opposed to shape-shifting back into crows and taking flight. Small comfort.

"I take it that this wasn't part of your big plan?" he Jonah of Charles.

"We can make it work. More unpredictability can only be good for us. There!"

They both ducked into a ragged, years-abandoned shack with only half a door and all its windows missing. They crouched underneath the gaping holes that once held the windows and listened. For a fleeting moment, Jonah had the insane notion that the pursuing Deadfallen disciples might hear his racing heart.

"Breathe through your nose," advised Charles, who wrapped a cloth around his hand so that his staff wouldn't gleam copper and give them away. "You keep heaving gasps like that, they may very well wind up being the last ones you take."

Jonah did as he was told, feeling vulnerable and, truth be told, a bit angry along with it. It was the vulnerability that made him angry. He was in the middle of someone else's plan—a plan that really wasn't a plan—all in the name of inscrutability. Jonah could already tell that Barisford Charles was prepared to fight to whatever end, but he didn't know that Jonah would do the same, even if he was unendowed.

He had half a mind to see if there were any spirits or spiritesses around, but Charles, who had busied himself stealing glances out of the windowless holes, snapped his head Jonah's way.

"Don't even think about trying to summon any spirits or spiritesses."

Jonah looked at him in surprise. "Are you an essence reader?"

"Hardly. Years of experience just tells me that you were about to do something stupid and desperate."

"Stupid and desperate? What do you call this—?"

Once again, Charles silenced him with a hand gesture.

Not a minute too soon. Voices were close enough to be audible.

"They can't have gotten far." It was the same voice that had identified Jonah to his counterparts. "Rowe ain't even endowed and the Networker's getting slow in his old age."

"I wish Daynard was here," whispered another disciple. "She'd be able to smell the bastard's essence."

"We can do this without help," the first voice insisted in a cold tone. "There is no way they got far from us. Probably found a place to hide."

"What about that shack there?" asked another voice eagerly.

Jonah tensed. He saw that Charles had as well.

"Nah," said the owner of the first voice. "They aren't dumb enough to hide in there. Too obvious. Besides, Charles was endowed. I don't see any aura colors shining in there."

Silence for several agonizing seconds, then—

"Good point. Let's move on."

The footsteps began to move, got faint, and then faded.

"You see?" said Charles when everything was quiet again.

"See what might have happened if you had summoned some-body—had their luminescence brightenin' up the universe—"

"I got the point, man." Jonah rose from his knees. "Now, can we move on from here?"

Charles rose, removing the cloth from his hand so that his retractable staff gleamed copper once more. "We need to get to Elizabeth City. Let's use the *Astralimes* the minute that we get out of this shack—"

"Gotcha!" A Deadfallen disciple sprung from a nearby brush. "Knew you'd do the obvious!"

He tapped his throat with two fingers, relishing the very gesture. "*Per mo—*"

In a flash of copper, Charles bashed the man in the throat with his staff, instantly neutralizing his voice. When he gurgled and clutched his throat, Charles swept his feet out from under him and brought his foot across his face.

"Go, Jonah I'm right behind you!"

"Charles—"

"Go, damn you!"

Angry with himself for the compliance, Jonah stepped onto the Astral Plane and then took the second step. He now stood in the parking lot of a less than stellar mall. But he paid little attention to the details around him. The crappy mall didn't matter in the least.

"Come on, Charles," he said impatiently to thin air. "Come on, man!"

"Jonah!"

Alarmed, Jonah swung a baton in that direction, endow-ments be damned, but the owner of the voice blocked it. It was Patience.

God, he looked terrible. His brown eyes drooped, and his unshaven face looked so tired that his expression seemed to be one-quarter wakeful, three-quarters asleep. Still, there was urgency and firmness in his voice.

"You made it! Where's Charles?"

"He stayed behind, Patience! He said he was right behind me!"

Patience's droopy eyes narrowed. "What happened?"

"Some Deadfallen disciples were chasing us. We tried to hide in this old shack and thought they'd moved on, but one of them waited behind. Charles held him off long enough for me to get here. He wouldn't even let me help him fight! He said he was right behind me, man!"

Patience shook his head, as though it would make him more alert. "Was this still in Ruby River?"

"Yeah, but—"

"I'll find him. I got his back. Jonah, your next destination via the *Astralimes* is Windsor. That's in Bertie County. You will appear at the county armory. No one there uses it anymore, so you shouldn't be noticed. No one will be waiting for you there; I was supposed to go there with you, but it doesn't matter. I'll tell you the next stop. Wait in Windsor for five minutes exactly, and then use the *Astralimes* to Kinston. There, you'll see Felix, Terrence, and Reena. They will be with you for the next stop, which is the town of Rome and then, finally, the estate itself. Lord willing, I'll see you there in a few hours."

Patience said all of that so fast that Jonah couldn't believe he was drowsy. But Jonah was mightily concerned for Patience's well-being. If Charles, alert and wary, was having a hard time, how would sleepy, tired Patience fare?

"Patience, let me come back with you. I'm begging you, man. You are in no shape. Let me help you guys fight—"

"The whole point of this is to keep you safe, Jonah. As for my fatigue, it looks a whole lot worse than it is. Now, get going!"

Patience stepped back into thin air and was gone. Jonah very nearly used the *Astralimes* back to Ruby River to be an extra set of arms for the two Networkers, but he simply stared at the blank spot where Patience just stood. His impatience, confusion, and anger were slowly morphing into fear. This "plan" was way too disorganized. And there were already missteps. Charles was not supposed to stay behind to hold off Deadfallen disciples, just like Patience wasn't supposed to go and help him do so.

Hoping with everything in him that Patience and Charles could hold their own long enough to get away from those Deadfallen disciples, Jonah focused on Windsor, stepped onto the Astral Plane, and then took a second step into uncut, knee-high grass. The armory that Patience told him about was behind him. By this time it was six in the evening, but since it was summer, there was still light out. This armory had seen better days. But now, the area was remote. Too remote to remain in plain sight for the five minutes Patience mandated.

Jonah needed a spiritual endowment. He needed one yesterday. He was rattled by the encounters in the diner and the woods. Not being spiritually endowed made him feel like he had his hands tied.

He ran to the side of the armory, backed against the wall, closed his eyes, and took a deep breath, willing the curtain to rise and the actors to perform. Then, he opened his eyes again.

There was one spiritess. That was it.

But there was something odd about her.

She seemed dazed. Confused. It was almost like she was disoriented from a fight. Jonah frowned. He knew that spirits and spiritesses could be harmed, since they were still living beings. But this spiritess acted as though she had a concussion.

Was that possible for a spirit?

"Spiritess?" he called out. "Are you alright?"

"Get away!" cried the woman in terror. "You're one of his!"

"His?" said Jonah, confused. "Who?"

"Him! The evil one! The usurper!"

Jonah raised both of his hands. "No, no—I promise you." He tried very hard to put reassurance in his voice. "I'm not one of them! They're after me, too!"

He took a step forward, but she took a step back.

"You're lying. I just got into Spirit, and he was waiting for me. Told me there was no resistance and tried to take me. I ran. He sent you to bring me back!"

"That's a lie!" Jonah was suddenly repulsed. "I wouldn't do anything to hurt you! I'm the Blue Aura!"

At those words, the spiritess shrank away even further from Jonah, her eyes gaping with fear. "*He* is a Blue Aura! There are two of you? Two devils?"

Jonah made a choking sound. Literally. Her words stunned him. How could she come to that conclusion? Was there anything about him that was even remotely devilish? Just the thought of being compared to Creyton was enough to make him damn near vomit.

He took a deep breath. He needed her help, but she needed help, too. And more importantly, reassurance. "Spiritess, please listen to me. I'm not like him. I am the Light Blue Aura. The one that tried to hurt you is the Dark Blue Aura. He is chaos, I am balance. I am not the devil. Please believe me. I only want to help you. As a matter of fact, we can help each other."

The spiritess' fear hadn't left her eyes, yet she regarded Jonah. "Light blue ... balance. ... You won't take me?"

"Never." Jonah shook his head rigorously. "I want to help you. I will not usurp you."

The spiritess relaxed, if only by a fraction, and stopped cowering. Jonah sighed in relief and slowly approached her with the intent to further reassure her.

"He might not usurp you, but I sure as hell will."

Jonah whipped around and saw a Deadfallen disciple, with a black bandanna over the bottom of his face. He had been camouflaged perfectly; his dark attire blended well with the shadows of the growing evening. Before Jonah could react, the disciple raised his hands toward the spiritess, and they darkened to the color of night. Instantly, the spiritess began to scream and her composition began to wane.

"No!" Jonah ran forward. "Dammit, stop!"

Jonah had no chance of reaching the disciple or the spiritess in time. She was gone within a few seconds. Jonah bellowed in rage but the disciple was inches away from him before he could act further. After the usurping of the spiritess, he looked invigorated, like he'd had a hundred hours of sleep.

"I wouldn't worry about her, Rowe. I have to admit, though … it was kind of foul, you suckering her in like that, promising her safety, coaxing her into letting her guard down."

Jonah trembled with fury. It was not unnoticed by the disciple, whose eyes narrowed over the bandanna covering the lower part of his face.

"You might want to contain your emotion, Rowe. Because you need to focus on my words. You need to come with me."

"Tell me one good reason why I'd do anything you say," growled Jonah.

"Because your little plan to jump all around North Cackalacki to make your path impossible to follow has failed." The disciple's mouth was covered, but there was mirth in his eyes. "The Transcendent figured it out before you'd even left Ruby River; why do you think that the Nightmare Scenario's net is so wide? Besides all that, if you knew what awaited you in Kinston, you'd thank me for catching you here."

Jonah's eyes widened slightly. Oh, hell no. Felix, Terrence, and Reena were like deer prancing into a trap. A bonafide deadfall. And he still didn't know what had happened to Charles and Patience. And had Raymond made it back safely?

It was in that moment that he realized that he would escape this Deadfallen bastard. He still didn't have a spiritual endowment. But he was an ethereal human. Unendowed didn't mean he was entirely useless.

"Now, raise your hands so that I can bind you in ethereal chains." The disciple raised his weapon higher. "Now!"

Very slowly, Jonah raised his hands. He just needed the bastard to get to work, that was all ...

The man neared Jonah with caution, his eyes narrow the entire time. When he judged that Jonah had accepted his fate, he let down his guard.

And it cost him.

When he touched Jonah's arms, they crackled with blue sparks.

"Ahh!" The disciple was knocked back, but not off his feet.

Jonah ran forward, not even bothering to use his batons, and bashed his head full force into the disciple's nose and mouth. Despite the bandanna, Jonah knew the bleeding was instant.

The Deadfallen disciple was down and writhing in pain, but still very conscious.

Jonah was already running, well aware that the man wasn't out cold. It would take an actual endowment for him to have shocked him unconscious. Without that, all he could muster was a bad sting and some aggravation. Thus, the headbutt.

Jonah ran down a narrow two-lane road. Soon, he saw a sign that announced to him that he was nearing the Cashie River. That made him pause. A July evening plus standing river water equaled mosquitoes. He couldn't hide from this guy if he had to smack his arms and neck every three seconds. He'd have to get to Kinston via the *Astralimes*—at a running start.

He hadn't ever done that before; would running make things go wrong?

"You little bitch! Get back here!".

Jonah was about to find out.

He focused on Kinston as hard as humanly possible, and before he knew it, he was on the Astral Plane, and then in front of three people who all made exclamations of surprise.

"Jonah!" Terrence helped him to his feet. "Are you alright?"

"Yeah," huffed Jonah. "I'm good."

"Why were you running through the *Astralimes?*" The rebuke in Reena's tone was clear. "That is wildly unsafe—you could've come off of the Plane and slammed into a wall—"

"Hello to you, too, Reena," said Jonah.

"What took you so long?" demanded Felix, who looked at Jonah with frustration. "You're twenty minutes behind schedule!"

"What fuckin' schedule?" Jonah fired right back. "This isn't a plan, it's a joke! But you need to listen—"

"Where is Patience?" Felix's eyes were still ablaze. "He was supposed to be with you—"

"He and Charles were in Ruby River, holding off Deadfallen disciples. I hope they got away. Listen, Creyton figured out this ... thing you're all doing. Random spots mean nothing now ... Creyton spread the net almost statewide. The last disciple I saw said something bad was waiting for us here in Kinston, so we really need to leave—"

A hellish *caw* froze everyone. Jonah was the first to see a crow zooming toward them. Now, he was pissed.

"To hell with finding an endowment. I've got this."

He reached into his cargo pants' pocket and removed the apparatus with the black blade on the end of it, the weapon that he had reserved to use on Jessica the next time he saw her. He affixed the apparatus to one of his batons and then threw his eyes up at the crow, which wasn't too far away now.

The crow hit the ground, but the shape-shifting process was already underway, so instead of slamming into the dirt, a person took the impact in a full tuck-and-roll. It was a woman, and when she came to standing, she shook her wild hair from her face.

It was Jessica. Just the sight of her put murder in Jonah's heart. Evil bitch.

"Well, look who it is!" Jonah abandoned his friends. "There *is* a God!"

Jessica just tapped her throat and cried, *"Per mortem, vitam!"*

"We need to be gone!" grunted Felix. "You said that just now, Jonah!"

"I ain't leaving!" snapped Jonah over his shoulder as he broke into a run towards Jessica. "She's not getting away!"

For whatever reason, Jessica did nothing. She didn't draw a weapon or even brace herself. When Jonah was only inches away, a black man with an eye patch appeared directly in front of her. Jonah nearly barreled into him. Momentarily distracted, he paused, and the guy took advantage of his confusion by shoving him down. He then removed something that resembled a gun from his duster and fired it into the air. A beam of light flew from the gun-looking object and exploded when it reached a certain height. He then grabbed Jessica's wrist and pulled her back.

Jonah barely registered that he'd missed his chance to kill Jessica because some type of mist settled on him. It was the substance that was in the capsule that exploded when the one-eyed guy fired it into the air. It was odorless and tasteless—had no harmful effect at all.

But something had changed the second the substance

contacted Jonah's skin. Now, the air felt ... different. It felt heavy, like it was confining on all sides. Jonah had never felt anything like it in his entire life, yet he knew it was wrong.

And likely dangerous.

Some feet away, Terrence must have registered the same effects and he called out to the one-eyed disciple. "What the hell did you just do?"

Even from the distance, Jonah could see the man's smug smile. "Oh, just a successful experiment the Transcendent ordered me to make. That blocked feeling? The denseness of the air you feel? That is the feeling of life about to get really fucked up for you all. And you won't be able to use the *Astralimes* to get away from it. No ethereal travel at all for several hours."

Jonah felt his stomach churn. This was ethereality that he had never experienced before, so he had no reference. But the thickness of the air let him know that this guy was not lying.

"Sean, we're done here." Jessica was terse. "Let's bail."

Sean nodded, grinning at Jonah and his friends. Then he and Jessica melted into crow shape and flew off into the night. The silence left in their wake was deafening.

"What the hell?" said Reena. "Why'd they leave?"

No one had any answers. Felix pulled out a sterling-silver knife and a kama-style weapon. The latter one gleamed the slate-gray of Felix's aura color. "I don't like this." They've prevented us from using the *Astralimes* or any other ethereal travel and then just left? Make sure you're armed."

Reena removed the socket wrench from her pocket, which gleamed yellow. Terrence removed the gloves that concealed his steel knuckles, which gleamed burnt orange. Jonah looked at their aura colors with envy, but it was what it was.

"I know you're concerned about not being endowed, Jonah." Reena must have read him, which Jonah never care for.

"But we've got your back. What I want to know is why they wanted us stuck here. Clearly, they were stalling ... I want to know *why*."

"Indeed, they were stalling," said a new voice. "For me."

Jonah felt all sensations descend from his body. He knew that voice, but it couldn't be. There was no way their luck was that bad.

He turned, and out of the shadows slunk the owner of that voice. Jonah actually winced. While the voice was familiar, the face was anything but. The 49er's countenance was obscured by a cowl, but it was clear that over half it was badly burned, and the left eye was damaged. It looked as though the layers of skin had been burned away by acid or something. Shouldn't those wounds have healed by now?

But such musings didn't matter. Despite the damage, the erstwhile vampire looked more feral than ever.

"Jesus," said Terrence in a numb voice.

"Not quite." The 49er smiled, and his facial wounds made the smile look sickening. "Though an event like this does have similarities." He took them all in. "All of you were present the night I first infiltrated the estate grounds. The only one missing is the Chandler boy. I'll see him soon enough, I'm sure."

He moved in closer, shifting his focus to Jonah.

"I have to be gentle with you, Rowe, but *only* you. The Transcendent didn't say anything about the rest of you."

Felix, who was stiff with incredulity and shock up to that point, suddenly pushed Jonah away and sprang forward. Almost lazily, the 49er pulled a black-gleaming knife from his duster and stabbed Felix with it, just underneath his collarbone.

"Felix!" shouted Reena.

Felix roared in agony, but quicker than they expected, the

49er yanked the blade free and stabbed Felix again, almost in the same spot. Felix collapsed in a heap.

The badly scarred vampire took advantage of Jonah's, Terrence's, and Reena's shock and horror when he darted forward in an inhuman blur, knocking Terrence and Reena back like rag dolls. He was too fast for either of them to block or counter. They both landed numerous feet back in a large mess of garbage.

"No!" Jonah was scared for his friends, but he had his own problems. The 49er had his hands on him.

Instinctively, he jabbed the 49er with his knife apparatus into his undamaged eye. The vampire roared and clutched at it, which bought Jonah time to slap him in the face with his knife-free baton and conjure up paltry sparks to knock the lifeblood looter off his feet.

When Jonah tore off, a kaleidoscope of emotions ran through him: rage, because he didn't have the power to do more, concern for Terrence and Reena, and absolute numbing shock for Felix. It was just like when Jonathan had been vanquished ... he hadn't been able to prevent that. He'd been unendowed then as well ...

And, on top of all that, there was fear. Creyton had let that psychotic vampire out of the ground. How? Trip had claimed that they'd never find his body. But maybe that's what he got for listening to Trip, given the horse's ass he'd turned out to be.

Suddenly, Jonah had to stop running. He doubled over, sucking wind. His energy seemed to drain with each gasp. Where had this come from? He hadn't experienced fatigue like this since before he started trimming up at the estate. It also felt like he'd just relinquished a spiritual endowment. But he hadn't had one to begin with, so why did it seem like his adrenaline decided to make an untimely exit? It was most inopportune, seeing as he hadn't yet escaped ...

But he had to keep going. He'd better not run, though. In this state, he might fall and bust open his head. Then, with his luck, the 49er would smell the lifeblood and forget that Creyton wanted him alive.

He somehow managed to drag himself into an abandoned store, full of empty boxes, debris, and extremely dusty mannequins. Strangely, the door still had a lock, so he locked the door after shutting it. He had to pause again; each movement was more draining. What was wrong with him?

After several minutes, he dragged himself over to a space of wall that wasn't lined by boxes. It was comfortable enough. Then he nearly lost his balance and grabbed hold of a nearby pipe. With much effort, he righted himself.

He released the pipe and frowned. Where his fingers had lopped it were traces of blood. He inspected his arm to discover that he was bleeding from the wrist.

The same wrist that the 49er had grabbed earlier. The bastard hadn't been trying to attack him when he'd gotten hold of him.

Raymond was right. They'd been herding him the entire time, but to a specific bag of tricks. The guy in Windsor must have gotten greedy, because he tried to stop the buck there. But Jonah knew that this had to be the grand plan. Get him to Kinston. Where that one-eyed guy could spray them with his little ethereal travel prevention juice, and then leave him to the 49er.

To poison him. And then cart him off like a sack of potatoes to Creyton.

And all Jonah could do about it was be grateful that the 49er didn't use any Haunts or had the damned bonesword of his.

Were Terrence and Reena okay? He hadn't been in any position to fight or check on them. It was clear that Creyton and his disciples viewed his friends as nothing more than pieces on the field to be removed. And despite all their efforts, he still wound up right where Creyton wanted him.

"Finally, you got here," said the 49er quietly.

Jonah slowly turned his head, not even surprised. He didn't know how long the vampire had been there. It didn't even matter.

"I've been mentally linked with you for a bit. I must say that it took you long enough to figure out the poison. But it would have been easy enough to follow you, either way. You've been leaking lifeblood for the past twenty minutes."

Jonah blinked very slowly. His brain actually managed to register confusion. Twenty minutes had passed? He must have blacked out for a bit when he sat down. But if he'd been that easy to find, why had the 49er allowed that much time to pass?

"I wanted every drop of fight out of your system." The 49er's horrific face twisted into a smile once more. "It just makes things that much easier. Now, let's get going. You're my ticket back into the Transcendent's good graces, after all."

He was about to hoist Jonah up when the locked door was bashed off its hinges.

Felix stood there, dripping with water as well as fury. He leered at the 49er and practically growled with every chest heave.

"You won't kill me like that, bitch. It'll take a whole lot more than that to stop me."

He aimed a crossbow at the 49er's throat and fired one of his trademark silver nails at him. The 49er had been so stunned by his appearance that he hadn't lifted a finger to defend himself. When the silver nail hit him, his hands immediately rose to his throat. He had trouble extracting the nail because the silver burned his hands just as much as his throat. With an anguished gurgle, he crashed to the ground, bringing several mannequins with him.

Felix spat at the heap then came to Jonah's side and pulled him to his feet. He noticed Jonah's bleeding wrist.

"Poison, but not fatal. Unfortunately, that silver nail isn't going to kill him. Hopefully, Creyton will do that for us."

Jonah just looked at Felix. His consciousness faded more and more with each moment. "I thought ..." he slurred, "I thought you were ..."

"Nope." Felix shook his head. "Nope. Got an open wound that stings like a dozen bees and the granddaddy of all headaches, but I'm still here. Now, let's get you home, brother."

Jonah nodded his head, but he didn't have enough strength to pull it back up. The last thing he remembered was Felix preventing him from falling on the floor by grabbing him with two hands.

4

THE GHOST IN THE ROOM

Jonah felt a myriad of sensations. He had the impression of hurried conversations, movement, and hands at his throat, arms, and chest. Despite the largely unintelligible state of mind that he had during this semi-consciousness, he knew that he was in a safe place. He couldn't tell exactly how he knew, but he knew that this was a safe place.

His brain computed things at a much more improved rate from there. Things were more comprehensible. He felt a firm but familiar surface underneath him. This was an infirmary bed.

Christ, he seemed to spend more time in this place than out of it.

A soft hand clutched his, which made him half-smile. No doubt who that was.

"Liz, you don't have to hold my ha—"

Jonah opened his eyes and froze.

"I'm not Liz," said Vera, "but I'm relieved as hell that you're awake." Her voice elevated. "Lizzie! Jonah's up!"

Jonah heard the hurried shuffling of feet but didn't look

that way. He only had eyes for the woman who'd just returned her gaze to him.

"What are you doing here, Vera?"

"Hardly important right now. But let me back up, let Liz do her thing."

She rose and freed her fingers from Jonah's. As always, she left traces of lavender in her wake. Liz was now at Jonah's side, her face tight with concern.

"Jonah, I hope that you aren't too woozy. I also hope that that poison wasn't more potent than Felix initially said—"

"It wasn't." Jonah finally did turn and saw Felix seated in a chair. "Etherarè only subdues, and now 49er sees fit to use it."

Jonah sat up slowly and cautiously, so that his head wouldn't throb as badly. "What did you call it?"

"That poison that 49er used on you is called Etherarè," Felix repeated, his bottle of Distinguished Vintage in his lap. "It's basically curare laced with ethereal properties so that it doesn't asphyxiate you. Don't ask me how; you don't want to know."

"Why was he using that?" asked Liz. "Can't vampires charm prey, or something?"

"Oh hell yeah, they can. But the 49er isn't charming anyone with that mug he's sporting now."

"Not following." Vera this time.

Felix grimaced as he used his injured arm to place the Vintage on a nearby table. "Creyton may have been merciful enough to get that lifeblood looter out of Trip's transient ground prison, but his mercy stretched no further. He burned the 49er with a strain of liquid silver that I've never seen before, and it looks as though it will never heal. Sucks for him, because the irreversible damage happened to be on over seventy percent of his face."

Liz sucked her teeth, Vera winced. Jonah shared neither of

their reactions as he lay back to rest his aching head. "Serves him right. He tried to obscure the damage with a cowl. Epic fail."

He flexed the fingers of his left hand, then the arm that the 49er had pricked with the poison. That entire arm was sore. He made himself as oblivious to it as possible and turned back to Felix. "What happened after the 49er attacked you?"

Before Felix could answer, there was a commotion at the door. Daniel walked in, followed by Raymond, Terrence, and Reena. When Jonah saw his brother and sister, he jumped from the bed, ignoring Liz's protests and his aches, and wrapped them in a group hug.

"You two alright?"

"Still in the physical." said Reena. "That's always a victory."

"Yeah, I'm good." Terrence.

There was something in Terrence's voice that made Jonah frown slightly, but he couldn't address it at that moment, because Daniel cleared his throat.

"If the love-fest is quite over, we all need to talk."

Jonah backed away from Terrence and Reena, ready to speak, but the absence of some people made him pause.

"Shouldn't we wait? For Patience and Charles, I mean?"

Suddenly, the wind picked up in the infirmary, and Patience stepped out of thin air.

"Patience!" said Jonah, relieved. "Where is Charles?"

Patience's eyes were hard. "He ain't coming."

The room seemed to lower in temperature as the realization dawned on everyone present. Jonah felt his mouth slowly open. He had only known Charles fleetingly, but he had come to respect him in that brief period of time.

Patience dropped into a chair, hands at his temples. He didn't sob or bawl, but he looked shell-shocked. Stunned. "I helped as much as I could," his voice was mechanical. "Right after I told Jonah where to go from Elizabeth City, I went to help Charles. Jonah told me that Charles stayed behind to give him a head start. I used the *Astralimes* to Ruby River and was instantly in a fight. Charles had already killed three of them by that point, but those that were left were like rabid dogs. He got into a fight with Charlotte Daynard, and she faked a grave wound, but when he went in to finish her off, she sprung up with that hook-shaped blade of hers, and ..."

His voice trailed off, and he lowered his head, inhaling and exhaling through his nostrils. That was okay—no one needed him to finish. Maybe he couldn't.

Felix regarded Patience in silence for a minute, then spoke. "My dad always spoke highly of Barisford Charles. It's been years since I've heard those stories, but I've never forgotten them. Dad said that he and Charles started their first campaign together, and Charles was one of the few who wasn't prejudiced against him for being a sazer."

Terrence shook his head. "That was one of Dad's closest friends. I ain't looking forward to that conversation."

"Before anyone does anything," said Daniel suddenly, "let's show some respect to the fallen."

He walked to the center of the group and pulled out an arrow as he did so. He held it out straight for all to see. It gleamed with the gold of his aura, which abruptly began to increase in brilliance.

"To Barisford Charles. Networker, braveheart, and ally. A thousand praises upon him for giving up his physical life in valiant battle, and may his celestial journey be rich with peace, tranquility, joy, and honor. Life never ends."

"Life never ends," everyone intoned.

Daniel's arrow burst into a golden flame, and soon burned to nothing in his palm. He patted the same palm on his shoulder, and the flames were gone. Jonah's eyes stayed on the spot where the flame had been, his teeth clenched. Yet another pine box on his conscience.

"Felix." Daniel was all business once more. "You mentioned something about the Deadfallen disciples having a substance that prevented using the *Astralimes?*"

"What!" Patience and Liz said it at the same time. Vera looked at Jonah for validation, and he nodded at her. There was no way he'd forget the dense, heavy feeling that the air had taken on after he got hit with that mist. It was like he was claustrophobic while in an open space.

"Yeah." Felix winced as he flexed his arm. "I'm thinking that the 49er was the ultimate trap for Jonah in the Nightmare Scenario. We were distracted by that skank Jessica Hale—"

Felix abruptly ceased and along with everyone else looked Vera's way in an awkward sort of manner. She waved a hand, indifferent.

"By all means, keep going. I've had ample practice numbing out when it comes to my sister."

Felix contemplated her, shrugged, and continued. "Hale baited Jonah...he looked like he was headed to do her some serious damage...but then Sean Tooles showed up in front of her, shot something in the air that made that crap rain down on us, and then the two of them blazed. Then the 49er popped up, hoping to swoop in and collect Jonah for Creyton."

"How did you manage to use the *Astralimes?*" asked Jonah, whose mind went from Charles to his missed chance concerning Jessica. "You didn't have that crossbow on you when I first saw you."

"I bashed a nearby fire hydrant and doused myself with water," answered Felix. "Tooles' mist must not have been waterproof, because it was nullified almost as soon as the water got on me. I used the *Astralimes* to one of my stashes, got the crossbow, and came back for you, Terrence, and Reena."

"Felix," Liz who looked concerned, "I don't like you still in those wet clothes. The last thing you need is a stab wound *and* hypothermia."

"You can get hypothermia in summer?" asked Terrence, astounded.

"You're joking, right?" Reena looked at him in disbelief.

Something that Jonah couldn't place flashed in Terrence's eyes.

"Yeah, of course." Terrence's response was dull.

Liz headed toward Felix. "Let me look at that again—"

"It can wait, Lizzie." Felix stood up. "We all need to meet up with everybody downstairs." He looked at Jonah. "I know you're still healing, man, but get your ass in gear. We finally need to address the Ghost in the Room."

Jonah closed his eyes tightly. His head had improved, but that didn't matter. He'd been bummed out, humiliated, tricked, chased, and poisoned that night. He'd gladly relive all of that if it meant he didn't have to deal with that subject.

"You guys all head downstairs." Jonah kept his eyes closed. "I need to change my clothes."

Everyone left. Terrence and Reena both went to their rooms, no doubt wanting to change out of their damp clothing, too. It was just Jonah and Vera now, and Vera looked confused as hell.

"Am I missing something here?"

"Liz hasn't told you?"

Vera shook her head. Jonah sighed.

"There is a plan in place for everyone to relocate, lie low during ... whatever Omega will bring. There is a plan on paper, but it won't be implemented until I say so."

He closed his eyes once more. He still didn't want to be the

68

one that made these decisions; what he just told Vera didn't even sound right coming out of his mouth. He hurried on. "I can tell you with complete certainty that a lot of people here have a very definite opinion on the call I should make, but I've been putting it off. I admit it. This matter has become that subject that everyone thinks about, but no one verbalizes. So, we started referring to it as the Ghost in the Room, because under the circumstances, *Elephant* just didn't measure up."

He chuckled in spite of himself, and grabbed some spare clothing that Liz, Akshara, and Skylar always put in the infirmary. He made to step into the bathroom to change, but Vera raised a hand to stop him.

"Seriously, Jonah. We've had sex."

Jonah snorted. It wasn't like he'd forgotten. "Very true."

He began to undress right there, wondering why he'd had any misgivings. There were threats to the ethereal world, after all. It's not like someone seeing his ass (who'd already seen it, after all) was that big on the radar. Vera had no awkwardness about it, either. She simply pulled out her phone and began to play on it.

"Speaking of sex," she said without looking up from her phone, "what happened with your no-strings arrangement? Your benefits friend? Lila? Lala?"

"Lola." Jonah as he discarded the ripped and ruined shirt. "And how exactly did you know about her?"

"Liz, of course."

Jonah shook his head. "I love Lizzie from the bottom of my heart, but that girl loves to keep people abreast of everything! Which is why it's kind of odd that she didn't fill you in concerning the Ghost in the Room."

"Nice try, Jonah." Vera finally looked up from the phone. "But don't change the subject. What happened with your little buddy?"

Jonah sighed. "Nothing happened. She works as a news-caster, if Liz didn't tell you. She is damn good at it. So much so that about two months ago, somebody called her all the way from freakin' England. They wanted to know if she'd be interested in working for *London Tonight*. She took the job and moved there last month. We're still friends and everything; we keep up on *Facebook* and *Gmail* and all that."

"Huh." Vera's face was inscrutable. "Good for her."

"Why did you want to know?" inquired Jonah, who regarded her with very real curiosity.

Vera shrugged. "I just didn't think that a casual sex arrangement was a good fit for you. You're a grown man; you can do whatever you want. But the vibe that I always got off of you was that it wasn't good enough unless it was a serious relationship. So, the whole friends-with-benefits thing seemed out of character, my opinion."

Jonah didn't know what to say to that, so he let it pass. It was a little interesting to know that Vera gave the matter enough thought to have such an opinion on it. He had half a mind to ask about East but didn't like the bastard enough to be curious. "So, why are you here, V?" he asked instead as he pulled up the athletic pants. "It's very good to see you, but what's the deal?"

"Tours don't last forever, Jonah. Although it might feel like it. We toured for over a year and some change. This breather was necessary."

"Oh. Gotcha."

He frowned. He's always had a way with words, and he couldn't come up with a better response than that?

Vera didn't seem put off by the lame response, though. She walked nearer to Jonah, which forced him to steel himself. He wished that lavender scent wasn't always so damned disarming, but it was. And he had to remind himself, once again, that Vera was in a committed relationship—and it had been established that that relationship was with a prick. But that was beside the point. If anything, he hoped that East realized how lucky he was.

"We jumped off the subject." Vera put the phone away. "Back to this ... Ghost in the Room thing ... it's okay to not know what to do, Jonah."

Jonah took a deep breath. "Not when you're the one who's supposedly in charge."

Jonah and Vera went to the family room together and Vera sat next to Liz, who was of course next to Bobby. Some things never changed, and that made Jonah smile for a second. It was also comforting to see all his other friends there: Terrence, Reena, Alvin, Doug, Katarina, Spader, Magdalena, Nella, and Themis. It was also a comfort to see the other people who hadn't left the estate, like Xenia, Sebastian, R.J., and Jada. They hadn't run off, though they were well within their rights to do so. That kind of bravery was the primary reason that he didn't want to have this conversation.

But here they all were.

Daniel stood nearby, twirling a new arrow. Patience had composed himself, though he looked more fatigued than ever. Felix massaged the wrapping that covered his wound, but his eyes were on Jonah. Jonah felt the eyes but didn't look that way as he joined Terrence and Reena near the fireplace. Terrence acknowledged him with a nod.

"We're just waiting a few more minutes. Raymond went to get our parents, tell Dad the bad news about Charles—"

No sooner had Terrence said that, the wind picked up and three Decessio people stepped out of nothingness. Jonah looked at Mr. Decessio. By the look in his eyes, he was now aware of what had happened to his friend. His expression was stoic; it was if he chose to remain a pillar. Like if he dared show any emotion, he might break down. Jonah respected that. He'd been there himself. Mrs. Decessio looked more prone to emotion than her husband at the moment, but she too chose stoic for her demeanor. Jonah's heart went out to them both.

But unfortunately, now was not the time for mourning. Jonah gritted his teeth.

"We all know why we're here." He was suprised his tone was steady. "So, let's finally address the Ghost in the Room, shall we?"

He looked around at the faces. Some had tightened, while some deflated. He cleared his throat.

"I want to go on record—again—and say that I don't want to greenlight an exodus. I've always thought that abandoning the estate was a mistake—"

"And that is your first mistake, Jonah," interrupted Felix. "To see objectively, you need to dial it back. This isn't about abandonment; it's about letting people handle their safety the best way they know how. Make their own choices."

Jonah looked at Felix, turning the words over in his mind before he said them, attempting to find a way for them not to sting. "With all due respect, Felix, I really don't think your opinion is the best one to follow on this. You're a loner, after all."

Felix's eyes widened, but Reena stepped in before the sazer started emitting sparks.

"Nobody believes in this place more than I do. With Trip gone, I am now the resident who has been here longer than anybody. And I don't want to see us leave it. However, I am also a pragmatist. This isn't the time to make emotional choices."

"My thoughts exactly, Reena! This is not the time to make emotional choices. I see where you're coming from, and where Felix is coming from, but at the same time, this is riddled with emotion. I'm willing to swear that most of you guys are probably rattled by what happened tonight with that Nightmare Scenario."

"Aren't *you* rattled, Jonah?" asked Magdalena. "Can you honestly stand there and say that you weren't scared? Or say that you can blame us for being scared for you?"

"That's a good point, Magdalena." Katarina this time. "Jonah, imagine for a second that you had gotten caught tonight, and you had never made the call on this. We'd have lost you *and* been wide open to Creyton and his disciples."

Jonah closed his eyes. That hadn't occurred to him. Not only was the estate his responsibility now, he was also responsible for everyone in it. What *if* the Nightmare Scenario had gone as planned?

"Katarina, you're speaking as someone who wore the Curaie's blinders on their eyes for a lifetime," said Nella coldly. "So many things have happened in our favor because this estate is here."

"I see your point, Nella," Mrs. Decessio piped up, "and I am no fan of an exodus, either. But I have a perspective that you can't yet understand ... that of a parent. When times are hard, you want to keep your family safe, and close when possible. It's just the way that it is. That is why Maxine's mother didn't allow her to return when she had second thoughts about leaving here. It's why you and Liz keep arguing with your parents every night because they don't want either of you at the estate right now. We have no idea what Creyton is planning right now, but in regards to our families, we'd want to at least have them within reach when his plans come to fruition."

Nella fell silent. There was truly nothing she could say to that one. Jonah attempted to change tacks.

"Consider those of us who have nowhere to go. Like Spader. Like Prodigal and Autumn Rose. What about them?"

"I appreciate you thinking of me like that, bro," Spader did indeed look touched, "but I've always been able to take care of myself. Prodigal and his girl would probably tell you that they've been on their own most of their lives. As you can see, they ain't even here right now."

"Will you listen to yourselves right now?" said Bobby suddenly. "It makes me sick to my stomach to hear how so many of you are so willing to just bail hell on out! Trip must have had a stronger influence than I previously thought—"

"This has nothing to do with Trip." Magdalena surprised people when she spoke. "And it's not about his bunch of idiot friends, either! We all know Omega is near. We know that. And wondering when Creyton and his Deadfallen disciples will come for us ... it's like being held down, but water weight or something. We aren't being proactive at this moment; we're just ... here. And Jonah,"—she turned exclusively to him—"I'm with you every step of the way. I'm loyal, and I hope you know that. But Trip and his buddies aren't the only ones who left here. People that we actually cared about left as well, like Maxine."

"That happened after Trip sat there and messed with their heads!" Jonah was heated once more. "Need I remind you that Trip was planning a bully move all along? We've been here before. Remember how low our numbers were when the Curaie was trying to crack down on us and Balthazar Lockman was throwing around his lies?"

"This is worlds different—"

"No, it isn't!" Why couldn't they see? Why couldn't they understand that they all needed was to stick together? "It's us against an enemy! Same rules apply, then and now. And how did we get through it? We sure as fuck didn't scatter! That's what they wanted us to do. And we pulled through it—"

"Because of Jonathan, Jonah." It was clear by Felix's tone

that Jonah's labeling him a loner had stung. By his response, he must have felt like he was giving Jonah his receipt. But he didn't stop there. "Because of Jonathan. He never wanted anyone to scatter, but he isn't around anymore. We can't base our decisions on what Jonathan would do. Now, you know our views, but this is ultimately your call."

Jonah was furious. But it wasn't toward Felix. It was toward himself.

Jonathan did this day in and day out. Made it look like it was nothing. Then he passed it on to Jonah, who had experienced a vicious brawl, watched more than seventy residents leave, got chased across North Carolina, and had a highly respected Networker get killed in the line of duty protecting him.

All of that had happened under his watch.

So yeah, there was definitely some anger there.

"Alright." Painstakingly, Jonah kept his emotions out of his voice. "You got it. The exodus is greenlit."

Many faces looked relieved, others uncertain.

"*But*," continued Jonah rather forcefully, "it will happen after an event I've been thinking about, and not a second sooner."

"What's that?" asked Raymond.

"A party for Bobby, Liz, Nella, and Themis. They've all had their graduations, and I want to do an all-inclusive gathering for them."

Nella and Themis looked touched, as did Liz. Bobby looked slightly caught off guard because the gesture was unexpected.

For the first time, Daniel spoke. "Jonah, I never really understood the need you all have to celebrate every little thing, but a gathering like that would be dangerous. That would be the perfect time for an attack."

"I'm not as dumb as you think, Daniel." Jonah didn't even attempt to veil his sarcasm. "I've had Bast and all the other heralds shoring up protective measures all over the property. I have already made arrangements with Patience about getting some S.P.G. practitioners to do sentry duty for that entire weekend. The party would be Friday night, so the exodus can be the very next night. Nana used to always say that the greatest weapon against worry was celebration. We've got plenty of time to worry, so why don't we give the latter a shot, just for one night? This will happen, non-negotiable. Meeting adjourned."

"Not just yet," said Felix hastily. There is one more thing that I need to do."

Felix walked up to Jonah, Terrence, and Reena, a pen and pad in his hand. Jonah saw a change in his face. He'd looked tense and slightly combative earlier, but now his expression was warmer, even respectful.

"Reena, tell me somewhere that Kendall has always wanted to go."

"What?" Reena frowned. "Why?"

"If we are scattering, then your fiancée needs to be in a place where she can't be kidnapped, used, or hurt."

Reena rose when she realized what Felix meant. "No. I'm not cool with that."

"You're not cool with your girl being safe and far away?" asked Spader, puzzled.

"Stay out of this, or I will freeze your nuts off." Reena hadn't even taken her eyes off Felix when she snapped at Spader. "Kendall won't be away from me. Creyton would never—"

"Yeah, he would." Felix didn't miss a beat.

"He doesn't know about her!" protested Reena. "It's not like we have allowed anyone in our business!"

"Reena, you are one of the best friends of Creyton's mortal enemy," said Felix in a blunt tone, "who happens to now be the Overseer of the estate and the single best hope we have to survive Omega. Don't think for one second that Creyton hasn't made a point to know everything about you and Terrence both."

Jonah was curious now. Felix had just been so contentious and disagreeable, and then he turned around and gave Jonah a glowing endorsement? Was it just complexity, or did this dude have a split personality?"

Reena chose to ignore Felix's words. "I won't do it. There isn't a damn thing you can say that will change that."

Jonah had half a mind to ask Reena, "Where's your damn pragmatism now?" but the urge faded almost as soon as it had come. He was aggravated, but not evil.

Terrence placed a hand on Reena's shoulder which, surprisingly, she didn't shrug off. "Reena, you said that you wanted Kendall to be safe. You said that you wanted for the day to come where you two could be married and not have to worry about nothing. For that day to come, you both have to survive Omega. You can fight all comers. Kendall, on the other hand, would be no match against a Deadfallen disciple. Let Felix help keep her safe."

Jonah felt a huge upsurge of respect for Terrence. He said that far better than he could have.

Reena forcibly wiped tears from her eyes. "Tullamore," she conceded.

"Ireland." Felix nodded. "Nice taste." Then he turned to Jonah. "Jonah, your friends ... the married couple. Nelson and Tamara, was it? Think of a place."

Jonah shook his head. "I appreciate the gesture, Felix, truly, but they can't travel. Tamara is pregnant."

Felix looked pensive. "How far along?"

Jonah racked his brains. "Five and a half months, I think?"

"That's no problem." Felix jotted something on a notepad. "It's a good rule of thumb for an expecting mother not to fly after thirty weeks. She's got time."

Liz looked at Felix in amazement, as did several others, Jonah included. Felix rolled his eyes.

"Don't ask me how I know. Just accept that I do. Now Jonah, if you please."

"Um, they love the Poconos—"

"No good, not far enough." Felix shook his head. "What else you got?"

"Uh..." Jonah thought on it. "Nelson said that they would love to visit Vancouver."

"Better." Felix wrote something else down. "I'll take care of these people."

"Just hold on a second," said Jonah. "What are you going to do?"

"Your friends are winning free trips."

"But Felix," Jonah looked at him, "they need explanations to get out of work. And we don't even know how long they need to be away—"

"Pointless details." Felix pocketed the pen and pad. "Let me take care of it. You just get some rest."

"You shouldn't use the *Astralimes* with your injury, Felix," said Liz. "You might want to fire up the mobile bunker and drive."

"Uh, no, actually." Felix's response was a little hasty, but hey, he was a weird dude. "I can handle the *Astralimes*. You guys just do what you need to do to get this place ready for the exodus."

He stepped into thin air and was gone. Spader whistled.

"He might not be spoiled and bourgeois, but he still has this ... this *way* of flaunting that he's loaded."

"I think that that was selfless and considerate, Royal," said Liz. "You could learn a lesson or two."

"Oh, no doubt," murmured Spader, "because we all need the ability to fly folks 'round the world."

Conveniently, he didn't say it loud enough for Liz or Bobby to hear. Usually, that cowardice would have amused Jonah, but that was not the case tonight.

He excused himself without even bothering to invent a reason, headed outside, and didn't stop walking until he reached the gazebo. When he sat down, he looked up at the night sky, slightly insulted by its starriness and clarity. Unsurprisingly, there were footfalls behind him shortly thereafter. He didn't bother turning around.

"That must have been rough," said Terrence.

"Wow, you guessed."

The sarcasm was so halfhearted that Terrence didn't even acknowledge it. "It doesn't take away from you being a great leader, Jonah."

"Yeah, I'm a real natural. I'm so great at it that I couldn't even save my own friends."

"You are starting to sound a little whiny, Jonah." Reena, was stern. "Tell your ego to take a walk. You've got bigger fish to fry."

Now it was Jonah's turn to not acknowledge a jab. He lifted his eyes back to the stars.

"Reena, did you get that bump on your head checked out?" asked Terrence suddenly. "The 49er clocked you as hard as he did me."

"My head is fine, Terrence."

Jonah looked her way. "Reena, you have a bump on your head. You might have a mild concussion—"

"I am not getting checked out, for Liz's own good. Because if I went up there, let her check me, and then she saw fit to

Green Deal me before Felix sends Kendall away ... let's just say that she and I will have a massive problem."

Jonah and Terrence looked at each other and came to a silent agreement: Reena could have this one.

"Why didn't you say anything through all of this, Terrence?" Jonah asked.

That thing flashed across Terrence's face again. It had only happened a couple of times, but Jonah knew that he already disliked that expression very much. "You guys were doing just fine without my opinion. I sincerely hope that Creyton is off somewhere, burning up whatever is left of the 49er's face."

"Seconded," said Reena, massaging the back of her head.

Jonah said nothing; just stared straight ahead, to the trees near the gazebo. He vaguely remembered a conversation with Jonathan way back when about darkened paths not necessarily needing a bad connotation. After Creyton orchestrated Jonathan's vanquishing, Jonah wondered if that assessment could be disputed.

"Jonah, you can't let Creyton get into your head," said Reena firmly. Despite her minor head injury, it seemed that her essence reading was still very much intact. "He thrives—*thrives* —on that bullshit. But when you break it down to the lowest common denominator, he's no different from those pricks you were in school with all those years ago."

"There is one blaring difference, Reena," said Jonah, whose eyes were still on the trees.

"Yeah? What's that?"

Jonah took a slow breath through his nostrils. "Those pricks back in school weren't murderers."

5
DIGGING

Preparations for the exodus began the next day. It was slow work, but Jonah knew why. Most people shared his view and didn't want to leave the estate. It felt tantamount to uprooting everyone's lives. Uprooting lives that people had not only grown accustomed to but had grown to love dearly.

And now, things had to change.

Manpower proved quite changeable, as people had to accommodate school and work. Patience resumed his duties and also had the unenviable task of informing the Networkers about Barisford Charles' passing. The best thing that Jonah could do for him was tell him to reach out if he needed anything. It was rather paltry in his eyes, but Patience seemed touched and appreciative. Score one small victory.

After a conversation with Daniel, the former Protector Guide gave him a small bit of advice before he resumed his trademark taciturn behavior.

"Never judge the size of a victory. Sizes change, but the fact that it's a victory remains the same."

As the plan was to scatter, people needed to keep their

belongings slight. As such, everyone began to move the bulk of their personal items to their homes, which was very tough. The people that had no homes beyond the estate donated their things to the Brown Bag Charity up in town. There were more than a few tears shed, but most folks distracted themselves by throwing themselves into the work necessary to empty the estate.

On more than one occasion, Jonah caught himself observing Vera when he should have been hard at work. He couldn't get over how much she'd changed. Vera had always had that sassy, sarcastic streak, and that was still very much there. But the confusion, apprehension, and self-consciousness that had accompanied those traits back when they'd met at Colerain Place was long gone. Time had had a hand in that; everyone was now older and wiser. But that was only a small part. Vera was a lot surer of herself, carried herself better, and didn't give a damn who saw her facial scar anymore. She even wore a tank top that didn't obscure the scars on her upper arm and the top of her back.

"She has changed, hasn't she?" said Terrence from behind him, which made him jump.

"Uh, what?"

Terrence's eyes narrowed. "This is me, Jonah. Plus, you've already banged her. You don't have to hide behind justifications."

Jonah snorted. Had Reena been around, she probably would have smacked Terrence for saying what he'd said. But just between the two of them, it was what it was. He resumed gathering boxes. "Okay, fine. You saw me looking at her. And yeah, she has changed. I was curious what made that so. Was it one thing, or a series of things?"

"Maybe it's because she's gotten a taste of doing what she

loves," theorized Terrence. "Being in front of all those crowds made her stronger ... more confident."

"Maybe it took her leaving North Carolina," mused Jonah. "Small town-living doesn't work for everybody."

"Or maybe she finally grew up after no longer having the scepter of her secret family ties hanging over her head."

They both turned to see Liz, buried under her straw hat, with weeds in her hands.

"You know, Jonah, you could just go over there and talk to her. Beyond the random and scattered conversations you guys have had over the past couple days. And Terrence, I heard what you said about *banging*—" She dropped the weeds and punched him in the gut. "Must you be so damned uncouth?"

Terrence rubbed the area that Liz struck with a grin. "Oh, Lizzie, where would I be without occasional scathing rebukes from you or Reena? But with all due respect, the ones from Reena actually hurt."

"She ain't here," said a voice. "I am."

Stella Marie came from nowhere and tackled Terrence, pummeling him while he yelped and cried out in surprise. Jonah winced, well aware that a scuffle with a sazer wasn't fun. She then hopped up, snatched up the dirty weeds Liz had dropped, and dumped them on Terrence. He waved dust away and coughed.

"I heard every word," she grumbled. "You bang nails, not women. You earned my respect the first night I met you, but you are *such* a chauvinist sometimes."

Terrence shook dirt from himself, still disoriented. Stella Marie disregarded him and looked up at Jonah.

"Liz had a good point, Jonah. Why don't you just be a man and go talk to Haliday?"

Jonah took a deep breath at Stella Marie's wording but shrugged as he grabbed boxes. "You can see that I'm busy."

With a laugh, Liz walked off. Stella Marie shook her head, muttered *Elevenths,* and followed. Terrence rose and dusted himself off.

"You *better* leave!" he called after Stella Marie, then refocused on Jonah. "Don't pay them no-never-mind, man. You can't be faulted for respecting her relationship."

"Speaking of which," Jonah was suddenly curious, "I wonder what East thinks of her being down here. She hasn't mentioned anything about him."

"Maybe he's in Hong Kong or Tokyo somewhere, participating in a hostile takeover or whatever it is that corporate execs do." Terrence shrugged. "But look at it like this, man—Vera, Lola ... at least those women acknowledged your presence."

It took Jonah a few seconds to figure out who Terrence meant. "Rheadne? You still hung up on her?"

"How could I not be, Jonah? Woman was awesome, and fine as hell."

"But I thought she went down in your eyes after she left you trapped with those cannibals and all that."

Terrence shrugged again. "At the time, I was fuckin' pissed about that, but I've had time to forgive and forget. She had gone for help, after all. And you, Reena, and that Oxendine girl showed up a few minutes later. All turned out well. No need for a grudge."

Jonah shook his head. His brother was whipped by a woman several states away. A woman who didn't even realize that she had a hold over him. Jonah wished him luck. Anything was possible, after all.

A car came down the drive, which distracted them both, but it turned out to be Reena. She stepped out, glanced at them, but simply nodded. There was a fierceness in her eyes, but neither Jonah nor Terrence bought it.

"Did everything work out?" asked Terrence.

"Oh yeah." Reena was oddly formal. "Kendall and I had a long talk; she wasn't fully sold on going. Felix knew that I wouldn't be the most convincing of people, seeing as I didn't want her to go either, so he leveled with her before I could. In the end, she agreed. Felix fixed everything to a T. Strange thing was that he did it as soon as he left the estate that night we'd agreed to do the exodus. Kendall already had a passport, so that was no problem. The documentation and flight and everything were squared away. He even set her up with a flat in Tullamore. I didn't leave RDU until she was in the air."

Reena lowered her head. She looked to be seconds away from a meltdown. Jonah couldn't help but acknowledge the difference in reactions. When Nelson called him about the "extended trip abroad" he acted surprised, of course. But Nelson and Tamara were over the moon. Tam even reveled the notion of having her baby on Canadian soil. They were ecstatic, while Kendall had to be convinced. He understood why, but still viewed it with wistfulness: Nelson and Tam on an indefinite, all-expense-handled trip to Canada. Kendall headed for Tullamore, Ireland for who knew how long. And Lola was now living out a dream in England. He, meanwhile, had to abandon his home and figure out how to topple Creyton, who had all the odds on his side. It made him want to lower his own head. But he decided to help himself by helping his sister.

He stepped closer to Reena so that the other people working outside wouldn't hear. "Reena, this isn't Julia Gallagher. You aren't setting Kendall free. You're keeping her safe. And when this is all over, you can get back to her."

"And you're doing her a favor," threw in Terrence. "She is gonna love being away from all those old fuckin' fossils she can't stand in her department at L.T.S.U."

Reena actually chuckled. "I'll give you that one."

The brief levity faded.

"What if something happens to me? What if we don't make it through this? What if—?"

"Reena." Jonah grabbed her shoulders. "You will see Kendall again. You'll get married. All of those things will happen. Let's just get through this. You *will* see Kendall again."

Reena met his eyes, and Jonah instantly felt afraid and a little guilty. He was in no position to say that those things would happen. He didn't have a clue what might happen to Reena. Or Terrence. Or even himself. His words were merely affirmations. Far from guarantees.

Reena squared her shoulders, took a deep breath, and nodded. Jonah was glad to see that she had her dampener on, because it would have sucked something fierce if she'd read the doubt in his essence. "You're right, Jonah. I still am concerned for us all, but admitting defeat means that we've lost already."

Her eyes fell on her engagement ring and lingered there for a few seconds. Then she looked at Jonah and Terrence again but this time the fierceness in her gaze was legitimate. Jonah half-wondered if he'd done something wrong.

"Can you guys get away from what you're doing?" she asked suddenly. "I need to talk to the both of you about something."

"No problem." Jonah was relieved for the shift. "Need to go to Jonathan's study?"

"It's your study now, Jonah," Reena reminded him. "But no. The studio."

The place seemed foreign to Jonah. After Jonathan got vanquished, Kendall convinced Reena to put her paintings in storage. With them gone from Reena's art studio, the place just seemed ... naked. He had a vague memory of how empty the dorm rooms looked when it was time to move out for the summer. One simply didn't realize the attachments that they made to objects, or the feeling of wrongness engendered by their absence.

Reena walked straight through the empty space without a moment's hesitation and stopped at her table. On it was a stack of sketches, scribbled-on pages, and the Phantom Key.

"You're still using that thing?" asked Terrence with uneasiness.

Reena scoffed. "Of course. It's quite interesting and fun when you're not being drained of essence and required to recreate feelings of anger. But I brought you down here for a reason."

She walked to the opposite side of the table...a feat made possible by the lack of paintings around it...so the three of them could face one another.

"Jonah, when you became Overseer of this estate, you gave me free reign of the library in the study. I was reading and researching for hours in there."

"Me too," said Jonah. "You know that research is a hobby of mine."

"Well, I didn't." Terrence had zero shame. "I just looked over a few things. It's cool that Jonathan had records of every Eleventh Percenter who's ever been here."

"Funny you should bring that up, Terrence." Reena snapped her fingers. "Because I saw those, too. Pored over them, to be honest. When I read over the last thirty years' worth...the ones that would include us, I mean...there were a few pages of Phantom Cipher tucked in there."

She grabbed them from the table and waved them for Jonah and Terrence. Terrence recoiled, but Reena half-grinned.

"Don't worry. I tested a portion of the cipher before I cracked it all. Totally benign. Lets me know that it was Jonathan who did it."

Jonah looked Reena over, remembering how wan and

decrepit she looked the last time a cipher was malignant. Satisfied when he saw none of those symptoms, he nodded. "Alright then. What did you find?"

Reena held up a sheet of paper, which showed what seemed to be a random array of letters that, when looked at head-on, created a landscape. The top, written in Reena's handwriting, read: **SPAIRITIN COUSLAND**.

"Spairitin Cousland?" read Jonah. "Who the hell is that?"

"It's not a person, it's a place. A town. Inhabited entirely by Eleventh Percenters."

Jonah's eyes instantly abandoned the page and shot to Reena. "What!"

"Are you serious?" demanded Terrence.

"Serious as sin. Nothing but ethereal humans."

Jonah snatched the page from Reena's grasp and stared hard at it. "So, the letters aren't random. They shape out a location."

"Yes." Reena nodded. "Put it down on the table and let me show you something else."

Jonah did so, and the three of them leaned in as Reena placed her finger at the tip of one of the landscapes.

"They aren't just random letters used to shape out the location. They're the actual directions."

Jonah's eyes narrowed. Sure enough, the letters he thought to be trivial spelled out such things as *West* and *South* and so on.

"So, you know how to get to this place?" asked Terrence.

Reena sighed. "Yes and no."

"Huh?"

"I didn't say that to be esoteric or theatrical," said Reena hastily. "I truly mean yes and no. Yes, because the directions are there, plain as day. And no, because at this particular moment they are less than useless."

Jonah looked up from the pages. "Why is that?"

Reena pulled some other pages from her table. "Jonathan explained it here. These people have taken painstaking effort to remain hidden. Apparently, they function much like an isolationist nation; they are self-sustaining and have something like closed borders."

"Closed borders?" said Terrence, baffled. "Like ... like the Vatican, or something?"

"Not exactly," said Reena. "They probably have interactions with people around them, but it's likely minimal. They keep to themselves, and trust is as exclusive as platinum bars."

Jonah didn't know how he felt about that. Closed borders and minimal contact with the outside world put him in mind of backwater inbreds as naïve as Katarina Ocean. The change in his face did not go unnoticed by Reena, who shook her head.

"I highly doubt that it's an ethereal outpost of yokels, Jonah. Closed borders and limited contact with the surrounding people don't mean primitive; it just means that they aren't very impressionable and prone to be swayed by outsiders."

"Okay, that part I understand. No outside influences screwing you this way and that. It has its appeals, but also has limitations. How old is this place?"

"I don't think Jonathan even knew. Could be as old as Jamestown, Virginia for all we know."

"But could you imagine that?" Terrence was mystified. "Think of the history! The culture! The stories! Why didn't Jonathan ever tell us about this place?"

"He'll have had his reasons," said Reena. "Most of which would probably be to prevent people from trying to find it en masse and abuse and misuse their culture and way of life."

"Then why tell us now?"

Reena fingered her dampener. "Let's all be honest with

ourselves.We all know that Omega, however it starts, will not end without a fight. We're kind of at war already, so that's a given."

Jonah and Terrence nodded. Everyone was still on the same page.

"And we know that Jonathan knew pretty much everything that went on at the estate, as well as in the ethereal world," Reena went on. "He was a Protector Guide, after all. I'm willing to swear on the Vitasphera that Jonathan knew that Trip would try an insurrection, try to get people to leave the estate. This information on Spairitin Cousland was probably like some kind of ... of backdoor plan B to bolster our ranks in the event that Trip went forward with his runaway scheme."

"Sweet!" Terrence punched the air. "Hell yes! Jonathan thought of everything!"

Jonah kept his eyes on Reena. Something in her expression told him that she was only halfway finished. "What else?" was all he said.

"Think about it." Reena regarded the pages. "An entirely ethereal society uncorrupted and undiluted by outside forces. Veins of knowledge forgotten by many."

Jonah tensed. "You think Creyton's looking for this place as well."

The gleam in Terrence's eye faded. "Well, fuck."

"Exactly," said Reena. "The possibilities are endless. Creyton could find access to a forgotten, or even secret, ethereality. He could try to sway people to join the Deadfallen disciples like he did with the sazer underground, or he could—"

"Flat out destroy it," finished Jonah. It made perfect sense.

Reena nodded. "It would be stupid to think that he doesn't know about Spairitin Cousland, too. But I don't know if he knows where it is yet. And that's a very good thing. But if he finds them first, you can bet on two things with this: one, it won't end well for them and two, whatever happens, good or bad, will tip the scales in Omega."

"So, we go there before he finds it then," said Jonah. "They'd have to listen to us if they knew that we meant no harm."

"But both of y'all are forgetting something," said Terrence, wide-eyed. "Early on, Reena said that the directions to this place were useless. Why is that?"

Jonah scowled. He'd completely forgotten about that. They'd deviated far from that point.

"According to what Jonathan left in the cipher, the directions only work when you get near the place," said Reena with reluctance. "All those directions—east, southwest, and all that? They won't start to make sense until we get within about a hundred-mile radius."

Terrence made a wry face and shook his head. Jonah stared at Reena.

"You've got to be kidding."

Reena chuckled with little to no mirth. "Jonathan did write that these people took painstaking effort to remain hidden."

Jonah hung his head. "The ethereal world is full of surprises. And I swear to God, sometimes that isn't a good thing."

6
THE FINISHING TOUCHES

By Thursday, everything was in order. Heavy bags and belongings were all gone, and everyone had their scatter locations. Felix, Reverend Abbott, and Mr. Decessio (along with several of his contacts) set up safehouses all over, all funded by Felix. Jonah shook his head when he thought about it. He never actually knew how much money Felix had—he evasively said that he was "loaded"— but to have the ability to comfortably lodge so many people for an indefinite amount of time ... man. Loaded might be an understatement. He wondered if the second-generation-rich sazer would have been so accommodating had seventy people not departed the estate.

Every vehicle was gone as well. Jonah put a plan in place for everyone to use the *Astralimes* simultaneously on Saturday evening. There was fear that piecemeal departures would arouse suspicion. Daniel and the heralds would stay at the estate, as they had no other home base, and the belief was once all the residents were gone, the ethereality of the property would be that much stronger with less people to protect.

Surprisingly, no one had even entertained the possibility that Jonah, as Overseer, would stay behind.

"Can't happen, and it won't happen," Daniel told him. "Creyton wants you worse than any of us. You need to get as far away from here as humanly possible."

That stance made Jonah's plans for the near future that much easier. There would be no arguments when he, Terrence, and Reena headed out to find Spairitin Cousland.

The three of them made the decision not to tell any of their friends about Spairitin Cousland, because with Creyton looking for it as well, too many prying eyes would mean a higher chance of risk for the people there. They had no clue what to look for, or what to say to the people if they were lucky enough to find it. Unfortunately, further conversation with Reena yielded nothing.

"Jonathan took the exact location with him to the Other Side, because he sure as shit didn't put it here. All I know is that it's in North Carolina, near one of the borders."

Jonah grunted his frustration. "You realize how little that narrows it down? North Carolina is bordered by three states!"

"Three and some change," said Terrence. "Georgia shares a little bit at the southwest."

"Not helping," muttered Jonah. "The point is that that is a lot of ground to cover!"

"I know, Jonah," said Reena. "But we do have the advantage of the *Astralimes*. At least we won't have to road trip to all of these places."

Jonah didn't even want to think about any of that at the moment. Luckily, there were still several distractions—if he looked in the right places.

Spader killed time overseeing a Texas Hold 'Em-style poker tournament among the residents that remained. Jonah played a few hands, but unfortunately got eliminated in the first round.

He and Terrence killed a few hours watching the WWE Network, and then debated their top-ten lists of all time wrestling greats. They swapped upon completion, and Jonah scowled at Terrence's list.

"Terrence, do you realize that over half of your list is from the Attitude Era?" Did you actually watch professional wrestling before Stone Cold, The Rock, and D-Generation X existed?"

"That was a great time to be a wrestling fan!" said Terrence defensively.

"Hell yeah it was, but there were years of great acts way before that!"

"You've got your tastes, and I've got mine."

Jonah put the paper down on the table and sighed. "You aren't a true wrestling fan," he said sadly.

There it was again. That flash of hardness or shame or whatever the hell it was in Terrence's face. Jonah frowned when he saw it again. What was up with him? They'd bantered about wrestling a thousand times; when did he start taking it seriously?

He left before he said anything else the "wrong" way.

"Jonah!" called a voice in a loud whisper.

He looked around and saw Bobby in the shadows.

"Come here, man." His tone was mysterious. "Got something to show you."

Jonah approached him, curiosity piqued. Bobby saw the look on his face and laughed.

"Calm down, Jonah. It's nothing illegal."

"Okay, Bobby. What's up?"

Bobby looked around to make sure they were alone, and then spoke. "First of all, thanks for the mash-up party, man. I really appreciate it."

"No problem. I'd been meaning to ask you something; now

that you've graduated, what's next? It is your plan to go pro, right?"

"It is," nodded Bobby. "But I don't want to do that just yet."

"Really?"

"Really." Bobby nodded again. "The NFL is my ultimate goal, but I want to get as much seasoning and honing as I can before I pursue that. The last thing I want to do is go on to the big leagues and get humbled day in and day out. I'm going to keep up my developmental conditioning and reach out to some practice squads. Terrence's brother Lloyd has agreed to help me navigate things concerning that—of course he's got excellent contacts. Then, God be willing, I'll be able to make the jump."

Jonah regarded his friend, pleasantly surprised and impressed. "Huh. That's really responsible and mature of you, man! Sounds like you're truly invested, and not trying to be some stupid, club-hopping baller who's more interested in jetsetting than honing the craft. I'm proud of you."

"Thanks man." Bobby looked pleased with himself. "But that isn't why I called you back here."

He pulled out a small white box and opened it. Inside was a neat little silver ring.

"What do you think?" he asked.

"But Bobby," Jonah joked, "it's such short notice."

Bobby rolled his eyes. "Oh, ha-ha. But seriously ... what do you think about it?"

Jonah looked over the engagement ring. It wasn't anything fancy or ostentatious. But it had a grace about it, a joyous gleam and elegance to it that was subtle until you noticed it, and then it was the only thing you saw.

All of the things that entailed Elizabeth Manville.

"She'll love it."

Bobby looked so relieved that it was almost laughable.

Jonah didn't do so, though, because he knew how important this was to Bobby.

"Are you going to propose at the party?"

"Nah. It's way too important to do it for some shock-value shit. I'll hang on to it. I was thinking more in terms of a nice dinner or something, when all of this is over. Reena wanted to propose to Kendall in spite of the heat around us—good for her. I prefer to let Liz have this special moment while thinking of nothing but peace."

Jonah smiled. "She's really changed you, man."

"Not entirely," Bobby assured him. "But she's changed me enough to know that I'll never let her get away."

Jonah nodded at that. "Happy to know that you're taking her seriously. The commitment, the nuptials ... all legitimate. Looks like you've earned that wedding night."

Bobby snorted. "Jonah, the wedding night is so irrelevant that it ain't even funny. Liz and I have been having sex forever—"

"Alright, alright, alright!" Jonah held up a hand. He meant it in jest but had no desire whatsoever to hear Bobby elaborate. He viewed Liz as his little sister, after all. "Keep that to yourself, man. Don't kiss and tell, least of all to me."

Bobby grinned as Jonah clapped him on the back. They went separate ways, and Jonah made to head downstairs when he heard a sound. His head instantly whipped in its direction, his thoughts on some kind of threat. But all he saw was a flash of flannel. He shook his head, feeling a mixture of pity and annoyance.

Spader had heard everything they'd said.

Poor boy. He must have thought that as long as there were no rings involved, he still had a fighting chance.

Jonah wished that he had realized that Liz was out of his

league from the second he met her. However, he kept up hope. Stubborn boy.

But when Jonah thought about it, was his hope of beating Creyton and making it through Omega any different?

* * *

11:30 P.M.

The night passed by leaps and bounds. And it didn't help that they'd all be hard at work, which killed even more time. A part of Jonah looked forward to the party, while the other part cringed at the realization that that brought them one step closer to the exodus.

Could life be any more complicated?

He walked the grounds to clear his head. It was pretty mild outside, and there wasn't a single cloud in the night sky. It was amazing to Jonah that, underneath the canopy, the moon and stars lay land and people at one another's necks in ethereal warfare.

Was this exodus the right call? It was much too late to renege, but Jonah couldn't help but wonder. Would people be safer on their own? With their families? Would they be even more vulnerable away from the estate?

He wondered if Jonathan had ever had to deal with anything like this. He hadn't been Overseer of the estate when he was killed in the Decimation, and he'd said that after seeing that—which he described as "true war on these lands"—nothing of that magnitude had happened since. Maybe Jonah could claim adherence to Jonathan's wishes in that regard. If the exodus from the estate meant things would end on another battlefield, then their home would remain untouched.

Jonah felt vitriolic hatred. He was the one who put the bug in everyone's ear about relocation. He'd been the one who was the sore loser when Jonah lost it and beat the shit out of him, and then had the last laugh with the pity party he threw, which swayed so many people to join him in abandoning the estate. It was such a Deadfallen disciple maneuver that he'd pulled. Laban could very well have been accurate when he said that Trip was his father incarnate. It just sucked that he chose such a crucial time to *show* it.

He looked at the plants that Vera, Liz, and Nella tended. He looked over at the gazebo. The courtyard, which was the site of so many conversations and meetings at one time, all of which had long since ceased due to fear of spies. It was all so peaceful, so calm.

And at that moment, Jonah froze in his tracks.

He just remembered that his current activity—perusing the estate grounds—was the exact same thing Jonathan had done the day he was vanquished.

Great. That was exactly what he needed in his head right now. Just the type of thoughts he needed to have right before a party.

Movement in Malcolm's wood shop distracted him. It was past midnight now; why would he be there at this hour?

Jonah knocked.

"It's open," said Malcolm, not sounding the least bit drowsy.

Jonah entered. Malcolm's wood shop jarred his emotions as much as Reena's art studio. He, too, had moved his creations off-site. He'd even moved the breadbox that Jonah once saved from looters. Jonah assumed he was up to something new, but then saw a book on his worktable.

"I take it you couldn't sleep either, Malcolm?"

Malcolm pushed away the book. "I'm too tired to sleep, Jonah. I keep going over it in my head. Sure, I get why we all have to leave, but I just don't agree with it. But hey, that's just my opinion."

Jonah sat down opposite him and glanced at the book. "Wars?" he questioned. "Surely, this doesn't relax you."

"Not in the slightest. It's just always been an interesting read."

"May I?" Jonah extended his hand, and Malcolm pushed the book over.

Jonah skimmed it and saw entries of wars of all kinds, fictional and otherwise. Wars from the Bible, Greek mythology, the Middle Ages, and so on.

"A part of me was wondering if this war we've got will end up in a book like this," said Malcolm. "Later on, of course."

Jonah nodded slowly. "One might assume so. But since the ethereal world is all but fringe, the facts would get fabricated all to hell."

Malcolm shook his head. "Even after you, Terrence, and Reena went on McRayne's show, the Eleventh Percent still remained all but secret."

"If there is anything a religious childhood taught me, it's that people choose what they want to believe and focus on," said Jonah. "It's just like Eva and the Greek mythology piece; it's so entertaining to them that they don't even acknowledge that that is her real life. And we aren't in people's faces like Eva is, so of course the Eleventh Percent would be treated as flavor of the month, and pretty much forgotten. And dude— remember that Eva is married now. She has eschewed her maiden name. Call her McRayne nowadays, and she is liable to slap you."

Malcolm grinned. "She adores that guy, doesn't she?"

"Worships him. They're on a honeymoon tour right now—a different place every night for a whole month. It's why she won't be at the party, but she sent her love and well wishes."

Malcolm shook his head and laughed again. It was fun talking about Eva for a few moments, but then reality set back in. Sucked how that happened every time.

"I've read this book a million times, Jonah, and there is always one recurring theme."

"Yeah?" Jonah allowed his voice to get just a bit maudlin. "What's that? That the good guys don't always win?"

"Pretty much. And also, if the heroes manage a victory, it comes at a steep, steep price."

7
PARTY TIME

Thursday flew past in a whirlwind, and now it was Friday. Jonah woke up but took his ever-loving time getting out of bed. He looked around the all but empty room, still not entirely sold on the decision he'd greenlit. As he no longer had an apartment; his belongings were now in storage. Fewer things to carry.

Now, if only his brain were that simple to unload.

An insistent scratching at the door pulled his attention away from his thoughts. Shortly thereafter, words, just as insistent, splashed across his mind.

"I know you're awake, Jonah. I could feel your essence from downstairs."

Amazed, Jonah leapt from the bed and opened the door to see Bast. "I thought you needed to look into my eyes for messages."

Bast blinked slowly. *"With all the conversations we've had, Jonah,"* Jonah saw in his mind. *"It's quite simple to communicate with you, no matter the connection. But I came to tell you that you have company downstairs."*

"What? This early?"

"Jonah,"—Jonah could feel the sternness in the words even though they weren't spoken—*"depending on one's perspective, the hour could be viewed as quite late."*

"Point made, Bast. I'll be right down."

He grabbed a T-Shirt, pulled it on, and went downstairs, wiping sleep from his eyes. If only he'd had time to wash his face.

When he reached the family room, six people were there, four men and two women, along with Daniel, who stood nearby, toast in his hands. It was always amazing to Jonah just how marked Daniel's presence was. He even made eating toast look badass.

A man on the loveseat came smoothly to his feet when he saw Jonah. The others followed suit, but since this guy rose first, Jonah assumed he was team leader. He was probably a few years after thirty, with a medium build, shoulder-length hair, and watchful eyes. Despite that, he looked friendly enough, a notion that he accentuated by extending his hand.

"Pleasure to meet you, Rowe. It's a great honor. I'm Clive Jessup, S.P.G. Practitioner, First Grade. This is Halima Rashid, Kara Maxton, Riley Jordan, Peter Chambers, and Ira Savage, all S.P.G. First Grade as well. We've been assigned to this estate to provide security for your festivities tonight."

Jonah took his hand and shook it. "It's a pleasure to meet you all, but the party isn't for another nine hours. Why show up now?"

"Just to get a feel of the place," Clive explained. "Patience already told us how your heralds have been shoring up defenses as well—we just want to be in concert with that and familiarize ourselves with the lands."

"Speaking of Patience," Daniel piped up, "why didn't he just assign some of the Networkers to this?"

"The Networkers are putting out Creyton's fires all over," said Clive, sounding annoyed and slightly affronted. "I assure you Daniel, we are up to the task."

Daniel sniffed and returned to his toast. Jonah cut his eye at him, and then returned his attention to Clive Jessup. "That's all cool. You guys have free reign of the place. You're welcome to food, drinks—whatever. As a matter of fact, my pal will be up soon, making breakfast for everyone. Help yourself as much as you like. And let me know if you need anything."

Clive nodded, throwing a cold glance at Daniel. "When all of that is ready, rest assured that we will partake. Until that time, we'll be spending the morning learning the lay of the land."

Jessup went outside. Jonah exchanged friendly words with his comrades as they followed him. Then his eyes fell on Daniel.

"What was that about, man? What are you thinking?"

Daniel finished his toast. "They're pensive. Alert. More akin to be cautious than curious. All good things."

"Why did you knock them, then? I feel like a 'but' is about to follow all of those compliments."

Daniel cleaned his glasses. "I was a Protector Guide for more years than I can say, Jonah. New elements have their benefits, as well as their mystery. You have to always be observant of fresh components, because it's important to glean how well they mesh with the established whole."

"Wouldn't it have been easier to just say that you don't trust new people, Daniel?" asked Terrence, amused. He and Reena were at the top of the stairs.

"Not really," answered Daniel, regarding Terrence. "Must every situation be simplified, Aldercy?"

Terrence rolled his eyes. "Way to completely miss the

point, Legolas. But Jonah, if you want my opinion, I think they're an awesome batch. We're gonna have a nice night."

Jonah agreed but didn't want to say anything in front of Daniel. Instead, he looked at Reena. "And you, sis?"

"Seemed like a decent collection of people. I don't have any reasons to object."

Daniel grunted. "Oh, to be young. And so forthcoming with trust."

He grabbed his bow and arrows and went outside. Reena's eyes narrowed at the jab.

"I never said I trusted them blindly. You both know that I give folks a trial run—"

"We know that, Reena," said Jonah. "Just let Daniel be ... Daniel."

"I couldn't agree more," Terrence told her. "And Jonah, you'd better go shower and get dressed. I think I heard you volunteer my services for breakfast. So, for that, I'm volunteering your help."

The day passed in an enjoyable way, gearing up for the party and making food. It was fun to see Reena and Terrence snipe at each other about the party food. Liz enlisted Vera's and Nella's help with the grounds once more, though Jonah had no idea what she hoped to achieve in a handful of hours. Bobby, Alvin, and Malcolm killed time with weights, football stats, and ragging on Alvin's two left feet when it came to dancing. Themis spent the day compiling a track list for the party. Terrence took a break from party-food prep to track her down and hand over every alt-rock album he owned, and Reena went right behind him and grabbed them all back.

Katarina did Bobby's, Liz's, Nella's, and Themis' names on a huge banner in Kirie design, while Spader and Magdalena oversaw setting up the party site on the grounds. Magdalena was such a detail freak that she was nuts at times, so it was great work for her. Spader seemed to have this one-dimensional energy since he'd overheard Bobby's plan to propose to Liz. He was practically a machine. Jonah didn't mind, though. If he had pent up emotion, why should it not be channeled through physical activity?

Jonah spent time in a chess game with Douglas. He played what he thought was a methodical, clever game, but after a small sequence of time, Douglas gave him a piteous look.

"What?" frowned Jonah.

Douglas chuckled rather sheepishly. "I've got checkmate in three moves."

Jonah gaped at the board. He'd paid attention to everything! "No, you don't. I've been playing smartly, carefully! I've done well!"

"Oh yeah!" said Douglas hastily. "You've done very well! It's just ... I've still got you."

Jonah scoped the board once again. Slowly but surely, it became clear to him. Douglas was right.

"Do I have a chance?"

"Well, you know, anything is possible—"

"Do ... I ... have ... a ... chance?"

Douglas gave him that piteous look once more. "No."

Jonah scowled, but then laughed. He wasn't actually angry, anyway. Doug had been at this since the cradle, after all. "I'm going to miss this, Doug."

"Me too." Douglas gave him a wistful smile. "Here's hoping that we won't have to miss it for long."

Jonah smiled, hoping the same.

He clapped Douglas on the back and walked to the gazebo. One of Jessup's counterparts—Kara—walked past, sharply scoping everything in sight. When she saw Jonah, she allowed herself a smile and nodded in his direction. Then, just as quickly, the smile slid off her face and she resumed patrol.

Jonah seated himself in the gazebo. The number of times he'd come out here just because it was quiet! Just so he didn't have to see Trip! If this wasn't a safe haven, he didn't know what was.

It hadn't changed in detail at all, which Jonah enjoyed. In a time of such cataclysmic change, it was nice to know that some things remained the same. He laughed to himself as he thought about whether he'd have any literary inspiration right now if he had a pen and pad.

"I was wondering when you'd make it here."

Jonah turned and laughed when he saw Vera. She was a sweaty mess but looked quite pleased with herself. Liz and her horticultural therapy stuck again.

She sipped water as she seated herself and dispensed with a straw hat. Jonah laughed

"Liz running you and Nella hard?"

"She's got Albie, Laurel, and Burton out here, too," sighed Vera. "She has it in her mind that a natural motif is much more decorative than gaudy lights and such."

Jonah thought on that. "Love that girl."

"I do, too," grinned Vera.

Vera looked like she wanted to say more and used talking about Liz as a distraction. Jonah contemplated her. "Did you come here to hang out?"

"No, actually. I just wanted to take a breather. We will converse more at the party, I'm sure. See you later."

She left. Jonah was a bit baffled. She'd come way out of the way to take a damn breather. So, clearly, she'd desired to speak further.

At this point, what could have possibly held her back?

* * *

Several hours later, it was time for a party.

Jonah hadn't been the biggest party-hopper, but he thought his black Old Navy polo and tan slacks were sharp enough to suffice. Magdalena deemed his five o'clock shadow fashionable, so he didn't bother shaving.

Terrence had on slacks of his own but ruined the ride with a sleeveless Duke University T-Shirt. In the name of festiveness, Jonah said nothing, but made a point to flash his UNC wrist watch whenever Terrence was around.

Reena had on a sleeveless shirt as well, a dark red one. She actually had her hair down. Jonah couldn't help but notice that she was quite a beautiful woman when she chose to accentuate it. But he was also smart enough never to tell her.

Terrence had outdone himself with the food as usual, even with the party food: Buffalo wings, fried chicken drummettes and wingettes, chips and French fries, deviled eggs, nachos and onion dip, pinwheel sandwiches, finger sandwiches, and sweets of all kinds. At Reena's insistence, there were celery sticks, fruit, and rice bread. Terrence snorted in clear derision when he saw her health options, but no one complained, so he didn't say anything about it.

Jonah didn't want to admit that he had some apprehension about Themis manning the music, but she pleasantly surprised him with a variety that pleased everyone. She even accommodated Terrence with some Nirvana, Our Lady Peace, and his beloved The Incline Down. Jonah also saw to it that she didn't stay with the music too long, as she was one of the guests of honor. He wanted her to get just as much attention as Bobby, Liz, and Nella.

The rest of the Decessio family was there as well, as were Patience, Reverend Abbott, Prodigal, Autumn Rose, and Prodigal. Felix was there, too, and beckoned to Jonah as soon as he got the chance.

"I know you've spoken to Nelson and Tamara."

"Oh yeah. They were ecstatic."

Felix nodded. "Two of most easygoing people I've ever met."

"Dude, Nelson is an accountant and Tamara works in the mall when she'd rather be home for her pregnancy. Your trip was probably the biggest lifeline on earth to them."

Felix almost smiled, but then looked at Jonah with a very nearly somber expression. "Have you heard from Maxine lately?"

Jonah looked at him curiously. "She's good," he told him. "She's back with her mom and sister in Arkansas."

Felix nodded once and walked away. Terrence and Reena caught up with Jonah shortly thereafter.

"Did I hear Felix asking about Max?" asked Terrence.

"I know, right?" said Jonah. "Thought he didn't care."

"It's not that he doesn't care." Reena sipped on her cucumber lemon water. "It's the fact that he doesn't want to."

Jonah smirked. So, Felix did have a heart. Somewhere behind the "tough stuff" that made up what a sazer was.

He then overheard Nella speaking on her plans with Mr. Decessio.

"Nah, no LTSU for me. I'm going to UNC-Greensboro. They have a music therapy program there. I'd love to do that, and maybe work at Valentania York later on."

"And what about you, Liz?" asked Sterling.

"I think I'll apply my pre-med knowledge to more ethereal healing practices," answered Liz. "The Spirits of Mercy have opportunities for that, but unlike traditional Tenth med school, it won't take eight years before I can practice it."

"That's very responsible of you kids," said Reverend Abbott

with approval. "And when Bobby tries for the pros, Lizzie, I'm sure you'll have no problem making sure he keeps up with his conditioning."

"Oh, no doubt, sir," said Bobby, who grinned at Liz. "She'll keep me in line."

With a roll of his eyes, Spader headed towards the refreshments table.

"Want more wings. Kinda hungry."

"Seriously?" said Magdalena. "You just had eight of those things!"

Spader ignored her.

"Hey, Jonah," said Terrence with a smirk, "Katarina still won't trust herself to navigate the meat without Doug. She has only had celery and refuses to touch the wings or pinwheel sandwiches."

"You should have done more to accommodate her, Terrence," said Reena.

"What the hell was I supposed to do?" cried Terrence. "Fry her fish bites?"

"You should have been more considerate of her," said a voice nearby. "Is that so difficult to accomplish?"

It was Halima. She had taken the briefest of breaks from patrol to refill a punch cup. But she looked at Terrence with hard, critical eyes. Terrence appraised her and grinned sheepishly.

"It was all in fun," he said in a register that Jonah could swear was lower than it had been moments ago. "Katarina and I are friends."

"Mmm. So that is how you treat your female friends? Joke and heckle them behind their backs? Make light of their challenging transitions for lifelong-held belief systems?"

The smile slid off Terrence's face. Jonah wanted to help his brother so badly, but something told him that silence was the best thing he could do for himself at the moment. "I...I don't treat my friends like that at all! I love women! I compliment them all the time! Like ... like you for example! You have a nice—"

"What?" Halima's eyes held a silent warning in them, and she lowered the punch. "I have a nice *what?*"

"Um-um..."

Terrence was in flames, and Jonah silently begged him to just tell her never mind or something. He hoped he would with every fiber of his being.

But he didn't.

"Hijab," Terrence managed at last. "You have a nice hijab."

Halima snorted. "And you have a nice foot."

"What?" said Terrence, puzzled. "I'm wearing Dockers ... you can't see my foot."

"Oh yes I can, little boy," Halima told him. "It's in your fucking mouth. Now, if you'll excuse me."

She about-faced and resumed her duties. Terrence looked ashamed, emasculated, and a little dejected. Jonah wanted to give words of support, but Reena clapped him on the shoulder.

"Smooth as silk there, Ter! Your charms are swoon-worthy!"

Terrence gritted his teeth, and Jonah decided that the best thing to do was just get away. It was at that moment that he saw Clive Jessup refilling his cup. If there was a more welcome distraction to the momentary tension, Jonah didn't know what was. He walked up to him.

"How's everything, Clive?"

"Aces, Rowe. It's pretty quiet, which is good. Daniel has stayed out of my face, which is even better. Your party seems to be going without a hitch as well."

"Oh yeah! No complaints whatsoever."

With a nod, Clive sipped his drink. "This may seem

random, but are you familiar with the Deadfallen disciple named India Drew?"

"Yeah, I am. She is on the Plane with No Name, right?"

"She broke out," revealed Clive.

"What!"

"Worry not, man," said Clive hurriedly. "She got caught again not too long after her breakout."

Jonah was taken aback "Really? That's pretty sloppy for a Deadfallen disciple, don't you think?"

"Or pretty efficient for us," countered Clive. "She was put in a high security district on the Plane. No way in hell she'll get out of there."

He nodded at Jonah and resumed his patrol. Jonah stared after him, and then at Halima, Kara, Riley, Peter, and Ira. He was glad of their presence, whatever Daniel said. But he had to admit that that information about India bothered him. It was all well and good that she got apprehended once again, but how the hell did she get off the Plane in the first place?

Fingers wrapped his wrist.

"Dance with me." It was Vera. She practically commanded it. "This is one of my favorite songs."

Jonah blinked in surprise. His mind was on India Drew, so he hadn't realized that Themis switched the track list to slow songs. Before he could process it all, he and Vera were already in the midst of dancing people.

Damn.

Terrence, who looked recovered from his humiliation, caught his eye, and mouthed, *"Roll with it,"* and carried on.

Jonah sighed and wrapped his hands around the small of Vera's back.

"Much better." Vera smiled with appreciation. "Being cooperative doesn't kill anyone."

Jonah snorted. "I guess not. So, tell me, how exactly did Moonlight Serenade become one of your favorite songs?"

"Mom played it all the time when I was a kid. But I wouldn't judge, Jonah Rowe. I've seen your workout playlists. You have more Frank Sinatra and Tony Bennett than you do any other artists."

Jonah nodded in concession. "Got me there."

Vera smiled, which made Jonah frown. Something in that smile...and her demeanor...was off. It'd been that way the whole time she'd been at the estate.

Well, she'd said that they could speak further at the party. No time like the present.

"Vera, we haven't really been able to converse since you've been here. How are you doing? How is life?"

Vera sighed. "What do you always say, Jonah? It is what it is? That would cover my life as of late."

Jonah looked into her hazel eyes. "Did something happen with *Snow and Fire*? Did you get booted, or something?"

"Oh hell no. It's nothing to do with the play. The play is an open run; we can pick it back up tomorrow and tour if we wanted. We just wanted a little break from the grind. We were on the road a long while."

"Oh, okay ... well, what is it?" Jonah pressed. "Has East been supportive?"

Anger flashed in Vera's eyes. "East and I are done."

Jonah started, stunned by the reaction. He removed his grasp from her waist and grabbed her hands. "Come on."

He pulled her away. The damned dancing was for the birds, anyway. They sat away from everyone, and Jonah did a double take to make sure that none of the S.P.G. practitioners were around. When he saw no one, he focused on Vera.

"Talk. What happened?"

Vera remained silent for several seconds, and then sighed.

"Something had been off for a few months. I could tell. East had been working late a couple nights a week. No blood, no foul...I was doing one-woman shows, so we were both busy. But then he started acting strangely. I mean, he'd snap over stupid things. He'd shoot down suggestions of mine with this ... this cold air about him. You know me, Jonah...I'll never back down. We had our share of arguments. I thought that I'd done something wrong, but I couldn't think of a single thing. So, I told him that we needed to sit down, be adults about it, and discuss where we stood. We'd been together for more than a year, after all. I wouldn't do anything like that if I weren't in it one-hundred percent. He agreed, and we made plans for P.F. Chang's—"

Jonah raised a hand. Vera looked puzzled for a second, and then understood when she saw Kara pass near their spot. When she was gone, Vera continued.

"The problem was that, on the night that we chose, East didn't show. I was there for almost three hours. Now Jonah, we've seen some wild things as ethereal humans, so my mind automatically went to every horrible scenario imaginable. For a crazy second, I even thought Jessica had found him. I was frightened as hell. So, I didn't call a cab. I used the *Astralimes* to his office building, making sure to step out a floor below so no one saw me."

Jonah swallowed. "Was he alright? Had something actually happened?"

Vera sneered. "I wish."

"Excuse me? You want to run that by me again?"

"I found him in his office, Jonah. With his skank of an intern."

Jonah stared. "No fuckin' way."

"Yes, fuckin' way," grumbled Vera. "He had her flipped tits over ass and was hammering her like a damn nail."

Jonah winced at the mental picture, but Vera wasn't done.

"It gets better. They'd been at it for months ... that was the reason why he was coming home late. He actually said that he never meant for me to find out like that."

"As if there could be a *better* way to find out?" Jonah demanded. "What happened then?"

"I...I attacked him, Jonah." Clearly it took Vera a lot to admit it. "I lost myself for a moment. I shoved that little bitch aside; she fell and sprained her ankle because she tripped over a Ficus. I punched East so hard in the chest that my ring's stone broke, and then I broke his jaw. He hit his desk and fractured his wrist."

Jonah nearly snorted but stifled it. "Was the intern crying?"

"The bitches were both crying."

"Vera,"Jonah's anger abated somewhat after he heard what Vera did, "That's amazing. But aren't you afraid that East or his little friend will come after you with an assault charge? I mean, if you explain the situation to Patience, maybe he could—"

"Not necessary, for two reasons. First, East is superficial, neurotic, and inanely proud and vain. They are flaws I was blind to when we were together. He'd never admit that a woman beat him like that. And second,"—there was suddenly a note of savage pleasure in her voice—"they'd look like idiots if they said anything, because when I left the office, I used my Time Item ethereality to manipulate things so it looked like I was still at P.F. Chang's when they got roughed up."

Jonah actually laughed. "You are so freakin' awesome!" he exclaimed, clutching Vera's hands. But the humor faded shortly thereafter.

Vera lowered her head. "I know we aren't supposed to use our ethereality like that, but he hurt me, Jonah. That really messed me up. Jonathan taught us better than that, but when I saw them—like I said, I lost myself for a moment."

Jonah nodded slowly. "I'm so sorry that he did that to you, Vera. He was a complete and utter dick for cheating on you and hurting you. For blowing off something authentic and substantial for some intern. I know that you won't heal overnight, but you deserve so much better."

Vera almost smiled. "I know I do. But I can't worry about searching for 'better' right now. I need to get that asshole out of my system, and we all need to get through this war. I have to get myself right, all over again."

Jonah's jaw tightened. With everything that Vera had experienced in her life, the fact that she'd made progress once she was on the stage again was a great thing. Jonah did his level best not to think about the awkward departure that saw her return to Seattle, because this particular moment was not about him. Vera had followed her dream and was happy. She started to like herself again. She no longer defined herself by her blood relations...seen past her scars. If East's actions had halted that growth in any way ... well. Vera's assault might not be the only one that the bastard experienced.

"But let's focus on other things," said Vera boisterously. "Like the fact that you got your wish! The party is nearly over, and there hasn't been a single snag!"

Jonah smiled at that. He couldn't help it. Vera was right. The party was almost at its end, and all had gone well. Everyone was relieved and overjoyed about that, himself included. He wondered if the sentries from the S.P.G. were relieved as well, or disappointed that there'd been no action. Oh, well. Personally, Jonah didn't mind the lack of action.

He and Vera rose at the same time, both heading back to the near-finished festivities. Jonah started to move forward when Vera barred his path.

"Thank you, Jonah. Besides Liz, you are the only other person with whom I was comfortable discussing this. You've always been so great at listening and helping when necessary. Means more than you know."

She stepped into his personal space and kissed him. Her lips lingered on his for a few extra seconds, and then she returned to the party.

Jonah stared after her, lifting his hand to his mouth, where he could almost feel the imprint of her lips. He'd wanted a drama-free party and the chance to converse with Vera. Both had occurred. Batting a thousand on both fronts, with the bonus of a kiss.

Daniel said to take victories where you could, no matter how big or small. And this was a victory.

Victory was a very sweet thing.

*　*　*

The high from the party continued into the next day. But by half-past six in the evening, it was time to go. Jonah had decided on early evening as the time for everyone to leave, as that was the time when the spirits and spiritesses had enough strength to appear and see them off.

All was in order. No one had bags to carry; they'd spent the whole week making sure that no one had those burdens. They had it down to a T; everyone would exit simultaneously, get to their destinations, and lie low. The puzzle pieces all fell neatly into place. But it was bittersweet.

Jonah took in the estate. Every piece of it. It was funny how quickly this place became his reality. The only place on the planet that he wanted to be. He could honestly say that he loved the estate as much as he loved his family.

"It won't be the last time we see it, Jonah," said Reena. "We will get through this. That's what you told me and now, I'm sending it back to you."

"Yeah, man." Terrence patted Jonah on the back. "Look at today. Everything fell into place. Sentries are here, and the only thing that was off about them was that Riley guy showing up late as hell."

"Yeah." Jonah glanced at the S.P.G. guy near the trees. "Too many damn drummettes."

"Not my fault if he ate too much," shrugged Terrence. "But my point is that we're rolling. And in about five minutes, we'll be at the safe spot Felix assigned for my parents, hang out there for a few days, and then we'll start looking for Spairitin Cousland."

Jonah chortled. "Thanks to you both."

Reena nodded with a small smile, which illustrated her own mixed emotions. Terrence, on the other hand, looked pleased.

"That's my job."

"Now, Jonah," Reena adjusted her backpack, "I think it's time to get everyone's attention so we can do this."

"Right. On it." Jonah rose his voice to a bellow. "*Everyone! All eyes on me!*"

All conversations desisted and everyone looked Jonah's way. Jonah took a moment to look at all of them. All his family. He didn't pray very much, but he issued a silent prayer that they would safely reunite here again one day soon—soon was both broad and vague, but still.

"We've done all the talking, and we've said our laters, because this isn't goodbye. I want you all to take care of yourselves. I know that you have worked out an arrangement with a spirit or spiritess of your choice for long-term endowments, so stay spiritually endowed at all times. Don't relinquish them for any reason. And when the time is right, we will meet here again, all of us. Right here, on this spot."

There were nods, smiles, and quiet words of agreement.

Jonah took a deep breath. The exodus was real. It was actually about to happen.

But the thoughts only served to delay things. Time to get on with it.

"On my mark, we hit the *Astralimes*," he announced. "In five, four, three, two—"

The wind picked up, which distracted Jonah from his count. Someone had just used the *Astralimes* to come there. Jonah hadn't figured out who it was when the Riley guy suddenly growled and tore off towards the huddled figure.

"Get him!" he snarled. "Get him!"

Clive restrained his ally, but the man fought tooth and nail.

"Riley, what's wrong with you, man? Riley, chill!"

"No!" Riley struggled against Clive's grasp harder. "Stop that guy! He's a damned liar!"

"Liar?" Jonah looked at Riley in confusion. "The man hasn't said anything!"

Jonah approached the unsteady figure and then felt an invisible blow to his gut.

It was Elijah.

And the man was a complete mess.

His left eye was missing. Copious amounts of blood dripped from his head, and he was unsteady on his feet. Jonah and Terrence grabbed him to keep him upright.

"What the hell? Liz, Akshara—!"

"No!" Elijah, blood spurt from Elijah's mouth as he spoke. "Don't worry about me! I heard Riley Jordan's voice just now! Kill him! He's a Deadfallen disciple!"

"Liar!" Riley bellowed right back. "You're a damn—"

"Shut up!" shouted Jonah, whose eyes never left Elijah's bloody face. "Elijah, what are you talking about? What's going on?"

"No!" Riley cried, who tried to wrestle free from Clive, but

Ira and Peter rushed forward to help him, and they forced Riley to his knees. All eyes were on Elijah.

"Rowe." It seemed as though Elijah had to labor to use his voice as he focused on Jonah almost exclusively. "The Plane with No Name has been dismantled. Emptied. Creyton used that India girl to free everyone ... gave 'em all a Get Off the Plane Free card. All my people there...all the Gatekeepers... they're gone. That Riley boy tried to kill me. But he didn't finish."

"He's ly—"

Riley attempted another yell, but Clive conjured an ethereal gag over his mouth.

Jonah barely registered that. He heard sounds of shock in the crowd at the information that he couldn't grasp. The Plane was empty? How in the hell had that happened? "Somebody!" he looked around. "Clive! Patience! Contact the Curaie—"

Elijah's grip on Jonah's arm tightened. "There ain't no Curaie."

"What!" Patience and Clive demanded simultaneously.

The voices of shock were even louder this time. Still, Jonah ignored them. He needed to know more.

"What did you just say?" Jonah's voice was lower than Clive's and Patience's, but the incredulity was identical. "The Curaie is gone?"

"Yes, boy." Elijah snapped the words, though his voice was weak. "Creyton took them all out. Vanquished 'em all, even Engagah. They're gone. Just ... gone."

There were even more gasps all around. Clive's, Ira's, and Peter's grasps must have gone slack with shock at the news, because Riley managed to break free and charge at Jonah, Terrence, and Elijah.

"Scum! Dilettantes!"

A burgundy arrow pierced his chest. Jonah and several

others looked for the source and saw that it was Halima. She'd just shot one of her own allies and looked absolutely stunned that she had to do so.

Riley fell to his knees. His expression was slack, but his voice still managed defiance.

"P-Per mortem," he whispered, "v-vitam."

And then he fell.

Jonah looked at the physically lifeless body in shock, but then Elijah slapped his face. It was a weak slap, more distracting than anything else. His face shot back to the Gatekeeper, who appeared lightheaded now. His rapid breathing had slowed considerably.

"Hell is here, boy. Fix it. You gotta fix it. Or Creyton'll wipe us all out."

Elijah's remaining eye rolled back, and he went limp in Jonah's and Terrence's arms. He was gone.

Jonah looked at every horrified face, sure that their expressions matched his own. The stunned, terrified silence was shattered by Felix.

"Get out of here!" he shouted. "Ya'll aren't prepared for an attack! Run!"

Felix's shouts were drowned out by what sounded like dozens of caws in the night sky. Those bird calls had sources soon enough, as crows were upon them like some sort of plague.

The Deadfallen disciples shape-shifted some feet above the ground, so for a moment, it looked like people rained from the dark. Their faces were masked, Old-West bandit style. But no one cared how they looked.

The scene devolved in seconds. People ran, struggled, and fell attempting to escape. Jonah and Terrence were forced to let Elijah's body fall. Jonah hated having to do that, but the first thing he saw was a Deadfallen disciple gear up to spray that liquid that prevented *Astralimes* travel. Jonah was on him immediately, bashing his arm and kicking away the liquid canister. He then punched him down, but Jonah hardly felt victorious. He knew full well that he'd only gotten the upper hand because the man was distracted due to his attempt to trap everyone. When Jonah looked twenty yards away, he saw a knife, ivory in sheen, slashing left and right to keep enemies away. Automatic panic rose in him at that sight.

"Vera!" he screamed.

He tried to run her way, but a sharp, fiery sting erupted just above his collarbone. He grunted in pain and looked down, only to see something like a steel dart lodged in his flesh.

Then a similar sting hit him in his lower back. It was at that moment that a foreign, but very familiar disorientation hit him. Jonah tried to shake his head free of the seemingly immediate cobwebs, to no avail. He fell to his knees, despite his body having no desire to do any such thing. What the hell?

From a short distance away, he heard a roar from one of the Deadfallen disciples who'd seen him fall.

"Package is prepped!" the man shouted. "Get Rowe! Fuck everyone else!"

"Oh, shit!" That was Reena, who was at Jonah's side. "Terrence! You heard that!"

"Hell yeah, I did!" Terrence nearly tripped over someone's crawling form to reach Jonah and Reena. "We need to blaze!"

"Jonah, we're getting you out of here!" Reena clutched his good shoulder.

"No ... no ..." Jonah was weak as hell, but he had no intention of leaving. "We need to fight ..."

"Jonah, this is a big distraction!" snapped Terrence. "They don't give a damn about any of the rest of us! They came for you! It's probably poison you feel in you ... they want to take you, sever us at the head!"

"I—I don't care ..." Jonah still attempted to struggle from his friends' grasps. Though feeble, he kept it up. "We're needed here ..."

"Jonah, we need to go!" Reena easily stamped down his struggles. "Four disciples are headed this way with that damned spray!"

"We can't leave!" Jonah managed to get some bass in his voice, but he paid for it, because a lot more strength left his body. "I'm needed!"

"Today is not that day, Jonah!"

"Wait ... *Wait*—"

Terrence forearmed Jonah across the face. He didn't knock him unconscious, but it was enough to stop his struggles.

"Sorry, man." Terrence apologetic tone was sincere enough. "Now, where're we going, Reena?"

"Away from here! Grab his other arm!"

Even in Jonah's groggy, pained state, he registered frustration and anger as he felt himself dragged by his two best friends into nothing. He wanted more than anything to fight them off, but he wasn't good for anything. The chaotic scene on the estate's grounds faded from view as they disappeared into the winds and mystery of the Astral Plane.

OMEGA BEGINS

8
SHOTGUNS & PHANTASMS

They'd used the *Astralimes* a million times in the past. But all those other times, Jonah hadn't been out of it while Terrence and Reena dragged him along.

The three of them collapsed in a heap somewhere that Jonah didn't recognize, but then again, he was poisoned and disoriented. He saw Reena immediately rise to her feet.

"What in the hell are we supposed to do, Reena?" Terrence spat. "It's not like we grabbed any Green Auras by the hand on the way!"

"Shut up, and hold Jonah up. I've got this."

Terrence propped Jonah up, sending pain through his wounds. He grunted dully, and Terrence made to remove the darts. Reena clasped his hand so tightly that his wrist popped.

"Ow, woman! Damn it!"

"Man up, Terrence. You got bitten by a vampire once, remember? Garlic was burning up your insides. Now you can't take a negligent bruise? Don't remove the darts. Not until I've gotten started."

"Wh ..." Jonah didn't have the strength to finish the word. "Wh ..."

"Save your energy, Jonah. You'll be great in a second."

In Jonah's blurred vision, he saw Reena's hands gleam yellow. She placed one above the dart in Jonah's collarbone, and then placed the other hand elsewhere behind him.

"Remove them now, Ter."

Terrence did so, but Reena didn't remove her hands. She made a sound in the back of her throat as her brow furrowed in concentration.

Suddenly, Jonah's disorientation lessened. His vision came back into focus, the pain began to fade, and his strength started to return. He looked at Reena's hands and noticed that liquid seemed to be lifting out of the puncture holes the dart made.

"Reena, what are you doing?"

"Foreign substance extraction. It's one of the first ethereality maneuvers I learned. Practiced it eight times a day when I first got to the estate. Now, let me finish."

Soon enough, all the poison was out of Jonah's system. He felt no pain in his collarbone or his lower back. Reena held the poison from both sources with her ethereality; it seemed to hover over her hands. Then with a sweeping motion, she tossed it away from them.

Jonah sat up, good as new. He looked at Reena in surprise. "What was that poison?"

Reena shook her hands out as though she'd just punched someone. "That was the same poison that the 49er hit you with in their little Nightmare Scenario."

"Why didn't you do that for Jonah then?" questioned Terrence.

"Because I was flat on my ass, Terrance, same as you."

"How did you learn to do that?" Jonah asked. "I just heard

—or I think I heard—you say that you practiced it eight times a day at one point?"

"Yes."

"Why?"

Reena gave Jonah a cold, firm glance. "None of your business."

Jonah blinked. "Alright then. Whatever." Why the hell did Reena have to be so damn mysterious now, of all times? "Thanks."

"You're welcome," said Reena, cognizant of his tone change.

Terrence stood and looked around. "I think we're in someone's barn. Were you thinking about a barn, Reena?"

Reena didn't answer, and Jonah didn't expect her to. He didn't feel up to many more words at the moment, either.

Because the reality of the moment settled on them.

Jonah didn't know what to think. The entire status quo had changed. In a matter of hours, everything had changed.

The Curaie was gone. The Plane with No Name was empty. What did Elijah say?

"Hell is here."

Creyton played a patient game. He made *everyone* look like fools.

Everyone thought that if something might happen, it'd be at the party. People were alert and wary at that time. And the whole thing had gone off without a hitch. Creyton lured them into a false sense of security—had his little spy there the entire weekend.

Riley, that bastard ...

The man got shot through the heart with an arrow and still had enough strength to say that damned phrase that everyone could hear, but only Creyton and his disciples could say.

What state was the estate in right now? The attack had

caught everyone off guard, but the only person that Jonah had been near enough to see was Vera. Christ alive, what if something had happened to her?

Out of nowhere, Reena grabbed his wrist.

"You are not going back, Jonah." Her tone was firm.

"Let go of me, Reena." Jonah, attempted to wrench himself from her grasp. "I've got to help; I'm the Overseer of the Estate!"

"And the primary target of every Deadfallen psycho there right now! Those darts that hit you were debilitating wounds, Jonah. They roughed us up, but you were the only one hit with poison. Going back is suicide!"

"I don't give a shit. If you won't come with me, then fine. But I'm going back—"

Jonah had his mind on his destination, but Terrence blocked his path before he could take a step to the *Astralimes.*

"Jonah, Reena is right, man. You are the priority. You have to stay away."

"Our family needs help—"

"Dad, Daniel, Patience, and the S.P.G. practitioners that ain't up Creyton's ass were all there," Terrence reminded Jonah. "Besides, you act like our friends are some useless bitches. You act as if we haven't trained for years! All it takes is two steps to get away. They'll have gotten out."

Jonah looked at his brother and sister, equal parts unconvinced and incredulous. "Do you hear yourselves right now? Aren't you the least bit scared?"

"What the hell do you think, Jonah?" Terrence demanded. "I'm scared out of my mind! But we ain't ready for a straight-up fight! We can't lose you! In case you didn't hear poor Elijah, Creyton wiped out the Curaie! Emptied the Plane with No Name! How stupid would I have to be to not be afraid right now?"

Jonah took a deep breath as common sense and reason returned. It was foolish to assume that Terrence and Reena weren't as afraid as he was. How stupid was it to think that they were actually calm? "I'm sorry. Reena, thank you for getting that crap out of me."

"You're welcome."

"Now, are you gonna tell us how you learned to do that?" Terrence again.

"No. Now let it go before you piss me off."

Terrence looked dumbfounded, but Jonah decided not to force the issue.

"Reena, if you won't answer that question, then I hope you're willing to oblige us with this one. Whose barn is this? Terrence wanted to know earlier, but you were helping me out. Did you think of a barn?"

"I didn't." Reena looked as though her mind were in a million different places. "I focused on a fixed point three-hundred miles from the estate. Nothing specific, just any place but there. And we wound up in this barn."

"Nothing specific? Three-hundred miles is quite specific. Why that distance?"

"I figured that three-hundred miles away was a safe enough distance for Jonah to avoid another Nightmare Scenario."

Jonah shook his head. Even in fight or flight mode, Reena was rational. "Greatly appreciated. Now, we better—"

A shotgun cocked, ceasing Jonah's words at once.

"I've got a gun aimed." The woman's warning was unnecessary as they'd already heard the thing get cocked. "Move, and I'll turn you into blood-and-bone pie."

Jonah frowned slightly at the imagery of that, but he breathed more easily. On the one hand, this wasn't Creyton or a Deadfallen disciple. It was a Tenth. On the other hand, the Tenth had a shotgun.

"Turn around," commanded the woman. "Don't play with me. Been shooting this thing since I was nine."

Jonah turned around and saw that Terrence and Reena had done the same. The woman that had the shotgun trained on them looked to be in her early fifties, shorter than Jonah expected, but she didn't look the least bit afraid. Despite the situation, Jonah's respect for her rose.

"Now, who the hell are you? And what are you doing in my barn?"

"We aren't a threat to you whatsoever, ma'am," said Reena before Jonah could say anything. "That's the honest to God truth. But now, you have to be honest with us, too."

"Are you *crazy?*" hissed Terrence, but the woman paid him no attention. She simply glared at Reena.

"And just what exactly makes you think you can tell me how and what to be? Who here is trespassing? And who here has the gun?"

Jonah wanted to glance at Reena but resisted the urge. Last thing he needed was for the action to be interpreted as a sudden move.

"We're not a threat to you, ma'am," Reena repeated and, for whatever reason, she was completely calm. "Yes, you are the one with the gun. But you aren't going to shoot us. You would have already if that had been your plan."

Jonah didn't know what to think. He heard Terrence make a sound in the back of his throat, like a mild choke or scoffing sound.

The woman looked at Reena closely. "Are you sure about that?"

"Yes." Reena didn't hesitate. "I'm sure."

The woman continued to stare at them, shotgun still trained in their direction, for about fifteen more seconds.

Twenty. Jonah's raised hands ached him something fierce by that point.

Then she lowered the shotgun. Unless Jonah was mistaken, she looked relieved to do so.

"Y'all didn't seem like dangerous people. But I can't be too careful. The T.V. said that some fools done up and escaped from a prison detail in the next county. Forgive me, but the three of you look like y'all been running from something."

"No, ma'am," said Jonah hastily. "We're not actually running. We were camping and lost our way. That's why we have these backpacks. We were looking for help, but we've been walking for a good little while, and ... legs got tired. We just came into the barn because it looked like it might rain. We meant no harm."

The woman shook her head slowly. "Bless your hearts."

Jonah didn't respond. He had heard that as a compliment and as an insult. He wasn't quite sure which one this lady used it for.

"How long y'all been lumbering around looking for help?"

"Couple days," lied Terrence. "We're hungry, tired, and have no phone reception."

Jonah nodded. It wasn't like all those things weren't true.

"Naw," said the woman. "Them things won't work out here. But you're lucky you wound in my own barn; other folks 'round here might not be so understanding. Come on."

She clutched the shotgun, turned, and walked out of the barn toward her house. Jonah glanced at Reena.

"You're either very badass, or very crazy."

"Jonah, I wasn't wearing my dampener. Her essence was practically screaming at me."

Jonah was about to respond, but a sudden thought occurred to him.

Reena was an essence reader. Without her dampener, that ability was full force.

So why hadn't she read Riley's treachery?

The guy was at the estate, around Reena, for most of the weekend. She hadn't gotten a glimpse of who he truly was?

Now probably wasn't the best time to bring it up, though. Emotions were still high.

With effort...he was still pissed at Reena for dragging him away from the fight, though he understood the reasons...he filed it away.

"Oh yeah," said the woman suddenly, "watch out for—"

Terrence tripped, swore, and would have face-planted had Jonah not grabbed him.

"Markers," the woman finished with a snort.

Jonah's eyes narrowed. Place markers? Surely that wasn't what she meant. The lady saw the change in Jonah's face and shook her head again.

"Not grave markers, boy. My land is deep sunk in a bunch of places. I have to throw dirt in them, raise 'em up. But I had to mark the places so I wouldn't forget where they were. Mind ain't what it used to be. So, there are bricks in places. I was trying to warn you—"

"Why haven't you filled them yet?" demanded Terrence, who twisted his foot this way and that. "That brick looked lodged good and tight in the ground! That wasn't recent work!"

The woman was at her back door by that time. At Terrence's question, she paused and turned. Jonah expected her expression to be annoyed or angry, but it was wistful.

"My mind ain't what it used to be," she said again. "And my heart ain't what it used to be, either."

Terrence lowered his eyes. He looked guilty as hell. "Sorry."

"Forget about it." The woman's face was mostly clear of emotion by that point. "Come on in."

"Way to go, Terrence," snapped Reena as they followed the woman into her home. "The ethereal world is in hell, and you're bitching about your foot."

"I said I was sorry," said Terrence through gritted teeth. "What else do you want? Me to coordinate a telethon for the lady?"

Jonah paid them no attention. He just looked over the woman's house.

It was pretty neat; the only things on her floor were stray newspapers. More newspapers were spread over the kitchen table. It appeared that the woman was polishing silverware prior to their arrival. The pictures on the walls were few. After a few moments, Jonah realized that it wasn't the detail that stuck out. It was the feel of the place. This clean, neat home felt neglected. Like a remnant of forgotten days. Long since passed days.

Kind of like the estate felt in the weeks that preceded the ill-fated exodus. There hadn't been much joy. Hadn't been much contentment. Until the night of the party, Jonah thought that if the exodus had to happen, then it could happen on a high note. But now that he knew that it had all been a false sense of security, Creyton had had the whole surprise attack planned out ...

"Jonah," said Reena. "Keep it together."

Jonah looked at her. They were all at the woman's table. Jonah didn't even remember seating himself. But that didn't matter. What Reena said made him frown. How well was *she* holding up, huh? With her fiancée in Ireland and the invasion of her home of almost two decades?

Terrence had a hard gaze on the woman's shotgun. The expression wasn't missed.

"I take it that you don't like guns?"

"Nope." Terrence's eyes hadn't left the thing. "Sure don't."

"Let me show you something," said the woman with a sly smile.

She lifted the shotgun for all of them to see. She then clamped one hand on the butt and the other on the barrel, gave it a sudden wrench, and the thing parted with an audible click. The shotgun was fake.

Jonah looked at it, stunned. Terrence stared at the separate parts, dumbfounded.

"I don't like guns either," said the woman. "It's all for show."

"Told you that she wasn't going to shoot us." Reena was unsurprised.

"You can't have possibly known that it was a fake," said Jonah. "The thing even cocked!"

"Of course I didn't know," said Reena, "but I knew that she had no intention of using it."

The woman turned her eyes to Reena. "How did you know that, exactly?"

Jonah's eyes narrowed, but his sister wasn't cornered in the least.

"Female intuition."

That seemed to be enough for the woman, who nodded. "Same thing happens with me, even though it ain't too often anymore. Well, since y'all are in my house, we might as well know each other. Starting with you three."

Jonah was thankful for the refuge but could do without the small talk. His mind was in other places, and this did nothing to help. But they were guests in the woman's home.

Therefore, shit.

"Jonah."

"Terrence."

"Reena."

"Patty," said the woman after they all finished. "Y'all want something t'eat?"

"Would love it!" Terrence, because of course...

"Wait one minute." Reena smacked Terrence's arm for being so zealous. "What do you have in there, Patty?"

Patty looked at her, her own eyes lowered. "Little lady, you don't look to be in a position to be choosy. One would think you'd take the first plate put in front of your face after not eating for the past couple of days. What was the last thing you had in that camp of yours?"

Reena didn't answer directly. "I'm not choosy. I'm just cautious."

Either Patty respected the fact that Reena didn't back down, or maybe she wanted to stick together with the only other woman. Jonah didn't know. But she relented. "Mainly frying parts, venison, fried potatoes, got some cured ham in there—"

Reena looked as though she might faint. "May I ask how you plan to cook?"

"Reena baby," said Patty, "there ain't nothing in this world that wouldn't taste good in lard—"

Reena shot up from her seat. "Apologies for my boldness, Patty, but you're not cooking our food. If you'd be so kind as to lead me to your kitchen, I will do it."

Patty looked put off for a second, but then shrugged. "Fine. But you'd better mind how messy you get. And you're gonna wash every single dish you use. I like to keep a clean house."

"That won't be a problem."

The two women disappeared into the nearby room. Jonah and Terrence were alone.

"You know," said Terrence as he stared behind the two

135

women, "it was always clear that Reena was direct and forth-right, but to commandeer the woman's kitchen? Wow."

"I think Reena needed something to do." Jonah's mind was still too far away to marvel at what had just transpired. "What with Kendall in Ireland and us being forced to flee our home before we could help anyone."

Terrence correctly interpreted the hardness in Jonah's voice and spoke up almost instantly. "Jonah, as messed up as it was, Reena made the right call. The main thing was your safety."

"At the cost of everyone else?"

"We've already been through this, Jonah. It wasn't like we're punk bitches, man. We can look out for ourselves, or at the very least, know how to get away using the *Astralimes*. But like I said—we've been through this already. You needed to not be there. Creyton must view you as like ... a level-seven threat now, or something."

"What about Riley, huh?" asked Jonah, equally as sharp with his words. "I'm the one who greenlit the S.P.G. practi-tioners to provide sentry duty at the estate. That means that it's my fault that things went to hell."

Terrence pushed back his chair and stood up. "Well, if you're gonna sit there and shoot down and counter every damn thing I say, then fuck it, I'm done. Better off making sure that Reena doesn't make rabbit food casserole."

"You're just going to leave?" Jonah eyed him, taken aback. "What is with you, man?"

A sharp knock on Patty's door halted the argument. Jonah and Terrence both turned to the door, wary and alert. Reena hurried out of the kitchen, followed by Patty. Both of them looked wary as well; Reena for the same reasons as Jonah and Terrence, and Patty because she had already had an interesting enough night as it was and probably wasn't in the mood for much more. Still, she squared her shoulders, cleared her throat, and walked to the front door.

Jonah, Terrence, and Reena stayed close to each other. Jonah couldn't speak for his friends, but the urge to yank out his weapons was strong as he didn't know what.

"Who is it?" requested Patty in a clear voice.

"Deputies, ma'am," drawled a lazy voice. "Just needed to ask a couple questions."

Patty looked back at Jonah, Terrence, and Reena, nervousness in her expression. "You honestly ain't hiding anything from me?"

"We aren't the prisoners that broke out of that prison detail, Patty," said Jonah. "We're displaced campers. That's it."

Jonah felt no guilt whatsoever. No, they weren't campers, and yes, they were hiding something. But it wasn't the fact that they were prisoners.

The knock came again. "Ma'am?"

Patty turned back to the door, and invited the deputy sheriffs in. Jonah breathed a bit easier, but he was apprehensive again. Here they were, huddled and rumpled, as if they were on the run. One of the deputies noticed that fact and frowned at them.

"Y'all a tense bunch. Got a reason to be?"

"These are my young friends from Bible study, deputy," said Patty hastily. "No tension. Just a little curious as to why the police are out and about."

The taller deputy kind of shrugged, as if the question was fair. "You might have heard that some prisoners escaped custody in Guster County. Seen the news?"

Patty nodded.

"Well, what the news didn't say was that they got an almost hour head start before anyone knew anything was amiss. Makes the search area a bit wider. So, Guster County asked the neighboring counties to help out with the search. Have any of you seen anything suspicious?"

"No, sir," answered Patty. "I can't say that I have."

Jonah glanced at Patty and grimaced. He wished that she looked calmer. These two deputies were not like the lovable, bumbling imbeciles that entertained him on old T.V. shows. They both looked watchful and suspicious of everything. Jonah was beyond ready for them to leave.

"What about your Bible study friends here?"The second deputy, who displayed some of the very suspicion that unnerved Jonah. "You three notice anything strange tonight?"

"No, sir." Jonah kept his tone neutral. "Nothing we can speak of."

The deputy didn't look entirely convinced, but that might be okay. As tense as he was about their presence, there was always a default edge on things when police were involved. It went with the territory. On top of that, it was clear that the deputy didn't have a way to prove whether Jonah was lying. That was a very good thing.

"Ma'am, we'll to be out of your hair soon enough," promised the taller deputy, "but we would like to look around just a little before we go?"

"He needs a warrant for that," whispered Reena.

"Warrants in the sticks?" Terrence whispered back. "Thought you were the smart one, Reena."

Jonah said nothing as Patty swallowed. "No problem."

The deputies walked further into the living room. Jonah lowered his head. He had no desire to look the nosier deputy in the eye. A half-second later, he shot his head back up, yanked a baton from his pocket, and flung it at the face of the nosey deputy. With a cry of surprise and pain, he crashed against a china cabinet and fell to the floor.

"Jonah!" Reena shrieked. "What the hell have you done?"

"They're Deadfallen, Reena!"

With a snarl, the taller "deputy" grabbed a stunned Patty and flung her into a nearby recliner. The force sent the chair completely backwards, and she rolled to the floor.

"Don't know how you figured it out, Rowe, but oh well!" said that same deputy, dropping the heavy drawl. "It's more fun this way!"

He threw something in the direction of Jonah and his friends, which exploded and sprayed them. Within seconds, the air felt heavy and dense once more. It was that anti-*Astralimes* crap, the creation of Sean Tooles. The disciple then produced what looked like a boomerang, but its two sharp tips made its appearance far from recreational. The thing immediately gleamed black in the disciple's hand, and he lunged for Jonah, in no mood to speak further.

Jonah backed away, swinging blue-gleaming batons as he did so. Reena ran to Patty's side, while Terrence made for the other disciple, who was up to his knees. The kneeling disciple screwed up his eyes as though his head still bothered him. But after several seconds, a fully formed corporeal shadow sprang from him. Judging by the audible footsteps, it was as solid as a true person. The shadow charged Terrence and caught him with a double-leg takedown, which Terrence was too dumbfounded to counter.

Jonah was just as shocked as Terrence—what the hell was *that* thing?—and took his focus away from his opponent.

That cost him.

He felt fire across his chest as the boomerang-style weapon slashed through his shirt. With a growl of pain, Jonah returned his attention to his own fight. He slammed his foot into the disciple's shin, which brought him down to one knee. Jonah then focused electrical current from his body into his batons, hoping to "tase" the Deadfallen disciple, but the man was no fool. He swung his weapon upward, which upset Patty's mantle and spilled pictures, vases, and a rather dense wooden clock onto Jonah. As if by reflex, Jonah dropped his batons to protect his head. Those objects were not only distracting, they hurt like hell, especially the clock. The false deputy smirked as he rose to his feet, ready to finish Jonah off.

Jonah allowed instinct to compensate for his dropped batons. He willed as much wind current as he possibly could, which was a damn great deal when he focused. He then extended his arms in front of him and splayed his fingers, releasing what he'd gathered. The resulting gust slammed the Deadfallen disciple against the wall. Hard. Harder that Jonah anticipated, because when the man slid down the wall, he left a trail of blood in his wake. Whether he was unconscious or worse, Jonah didn't know. However, he was more concerned about the other Deadfallen disciple, who had recovered enough from the head wound to stand. Unfortunately for him, he was still disoriented from either the injury or the ethereality he'd done, or both. He wouldn't get much comfort, though—Reena left Patty's side and slammed him from behind with her yellow-gleaming socket wrench. He crashed to the floor again, as motionless as his comrade.

Feet away, the shadow that wrestled Terrence to the ground faded to nothing. Terrence scrambled to his feet, furious.

"What in hell's name was that thing?" he demanded.

"Just hang on a second, Ter." Reena's eyes were on Jonah. "How the hell did you know they were Deadfallen disciples?"

"Never mind that!" Jonah fired back. "You didn't notice something off in their essence, Reena? What the hell's with that?"

Reena's eyes widened. That stung her. Jonah had gratitude that Reena didn't get teary-eyed or weepy like Katarina Ocean or (if it were a truly serious situation) Liz. That didn't take away from the fact that that was a hurtful comment. Jonah wasn't about to back down but braced himself for Reena's warpath. Surprisingly, she didn't engage. She lowered herself onto a chair, took deep breaths, and then spoke in a lower, level tone.

"We need to calm down. We just shouted three questions at each other, and all had the word *hell* in them. I think that's a bit excessive. Let's answer them one by one, starting with me. Deal? Now then, Jonah, I don't know why my essence reading didn't compute with these Deadfallen disciples, nor do I know why it didn't work with Riley back at the estate—and don't act like you weren't wondering about that one as well. I'll inspect these guys, see if any clues are there."

Reena crouched down beside the disciple she'd just knocked out and splayed her fingers. The tips of them gleamed yellow.

"I'll get to you in one second, Terrence," she said idly. "But Jonah, once again—how did you know they weren't deputies?"

Jonah knelt alongside Reena and pointed at the closest disciple's feet. "I'm not the expert on police, but I'm pretty sure that police uniforms don't include alligator loafers."

Reena and Terrence gaped at the shoes. Reena actually abandoned her inspection to do so. Jonah continued.

"When they walked in, I dropped my head. When I did that, I saw that the nosey deputy had on alligator loafers. Tenth police bitch about their salaries all the time, and that's the city cops. So, how would some po-dunk deputy in an armpit town afford shoes like that?"

Terrence chuckled without mirth. "Been watching Sherlock, much?"

"Nope, I just know the difference between living beyond your means and wearing a disguise."

Terrence shrugged. "So, some of Creyton's disciples are

rich. Can't say I'm surprised. Now, Reena, answer my question. What was that shadow thing?"

"It's called a phantasm." Reena resumed her inspection of the Deadfallen disciple. "Spirit Reaper thing. A manifestation of one's mental picture, given form, substances, and purpose. I've never seen one that powerful before. Creyton must have schooled his followers well."

"So, Creyton and his cronies can make shadow versions of themselves?"

"Not shadows, phantasms," stressed Reena. "And yes, they can. Phantasm people, phantasm animals, phantasm insects and arachnids...you name it. Jonathan told me that when he was a teenager, he even saw a Spirit Reaper manifest a hybrid phantasm ... some kind of wolf thing with bullhorns or something. Not something I ever want to see."

"Uh-huh," muttered Terrence. "Why did it come for me?"

Jonah assumed the question was rhetorical, but then saw something change in Reena's face. Unfortunately, Terrence noticed it as well.

"What was *that*, Reena?" he queried.

"It's not a big deal, Terrence—"

"Damn it, Reena, spill it."

Reena cut an eye at him. "Phantasms go for the weakest link in the group. Or what they view as the weakest link. It could very well be speculative; one can't believe everything they read—"

"Save it." Terrence waved a hand to silence her. "I got the point."

"You made any headway with your inspection, Reena?" asked Jonah hastily.

Reena continued to run her yellow-gleaming fingers over the man. When she reached his upper body, the yellow of her fingertips blinked and faded out.

"What the ...?"

Reena's eyes narrowed. She grabbed the badge off the disciple's shirt and flipped it over. Inside was a material darker than the material that made up the badge. She tossed it across the room.

"The badges are chock full of Jarelsien. It's the same material my dampener has in it. *That's* why I couldn't read their essence."

Jonah's eyebrows rose. Since when could they do that? "What about Riley?"

"S.P.G. practitioners have badges as well. No doubt his was fixed against me, too. If Elijah hadn't hung on long enough to warn us, Riley would've have never been revealed as a disciple, and the ambush would have been a complete success."

Jonah's mind wandered to something Felix had said to Reena the night he'd convinced her to let him send Kendall abroad. That night already seemed so long ago.

Reena, you are one of the best friends of Creyton's mortal enemy. Don't think Creyton hasn't made a point to know everything about you and Terrence both.

Creyton knew about Reena's essence reading. The Deadfallen disciples he sent after them had protection against it. Then one of the fake deputies produced a phantasm thing that pegged Terrence as the weak link. Terrence already struggled with self-worth issues. Was there actually dark ethereality that preyed on self-doubt? That would only mess worse with Terrence.

What the hell had he gotten his brother and sister into?

"What about Patty?" he asked rather forcefully. "You didn't mention anything."

Reena's expression remained angry, but Jonah was surprised to see a single tear fall down her face. "She's in Spirit.

Went into cardiac arrest when that disciple over there threw her over that chair. There was nothing I could do."

Jonah felt a thud in his gut. His eyes drifted to the poor woman's physically lifeless body. She'd held them up with a phony gun just as a fake show of force. Then she invited them into her home and offered to feed them.

And these Deadfallen pricks threw her to the side like she was nothing.

Another innocent person swept up into his mess.

Just like Mr. Steverson.

Jonah shot up from his knees. "What do we do now?"

Reena's eyes were on Patty as well. "Wish I could tell you."

"I'll tell you what we'll do." At that very moment, Terrence came back from the kitchen, a dishrag in his hand. Jonah hadn't even realized he'd left. "I'm going to wipe down this room. We were never here. Then, we call 911 and tell them about disturbance we heard. These bastard bitches are the reason Patty is in Spirit, so why shouldn't they answer for it? Besides, I don't even know if that one over there is still physically alive, way his head is bleeding. Then we can use the *Astralimes* to go—"

"Nowhere," hissed Jonah. "We got hit with that anti-*Astralimes* shit."

Terrence scowled. "I forgot about that. We'll need to find a gas station and hose ourselves down—"

"No." Reena shook her head. "I don't think that will work. I could read the guy's essence once the badge was off. There was this—this evil glee in it. Even unconscious, I could read that glee. I think that Tooles guy perfected the solution. No Etch-A-Sketch showers will get rid of it. And I don't think that it will wear off in an hour. My feeling is that it'll take a while."

"That's just swell." Jonah's mouth twisted. "I'm open to suggestions."

"After Terrence wipes the room down, we walk into town,

find a car, and leave," said Reena. "I hate to have to steal, but we need to get out of here. Leave the state."

"Wait, what?" Jonah looked at Reena. "We need to start looking for Spairitin Cousland! We can't do that if we're off in another state!"

"Jonah, let's not forget that the *Astralimes* are our ace in the hole for not only finding that place, but staying ahead of Creyton and his followers," Reena reminded him. "We can't travel like that right now. Which means that we need to be away from here until this crap on our skin fades. And, uh, there is something else you need to know."

Jonah didn't like Reena's expression. At all. "Yeah?"

"I know how they found us here. Weren't you two wondering about that?"

Jonah said nothing. With all that had just transpired, he hadn't given it any thought. But Terrence didn't keep his mouth shut.

"Uh, yeah! Kinda."

Reena rolled her eyes. "Anyway, Jonah, the darts they hit you with to debilitate you weren't just meant to poison you, they were trackers."

Jonah blinked. "Say what?"

"Ethereal steel trackers. They are activated by Lifeblood. That's why I told Terrence not to take them out when I sifted the poison out of your system. He would have thrown them aside in that barn, and they could have continued tracking us. I've destroyed them. Those two Deadfallen disciples were the only ones who picked up our trail. Had I not destroyed them when I did, more may have come."

Jonah gritted his teeth. Creyton just didn't quit! "So, we're safe for the moment then?"

"Theoretically."

"I'll get to work." Terrence was already wiping the back of

the chair where sat. Somehow, it had survived the fight. "I don't want to stay long enough to test that theory. But just out of curiosity, where out of state are we going?"

"I know where we can go," said Jonah.

"And where would that be?" asked Reena.

"The one place none of us ever thought we'd go again." Jonah cracked his neck muscles. "Dexter City, Maryland."

9

BACKPEDAL

Escape was a test in morals, nerves, and judgment.

At least those were the things that ran through Jonah's mind.

They walked several miles from Patty's house after praying that her spirit's sojourn to the Other Side was a peaceful one. Then, after they put as much ground between them and the property as possible, Jonah made the 911 call. He made a point to embellish and was as histrionic as possible, for one reason only. He knew what Deadfallen disciples were capable of doing to anyone, let alone Tenths. If one officer went to investigate, or even two, they would be eaten alive. However, Jonah figured that if they made as big a show of force as they could, then the better off they'd be. The Tenth police might even stand a chance against the two ethereal humans, one of whom had a bad head wound. They should have a chance if they went in heavy duty.

Or as heavy duty as a backwater sheriff's department could be.

The next step was to secure transportation. Reena decided

on a Jeep Grand Cherokee from a local car dealership. She and Jonah were well aware that leaving town was necessary, but both had serious misgivings about actually taking the Jeep. Terrence told them that this was the best time to do so because in all likelihood the sheriff's department had to empty to make the show of force that Jonah begged of them.

"The town is empty of law enforcement," Terrence reasoned. "This is a sweetheart opportunity to take a vehicle."

"Did I just hear Spader's voice coming out of your mouth?" Jonah asked wryly.

"Nope. Just the voice of a guy who was homeless for a year and a half and never forgot the experience."

So, shortly thereafter, they were on the road. Jonah volunteered to drive first, with Terrence riding shotgun and Reena in the back. In hindsight, Jonah felt that should have let one of them drive. Because when you were on a long road trip, your mind wandered. Guaranteed.

And damn, did it wander.

It didn't help that, initially, the trip was virtually silent. The three of them were in their own minds. For Jonah, that was hell. What had happened at the estate after Terrence and Reena pulled him through the *Astralimes*? Sure, there were plenty of people there who could hold their own, but did that matter in an ambush? Did they all get away? Did anyone *not* get away?

And Vera. Slashing her knife this way and that in an attempt to keep Deadfallen disciples at bay. He prayed that her efforts worked. The fear that she fought valiantly and fell quickly almost robbed him of his breath.

Why hadn't he listened to Daniel? The former Protector Guide vilified the need for a party from minute one. Jonah did it anyway.

Wait.

Nothing happened at the party. The party went perfectly!

But Jonah made the call to get protection around the estate for the party and for the exodus. Which brought Riley into the picture, the hidden Deadfallen disciple who'd covered all his tracks ... he'd even hidden his essence from Reena—

"That's why he was late," Jonah growled aloud.

Terrence frowned at him. Reena raised her head and did the same.

"What are you talking about, Jonah? He who?"

"Riley. The reason why he didn't show up with Clive and Halima and the rest of them. He wasn't sick because he ate too much fried chicken at the party. He was part of Creyton's raid on The Plane with No Name."

"Oh." Terrence's expression darkened. "Yeah ..."

"There is something I don't understand, though," said Reena. "Elijah said The Plane with No Name had been emptied. He was one Gatekeeper; there were four. And that's not counting the other guards who patrolled the place. There should have been more chaos. More resistance. It just seemed like it was too damn smooth...like it was organized from the inside."

Jonah remained silent, his eyes on the highway. Then another infuriating thought fell into his head. He actually banged his fist against the dashboard.

"Fuck!"

"Whoa!" Terrence exclaimed. "Keep it together, man! What's up now?"

"Reena's right! It was organized from the inside! By India Drew!"

"What!" said Terrence and Reena together.

"That night at the party, I was conversing with Clive Jessup about how things were going. He told me that India Drew had escaped The Plane with No Name, but he said the

Networkers caught her a few weeks later. I thought that was really sloppy of her to get caught so soon afterward, but now I get it. Creyton got her out of there, told her what to do, and then made her put herself out there to be caught again! She was Creyton's inside person among prisoners, and Riley was his inside person among the authorities. Creyton probably told India to round up all of his disciples in there, coordinate some signal—no, that was probably Riley's job—and then wait for a sign or something."

"I'll be damned." There was anger in Terrence's eyes. "Reena, there was little to no chaos because India had already spread the word about what would happen. How they were supposed to behave."

"My God," breathed Reena. "Creyton gave all of them a pass. Not just the Deadfallen disciples that were in there, but all the Spirit Reapers in there. All those psychos ... sadists ... they're all free."

"And they'd have wiped us out if Elijah hadn't hung on long enough to warn us," said Terrence. "Is that a miracle? The fact that he stayed physically alive long enough to warn us?"

"If *that* was a miracle, then I'd rather be free of any more of them," declared Jonah.

They were all silent again. Maybe a full hour passed in silence. They crossed the state line into Virginia when Terrence broke the silence once more.

"We need to eat. Gas station'll do. I know you're leery of all diners now, Jonah."

Jonah nodded in agreement but didn't say anything. They stopped at a gas station joined with a Hardee's. Jonah and Terrence racked up fast-food breakfast items, while Reena went into the gas station and grabbed granola and green tea. When they'd returned to the Jeep, none of them relaxed until they'd all gone into Spectral Sight and saw a decent number of spirits and spiritesses. They were good for the moment. So, they dug in.

Or so Jonah thought.

A random glance in the rearview mirror revealed that Reena's breakfast, though small, was nearly untouched. She stared out of the window with unreadable eyes. Feeling for her, he tapped Terrence.

"You'll see her again, Reena."

Reena looked at Jonah in surprise. "What?"

"Kendall. You'll see her again."

"Why are you—? Oh."

Comprehension dawned on her face. Reena almost smiled. Jonah raised an eyebrow.

"You thought I was thinking about Kendall just now. She's never far from my thoughts, trust me. But, at that moment, I was thinking about something else."

"What?" nosed Terrence.

"That sign over there." Reena sighed. "The one that says how far we are from Charlottesville. That's where my family lives."

Now Jonah realized why she had that look on her face. "Oh. Gotcha."

"What, you want see them or something?" asked Terrence.

"Oh, hell no." Reena's contemplative voice hardened. "I never want to see them again."

"Reena, you're not the only one with daddy issues—"

"For your information, Terrence, I had *mommy* issues. My stepfather was too much of a coward for me to have issues with him. Don't tell me that it could work out for the best. They turned their backs on *me*."

Terrence fell silent, guilt on his face. The funny thing was, Jonah couldn't blame Terrence. He was curious about Reena's family, too.

"Reena, you said you had sisters, right?"

Reena took a deep breath. "Yeah. All younger. Kai, Myleah, and Tempie. Tempie was named after Mom."

"What was your relationship like with them?"

"Kai and Myleah? I suppose we got along fine, at least until Mom turned them against me. But Tempie, my baby sister, was the one I was closest to. We were the best of friends. She was nine when Mom threw me out. Tempie was bawling the whole time and wanted to come with me. I told her that she couldn't, and when she tried to hug me, Mom yanked her back, just in case I was 'contagious'. She didn't let me go quietly."

"Were any of them Elevenths?" asked Terrence.

"Don't know." It was clear that she didn't want to keep the conversation up much longer. "I didn't even know I was one myself until I met Jonathan—"

"Hold on, Reena," interruptedd Jonah. "I hate to say it, but you just contradicted something you told me when we first met."

Reena's eyes narrowed. "Which was?"

"You told me that your Uncle Kole was the only family member who cared about you. You never mentioned that your baby sister didn't want you to leave."

Reena's gaze returned to the window. "I never mentioned it because it doesn't matter. Like I said, Tempie was nine back then. That was about a decade and a half ago, which means our mother has had about fifteen years to poison her against me ... like she did Kai and Myleah. It's in the past now. End of story. Just forget it. It's not like we don't have enough on our plates right now."

Jonah let Reena's words sink in. He didn't like his relatives; they were all idiots. The only family he loved and cherished was now on the Other Side. Terrence had made amends with his adoptive brother and, as such, had created a bridge between his past family and the Decessios. And now, Reena had just revealed that one of her sisters was heartbroken to see her leave. What if Reena was wrong? What if her stupid mother hadn't succeeded in poisoning Tempie against her?

The moment was interrupted by a buzz that made them all jump. It was a text message.

Messages.

All three of their phones buzzed nonstop with new ones.

Jonah, Terrence, and Reena looked at one another, hesitant to read them. Terrence was the first to take the plunge. He read a message and laughed with relief.

"It's Dad! Everyone got away! My whole family's good at the safehouses Felix set up for them!"

"Thank God!" exclaimed Jonah, who grabbed his own phone. That good news infused him with courage.

He read the text and closed his eyes with relief.

"It's from Vera. She got out. She's back in Seattle, but I think she'll be cool. With the success of *Snow and Fire,* as well as her one-woman shows, her profile might be a little too high for them to mess with her."

"But?" said Reena, eyeing Jonah.

"But she isn't stupid. She's taking a trip and didn't tell me where."

Reena nodded. "Good girl."

They all returned to other text messages they had. They were from Bobby and Liz, Malcolm, Douglas and Katarina, Nella, Spader, Magdalena, Themis—a bunch of them. It seemed that almost everyone instantly realized the situation and ran for it. The three of them spent several minutes digesting the hugely welcoming information about the safety of their friends. There were still concerns, though—there were several phone numbers they didn't have—but the messages they got were such a boon to them. They tided them over greatly.

"All the text messages seem to have the same gist, Jonah," said Reena.

'What's that?"

"That you need to be as far away from Rome as possible."

Jonah sighed and lifted his phone. "Vera said the same thing. Let's finish this food, and head on."

* * *

They reached Maryland several hours later. By that time, Terrence was the one behind the wheel; he'd taken over from Reena two hours prior. Once they passed the "Dexter City Welcomes You" sign, Terrence laughed.

"When we were here last time, that sign touted how Balthazar Lockman was a famous citizen. Wasn't anything like that on that sign now."

"Jonah, coming here was your idea," said Reena. "What was your plan once we got here?"

"I thought we could keep a low profile at that foreclosed house where we found Prodigal and his buddies way back when. We could find a place to hunker down while this anti-*Astralimes* crap wears off. We're much more adept at keeping our heads down than teenaged sazers were, with a pregnant girl in their midst."

"That's not a bad idea, but we can't know if that place is still in foreclosed status—"

"It is," said Jonah. "I looked it up after I made the suggestion to come here."

"You knew the address to that place?" Terrence sounded both surprised and impressed.

"Yeah. I memorized it back then. 1603 Prinesdale Road. Still no buyers. According to what I found, people think it's haunted."

Reena laughed. "I conversed with the spirits and spiritesses around that house when we found Prodigal there. They were too afraid of the vampires taking their lifeblood in that town to be interested in trying to 'haunt' people. Some Tenths can be so dense."

"One problem," said Terrence. "We got a very early start on this drive—it's still daytime. We can't go to a foreclosed house right now. Have to hang out elsewhere until it's dark."

"Already thought it through," said Jonah. "We can whittle time away at the library. It's on the same street as that stupid police station where Lockman's lackey had me in holding. Nothing at all suspicious about poring over books in a library for several hours. Then, we can go to the house on Prinesdale Road."

* * *

The hours in the library were quiet. Jonah, Terrence, and Reena spent the majority of the time replying to texts. Jonah replied to all his, and then thumbed through magazines to take his mind off things. He was pleasantly surprised to see something about *Snow and Fire* in one of them, with pictures of the whole cast and Vera in front. He affirmed and reaffirmed that he'd see her again, much like he'd seen Reena do a time or two concerning Kendall.

When darkness fell, they set off, Jonah behind the wheel once more.

"I really wish those pricks hadn't hit us with that spray." Terrence looked like he wanted to hit something. "That one that sicced the phantasm on me? If I ever see him again, I will end him."

"Good," said Jonah. "And I will end Sean Tooles for making that crap in the first place."

Reena must have heard the hardness in his voice.

"Jonah, none of this is your fault," she insisted. "Creyton was bound to make a move. We all knew Omega was coming. I hope you believe that because it's true. And also ..."

Reena's voice trailed off, and she glanced away. That look that was on her face when she read the Charlottesville sign was there once again. "I hope that you'll forgive me for pulling you away from the estate. Under normal circumstances, I couldn't give less of a damn if anyone's mad at me. But—you had poisoned wounds, Jonah. I was trying to save your physical life. If we lost you ... I was just trying to save your physical life."

Jonah couldn't lie. Reena pissed him off when she did that. He understood why, but it still pissed him off. And he still had salty feelings about it. But he got the point. "We're cool, Reena. And thank you again. God only knows what would have happened if you—"

"Jonah, watch out!" Terrence shouted.

In a panic, Jonah refocused his attention on the road. How had he not noticed the person in front of him?

Wait.

Because there hadn't been anyone in front of them! The guy just appeared!

Before Jonah could slam on the brakes, the tall figure swung out his hands in front of himself and halted the Jeep. He actually stopped the Jeep with his bare hands. The act was so forceful that Jonah and Terrence might have gone through the windshield were it not for the seatbelts.

Jonah shook his head to clear cobwebs and stared at the attacker. He was freakishly tall, ruddy in complexion, with a face so gaunt that he looked malnourished.

But that was in looks only. The lifeblood that dripped from his mouth proved that much.

"Aw, fuck," Jonah groaned. "We'd just been talking about vampires in Dexter City."

"Maybe it's random." Terrence sounded hopeful. "Maybe he's a scavenger and hasn't thrown his lot in with Creyton—"

"*Per mortem, vitam,*" rasped the vampire, which widened Jonah's eyes. The vampire heard them through the windows? "Does that tell you my allegiance?"

"Jonah," Reena hissed, "hard reverse *now!*"

The vampire must have heard her as well because he tightened his grip on the hood. His fingers actually caused indentations in the metal.

"Unwise," he whispered. "And just to prevent you from trying to escape me—"

The vampire heaved with little to no effort and hurled the Jeep through the air.

10
THE FIRST THING TO GO

For Jonah, the dangerous moments flying through the air in the Jeep brought about the most disconcerting feeling of no gravity. It was as if time itself achieved sentience and shuffled all essence, while he, Terrence, and Reena remained in brief suspended animation.

But as quickly as that feeling registered, it was over.

All sensations righted themselves as the Jeep slammed to the ground many feet from the point of the throw. The vehicle landed upright somehow but that was so small a comfort, it was immaterial. In fact, it landed with such force that all the tires burst. Jonah felt a sting at the top of his head and there was discomfort in his back, but he was still physically alive. Had it not been for the seatbelt, he'd probably be the opposite.

"Terrence? You alright?"

"Head's buzzin. But I'm good."

"Reena?"

"Of course ... I am," Reena answered faintly.

But Jonah tensed. There was something in her voice that

let him know her statement was a false one. He turned around to look her over.

"I said I'm fine, damn it!" Reena insisted with impatience. "We need to get away from that damned vampire!"

Jonah looked through the cracked windshield. The vampire stood in his original spot. He hadn't moved and seemed quite amused.

"We got anything silver?"

Neither Terrence nor Reena replied, which answered that question.

"Swell," Jonah muttered. "But we got to do something."

He undid his seatbelt, which mercifully wasn't jammed, and fished out his batons. They gleamed blue, but the vampire laughed, which Jonah could hear from many feet away.

"Really, boy? Steel is useless against me."

Jonah struck the windshield with his batons. The ethereal steel knocked it completely free. He began to maneuver himself out.

"Alright, Terrence, we don't have any silver, but I got blue steel, and your brass knucks might make a difference—"

"Let me help Reena, man. Stall him, and I'll get to you."

"Wait, what—?"

That was all Jonah managed to say before the vampire closed the gap between them, grabbed him by the collar, and pulled him out. A punch knocked him to the ground.

The vampire grinned. Clearly, he enjoyed their dilemma.

"Pitiful. And *you* are supposed to be the last best hope of the dilletantes?"

Furious, Jonah focused an electrical current from his palm into his left baton, which then flew to the vampire's face. The electricity blinded him, which bought Jonah enough time to leap in the air with both feet and dropkick the vampire, a move meant to put some distance between the thing and Jonah's friends. It seemed a good idea at that moment, but when Jonah landed on the ground on his already sore back, he cursed out loud at his rashness.

The strike knocked the vampire to both knees. Jonah glanced at the Jeep. Why the hell was Terrence taking so long? He seemed to be in no hurry to extract Reena from the back seat. What was wrong with her?

Jonah refocused on the task at hand and hoped to press his advantage, however slight it was. But then a pain buzzed at the back of his skull. Jonah thought that he was more injured than he'd previously thought, but then realized that the vampire had just done one of Creyton's Mindscopes. Though temporary, it hurt like the grandfather of all headaches, and paused him enough to allow his enemy to recover.

The vampire struck him in the chest with enough force to knock him onto a car. It wasn't the most severe of strikes, but Jonah's lower back was killing him, and the strike didn't help matters. Now it was Jonah who collapsed to his knees. The vampire wasn't even winded.

"This is just wonderful." The vampire sounded jubilant. "And I wasn't even looking for *you* tonight!"

He raised his fingers to tap his throat, but at the same moment, what looked like silver bands wrapped him from his upper body to his ankles. He swayed for a second or two, and then fell to the ground. Jonah raised his eyes and couldn't believe it.

It was Felix.

"You're here, Felix?" murmured Jonah through the various pains. "Fancy ... fancy that."

"Yeah, Jonah, fancy that. Now, get up."

Jonah struggled to his feet. "What are you doing here?"

"I live in Dexter City at times. Call it a seasonal residence if you want. And you?"

"Long story. Come with me. Need to check on Terrence and Reena."

They left the writhing vampire and headed back to the wrecked Jeep, where Reena stubbornly pushed Terrence as he tried to help her. She hadn't even exited the back seat, despite the fact that Terrence had wrenched open the door.

"Let me help you, Reena!" he snapped.

"I don't need your damn help! I'm fine! Just—just give me a minute!"

Jonah looked at his sister, concerned. Something was up and despite Reena's insistence, her face made it clear that she was anything but fine.

Felix pushed Terrence to the side and looked at Reena more closely. His previously unreadable face tightened.

"Damn. No wonder you haven't maneuvered yourself out of there yet."

"*What is wrong with her?*" demanded Terrence and Jonah at the same time.

"Her right arm." Felix was calm. "It's completely out of the socket."

Pain shot down Jonah's own right arm, even though he knew that he couldn't possibly fathom how Reena felt right now. Terrence winced.

"No Greens around! Ain't that a bitch!"

"Terrence." Felix cut his eyes that way. "What have I told you all about relying on ethereality too much? You don't need a damned Green Aura. I'm a pretty solid medic. You have to be when you're a bounty hunter." He turned back to Reena. "Now, Reena, listen to me, and listen clearly. I get that you're proud and all that, but ... oh."

Jonah and Terrence peered in. Reena had passed out. The pain must have been unbearable.

"That makes things easy, I must admit," said Felix. "I'll

carry her. Terrence, I want you to grab that vampire by those bands and drag him. Don't worry, he won't resist—that silver burns him too badly. Jonah, you just follow. When we get to where we're going, I'll give you something for your back."

"Wait," said Jonah, "where are we going? We can't use the *Astralimes* right now—"

"You don't have to. We are literally walking distance from our destination. I have a place."

"Seriously?" asked Terrence. "You really want to walk into your place with a conscious vampire in tow, taking in details?"

"Doesn't matter what he sees," Felix told Terrence. "He won't be telling a soul."

Jonah regarded Felix, curious. There was something weird about him that he couldn't place. "What are you going to do, Felix?"

Felix carefully positioned Reena in his arms. Then he looked Jonah in the eye. "I'm going to fix Reena's arm. And then I'm going to fix your back. And then I'm going to torture this vampire and kill him. That work for you?"

If this wasn't the most bohemian band of people Jonah had ever seen, he didn't know what was. Felix, who led them, carried Reena, who still hadn't regained consciousness. Terrence dragged the vampire behind him, who was in so much agony from the silver that he couldn't speak. Last was Jonah himself, who did everything in his power to make himself oblivious to the pain in his back. He hoped that the walk wasn't long. There was no telling what someone would think if this motley crew were seen. It looked like a cross between a half-finished mob hit and a Monster-of-the-Week episode of *Supernatural*.

About five minutes later, they were in front of a very old

building that stood underneath an illustration of a soaring film reel with a shower of stars in its wake. Below the illustration, in ancient crumbling letters, read *Astro Cinemas*. The place looked as though it had been a regal establishment at one time. But now it was abandoned, forgotten, and surely condemned.

"What the—"

"Trust me," Felix interrupted Jonah. "Come on."

When they reached the doorway, Felix paused.

"Mind your step for the first ten feet or so. It's pretty rickety."

"It's only rickety for the first few feet?" laughed Terrence. "What, you've fixed the rest?"

"Mmm-hmm."

"Why didn't you—I don't know—fix all of it?"

"Because if trespassers walk in just the first few feet and feel how unstable it is, they will be disinclined to go further," Felix explained. "No one wants to be in the middle of a cave-in."

Jonah mulled that over. "Clever. I'll give you that."

Felix walked in, Reena in tow. He moved gingerly on the unstable floor, but still had the confidence of someone who had done it many times. Terrence moved uncertainly, dragging the vampire along. Jonah followed suit. The ramshackle floor felt like crushed cereal underneath his feet, and he felt he was tempting fate with each movement.

After about six or seven dubious minutes, the floor became solid. Jonah could have knelt and kissed it. He took in this new place, as did Terrence. Felix rounded what used to be a concession stand and disappeared behind it.

"Wait right there," he called. "Don't go anywhere; just stand there. I don't want you to get hurt. I'll be back."

They heard the footsteps fade.

"I don't know 'bout you, man," said Terrence in an aggravated voice, "but I'm damn sick and tired of all these dramatics. Where the hell are we? This movie theater looks older than my mother—not that Ma's old."

Jonah agreed, but he wasn't really focused on that. Now that he and Terrence were alone, something else came back to mind. "Terrence, what happened out there at the Jeep?"

Terrence looked at him. "What are you talking about?"

"I'm talking about when this vampire attacked us." He jabbed a finger at the bound lifeblood looter. "I went to try and stop him. You stayed with Reena. I get that. You wanted to make sure Reena was safe. But after Reena refused to deviate from her usual self, you still didn't leave her be. You knew that there was nothing you could do for her at that time, but you kept trying to get her out of that backseat. Why didn't you come to help me?"

Terrence frowned, confused, but also messed up. His eyes had widened a second before the frown and Jonah had caught it. Before Terrence could pull something out of his ass, Jonah raised a hand.

"You and I both know that the next thing out of your mouth will be a lie. So, just like you told Reena this morning: spill it."

Terrence sighed. "Jonah, I ain't really comfortable around vampires. Not since I almost became one. You already know about my aversion to garlic. I think I might be ... a little afraid of vampires now."

"Seriously? Terrence, that can't be right. We've been around vampires since then! Remember when we rescued those S.P.G. practitioners?"

"I didn't go anywhere near that thing!" Terrence shot back. "Why do you think I bashed that Deadfallen disciple in the mouth? That vampire lost all interest in us. That was the goal. I don't want them or their fuckin' fangs within biting distance of me. Call me a bitch all you want, but vampires ain't my gig. I didn't even want to drag this thing in here."

With a jolt, Jonah realized that Terrence had been hesitant as he'd dragged the vampire. Jonah assumed that it was because he, like him, was apprehensive about being seen. He had no idea that Terrence was—

"Afraid of vampires?" Felix was behind them. "Grow a set, boy. For Christ's sake, if you're jumpy about a damn lifeblood looter, you're going to get eaten alive as Omega rolls on."

"That's not fair, dude." Jonah instantly snapped his gaze to Felix. "None of us knows what Creyton has in store."

Felix ignored that. "To business ... I fixed Reena's arm. She'll be pure gold in a day or so. This place is the former *Astro Cinemas*. It's been closed for thirty-two years. I bought it for a steal, set up shop, and sometimes use it as a safe house for sazers. Call me the Harriet Tubman of sazers if you want."

Jonah and Terrence looked at each other. There was something very odd about Felix. Initially, Jonah simply suspected it. Now? He was pretty sure.

"Well, Terrence, since your balls have fallen off and all, I'll carry the vamp."

"What did you say?" asked Terrence, suddenly heated.

Once again, Felix ignored him as he grabbed the vampire who, like Reena, had passed out from pain. "You two follow me to Theatre Nine."

Terrence sneered but followed the sazer. Jonah wondered, but walked on. Theatre Nine wasn't very far from where they were. The old letters below the number Nine read *The Last Resistance*.

"My God," breathed Terrence, distracted from his anger. "That movie? I watched that on VHS when I was like, fifteen. That movie sucked balls."

Felix didn't respond as he carried the vampire inside the

theater. Jonah hadn't ever been in an empty movie theater and found himself less than thrilled by the experience. The seats, after years of neglect, were in a derelict state; some were on the ground. The huge screen was a nasty beige color due to age and was cracked and torn in many places and looked to be fibers away from peeling off entirely.

Felix paid no attention to this. Jonah watched him walk to the thirteenth seat in row M, although so many seats were gone by now that it hardly qualified as a row anymore. He undid the silver bands around the vampire and strapped him to the seat with what looked to be ordinary leather.

"Um, what are you doing? Why did you put him in that particular seat?"

"You'll understand in a few moments, Jonah. Why don't you come here and take a look? You too, Terrence, if your panties aren't too tight."

"Look, mother—"

"Dude." Jonah was tired and sore. The drama was worrisome. "You know that Felix is caustic at the best of times. It's not worth it. At all."

Terrence's nostrils flared, but he fell silent. They walked to Felix, who waited until they were next to him to speak again.

"As I've already told you, I'm going to torture this piece of shit. Let me explain myself before you two judge me as harsh and piss me off."

Jonah stepped back. What the hell was Felix's problem?

"This vampire is named Tieran Gregory," Felix told them. "He had been on The Plane with No Name and is one of those broken out at the start of Omega. He was also in the ambush at the estate—"

"Do you have any more info on that?" demanded Terrence. "We got texts from a bunch of folks, but we wondered if you might be able to tell us more."

"No, I can't. When I saw Tieran, I lost sight of everything. He used *Astralimes* to get away, and I followed."

Jonah frowned. Was he serious?

"Tieran Gregory was taken prisoner by the Networkers some time ago," Felix continued. "They felt that skewering him through the heart would have been kindness."

"Why? What in the hell did he do?"

Felix's jaw twitched. "He is what vampire hunters...the ones that are sazers, anyway...would call a herder."

"What's a herder?"

"Simply put, a herder is a vampire planted where the most naïve of Tenths or Elevenths are congregated. Vampires cause disappearances in numbers you can't possibly imagine, but when they usually involve college girls or children from school-yards, they are usually the work of herders, like Tieran here. Girls and children are always prime targets to turn into vampires, because they can always trap more victims. Who isn't moved by a charming girl or a defenseless kid in need of help?"

The vampire instantly made Jonah's blood boil. "What's this have to do with Creyton? I thought he had no more use for vampires after what the 49er did."

"Yet Creyton brought him back into the fold after beating the shit out of him and burning him beyond recognition," countered Felix. "Anyway, like I said, Tieran was on the Plane with No Name when 49er hijacked Creyton's plans a couple years back. He wants to prove that vampires can be loyal to Creyton, and integral to his occupation. Creyton has him at arm's length, and is giving him a trial run, if you will."

"For what reason?" asked Terrence. "What's he doing for him?"

"That's why we're here." Felix turned back to Tieran's unconscious form. "Wake up, bitch!"

He kicked the vampire across the face. The beast awoke

instantly, his pale head darting this way and that. Then he looked at the three men in front of him, and down at his bound form.

"Leather?" he demanded. "You should have kept the silver on me, Duscere! Would have been easier for you!"

"Don't bet on it, Tieran. We're going to play a game of Twenty Questions, assuming I want to go that far. But it will be much easier for you if you're cooperative."

Tieran hissed. "Crawl back to your hole and die, sazer."

Felix's gaze froze over. "If I were you, Tieran," his voice was as icy as his gaze, "I would be more forthcoming with information. This could get very painful if you aren't."

Tieran continued to sneer, but his features betrayed the slightest hint of trepidation.

"Now listen. That leather that you spoke of so poorly? It's been soaked with garlic. That means that if you struggle, not only will they tighten, but your movements will leak more garlic on your skin. Now, unless what Creyton did when he burned the 49er has created a vogue among vampires, I would assume you don't want to get burned too much."

Jonah felt Terrence shudder next to him. Garlic and vampires both? He must be really hating this.

Tieran looked at Felix with a hard expression, which Felix matched with indifference.

"Q and A begins now. Now, you happened across Jonah, Terrence, and Reena, but you were actually looking for me. I want to know why."

Defiantly, the vampire spat at Felix. Jonah saw that Felix was instantly furious and he pushed a button near his belt. Garlic seeped from the leather straps and the vampire's skin steamed, hissed, and burned. Tieran released a howl, followed by a string of oaths. Felix threw a look Jonah's way, and Jonah shrugged.

"You were going to attack him. Damage would be counter-productive to Q and A, don't you think?"

Felix relaxed somewhat. "Point." He turned back to Tieran. "Now you know that I'm not playing with you, bitch, so answer the question."

Tieran made a sour face, but his steaming flesh made him think twice about further defiance. "The Transcendent asked me to use these nights to hunt you down and kill you. You and that sazer boy keep trying to sway sazers to be heroes, and he can't have that. You're a bane."

Felix scratched his stubble. "Very good. Next question: how exactly does Creyton have sazers and vampires working together? I haven't been able to find that out. What's he done to make natural enemies co-exist?"

Tieran winced. Jonah saw that Felix had tightened the leather a little more.

"He got through to us. He told us that we've been natural enemies all this time because that worked better for the weak. He said that we've spent years and years hating each other when we should have hated Eleventh Percenters for making all of our lives hard. And he was right."

Felix closed his eyes. Jonah glanced at Terrence and knew that they shared the same thought. Fighting the good fight wasn't appealing when you got oppressed at every turn. Even Felix himself held anger and resentment toward bigoted Elevenths. For a quick second, Jonah wondered if the Curaie might still be around if they hadn't been so resistant to change and learned to flex with the times.

He had to admit it: Creyton truly was a master.

"What is Creyton's next step?" Felix was trying very hard to maintain composure.

Tieran hissed once more. Jonah heard Felix make a growling sound in the back of his throat.

"I'll see your hiss, and I will raise you one of these."

He lifted one of his trademark silver nails from his pocket and held it inches away from Tieran's heart. The vampire looked afraid, and Jonah couldn't blame him. Felix, by this time, was scaring *him*, too. The vampire swallowed.

"All I know is that he is looking for something back in North Carolina. Something that was lost. Something no one's been able to find for a long while."

Jonah stiffened. Terrence's mouth parted. Could it be? Creyton was searching for Spairitin Cousland, as well?

He shouldn't have been surprised, but the fact that he now knew that he and Creyton pursued the same goal made it that much more real.

And that much more vital to find it first.

"He's looking for something in North Carolina." Felix looked about ready to chew bricks. "Something no one has been able to find. That is by far the most useless piece of information I have ever heard in my life."

Jonah stepped back once more as Felix roared and got in the vampire's face.

"What is he looking for?"

"Well, if I knew that ..."

Felix tightened the leather again. The vampire roared.

"Don't get cute. I literally hold your existence in my hands."

"What is this, Duscere?" whispered Tieran. "Do you really care what the Transcendent is doing, or are you just trying to let out pent-up emotion because this has been a traumatic time for you?"

Felix froze. Jonah and Terrence looked at him curiously. Tieran actually laughed. In front of this seething sazer and two Elevenths, he *laughed*.

"At least I can admit my fallacies. You, on the other hand,

are nothing short of pathetic. That was the true reason why you failed, and why you're taking your failure out on me. And ... wait ..."

For some reason, Tieran's nose twitched, and his eyes narrowed. Jonah frowned at the beast. What the hell was going on here?

"Oh, Duscere." Tieran sounded mocking. Disappointed. "Felix Betran Duscere. I thought your previous failure was bad enough, but I had no idea ..."

Felix's eyes bulged and he reached into one of the old theater seats nearby and yanked up a huge contraption.

"And just like that, Gregory, you failed."

He flicked a switch at the back of the contraption in his hand and a blinding white light shone on Tieran Gregory. Jonah and Terrence had to shield their eyes, but that didn't blank out Tieran's scream. It was dreadful, piercing, bone-chilling ...

... and then it was over.

Felix switched off the UV light and carelessly threw it to the side, like the twenty-plus just like it. Jonah looked at the seat that had been occupied by the vampire. The garlic-laced straps hung limp, and behind them was nothing but ash.

Terrence broke out of his shock first and rounded on Felix. "Dude! What the hell was that? I thought you were going to work him over and pump him for information! You said *Twenty Questions!*"

"Never mind that!" said Jonah. "Felix, what was Tieran talking about? What have you failed at lately? And what was the deal with him pausing like that and saying your previous failure was bad enough? What's up, man?"

Felix glared at the remains of the vampire. For a tense moment, Jonah expected his eyes to flash red. But then, slowly but surely, Felix turned his eyes to them.

"Nothing. Forget you heard that. I did tell you once before that vampires are liars. Now, come with me. Jonah, I'll give you something for your back like I promised, and then I'll show you where you can sleep."

"You don't have to do that, man. We already have arrangements—"

"If you're talking about that foreclosed house on Prinesdale Road, forget it. First of all, I don't want Reena to move until her arm is completely healed. Second of all, that place is being watched. So, get it out of your mind. You're sleeping right here."

He turned and walked out of the theater. Jonah and Terrence didn't follow him.

"Jonah?" said Terrence quietly. "Are you thinking the same thing I'm thinking?"

"Uh-huh." Jonah didn't even hesitate. "That vampire was about to reveal something Felix doesn't want us to know."

Terrence nodded. "Exactly. Can't imagine what that might have been."

"Your guess is as good as mine, man."

Felix dipped his head back in the door. "You coming?"

Jonah and Terrence glanced at each other. Just like before, their thoughts were the same. Suddenly, Felix's presence didn't seem much like a relief anymore.

"Yeah, man. We're right behind you."

Some hours later, Jonah awoke. He guessed it was a powerful tonic that Felix gave him, because the second he drank it, he was out. He didn't even have much chance to take in where he was, which was Theater Twelve. It was so different from Theater Nine that it wasn't even funny.

Theater Nine was a ruin. Ancient. Theater Twelve, on the other hand, was completely empty of seats, but filled with cots along the wall and a well-worn workbench at one side. Three refrigerators were along the north wall. In addition to the cots, Jonah noticed a few bunk beds there as well. He couldn't tell if they were broken in or not, they were that clean and tidy.

He looked for Terrence, whom he knew Felix put on the other side of the theater. But his cot was empty. Jonah wasn't worried, though.

He knew where he'd be.

He rose and left Theater Twelve for Theater Fifteen. Felix told him right before he passed out that Reena was there. It was an easy walk to make, and on top of that, his back, after the tonic, felt great. Maybe his misgivings about Felix were premature. Maybe the man was stressed out, like all of them. The guy had just coordinated and bankrolled safehouses for over two dozen Elevenths, as well as two Tenths. That couldn't have been the easiest thing to do. If it took vanquishing a murderous vampire to level out his head, who was Jonah to judge? Hadn't he just recently cracked a Deadfallen disciple's skull himself?

He went to Theater Fifteen and, sure enough, Terrence was there, seated next to a slumbering Reena. Felix had replaced her torn and bloody polo with a clean sleeveless T-shirt. Her right arm was heavily wrapped from the shoulder to the elbow. Seeing Reena like that, in such a peaceful sleep, made Jonah's misgivings about Felix fade even further.

"Morning."

Terrence snorted. "It's three in the afternoon, man. You were out for a good little while. Felix said you needed to be. Something about how your back would have a much smoother time fixing itself were you not up, moving around. How is it, by the way?"

"Good as new. Has Reena been awake yet?"

"Once or twice, but she is sleeping off some stuff, too. She's doing well, though. It's nice to see her arm attached like it's supposed to be."

Jonah nodded in agreement. Seeing Reena's arm dangling like it was prior to Felix fixing it wasn't the prettiest sight.

"I was thinking just now—and especially after seeing Reena's repaired injury—that Felix might be just a bit frazzled," said Terrence. "How about you?"

"Right there with you. But I wonder what this place is exactly."

"It's a Plan B."

Felix was there, a syringe full of reddish liquid in his hand. "I told you that I bought this place for a steal. I was thirty at the time. They were going to demolish it. Seemed like a place that could be useful, and I wouldn't have to worry about prying eyes. Sometimes I house sazers or homeless Elevenths—I'm not discriminant, like the Curaie is. Or should I say, was."

Jonah glanced at Felix, and Felix knew the look. He nodded.

"I can't really find pity in my heart concerning what happened to them. Not after how they treated my father and countless others who didn't fit their mold."

He walked up to Reena, inserted the needle into an exposed place near her collarbone, and injected the entirety of the liquid into her arm.

"That's the last thing she'll need. Putting her arm back in place was easy. It was getting everything else right again—tissues, ligaments, and the like. In a few more hours, she'll be fully recovered."

"Awesome," said Jonah with a grin. "But all this, Felix,"—he waved his hand to indicate the theater—"how'd you do this?"

Felix trashed the needle. "Well, I was basically a rich man who had no interest in the finer things in life. Money has to be spent somewhere; it's not like you can take it with you. Why don't you come on back to Twelve? We can talk there and let Reena rest while her arm finishes healing."

Jonah thought that was a decent idea, so he and Terrence followed Felix back to Theater Twelve. Once there, Felix went up to one of the refrigerators and grabbed some bottles of water, which he tossed to Jonah and Terrence. Terrence pulled fruit snacks from his pocket and passed a pouch to Jonah.

"Why didn't you get some water, Felix?"

"Already hydrated." Felix settled at the workbench. "So tell me, what happened to you guys after the exodus got ambushed?"

The feelings of relief about Reena's recovery dulled somewhat when Jonah recounted the story, but it felt good to get it off his chest.

Felix nodded. "Sharp wit identifying that fake cop, Jonah. That will take you further than ethereality sometimes, mark my words."

"Shit," said Terrence, shaking his head. "Creyton wiped out the Curaie, emptied the Plane with No Name, and sent fools after us. A trifecta. It was like Michael Corleone solidifying his grasp on power."

"*Creyton* is Michael Corleone in this situation?" asked Jonah, annoyed. "Who does that make me? Fredo?"

"Nah," mused Felix. "You'd probably be Sonny."

Jonah had to end this quickly. Being called Sonny Corleone...the impulsive, violent one...didn't sit well with him. Not after the botched exodus. "What about you, Felix? You can't tell us anything that happened?"

Felix scratched his chin. "Told you that my entire focus went to Tieran when I saw him. He ripped the head off of one of the heralds—"

"What?" Jonah spat out water. "Which one?"

"The only name I ever bothered to remember was Bast's but the herald was … Aegean breed?"

Jonah closed his eyes. "That was Naphtali. Vera's favorite herald."

Terrence looked down and shook his head. Felix spoke again.

"I figured that Tieran showed up to kill me, so I gave chase. That's why I'm here in Dexter City. I wanted him to come looking for me, but in a place where I knew the lay of the land. You guys were an added bonus. But is there any particular reason why you chose Dexter City?"

"We wanted to get out of Rome while the anti-*Astralimes* crap wore off," grunted Terrence. "Reena read something in one of those disciples' essences that gave her the feeling that that Tooles guy had perfected it. No more washing it off or having it fade in an hour."

Felix took a settling breath. "She'd be right. Creyton's changing things across the board. You touched on phantasms," —Terrence's eyes flashed at the mention—"and I haven't seen one of those in years. But the anti-*Astralimes* stuff? That silver that caused those irrevocable burns on the 49er? It's a new ball game. I don't know what Creyton's ultimate goal is. Wait, yeah, I do. I just don't know the mechanics of how he plans on getting there."

Jonah lowered his eyes to his hands. Elijah's words moved about his head.

Fix it. You gotta fix ii.

And here was Felix, mentioning ethereality that either hadn't been seen in years or hadn't ever been seen at all. Jonathan hadn't even mentioned phantasms to him before.

"Where will you go from here?" asked Felix.

"Back to North Carolina," said Jonah "Air feels a little

clearer ... stuff must be wearing off now. Then we can use the *Astralimes* again—"

"Color me curious, Jonah," interrupted Felix, who didn't seem to realize that Jonah hadn't finished answering his question. "What are you guys trying to do? Perhaps I shouldn't wonder about Creyton. What's Mr. Light Blue working on?"

Jonah regarded Felix, put off. The question was a bit odd. Felix noted the reaction.

"So, you guys are up to something." The sazer's voice sounded almost greedy. "What is it? Tell me. You just might need the services of a certain friendly neighborhood sazer."

Felix had shifted his weight as he spoke. He was invasively and uncomfortably close to Jonah by this point. Unfortunately, the liquor bottle fell from his pocket. Reflexively, Terrence caught it.

"You need to dial it back, man." He frowned at Felix. He looked as put off by his behavior as Jonah. "What if this had been your wallet that fell out of your pocket? You'd have never noticed ..."

Terrence's voice trailed off.

"Something ain't right."

"How many times have I told you guys not to concern yourself with that bottle?" demanded Felix. "I'll have it back, thanks."

He snatched it from Terrence but as soon as he did, Jonah opened his hands, focused on the air, and mentally said, "*Here.*" The wind that he manipulated slipped the bottle from Felix's grasp and it flew into his open grasp.

Felix inhaled methodically; it was reminiscent of a bull inhaling heavily at viewing the sudden presence of red. "Jonah, give that back to me ... *now.*"

"This is not the Vintage, it's vodka. What happened to the bottle you had all those years?"

Felix's eyes never left Jonah's face. "It got smashed."

"You had that bottle for damn near a decade, Felix, so you said." Jonah's bullshit meter on full blast. "Through all the vampires you've vanquished, the Spirit Reapers and Dead-fallen disciples you've stopped, and the skirmishes at the estate. Hell, even during the exodus ambush you had that bottle of Vintage. And now, after all that, you expect me to believe that you just broke it?"

"Crazy times we're living in, Jonah." Felix's voice was stoic. "Things happen."

"I wondered why we hadn't seen it," said Terrence. "Every time we see you, you place it in front of you like it's a focal point or something. Didn't happen this time."

Felix's eyes were so hard, they could have been obsidian. "Give me back the bottle. Now."

Jonah's body began grow numb. Suddenly, those prickles of caution he'd had around Felix earlier began to make sense. There *had* been something off about him. When Jonah spoke again, his voice mirrored the numbness in his body.

"Felix, are you drinking again?"

Felix's expression didn't change. "I've got it under control, alright?"

"Oh, my God." Jonah stepped away.

He tossed the bottle away as if it were a contagious disease. It hit the floor and didn't crack, thus contradicting Felix's lie about the Vintage bottle.

Terrence buried his face in his hands. When he raised it again, there was disdain and contempt in every line and curve. "Why, Felix? How could you be so weak?"

"You could never understand." Felix's nostrils flared. "Neither of you! You have no idea how hard it is—"

"Don't give us that shit!" Jonah fired back. "You don't get to bitch about not staying on the wagon, Felix! Not after all the grief you gave me about focus during those Haunt sessions! You had a ten-year run of success! Ten years! All that progress, thrown away by you! Hard? Sounds like it was quite easy!"

"You're making a bigger deal of this than it is!" Felix shouted. "I've only been doing a little at a time! I'm not even drinking to get drunk! A half glass here, a couple of swallows there—that's nothing! If you'd known me before, you wouldn't call what I've been doing drinking. Trust me."

"Trust you?" cried Jonah, incredulous. "Trust you?! How can we ever trust you again, Felix? You've fucked up!"

"How have I fucked up? Sending your friends to safety? Sending Reena's little girlfriend to safety? Not to mention the safe and seamless relocations of Eleventh Percenters all across the country? Where exactly have I fucked up? Enlighten me."

Jonah opened his mouth angrily, but Terrence raised a hand to stop him. When he spoke, his own voice was far quieter than Jonah's would have been.

"I remember a certain day at the estate, nearly two years ago. When Lockman's flunky was spying on us. You had that bottle in front of you, like always. Magdalena asked you why you carried it around, and you told her that it was a reminder that you were powerless—"

"I know what I said," growled Felix. "I was sitting there when I said it."

"Don't get cute, as you would say," snapped Terrence. "You also said that you respected alcohol like one respected poison. You said you respected the capabilities of poison enough not to want to put them into your body. You said that. So, bearing your own damn words in mind, why are you taking in bits of poison?"

Felix's eyes fell on the vodka bottle. Maybe at this point, Jonah wasn't really thinking straight and could only see things he feared. But he could swear that there was longing in Felix's eyes, despite what he said about control. "I am still part of AA's success rate. You've got this backwards. I may be drinking again, but I am still successful because I have yet to have gotten drunk."

Terrence threw up his hands. "He's gone, Jonah. The man is fuckin' gone."

Felix scoffed. "Fucking babies. I'm getting my damn bottle."

Jonah didn't know where he got the courage, or the balls, to do what he did next.

He moved faster than Felix did and punted the bottle. It flew in a wide arc and gained enough speed and momentum that when it hit the ground this time, it shattered.

Felix's incredulous eyes followed the action from beginning to end. When the bottle shattered, those eyes lingered on the foamy, glassy mess for several seconds. Then they raised to Jonah and Terrence.

After they flashed red.

"That's your ass, boy."

Jonah had his batons out, ready for whatever might come, but before Felix could attack them, something wrapped around his upper torso, legs, and feet. Bound, he fell back against the workbench.

Reena had done it.

Using her left arm, she'd flung Felix's own silver bands at him. When she came to join Jonah and Terrence, Felix looked ready to spit sparks.

"You fucking bitch! After I sent your skank to safety? After I fixed your damned arm?"

"Aw, shit!" Terrence looked at Reena, terrified. "He did medical work on you! Are you alright, Reena?"

Jonah and Terrence both regarded her with concern, but

Reena shook her head and massaged her newly repaired arm with only a mild wince.

"Pain is fading more and more. I'm guessing Felix is high-functioning when he drinks. Suppose I should thank him for that much, at least."

"High func—wait, you *knew* he was drinking again?" asked Jonah.

Reena nodded and sighed.

Felix looked at her, enraged. He struggled in the bands but made no progress whatsoever. Clearly, he'd done too good a job creating them. "How could you have possibly known, Katoa? I didn't tell anyone—"

"Not verbally, no," said Reena. "I read it in your essence. I didn't have my dampener on me. The essence of an impaired person feels like a ... fog in my consciousness. Plus, when you were fixing my arm, I smelled your breath. You went overboard with the mint. Massively so. Sure-fire sign that you were hiding that telltale breath."

Felix's gaze was off-putting, but Reena turned her back on him and faced Jonah and Terrence.

"A lot of things make sense now. Remember that night when we decided to proceed with the exodus? Liz asked Felix if he would rather drive than use the *Astralimes* due to that stab wound the 49er gave him. Felix shot down driving a little too quickly. I'm willing to bet that he had vodka to dull the pain; the Vintage had likely been long-since consumed. He's a sazer, so a glass wouldn't do it. He probably had a few bottles."

Felix looked stunned. But Reena wasn't finished.

"The night you threw the party, Jonah. Felix showed up to tell us about the travel plans for Kendall, Nelson, and Tamara. You know how he is usually brooding, but that night, he was sociable, friendly ... dare I say, loose. I didn't peg it because a bunch of people had a buzz going. But Felix were among the ones that were drunk."

"How could he be lit, and no one know?" asked Jonah. "He seemed completely on the level!"

"Sazer, Jonah," Reena reminded him.

Felix looked away. It seemed that his Red Rage was gone. Now, there was nothing but shame.

"You should have seen him last night, Reena," said Terrence. "He was torturing that vampire and, even by his standards, it was vicious. He spoke about Creyton having wiped out the Curaie and said he didn't give a shit."

"I told you why, Terrence," snapped Felix. "Everybody knows that I hated the Curaie. They've had it in for people like me for years. Did you expect me to suddenly weep for them because they were obliterated by a force they didn't do enough to stop?"

"Absolutely not," said Jonah. "And the Curaie had times where they were world-class pricks. But Felix, I never forgot those ostentatious crystal-blue roses you got Vera. You researched my dad just to help me get closure. You might have your rough and ruthless moments, but you're not heartless. Certainly not heartless enough to know that thirteen Spirit Guides got usurped by the man who ordered the murder of your father, and not give a damn."

Felix looked away again.

"And that vampire that you were torturing." Terrence once more. "He must have smelled the liquor on you. You might have buried your breath in mint, but the vamp still picked it up. And he was gonna snitch on you. That's why you pulled out that little UV hell light and blew him up. Wrote it all off by saying he was lying."

"With vampires and addicts, the first thing to go is the truth," said Jonah softly, which prompted Felix to look up at him. "I never forgot that, man. Why would you open yourself up to that again?"

"My mentality has changed," said Felix shortly. "Ever since Creyton achieved Praeterletum, I had trouble sleeping. That night when I took my first drink in ten years? Slept like a baby."

"Another lie, Felix." Reena's response was immediate. "This relapse had nothing to do with Creyton's Praeterletum, or you'd have started drinking again when he first returned from the grave. So, stop making a fool of us, and try again."

Felix looked as though he wanted, with every fiber of his being, to be defiant. But then he just sighed. "Let me take you back. As you know, I didn't take it well when my dad was killed. On top of that, Trip, about the only guy I would have called my brother, became a mortal enemy practically overnight. Three years later, my mom passed into Spirit. And— you also know this, too—I had a tainted record, though I was free. The only time I had peace was when I drank. Never for the taste—for the feeling. I craved that feeling, but my biological makeup would make me burn right through the liquor, every time. That's why I became a heavy drinker. Vodka and the Vintage were the only liquors hard enough to numb me. So, I drank it all the time. I had control over the family fortune by that time, but all I did was drink. In fact, from age twenty to twenty-three, life was a haze of Vintage, vodka, and painkillers. It's a miracle that I didn't piss away Mom and Dad's money. Then I met Camille."

Felix closed his eyes.

"Millie was what everyone called her. She was a Tenth woman I met who was going to AA. She might have been two years younger than me, but she was an old soul. Far more mature than any other twenty-one-year-old girls I'd ever met. I don't believe that her drinking problem was as bad as mine, but she made the conscious effort to quell the issue. It was quite inspiring. So, I started going with her to AA. Five minutes later, we were in love. Five minutes after that, she was pregnant. And it was a Tenth baby. Can you believe that I sired a Tenth baby? It was so exciting! Scary, yeah, but exciting. I figured that fatherhood and love were great incentives to start anew. So, I made arrangements for Millie and me to just go away. I remember it like it was yesterday. She wanted to spend time in Baja, and then retire to Sao Paolo. I handled everything, even found out how far along a mother could be before it was unsafe for her to fly."

"So that's how you knew Tamara could safely fly to Vancouver," said Jonah.

"Yes." Felix didn't look at him. "I was ready to forget everything. Trip, the 49er, Creyton, Networkers, ethereality—all of it. Then, the night before we were supposed to go to Baja, Millie and our unborn son were killed."

Jonah felt, once again, that someone had punched him in the gut. Terrence closed his eyes. Reena shook her head, pained.

"I never knew the name," mumbled Felix. "I just know that it was a vampire and a Spirit Reaper together. Millie was completely drained of blood, and both her spirit and that of my son were usurped. After that, I withdrew from everything and Ol' Man Vintage was back."

Jonah looked over at the foamy mass of spilled liquid. How could such a substance have such power? Felix experienced a terrible loss, and that was the first thing he grabbed? But Felix wasn't finished. Apparently, the dam was completely broken, and he'd see it through.

"I spent six years vampire hunting, doing contract jobs for Eighth Chapter crimes ... and I don't remember half of them. Vintage, vodka, and painkillers. Of course, there was weed, but liquor and painkillers were the main things. Jonathan brought me back from the brink. Not once did he give up on me. He said I was worth more than the reckless things I was doing to myself. He said that I needed to stop using the ink of my past to write the story of my future. He always had this ... this way of packing endless meanings into words."

Jonah and Terrence looked at each other. Once again, a single tear ran down Reena's face. Just the one.

"I gave it up again, with Jonathan's help. I achieved my longest period of sobriety yet. And now, Jonathan's gone."

Felix's words were like a jackhammer that bashed Jonah's coping mechanisms. He gave himself a mental shake and listened.

"Do you get what I just said? Do you? Jonathan is gone. Dad, Mom, Millie, my unborn boy ... all gone. And Creyton is back. He found a way to screw the laws of life and return from the fuckin' grave. Those wonderful people on the Other Side, and *he* comes back? He even dug that bastard 49er out of the ground. Burned him half to hell, sure, but he's here. After that, I began to understand. There is no point to responsible living. No point. Great men and women fall left and right, and Creyton and his disciples just rise higher and higher. So, I said fuck it. To hell with life. All life has ever done is take from me. So, I bowed to the inevitable."

The story saddened Jonah. Indeed, Felix had been through a lot. Hell, that put it mildly. All those losses. Jonah almost felt sorry for him. But while the story saddened him, it didn't blind him.

"All those things were terrible, man. And losing Jonathan hit all of us hard. But you made a conscious choice to start drinking again. We could have helped you cope. We were all going through hell together—"

"I didn't need your damn help. Because your help means less than nothing. Sweet and profound words and gestures won't bring any of them back any more than they will make Creyton weaker. The fucking Curaie tried to hand-hold, and they got demolished. Creyton always wins, so to hell with it all. Liquor is not my addiction, it's my savior. The only thing in my life that has never let me down is the bottle. It's the one and only thing that can't be killed or usurped."

"Just abused," said Jonah. "You're blind, Felix. You're hurting, and you're blind. And you don't even know it. This isn't about your parents. Or Millie and your kid. Or even Jonathan. It's all you, Felix. You drank the liquor here. They didn't make you fall off the wagon. You can't even blame Creyton for that. This is about you." He shook his head. "I respected you, man. We all did. I had even put you up on a pedestal."

Felix shrugged. "I didn't ask you to. Your proclivity to go around deifying people isn't my fault, Rowe. I'm human. Human enough, anyway. And humans disappoint. I will not apologize for being sick and tired of being sick and tired. Not my fault that you admired me."

Jonah looked at Terrence, who shook his head in contempt. He then looked at Reena, who seemed within seconds of smacking Felix. In his own mind, he couldn't really ascertain his feelings. Disappointment superseded anger. Superseded betrayal. He almost wished it were anger. That, at least, was easier to stomach.

He dropped his batons on the floor, which he'd clutched them in his hand the entire time and knelt so that he could look Felix in the eye.

"You're right. I shouldn't have put you on a pedestal. You're no better than me. But you want to know something? I'm not the one using loss as an excuse to destroy myself. In no way will I discredit or belittle your pain. But *you* are the one drinking yourself to hell. You are the one popping painkillers. This fuckup is one hundred percent on you."

Jonah undid the silver bands. Felix rose, regarding him with surprise. Terrence and Reena stepped back.

"Jonah," Reena hissed, "what the hell are you doing?"

Jonah ignored her. He looked Felix straight in the eye. "You weren't easy with me when you taught me how to destroy Haunts, and I won't be easy with you now. As such, here is the truth: we don't know who you are. We don't respect you, and we sure as hell don't trust you. Get out of here. Don't ever come back. Felix Duscere will be welcome. His help will be invaluable against Creyton. *You*, on the other hand, can go to hell."

Felix glared at Jonah. "I put up all your friends out of the goodness of my heart. You realize that your actions here could prompt me to undo all of that?"

"You won't." Jonah was neither unmoved nor undeterred. "Because deep down in there, you still want to make Jonathan proud. And you know good and damn well he wouldn't approve of you undoing a good deed due to pettiness."

Felix looked speechless. Then he turned away pointedly and headed for the door. He was actually complying with Jonah's order to leave.

"Oh yeah, one more thing," said Jonah abruptly, "if you go anywhere near any of our friends in the current state you're in, you and I will have a massive problem."

Felix, who was at the door, looked back. "Did you just threaten me, boy?"

"You're goddamned right I did. Our friends have enough going on in their lives without a pissy drunk sazer messing around them. Stay the fuck away from everyone, or you deal with me. I don't care if you're a dangerous sazer. As you are well aware, I can be quite dangerous as well, should I wish to be."

Felix looked at Jonah for several more moments. Then he

pushed open the door and edged out of it. Because the place was so quiet, they heard his footsteps until they faded.

Then, there was total silence. Terrence was the first to break it.

"Damn, Jonah." He was in complete awe. "It takes balls to kick Felix out of his own place."

"That wasn't Felix Duscere," Jonah told him. "I would have never said that stuff to Felix; I owe Felix my life. But I don't owe that excuse-making drunk who just left a damned thing. Now, let's get some sleep. One way or another, we're out of here tomorrow."

11

THE ENDURING ELEVENTHS

Adrenaline was a funny thing.

It was almost like a spiritual endowment in many regards. Once it was in your system,

you felt on top of the world. You were faster than fast, mentally, and physically, and could even surprise yourself sometimes.

But just like spiritual endowments, once the adrenaline was gone, then came the fatigue.

And the aftereffects.

And the realizations.

Jonah was at that point. What made it worse was the sleep. After he'd sent Felix away, he fell asleep with an intractable state of mind, full of righteous conviction. When he awoke the next morning, however, he felt anxious, awkward, and doubtful.

He'd thrown the man out of his own safe house. The disappointment and disgust he felt towards Felix was insurmountable and plowed over anything rational. Or maybe it was anger and disappointment in equal parts. Either way, an adrenaline-fueled ride.

But now, hours later, he felt the realization of what he'd done.

And why he'd had to do it.

Jonah was very shaken by what had happened with Felix. He couldn't deny that. Felix threw away ten years of sobriety. Ten years. He was full of excuses and justifications, each one hollower than the next.

Or were they?

Jonah was not an alcoholic. He didn't understand the disease of alcoholism. And he hadn't had the love of his life murdered. But Felix taught him to make anger work for him with the Mind Cages. Felix was a sazer who was damn near bulletproof when it came to prejudice and strife.

But it wasn't the pains of the past that he said made him relapse.

It was the vanquishing of Jonathan.

The pull of that one thread had unraveled the entire tapestry of so many things. He and Trip bloodied each other. Trip did his little sermon, and the population of the estate dropped. Then the damned exodus, which got ambushed.

But Felix resumed drinking because Jonathan was gone.

Jonah could understand the hurt of that loss. He could. But he couldn't fight the feeling of betrayal. He'd looked up to Felix. Trusted him. But his mind was screwed up in a haze of booze and unresolved grief.

Despite those feelings, it now dawned on him that he'd cast out Felix Duscere.

What did this mean for Omega?

It felt like Felix's departure literally snatched away one of the most invaluable allies against Creyton. And Creyton's influence, however indirect, was the reason. Was he giving Creyton too much credit? He wasn't the one making Felix drink hard liquor and down painkillers.

Jonah stood and stretched stiff muscles. His mind was as wild this morning as it had been the previous night. But while that had been anger and disappointment, what he felt now was confusion.

"Jonah?"

He turned. Terrence and Reena were there. They, too, looked highly shaken.

"Did I do the right thing?" he asked, trying—and quite possibly failing—to hide his need for validation. "I was so certain last night. But now—"

"I hope that you don't take this the wrong way, man," said Terrence, "but now probably ain't the best time to doubt it. It's done. Can't be taken back."

Jonah felt his lip curl. That wasn't a particular helpful answer. Terrence had just more or less said that it was what it was. Hardly a heartening notion.

"You have no right to beat yourself up, Jonah." Reena was stern. "Last night, Felix was a danger to himself as well as us. He's got his own demons to fight, and he's got to figure them out on his own. Until that time, he is of no use to anyone."

For a few illogical seconds, Jonah wondered if he should have taken Felix's word for it when he said that he had it under control. They needed all the help they could, after all.

But there was no point dwelling on it now.

"I don't think I'm going to be comfortable staying here another night. It was an act of charity on Felix's part, so it feels awkward now. Either of you got any ideas on where to go next?"

Terrence stretched his neck muscles. "We start looking for

Spairitin Cousland. A nice little boring search would be welcome after all of this crazy drama. Just one thing."

"Yeah?" asked Jonah.

"You realize that we didn't actually spend another night here, right? All the dark in this theater is misleading. When you threw Felix out, and we went to sleep? That was something like four in the afternoon. It's like, ten-thirty at night now. You sure you don't want—?"

"Hell yes, I'm sure," said Jonah promptly. "I'm done with this place. Vampires getting blown up, sazers in drunken rages—"

"Really, Jonah?" Reena was incredulous. "Felix needs to be held accountable, yes. But he's just a nameless sazer now?"

Jonah looked away and forced himself to let that go. Yeah, he was confused and disappointed as ever about Felix, but it wasn't Terrence's or Reena's fault. He had experience with taking his frustration out on those around him. But that contributed zero to anything and usually led to disastrous miscommunications. He took a deep breath and exhaled the sudden tension. "What I mean to say is that I don't think we should stay here, even for the night. Forget the awkwardness and all that, we know next to nothing about this place. Felix used it as a safehouse, which means he probably has defense mechanisms all around. He did say to stay close to him, so we wouldn't get hurt. He didn't brief us and was probably in no position to do so, anyway. Besides that, Felix may have walked away earlier, but what's to say that he didn't go somewhere, binge on liquid fortitude, and is planning to come back here in full rage mode? I can't speak for you guys, but I personally don't want to be anywhere around for that. We're already facing knives at every turn. The last thing we need is to spend the night here and risk being at the mercy of an inebriated sazer, my opinion."

Reena thought that over, then nodded in agreement. Terrence didn't look too thrilled about leaving free digs but realized that there was too much sense in Jonah's words to ignore them. He nodded as well.

"Alright then. Our bags are over there. Reena, Felix put yours in here, too."

They crossed the theater and retrieved their bags. Jonah opened his to pull out his reading glasses with half a mind to ask Reena which border to search first. But what he saw when he unzipped the backpack pushed the thoughts aside.

Cash. A pretty damn good deal of it.

Before he could say anything, Reena beat him to it.

"What the hell? Where did this come from?"

Jonah looked her way. So, she had a buttload of cash, too. But Terrence's reaction trumped theirs.

"Oh, my good Lord." He held up his wads. He seemed to forget the fact that he had other possessions in the bag. "This seems like a few grand! Ten, fifteen easy!"

"Huh." Jonah was wary. "Felix gifts us this before he got lit?"

"Couldn't tell you, man! It only makes sense, right?"

"No."

Jonah and Terrence looked at Reena. She looked tense and little unnerved.

"What's up?" asked Terrence.

"Felix did this recently, guys. You told me that Felix put my bag in here with yours and Terrence's, Jonah. But I heard you guys arguing with Felix; my bag was still in the theater where he fixed my arm."

A chill went down Jonah's spine. "So, your bag would have still been there when I kicked him out."

Reena nodded. The glee faded from Terrence's face.

"So, he slipped back in here while we were asleep, put this

cash in our bags, and then put them in a neat little row, hoping that we wouldn't notice."

Jonah was speechless. It disturbed him greatly to know that Felix had returned when they were all asleep. He could have done anything and everything, completely unopposed.

But he didn't attack them. He put money in their bags.

Of all the things he could have done, that was what he did.

Suddenly, Jonah was furious.

Felix was a real piece of work right now. His relapse was out in the open. He was well aware that he was a total disgrace to three people who'd trusted him. And after the heated exchange, he hadn't lashed out when he had a golden opportunity. He put thousands of dollars into their bags. The bastard had tried to buy an apology, like an adult who used presents as damage control to appease angry children, or an abusive spouse who used purchases to get back into an abused spouse's good graces. But Felix hadn't pissed off any children or abused any women.

He'd betrayed his friends when he'd betrayed himself.

And he'd hoped to compensate them for their trouble.

Jonah shook his head. He couldn't believe that he'd second-guessed kicking him out earlier.

Jonah got all the money out of his bag and threw it on the floor.

"Kiss my ass, Felix. I'll be damned if I take a bribe."

Reena, who looked furious herself, tossed hers on top of Jonah's. "My forgiveness isn't for sale either. Not now, not ever."

Terrence looked like he was at war with himself. Jonah and Reena glared at him. He went instantly on the defensive.

"Look, I get it. Felix putting this money here was a grimy move. But so what? We didn't have any qualms about taking

Turk Landry's blank checks, did we? We took those and did something good with them."

"This is worlds different, Terrence. Landry was a weasel. It was fun spending his money. This isn't fun. It's a different set of rules here."

"Oh, really." Terrence arched an eyebrow at Jonah. "How is that?"

"Because if you take that money, Terrence," Reena chimed in, "you're letting Felix off the hook. It means that all of the shock and betrayal that you felt earlier could be erased for the right price."

Terrence looked mildly disgusted, like the notion of Reena's words made him feel dirty. Very reluctantly, he dumped his own money on the floor.

"Point taken. Let's just—let's just get out of here before I change my mind. But how exactly do you plan for us to travel? Jeep's a pile of junk now."

Jonah smirked. "I was wondering when you'd get to that. Have you noticed anything since we've gotten up? Feel the air?"

Terrence frowned for several seconds and then his expression cleared when he realized what Jonah meant. "The air feels open again. We can use the *Astralimes* again. Nice. Can we leave now, please? That's like thirty grand on the floor. It's a powerful distraction."

* * *

After a brief conversation, Jonah, Terrence, and Reena decided that since they were flying blind, luck was the only ace they had. Given the hour, plus the fact that the random sleeping pattern had thrown them off, they agreed to check into a motel wherever the *Astralimes* led them, if the directions to Spairitin

Cousland didn't start to make sense. Before they left, Reena affixed a shoulder apparatus to her newly mended shoulder. She preferred to be safe than sorry.

"Felix did a great job, despite everything," she conceded. "But still, he was drunk."

At long last, they were ready. As one, Jonah, Terrence, and Reena stepped into nothingness. The brief, unblinking glimpse of the Astral Plane never looked so good to Jonah. But it was gone as quickly as it was seen, and they stood near a shopping center, a Taco Bell, and a quaint little motel named The King's Inn.

"Where are we?" asked Jonah, puzzled. "I know we were going for random, but not like this."

Reena looked here and there, but it was too dark to see street signs. Terrence eyed the motel with a look of longing, but said in a pseudo-obliging voice, "How about it, Reena? Directions starting to click in?"

Reena pulled out Jonathan's pages and held her phone near them to illuminate them. Her lip curled. "No. Absolutely nothing has changed. Let's check in at that motel over there. It's been a tiring day, and it wouldn't hurt to figure out where we are."

Jonah had to admit that he had a small strain of nervous energy but realized that they probably wouldn't get far that night. So, he agreed and led them into the sliding doors of the King's Inn. The place was far from ostentatious, but the lobby was neat and clean. The lady behind the desk paid more attention to her Kindle than anything else. Jonah frowned at such lax behavior; what if they were a threat? At the same time, though, he envied the fact that the woman was in a situation where she could be so inattentive. He, Terrence, and Reena had to be watchful at all times nowadays.

The lady gave them more attention when they reached the

desk. She looked rather reluctant to do so, as though their desire for a room inconvenienced her. Reena noticed it and regarded her with a trace of aggravation.

"It's a great day at the King's Inn," she said in a tone of rote. "How may I help you?"

"It's evening, actually," said Reena coolly, "and we want a room. Non-smoking, two beds."

The lady punched something into the computer, accepted payment, and passed over keys. When she saw the engagement ring on Reena's finger, she grinned rather greedily at Jonah and Terrence.

"Which one of these is the lucky man?"

She pointed at Jonah and Terrence without a hint of shame.

"Neither of them." Reena pulled the keys from the woman's hand. "Now, where is our room?"

The hotel clerk blinked and her demeanor towards Reena changed instantly. "Follow this hall to the back." Her voice was saturated with judgment. "It's the door nearest to the stairs."

"Yeah." Reena gave the woman a cold smile. "Bye." She turned from the woman and was down the hall before Jonah and Terrence, both stunned, caught up with her.

"Reena, you could have elaborated to that woman."

"My personal life is none of that bitch's concern."

"But Reena," protested Terrence, "you could have easily prevented that woman from assuming that you're some whore from around the way!"

"She doesn't know me," Reena told him. "*I* know me."

"To hell with that, Reena!" said Jonah, still incredulous. "Do you have any idea what that woman might think of you now?"

"She can think whatever she wants. She will anyway."

Reena nearly kicked in the room door, flung away her bag,

and flopped on one of the beds, where she began to massage her temples. Jonah and Terrence looked at each other. Likely, the reminder of her engagement ring brought her missing Kendall into fresh relief. Jonah figured that she dealt with it as best she could, but the nosy, judgmental motel clerk hadn't helped matters at all. Reena sighed.

"If you two are done trying to gauge my thoughts, perhaps we can talk about what we will do and say when we find Spairitin Cousland."

Terrence sat in a nearby chair and unwrapped a Snickers bar. Jonah sat at the front of the empty twin bed.

"Well, we are well aware that we don't know what to expect from these people. Reena, you said that they probably weren't a bunch of yokels, but if they have closed borders—"

"Jonah, we've been through this." Reena had that hint of impatience again. "Closed borders do not mean they're Amish. It just means that they don't care very much for outside influences."

"Which sucks something fierce," Terrence threw in. "Because if we ain't outside influences, I don't know what is."

"We're ethereal humans, man. Those are the ties that bind. The whole *look out for your own* bullshit sounds a bit too Curaie for my taste."

"I don't think they're being so overprotective out of malice." Reena and sat up on the bed. "Creyton has been wrecking things like an EF-5 ever since he returned from the grave. They very likely don't want to be exposed to things and people that could put them in his path."

"They had no issue with Jonathan," Jonah reminded her.

"Of course they didn't have an issue with Jonathan. It was Jonathan."

Jonah looked away. There was no need for further explanation. No need at all.

"Jonah, you're forgetting the best card that you have to play," said Terrence with wide eyes. "You can just go in face-first like you own the place and tell them that you're the Light Blue Aura! They'll practically be begging to help you then!"

"I'm not doing that, Terrence. How would it look if I went in there and made an ass out of myself for ego purposes? That's stupid."

"Wow." Terrence's face hardened. "You sure shot that one down quick-fast. Can't say I'm surprised, though. It's common-place to disregard the shit I say."

"What ...?"

Terrence rose ungraciously to his feet. "I'll be back. That Taco Bell across the street is calling my name."

He didn't even grab a motel key as he went out the door. Jonah stared at it for several seconds, completely baffled.

"What the hell is with him? When did he get so damn sensitive?"

Reena didn't even open her eyes. "Sensitivity had nothing to do with it, Jonah. The toughest man on earth would have an issue with their opinion being shot down with so little thought."

"But I didn't shoot him down! It was a dumb idea!"

"I'm not saying it wasn't. But Jonah, you are a writer, and a lover of words. So, surely you could have found a way to convey your opinion on the matter without simply writing it off as stupid. And by the way,"—Reena opened her eyes wide enough to regard Jonah—"take some of that bass out of your voice. You aren't the only one who is uncomfortable and riled."

Jonah lay flat on the bed and sighed. Now he felt like an imbecile. Again. Hindsight was always 20/20, and he thought of twenty different ways he could have rephrased what he'd told Terrence. Twenty different ways, too little too late.

Sometime later, a rather reluctant knock rapped on the door. Jonah rose and opened it.

"Did they have any specials?" he asked after a small delay.

"A few. But it's pretty cheap if you know how to order."

Jonah returned to the bed, and Terrence sat down on the chair.

"I got you some soft tacos. No tomatoes though. They'd make the whole thing cold."

He passed them over. Jonah could tell that it was a peace offering.

"Appreciate it."

Terrence nodded once, and then turned to Reena. "Reena, I—"

"I am very grateful for the gesture, Terrence, but I would rather fast than eat that."

Terrence smirked. "More for us, Jonah. And by the way, this town we've wound up in? It's named Laurinburg. A town named Raeford is about twenty minutes in that direction." He pointed to the wall, which didn't mean much. He didn't seem to care, though, as he was focused on the food.

He and Jonah ate in silence. Reena filled a paper cup with water, took an ethereal sleep aid she'd scored from Liz's stash, and fell asleep without another word. Both Jonah and Terrence were fine with that. Reena had mentally checked out a long time ago, anyway. When they were done with the food, they took some of the sleep aid themselves, and were asleep themselves within minutes.

The good news was that the aid did the trick.

The bad news was that Liz was good at her tonics. The aid worked too well.

Jonah opened his eyes, feeling better that he had in days. But he also felt odd. It was still dark. With a frown, he looked at his cell phone: 7:58 P.M.

They'd slept through an entire day. *Shit.*

"Reena!" he said loudly. "Terrence!"

Unsurprisingly, they both shot upright and looked wildly at Jonah.

"It's eight at night We've slept the entire day through! Reena, how much did you pay them for?"

"Two days. It just seemed like the smart thing to do."

Jonah sighed in relief. But he was still annoyed.

"Why did we sleep so long?" demanded Terrence.

"Fatigue," answered Reena as she watched him stretch. "It's a world-class bitch. Plus, you know Liz's sleep aids are effective. She wouldn't have it any other way."

"I had a plan for today!" Jonah grumbled in frustration. "I'd hoped that we could search for Spairitin Cousland as much as we possibly could! Now it's just as late as it was last night!"

"It just might work in our favor, Jonah," said Terrence. "We just slept almost a whole day. Night-searching might be best. How odd would it look if we stepped out of thin air in broad daylight? Yeah, we've done it before, but we actually knew where we were going at those times. We don't know where we'll turn up this time around."

Jonah thought on it. That made a bunch of sense. Last thing that they needed were prying eyes. He stood. "Sounds like a plan. Let's get going."

"Um, two minutes." Terrence stood. "I've been in one position for hours and hours, and gravity has riled the bladder."

Jonah snorted. Reena just closed her eyes and shook her head.

A while later, they were out of the door.

"Question." Terrence looked here and there. "I was wondering if you guys were planning on looking around Laurinburg to see if those directions will start making sense, or do you want to use the *Astralimes*? Or did you want to get another car?"

Jonah shuddered. Stealing that Jeep had been a hard

choice. He wondered if he would have made a different choice if he had to do it over again. Yeah, it was convenient, and they really needed to put road behind them, he wasn't too keen on doing it again. One top of the misgivings, he had the crazy notion in the back of his head that what happened with the Jeep might have been karma. That was a foolish notion, of course, but with all the things Jonah had seen, he didn't write things off anymore. "I'm thinking we can use the *Astralimes*. We've got to be leery of quieter places anyway. Reena, get the directions out. We can probably move about ten, fifteen miles from here. One direction first, the other direction next."

Reena looked as if she had serious reservations about this method but said nothing since they had nothing else at the moment. She removed the directions from her pocket. "I'm ready."

"Me too," said Terrence.

Jonah nodded again, and they all took one step onto the Astral Plane and a second step onto another patch of land the number of miles that Jonah suggested. Before Reena could consult the map, though, they were all distracted by a pained howl.

Maybe twenty yards away from where they stood, two men were savagely beating another man. They weren't even methodical about it; it looked as though their plan was to simply beat the physical life out of him.

Jonah raced forward and tackled the guy punching the prone man in the face. They tumbled to the ground. He followed his attack with a jab, made even more effective by the spiritual endowment, followed by a gut punch. The man choked out a lungful of air and rolled to the side. The guy may not have been unconscious, but he wasn't a threat. It was at that point that Jonah looked around for Terrence and Reena.

Reena had the other guy pinned under her knee as Terrence helped the badly injured victim to his feet.

"What the hell is going on?" snapped Jonah. "Why were you beating the shit out of this man?"

The dazed guy looked at him, livid. "Why did you stop us? You ought to understand! You're Elevenths like us!"

"Wait," frowned Terrence, "you guys are Elevenths? And you *know* we're Elevenths?"

"'Course we know!" cried the man pinned under Reena's knee. "We're in Spectral Sight right now, and none of you have spirits or spiritesses around you. So, you ought to understand."

"Understand what?" snarled Reena.

"That piece of shit is a sazer!" said the groggy man. "He ain't like us, mixed-breed bastard! We were reminding him of his place."

Jonah was further infuriated by those words. It wasn't the first time he'd encountered ethereal purists, but these fools could only be big men when they double-teamed somebody. Once everyone was on equal footing though, they bitched out. Typical.

"I know plenty of sazers worth ten of your sorry asses," said Terrence in an icy tone. "But there ain't a point speaking intelligence to you fools. Pearls before swine."

"Spare us the sermon," grumbled the pinned man with effort. Reena must have had him in pain. "We know we're right. Sazers are worthless. We ain't sorry about whipping their asses. That's what their asses is for!'

Reena couldn't take it anymore. She punched the guy in the back of the head, and he squealed like a pig.

Terrence helped the sazer straighten. The man winced, but only a little. Jonah wanted to assist, but he'd have to leave the seated man unopposed. Terrence saw the frustration on his face and shook his head.

"It's alright, brother, I got it," he said to Jonah before he turned to the sazer. "What's your name, man?"

"Denny."

"You're lucky, Denny. Well, these fools are, anyway. You could have gone into Red Rage and savaged them."

Denny shook his head. "I was too scared to be angry. I thought they were gonna kill me."

The seated man spat on the ground, very close to Jonah's feet. Jonah yanked out his baton, happy to see the blue flash on the man's face.

"Do that again. I dare you ..."

Jonah's voice trailed off as he noticed the guy staring at his baton. He didn't see fear or frustration on his face.

The man looked shocked at first. His eyes were wide as he rose to his feet. Then they returned to Jonah's surprised face.

"Blue," he breathed. "You're Jonah Rowe ..."

Jonah didn't know what to make of it. There was a kind of desperation in the man's eyes, which was mirrored in the pinned-down man's eyes and, oddly enough, the sazer's as well.

The man looked past Jonah, and his eyes fell on Denny. The sazer he'd just helped beat up.

"Truce?" he asked.

Denny pushed himself away from Terrence's support and said. "Hell yes."

Terrence looked between them. "What the hell is happening ...?"

"I'm in, too!" cried the man pinned under Reena's knee. "Get this bitch off me!"

Before any of them could react, the standing man made an X by crossing his forearms. What looked like a silverish wave shot from his arms and slammed into Reena, blasting her off the guy. Jonah's eyes bulged. The man had just used a Mind Cage weapon on Reena!

Denny wasn't half as methodical. While Terrence roared at what happened to Reena, the sazer kicked him in the groin. No ethereality whatsoever, just a pure, unadulterated balls shot. Terrence gave an abbreviated bellow and collapsed as though he'd been hit by a bullet.

The two men tackled Jonah and drove him hard to the ground. He could barely focus past the lights strewn across his eyes before one of the guys snatched the baton out of his hand and began to strangle him. Jonah attempted to struggle, but the other guy restrained his hands.

"Hurry up, man!" he shouted to the guy strangling Jonah. "I'm glad the bitch was wearing that dampener thing she's got! The other dude's the weak link, right? He's no problem just rolling around on the ground over there! Hurry!"

Jonah tried hard to shock the man who restrained his hands, but he couldn't focus. His vision blackened.

The strangler suddenly lunged forward, inadvertently head-butting the man that restrained Jonah. The head-butt must have been forceful as hell because it knocked the guy out cold. Jonah rolled onto his stomach, coughing furiously, but when he saw the guy who had throttled him with his own baton begin to stir, he buried the pain as far as it would go. He pounced on the bastard and proceeded to beat the hell out of him. The only issue would be restraint ...

"Jonah, that's enough! He's unconscious! Get Terrence and Reena and go back to where you were!"

Jonah swung around on his knees. "Patience? What are you—"

"We'll talk in a few! Let me take care of things here. Leave now!"

But Jonah hesitated. He remembered the Nightmare Scenario ... how Barisford Charles had promised to regroup with them, but never made it back. He wasn't about to abandon

Patience to a potentially similar fate. Patience saw the look in his eyes and impatiently shook his head.

"It won't be like that, Jonah," he assured him. "These two guys are out like a light, and that sazer ran when I turned up. Five minutes, tops."

"But you don't even know where—"

"Shut up! You don't know if any other Elevenths are around here listening! I'll find you!" He dropped a Tally into Jonah's shirt pocket. "Now, take them and *go*!"

Jonah stumbled toward his brother and sister. Reena clutched her shoulder, growling in pain. Somehow, Terrence managed to get to his feet. But his eyes were red, and his equilibrium was shot. Jonah grabbed them and guided them through the *Astralimes* and right back into their motel room, where he pushed Terrence into his chair. Reena leaned against the wall, where she still clutched her shoulder. Her eyes blazed with fury.

"Son of a bitch," she said through clenched teeth. "Mentis Cavea ... goddamned shoulder just healed ..."

Jonah barely heard her. He was angry, confused, and a little afraid. What the hell had happened out there? They stopped an ethereal hate crime, and then got jumped?

The wind picked up, and then the motel room had a fourth occupant: Patience was with them. He looked very tired, but he was uninjured. He regarded the three of them, relief in his eyes.

"Thank God, I found you guys. I tried to find you all sooner so I could warn you."

"What was that, Patience?" demanded Jonah. "What the hell just went down out there? We helped the sazer, and then he teamed up with the guys who were beating him to—"

"They'd have killed you, Jonah. They'd have killed all three of you."

"What? What are you saying, Patience? Were they Dead-fallen disciples or something?"

"No, Jonah. They weren't Deadfallen disciples, but they still would have killed you. Just sit down, take a load off. We've got a lot to talk about."

12

MEAN-SPIRITED

Jonah wanted more than anything to find out what Patience knew right then and there, but Patience checked on Terrence and Reena. While the Eleventh's Mind Cage didn't hurt Reena half as much as it would have if she'd been a Haunt, the blast knocked her directly onto her recently repaired shoulder. Patience looked her over (he wasn't a Green Aura, but he had ample first-aid training as a Networker) and discovered that nothing was reinjured. However, the fall did her no favors, and she'd have to ride out the soreness.

Terrence was still in pain. After brief inspection, Patience closed his eyes, shook his head, and made Terrence drink almost an entire bottle of tonic. When Jonah wondered aloud why that was, Patience didn't even look at him.

"There was swelling. You don't need to know any more than that."

About an hour passed before things were calm enough for conversation. Reena sat on the bed, an icepack strapped to her shoulder. Terrence remained in the chair, a bag of ice in his lap. Save for some inconsequential bumps and bruises and a cut over his right eye, Jonah was fine. But he couldn't care less about those injuries. He wanted to know what Patience meant.

"Patience, you look tired as hell," commented Terrence in a quiet voice. It seemed that he didn't want to speak too loudly, out of fear that it might require movement from his injured muscles. "With the Curaie gone, are there even Networkers and Spectral Law practitioners anymore?"

"Of course there are." Patience seemed affronted by the very notion. "The Spirit Guides couldn't watch us 24/7; we have structure and protocol to follow at all times."

"But who are you answering to?" asked Jonah.

"Some Very Elect Spirits have taken the reins as a temporary measure. There were contingencies in the event of the Curaie collapsing; we just never thought we'd have to use them. Whole damn thing is a mess."

There was bitterness in Patience's voice, but it seemed to run deeper than just the shit storm they were all in. Reena, who had removed her dampener when she applied the icepack, caught it first.

"Patience, what is going on with the Networkers?"

Patience glanced at the dampener on the dresser. His eyes showed irritation for a few seconds, but then he shook his head. "Doesn't matter. You guys never met my superior, Networker Team Lead Gene Stowe. Amazing man. Five campaigns. Got killed two months ago. Took seven Deadfallen disciples with him. But the Curaie had forbidden us to make it common knowledge, fearing that it'd send the wrong message and dampen morale."

Jonah shook his head. Reena murmured condolences, and then looked away. Terrence took a very heavy breath. Patience removed his hat out of deference and respect, but continued, a much harder edge in his voice.

"His replacement is a woman named Evelyn Tribby. And it was the biggest mistake they could have ever made."

Reena made a sour, suspicious face. "Forgive me, Patience, but it sounds as though you have an issue answering to a woman."

"Not at all, Reena. I have no problem answering to a woman. I have an issue listening to *that* woman. She is incompetent. She has no business whatsoever running the Networkers—I doubt that the woman could run water. She doesn't know what she's doing and has us working ninety-hour weeks. When we bring this up, she brags on and on about doing a full campaign without a day off. What she fails to mention is that she was twenty-five years younger at the time. I'd love to see her do that now."

Reena's indignation faded almost instantly. Patience finished a cup of water in seconds, and then looked at the three of them in turn.

"And don't worry, Reena, you will hate her absolutely when I'm done. Let me tell you what you need to know. Let you know what's happened in the ethereal world."

Jonah braced himself. It felt necessary.

"You want to know why those Eleventh men and that sazer did what they did tonight, Jonah? Unfortunately, their actions are the result of something else. What you need to know first and foremost is that the entirety of Spectral Law had to be relocated. Creyton has taken over the Median. It is now his base of operations."

Jonah felt his face go cold. Terrence and Reena looked stupefied. But the expression on Patience's face denoted that the worst was yet to be told.

"Creyton usurped all thirteen Curaie spirits and spiritesses, as you know. That has emboldened him like nobody's business. He has designated Deadfallen disciples all over the place looking for you, Jonah. He is so determined to find you that he has upped the ante."

"What?" prodded Jonah. "What has he done?"

"He's not only been using the Median as his base, he's also been using it as his own personal Threshold of Death," revealed Patience. "He's been taking men, women, children— bunches of people. He has a Gate Breacher, a newly recruited disciple. He's activated every Gate in the Median. The people are injected with Sean Tooles' anti-*Astralimes* solution—it works indefinitely now—and are then thrown through the Gates to God knows where."

"What!" Jonah, Terrence, and Reena said it all at once.

Jonah pushed past the exclamation. "What's happening to these people? Where are they going?"

"No one knows. But we've heard rumors. Some people get stranded on the Astral Plane, unable to use the *Astralimes* to get off of it. Some people are simply never heard from again. Some people were sent to what's left of The Plane with No Name. I've even heard that a few people were sent to rooms full of cannibal sazers."

Before any of them could respond, Patience reached the worst point. "Jonah, Creyton's got people petrified. I know it's been a short amount of time since Omega began, but time was never that big a deal in the ethereal world in the first place. People are scared. He has spread the word to everyone that if they find you and give you up, he will give them and their families immunity from his wrath."

Jonah stared. He couldn't believe what he'd just heard.

"Consequently, that leads to another reason why I hate Tribby," Patience added, glancing at Reena as he did so. "She knows that I'm friends with you, Jonah. She thought that it would be...beeficial for me to impress upon you the need to turn yourself over when I next saw you. She believes that—how did she put it? *If the Light Blue Aura is a true hero, he would make the tough decision.* Those were her very words. She even gave me her card to give to you if you wanted to meet her and discuss options. Jonah, she would turn you over so goddamned fast ... hell, she'd probably kill you herself. Just like the men tonight, who decided that killing you was more important than their prejudices, and the sazer, who decided that getting a free pass from Creyton was more important than standing up to bigots."

The words were no more than background noise to Jonah. He was full of fury that he could almost *not* control and had no desire to balance. This was Creyton's greatest power. The reason why his unbridled chaos was so polar opposite to Jonah's balance and equilibrium. He could make people do things without even telling them to do so. All he needed to do was plant a seed, and the waters of fear made it achieve bloom. Jonah understood that people wanted to protect their families. He got that. But to take it this far? To be willing to turn him over to Creyton even though it was obvious what would happen next?

It made his blood boil.

Perhaps if he had the luxury of not being the person in the hot seat, he could be calm right now. But of course, that wasn't the case. Trip ran his mouth, and so many estate residents left. Now Creyton made this grand proclamation and most of the ethereal world, the people he wanted so much to save from Creyton, had no issue handing him over on a silver platter.

Just how many fucking people would Jonah meet who had no reservations about compromising everything they believed in just for self-preservation?

Reena looked enraged. Her anger seemed to have made her oblivious to her shoulder pain. There wasn't enough anger in the state of North Carolina to take Terrence's mind off his groin pain, but he didn't look pleased with the citizenry of the ethereal world at the moment, either.

"Don't think everyone is out for your head, Jonah," said Patience. "You have many supporters. I, for one, have your back always. You've got people who would never let you down—"

"That's what I thought, too," murmured Jonah. "But my faith in people has been rattled since what happened with Felix."

"Huh? What happened with Felix?"

They told him about Felix's relapse and the aftermath of their argument. Patience closed his eyes and hung his head.

"He fell off the wagon after Jonathan's vanquishing. I had a couple drinks myself after that happened, too. Difference is I don't have an actual problem with alcohol."

Jonah said nothing. It gave him no pleasure to discuss Felix any further.

Patience stood up. "Jonah, Tribby advised me—hell, who am I kidding? She sweetly coerced me into giving you that message—and her card—the next time I saw you. Therefore, I haven't seen you. Haven't seen you since before the exodus."

Gratitude sprouted out of Jonah's anger, if only feebly. He stood up as well and shook Patience's hand. Reena joined him. Terrence, slowly but surely, did the same.

"Get out of Laurinburg at first light," the veteran Networker commanded. "I took care of those coward Elevenths, but the sazer will have told everyone he knows that he saw you in town. The motels in this town will not be safe for you, because they're the first places he and his buddies will look. Rest tonight, and then get out. Where are you guys heading next?"

Jonah looked at Terrence and then at Reena. They came to a silent agreement. He looked back at Patience. "If you don't know, you won't have to do any more lying to Tribby."

Patience nodded. "Understood. Whatever you do, and wherever you go, look out for each other. And above all else, *please* stay safe."

"You too, Patience," said Reena.

Patience stepped back into thin air and was gone. Jonah, Terrence, and Reena eyed one another.

"They knew about my dampener, Jonah," Reena whispered. "These weren't Deadfallen disciples. Three random *strangers* knew about my dampener."

"And once again," growled Terrence, "I got branded the weak link."

Jonah knew from their tones that they were all of the same mind. He was the one who verbalized the next part.

"If we don't find Spairitin Cousland soon, Creyton might become too powerful to stop. And if he finds the place first, he'll be frickin' powerful and will tear the place apart. It's been said a million times, and here's a million and one: what the hell have we gotten ourselves into?"

13

PORK AND PROMISE

Jonah had what was easily the crappiest sleep he'd ever had in his physical life, and that was saying something.

The succession of dreams he had made it even worse. The first was of him in some type of plastic wrapping, like an action figure, while people fought over who'd get the opportunity to give him to Creyton. That dream segued into another one, where he was in a group of complete strangers, with Terrence and Reena nowhere in sight. He was unendowed, but his fingers began to glow like he'd been Green Dealt, only his fingers glowed blue. In panic, he shoved them into his pockets, but the glow reached up to his arms, neck, and face. In the end, he resembled some sort of Glo-Stick. People swarmed him, fighting over who'd snag him first, but then someone grabbed him from behind. He tried frantically to see his captor and, enraged, realized that it was Trip.

"What the hell do you think you're doing?"

"What do you think, Rowe?" Trip shook his head at Jonah's ignorance.

Jonah felt the blood drain from his face. "Would you really sink that low, Trip?"

"It's just like all those nights when no one wanted to cook at the estate, Rowe," smirked Trip. "Every man for himself."

A muted thump awakened him instantly. It was a miracle that he didn't shout or swear, because it took him a few seconds to realize where he was. He was in the motel, and Terrence and Reena were still asleep. Good thing.

It was his cell phone that had made that sound. He had a text; his phone must have vibrated off the nightstand.

It was from a number he didn't recognize, and read: *Jonah, this is Vera. I know you don't know the number; this is a burner phone. Can't be tracked. Trying to be cautious and all that. I hope and pray that your phone is on vibrate, but I had to message you. Liz has been messaging crazy things to me. She said that Creyton has taken over the Median, and is using it as some kind of fucking exile chamber, or something? And he's promised that if someone snitches on you, then he'll leave them be? Does anyone actually believe that bullshit?*

"I'm worried about you, Jonah. I want you—all of you—to make it. I feel like I'm benched out here, and it's driving me nuts. My friends think that I'm still torn up over East. I've been able to clear my head somewhat, and I've got a few one-woman shows lined up. Snow and Fire *will be touring again in half a year, too. But you and everyone else are always in my head. Just get back to me when you can. Even if it's just a stupid emoji or something. Be safe. Please."*

Jonah looked at the phone for several seconds. A small part of him was glad that it was just the text and not a call. He had no idea what he could say to her that he was comfortable saying around Terrence or Reena. Another part of him was a little bummed out that he hadn't heard her voice. But the text would do just fine. It was refreshing that after everything that had occurred, she still bothered to message him just to tell him to be safe.

The whole ethereal world was in hell at the moment, but Vera cared for his well-being. That served as a type of balm for him, especially after those dreams.

But that nagging thing called reality crept back into his mind. He closed his eyes tightly. He would fight it with every ounce of his strength. Reality wouldn't strip him of the warmth he felt from Vera's words that quickly.

"Jonah?" came Terrence's curious, drowsy voice. "You alright? You ain't constipated, are you?"

Jonah rolled his eyes. Only Terrence ... "No, I'm not constipated. Just thinking. How's your—injury?"

"Much better." There was relief in Terrence's voice at those words. "If I ever see that stupid sazer again, I will fuck him up, and then pay him back in kind."

"I have no doubts about that." Reena rose and stretched as she spoke. "But I don't think that he'd be dumb enough to let you find him."

"Anything's possible, Reena. Any ideas where to go next?"

With a sigh, Jonah stood. The good feelings stirred up by Vera's text were shunted sideways by the task at hand. Reluctantly, he filed them away. "Well, the bull's-eye on my back puts things into perspective. Downside is the fact that it doesn't give us time to inspect stuff the way we want."

"That may very well be a good thing," said Reena. "It won't allow us to get lazy or complacent. May as well make a negative into a positive, yes?"

Jonah looked at his sister. Negatives into positives? That was easy for her to say. "If that's how you feel, Reena. Let's get this show on the road."

* * *

The searching was a lesson in patience, maintaining tempers, and ignoring the silent but nagging question in all their minds: *What am I doing this for?*

Jonah didn't know if it was Creyton's adverse effect on the ethereal world or what, but he, Terrence, and Reena got antsier, more detached, and more distracted with every fruitless search. It seemed as though every dead end took a piece of their determination with it. Reena appeared to be as sharp and focused as always, but more than five minutes around her made it obvious that her mind was in Tullamore, Ireland, far away from this seemingly unattainable town of Eleventh Percenters. She didn't whine or moan about missing Kendall, but she didn't have to. Jonah would see her from time to time, when she thought he was asleep or otherwise occupied. She was too proud and strong-willed to sob, but tears would fall unchecked. No matter the case, she always reapplied her mask of composure within minutes.

It was as though Terrence felt that he had no self-worth at all. He'd gotten so many blows to his confidence and value in such a short period of time. Jonah could usually crack through his brother's wall of self-doubt with humor and focused effort but this time, he had no luck. Right before the botched exodus, he had as much resolution as Jonah. Now, he simply seemed to go through the motions.

Jonah's state of mind was easily deciphered.

The world was wrong.

Everything about it was wrong.

He wanted to stop Creyton. Yet most of the ethereal world wanted to give *him* over. The allies he trusted were scattered all over, in safehouses that had been coordinated by a sazer who had relapsed into alcoholism. His two closest friends were lost in their own heads. In no way did he blame them for the ruts they were in. He just attributed it to the wrongness of the world.

All their border searching made anonymity all the more paramount. The three of them were spiritually endowed at all times, but they made a point not to use any ethereality unless absolutely necessary. Spectral Sight showed them that spirits and spiritesses played it safe as best they could. So few of them were around nowadays that Jonah sometimes felt like a plain Tenth, ignorant of the true nature of the world, yet aware of the fact that something else was there.

Aesthetic changes assisted as well. Jonah let his beard grow out once again, thicker than last time. Reena, begrudgingly, wore her hair down almost daily and because she didn't have hair dye, her scarlet highlights began to fade. Terrence allowed his hair and beard to grow out but warned that he'd trim it here and there.

"You don't want to see me with my hair and beard too long," he told them. "If it reaches a certain length, I'll start to look like a savage. Trust me."

At one point, they were able to find a motel with a kitchen. Jonah and Terrence allowed Reena to get the groceries, because they believed that it would do her some good to clear her head. Neither of them gave any thought to what they had done until the moment Reena walked in the door, with her arms full of fruit, vegetables, and a blender. Jonah's mouth dropped in horror and Terrence looked as though he'd collapse from shock.

"What the hell is *this?*"

"It's a juice fast is what it is."

"Who decided that?" Terrence demanded.

"I did." Reena's voice was cold. "We need to stay vigilant at all times, considering that we have Deadfallen disciples as well as much of the ethereal world on our asses. Fortitude is just as much internal as external. I've made concessions with food all these weeks and weeks; now, it's your turn. I'm helping us out here. We are all on a juice fast, beginning now. I know we're at this motel room with a kitchen for two nights, but that's fine. We don't need a kitchen for this blender. The juice fast will sharpen us like you won't believe. We'll take in the minerals and vitamins in juice form; they go straight into our systems without having to plow through carbs or processed shit. It will help with our concentration, mental acuity, and attention to details. Don't fuck with me on this, Terrence. It's nonnegotiable."

The intractable edge in her voice prompted Terrence to stop the complaints. Verbal ones, anyway.

* * *

Jonah had to admit that the concoctions Reena made weren't terrible. But then Reena had them on the fast second day. And a third. Fourth, fifth, sixth. A week. Three weeks. And several of those days coincided with them being forced to flee towns due to ambitious Elevenths. Terrence even tried to make Reena forget the blender. No luck. It was hard as hell to search for where the directions for Spairitin Cousland would make sense, elude the bastards, all while being meat-free and hungry for something not liquid. Jonah adored Reena, but he really wanted to throttle her at times.

And this smoothie fast, on top of everything else, was one of those times.

On day twenty-two of the damned fast, which was a day in early November, Jonah was awakened by insistent tapping. Something let him know that it was Terrence, and his intentions were meant to be secret. He opened one eye.

"Jonah, we used the *Astralimes* to Henderson, N.C."

Jonah opened both eyes. "Yeah, so?"

"There is a barbecue place about ten miles up the road," Terrence whispered. "I have been in meatless hell for three damned weeks, Jonah. And we almost got kidnapped again last night. I need a win right now, man. I'm losing my mind. I want some damn *food*."

Jonah looked at his brother. He did look a bit crazed and desperate. And he himself needed something that wasn't liquefied fruit or vegetables. He glanced over at Reena, who was in a deep sleep and didn't look as though she'd be easily awakened.

"Alright." he grabbed his wallet. "Let's go."

* * *

The barbecue restaurant was a cozy and comfortable place that wasn't too full. Jonah hadn't forgotten Ruby River, and he went into Spectral Sights before they walked inside. The place was decently spirited. When they walked in the door, he paused at the threshold and acted as though he needed to tie his shoe. When he was sure no eyes were on him, he pulled out a pocketknife and made a slit in the threshold itself. There would be no unpleasant surprises here.

Not long after that, Terrence looked bewitched when a plate of barbecued meat, hushpuppies, and potato salad was shoved under his nose, along with a huge glass of iced tea. Jonah didn't know if he wanted to go so wild after three weeks with no solid food, so he got Brunswick stew and lemon water.

"Terrence, do not wolf that down, man. We've been juicing for too many days, and your system might not be up to it."

Terrence disregarded him completely and devoured everything in his path. Jonah had had maybe five spoonfuls of stew when Terrence was done with his whole plate.

"I'm sorry," he said when he looked up. "What did you say?"

Jonah sighed. "Nothing at all."

Terrence ordered another platter of the same thing. Jonah pushed his stew aside.

"Now come on, man! You're going to get ... what did you call it... the Itis!"

"I'm perfectly fine, Jonah. You've been around me long enough to know that I'm made of steel when it comes to food."

"Yeah, I have," conceded Jonah. "But this is overkill!"

"I'm good! I'm built for this!"

Jonah protested no further. Terrence was in his element, and he may as well be talking to the wall.

After several minutes of further gluttony, Terrence slowed down with a grimace.

"I don't feel so good."

"I'd imagine not," said Jonah, annoyed.

"I don't need the scathing rebuke." Terrence winced as he clutched his stomach. "I need to take something. I need—"

A bottle of milky-looking liquid slid his way. He and Jonah jumped.

"You need that." Reena looked angry as hell. "You stupid, stubborn men ... I swear to God ..."

"Take that back, Reena," said Jonah heatedly. "I only had stew!"

"You're just as guilty, Jonah. You snuck out with him, didn't you?"

"We're grown men, Reena. We don't have to sneak anywhere."

"Why did you go while I was asleep, then?"

"Because it was easier."

Terrence, who seemed more and more disoriented with each passing second, grabbed the bottle Reena had slid across the table and drank half of it. His expression appeared less tense, but he still looked uncomfortable.

"We're going back to the motel," snapped Reena. "Good thing you've already paid. I'll take care of the tip."

She yanked her wallet from her pocket with such force that several receipts and the directions came out of there as well. "You two are something else."

Jonah shook his head. He wasn't about to be chastised when all he'd had was a half a bowl of Brunswick stew. Reena could be pissed all she wanted. He had complied with her juicing for three weeks.

He stood, as did Terrence, who looked a lot better, but Reena put a hand on each of their shoulders and pushed them back down in their chairs.

"What the hell, Reena?" asked Terrence. "You said to leave, and now you shove us back down—"

"Shut up." But there was shock in Reena's voice, not scorn. There was a wildness in her eyes that Jonah hadn't ever seen there.

"Reena, what is it?"

Very slowly, Reena pulled out a chair and lowered herself onto it so that she was eye level with them. "The directions," she whispered, pushing them forward for Jonah and Terrence to see, "they're making sense! We're officially a hundred miles away from Spairitin Cousland!"

14

SCHOOLED

Jonah, Terrence, and Reena were back at their motel room quicker than breathing. Unfortunately, they had to relinquish their spiritual endowments shortly thereafter. The spirits and spiritess who'd granted them appeared almost immediately after they returned, and desperately asked them to release the endowments. They had gotten it in their heads that endowments split their focus (though there was no evidence of that) and didn't want to increase the risk of being usurped. Jonah, Terrence, and Reena weren't too keen on relinquishing the endowments but did so willingly. Maintaining endowments against a spirit or spiritess' will was the one line they did not cross. It would make them no better than Creyton.

The resulting endowment release resulted in a very pronounced fatigue that would have required a few hours' sleep under normal circumstances. But the directions making sense had them way wired—wired enough to disregard their fatigue. Reena hurriedly pulled out the directions, fearing that the mileage between the barbecue place and the motel would affect something. To their relief, it hadn't. The motel was well in radius.

"I can't believe we just happened within range because we were running from stupid people," said Terrence for the tenth time. "Craziest blessing in disguise, ever!"

"Hmph." Jonah made a face at those words. "Call running for our physical lives a blessing if you like. I'm not even going to tell you what I think it is." He refocused on Reena. "When you say that the directions make sense, what exactly does that mean?"

Reena ran a finger across the paper. "When I first looked at this, it was just a hodgepodge collection of words and directions. But in the restaurant, the words gleamed gold, no doubt a final gift from Jonathan. The words began to shift and form sentences. The words must have continued to do so while we headed back here, but it's finished now. Look for yourselves."

Jonah put on his reading glasses and leaned in. Terrence did the same. Reena was right, it was no longer a jumble of words ... it made perfect sense now. Initially, the random words and directions made the words SPAIRITIN COUSLAND. But Reena was right. Many of the words and directions had turned gold and shifted positions. In fact, they were still gold. When those words and directions turned gold and shifted, the remaining letters no longer spelled SPAIRITIN COUSLAND.

They spelled SPI RIT LA ND with spaces in between. They all grinned. It was a nice touch. The directions in the golden letters were as follows:

- Head east for twenty-two minutes exactly. Follow the timeframe to the number.
- When you hit the twenty-two-minute mark, head west for twenty-four minutes. Again, follow the timeframe exactly.

- Third and final step. Head southwest for eighteen minutes. BE CAREFUL. You will be traversing territory that is not your own. Respect, tact, and caution will be your tools.
- And if it all possible, arrive without spiritual endowments. If the need is dire, by all means obtain them. But if you can do so without them, so much the better.

Peace and blessings.

Peace and blessings. Jonah hadn't heard that since Jonathan got vanquished. It filled him with a bit of hope. Jonathan always did that so expertly. It was true that direct contact was an impossibility now, but it still seemed as though Jonathan had reached out from the Other Side to say that he still had their back in some way, shape, or form.

"Hold up," said Terrence with a scowl, "after all we've been through, we can reach the place by following three damn steps?"

"After everything we've been through, Terrence," said Reena calmly. "After the botched exodus. After all of the border-hopping and fleeing. After happening across the radius at a damned barbecue restaurant. Do there really have to be any extra steps? We didn't get here easily, after all."

Terrence's face loosened. "Point. So, do we head out now? No time like the present—"

"No."

Jonah's response was so sharp and sudden that Terrence and Reena looked at him in surprise. He sighed.

"After all this shit we've been through, this is the opportunity that we've craved. It has to be as smooth and polished as possible. Like Jonathan said in the directions, this is new territory. We've got to be our best and look our best. We've got this room till tomorrow, anyway. Let's use that day to clean ourselves up. And also,"—Jonah steeled himself and took a breath long enough to roll over in his mind what he was about to say—"I think we should finish up the day with Reena's smoothie fast."

Terrence's eyes widened: Reena's eyes narrowed.

"And why would you want to do that?"

"To detox. We will need our minds as clear as humanly possible, right? Every advantage is an advantage."

Reena didn't look entirely convinced. Scratch that—she didn't look convinced at all. But she looked appreciative of the gesture. She headed for the door. "Fine. I'll go get some more fruit and vegetables, and some red hair dye."

She left, and Terrence looked at Jonah, skepticism written all over his face.

"Detox, my ass. You were just trying to butter her up and get her mind off of you coming with me to get some real food."

Jonah shrugged as he removed his electric shaver from his bag. "A happy Reena is a helpful Reena. Plus, I wanted to get her mind off of Kendall, if only for a bit. So yeah, I had my own motives, but my heart was in the right place."

* * *

The next morning, Jonah and Reena woke up to find themselves alone. They had very little time to speculate, however. A loud horn blew from outside. Jonah and Reena looked at each other.

"He didn't," said Reena.

"Lie to yourself if you like," Jonah told her as he threw open the door.

Terrence stood near a sun-faded Jeep, which looked a bit battered, or maybe hardened. He held up both hands and spoke loudly before Jonah and Reena could tear him a new one.

"Before you guys bring out the hate and scorn, hear me out. Road travel is the best way to do this. Those directions were pretty anal. I don't think using the *Astralimes* would help us much."

Jonah opened his mouth, but Terrence soldiered on.

"I filled this bad boy up. Full tank. Figured multiple trips to the gas station would bring unwanted attention to us."

Reena looked about to erupt, but Terrence continued, this time in a quiet, firm voice.

"And since you're thinking it, no, I didn't steal it. It was on the side of the road with an ancient cardboard sign that said, 'If you can fix her, you can have her'. I've been at work all morning and afternoon. You know Dad taught us all how to fix cars. If it's got wheels, I can fix it. I used some of the cash I saved up for this whole expedition and bought parts from Autozone and O'Reilly's and fixed it up. It's as good as new, get about forty miles to the gallon. No thievery whatsoever. So, does that cover everything you guys were going to throw at me?"

Jonah and Reena looked at each other again. Terrence had completely disarmed them. He was in the clear. Hell, he might have even redeemed himself for eating himself into a near-stupor the previous day. There was only one to say.

"Alright, let's do this."

* * *

Out of respect for what Terrence had done for them, they let him drive. Well, that and the fact that Reena was the navigator and Jonah wasn't all that comfortable driving a stick. Each of them had a job. Terrence was driver. Reena was navigator. And since the clock in the Jeep was deadlocked at 5:02 for some reason, Jonah was the timekeeper.

The first twenty-two minutes east were serene, same for the twenty-two minutes west. But during the last leg was when apprehension hit Jonah. He just didn't know what to expect, but he had ideas. A secret haven of Eleventh Percenters had a way of tugging on one's imagination. That went without saying. But as they rolled on, watchful for any sign or inkling, anticlimax began to set in.

The scenes were no different than one would expect during a countryside road trip. Nothing about it seemed remotely ethereal. Even going into Spectral Sight yielded nothing.

They passed a sign that read: *Welcome to Emerald Lakes, N.C. Enjoy your stay!* Jonah frowned at it.

"Emerald Lakes?" he demanded. "But Spairitin Cousland —Spirit Land, whatever—should be here!"

"We don't know what to expect, Jonah," said Reena, although there was something in her voice, too. "Maybe it hasn't been eighteen minutes to the number yet. Maybe other things will be illuminated when we near it, or something."

"There's a rest stop." Terrence looked about as annoyed and disappointed as Jonah felt. "Let's pull in there and give it some more thought. Maybe we missed something."

He pulled into the rest area before Jonah or Reena could object. It was well-kept and completely empty, save for them.

No, that wasn't right.

There was another person there, too.

A black woman was about eight or nine spaces from them, and seemed to be having a very hard time. Initially, she tried to hoist supplies, and the bag on her shoulder slid down her arm and knocked her box askew. She then rearranged the bag but some of the top supplies fell off the box. She swore softly and laid down the box and her bag. As soon as she did that, the breeze picked up and blew papers from her box. She stood and put her hands at her temples, tears of frustration in her eyes. Jonah felt for her, but there was no way she was going to recover those papers.

"Damn. And I thought that we were having an aggravating time of things—Terrence?"

Terrence didn't answer at first. He hadn't taken his eyes off the woman since he'd parked.

"That's a teacher," he said at last.

"What?" said Reena. "How would you know that?"

Terrence looked away from the woman and turned to Reena. "When you work around teachers, Reena, you know. I'm gonna go help her."

"Terrence, hang on! How do you think she will react if some strange man just waltzes up to her?"

"I'll cross that bridge when I get to it," said Terrence without looking at Jonah. "She needs some help."

He was out of the Jeep before any further words were spoken.

"Dammit." Jonah was confused about Spirit Land and irritated with Terrence at the same time. "Hasn't he learned his lesson about encountering strangers by now?"

"Come on, Jonah." Reena maneuvered out of the back seat. "Damage control."

Unfortunately, they didn't catch up with Terrence until he was already near the woman. It was at that moment that she abandoned her struggles and realized that she wasn't alone. The sight of three people startled her (because of course) and she stepped back.

"Ma'am, forgive me." Terrence raised his hands and spoke

in a calm and reassuring tone. "I just saw you having some trouble and thought I could help."

The woman calmed, but not by much. "Noble, but three people might be a little overkill, don't you think?"

"Three people?" Terrence glanced around to see Jonah and Reena. He rolled his eyes.

"We're his friends," said Reena before Jonah could. "Between the three of us, we figured that you wouldn't lose any more papers."

Jonah noticed that Terrence looked a little aggravated. He probably wanted to help the woman alone. She, on the other hand, looked amenable to the extra hands.

"Thank you. My car's unlocked."

She lifted the bag. Reena grabbed the papers that the wind hadn't taken away, Terrence picked up the box, and Jonah got the door. The thing took all of five minutes. The woman looked so pleased for the aid that it was almost amusing.

"You have no idea how much help you three have been to me." The woman was jubilant. "Thank you so much. Now, just one more thing."

She blinked. It was slow and pronounced. Jonah didn't think much about it until, very suddenly, he was disoriented and woozy. He attempted to say something, but he couldn't get his mouth and tongue to work. Terrence collapsed, out cold. Reena slid down the side of the car with just enough strength to give the woman a scornful glare. Jonah actually tried to grab the woman, but she clutched him at the wrist with a surprising amount of strength.

"Don't fight it. It only prolongs the inevitable."

Jonah collapsed to the ground. The woman released his wrist and walked away. Laboriously, he raised his eyes to hers. She looked at him, then Terrence, and finally Reena, seemingly going over something in her mind. She then pulled out a phone and placed it to her ear.

"Hey, it's me. I've incapacitated three people. Yeah, they're Elevenths. I think one of them might be Jonah Rowe. No, I don't need help. I got it."

15

HANIEL

Jonah woke up with a very dull ache at his left temple. He was in a bedroom, slightly dark because of the shorter days of autumn, and was propped up at the foot of a bed, in a kind of indented groove so that he was more comfortable. Weird.

The woman at the rest area was an Eleventh Percenter. She'd suspected who he was but had said, "I got it". Had he landed himself in the clutches of opportunistic ethereal humans, after all? After all the hiding and clandestine travel, had he wound up in a bad spot regardless?

But this wasn't his fault. Terrence had pulled into that rest area. *He* was the one who hopped out of the Jeep and ran to that woman's aid because he thought she was a teacher. What a load of horseshit that turned out to be. She freaking blinked and they were out. Jonah knew what it was like to have his body turn on him due to Haunt attacks. But what happened with the woman at the rest area hadn't necessarily felt sinister. Just incapacitating.

Once again, weird.

"Chicken chili," mumbled Terrence, which prompted Jonah to snap his head in the direction of his voice.

Terrence was prone across the bed opposite from Jonah. Reena was on the bed as well, nearer to the headboard. Neither of them looked injured, which was good.

Jonah neared Terrence and said, "What?"

Terrence bolted into an upright seated position and looked wildly around. "Who? What?"

His erratic movements roused Reena as well. She looked at them in confusion.

"Are you guys alright?" asked Jonah. "You have no wounds I see, but how are you feeling?"

"Oh, just dandy!" Reena bared her teeth like a lion. "Where the hell are we?"

"Somebody's bedroom." Jonah turned to Terrence again. "What did you say? You mentioned chili."

"Chicken chili."

Reena rolled her eyes before Terrence said anything else. "Seriously, Terrence? We could very well be hostages right now, and you're thinking about food?"

"No, Reena," snapped Terrence. "Someone is making chicken chili. The smell of it must have worked its way into my dreams, I guess. But whoever is out that door is cooking chicken chili."

Now that Jonah paid attention, there was indeed the smell of food in the air. Although it wasn't unpleasant, it gave him no comfort whatsoever. He looked Reena's way. "How did you not read the fakeness in her essence?"

"There was none to read, Jonah. She seemed completely clean!"

"Maybe she had Jarelsien on her somewhere," suggested Jonah. "Like the fake deputies, there might have been measures taken." He felt his pockets and scowled. "Took my batons."

Terrence felt his own pockets and his lip curled. Reena didn't even bother to check herself. There was no point.

"I'm damn sick and tired of these ambushes. I need to attack something, and I don't need my socket wrench. I don't have to worry about re-aggravating my shoulder anymore. I'm a hundred percent now."

Jonah was sick of it himself. He stood, the dull headache be damned. "I'm with you, Reena. I say we go out there, triple-team the bitch, and find out why she did what she did. We'll get our stuff back, and we're getting out of here. I'm sure you have the right type of chokehold for the occasion, Reena?"

Reena took a controlled breath. Clearly, she loved the idea. Jonah couldn't help but notice that Terrence didn't look cool with that for whatever reason.

He quietly opened the bedroom door.

The bedroom was on the second floor of a house and stairs were a few feet away. The smell of what Terrence had called chicken chili was more pronounced outside the door, and it smelled so delicious that it nearly took the edge off Jonah's focus. He mentally checked himself, and slowly and cautiously led his friends downstairs. He'd have loved to have gotten his hands on a weapon of some kind, but there were none to be had. They weren't spiritually endowed at the moment, but Jonah was no stranger to that situation. He hoped that he could bash someone in the face before his lack of an endowment proved a liability.

When they got downstairs, however, they found no threats at all.

The living room was empty, and the television was on The Weather Channel. The room opened into the kitchen, where they saw the woman from the rest stop at a stove, tending to a huge pot. She turned to them and gave a welcoming smile that didn't reach her wary eyes.

"Nice to see you awake, Reena." She looked at her. "Terrence." She moved her eyes to him. "And Jonah Rowe." Her eyes dimmed somewhat when she reached him. "I was just about to come get you; I could read in your essence that you were all awake and ready to come down here and attack me. There is zero need for violence, and since this is my home, I'd very much prefer not to have to resort to it."

Jonah frowned, but Reena asked the question.

"You're an essence reader, are you?"

"No, I'm not. But *you* are. You're doing the work for me."

Reena looked at her blankly, but the woman glanced at Reena's wrist. Jonah and Terrence did as well and saw a snug black band there. It looked unremarkable, but Jonah knew full well that looks could be deceiving.

"It's an ethereal inversion device," the woman explained. "It makes your ethereal abilities work for someone else if need be. In this case, your essence reading was a thing of value and could be used so long as I was within fifty feet of you. As long as I'm wearing this, of course."

She lifted her arm and revealed an identical bracelet to the one on Reena's wrist. It was clear to Jonah that Reena hated the contraption, and he distracted things before she flew off the handle.

"I mean no harm, lady, but you having us at a disadvantage has gotten old. Who are you, and why did you do what you did?"

The woman turned her back on them long enough to stir the contents of the pot, and then faced them once more. "My name is Haniel. Haniel Rainey. It's a pleasure to meet you all. Now, to answer your second question—"

"Hold up." Terrence look intrigued. "Rainey sounds familiar. A historical figure. Joseph H. Rainey, I think? Barber who worked his way to being the first black man to serve in the House of Representatives?"

Haniel looked pleasantly surprised. "Yes, actually. He's a distant relation of mine."

Jonah looked at Terrence, stunned. Terrence paid no attention as he went on.

"Well, Haniel, you might want to turn that chicken chili down. It doesn't need full heat anymore. Needs to simmer. And if you're planning on serving it to us, you should know that the spices are off. You need some more ground cumin in there to bring it 'round."

Instantly, Haniel looked affronted. "You don't know what you're talking about."

"Yeah, I do, actually."

Haniel turned her back on them, seemingly oblivious to the fact that Jonah still had a billion questions. She scooped a small portion of the chicken chili into a plastic spoon, tasted it gingerly, then looked at Terrence, thunderstruck. Terrence merely flashed her a pleasant smile.

Haniel grabbed a container of cumin and shook some into the pot.

"Okay. I'm going to pretend that that didn't just happen. But back to your second question, Jonah, what I did wasn't personal. I had a job to do, and I did it. Now, please sit down. The chicken chili will be done as soon as the cumin settles into it."

Jonah glanced at Reena, still unaware of what to make of this woman or situation. They all lowered themselves onto seats around Haniel's kitchen table. Terrence seemed detached from Jonah's and Reena's apprehension, though. He only had eyes for the woman, and his expression was a mixture of annoyance and disappointment.

"You had a job to do, huh? What job is that, I wonder? There I was, ready to swear that you were a teacher."

"I *am* a teacher. I teach ESL." Haniel then rolled her eyes and shook her head. "You probably don't know what that means. It stands for—"

"English as a Second Language," finished Terrence like it was the most obvious thing on Earthplane. "Who wouldn't know that?"

Once again, Haniel looked at Terrence, stunned. "You'd be surprised, Terrence. Now, let me check the chili."

Jonah glanced at Terrence, as did Reena. The man was in rare form tonight! After being down in the dumps for so long, he was now on all cylinders. Terrence caught their glances and scoffed.

"How many times do I have to tell you guys that I'm not an idiot?"

"Nah, man," said Jonah hastily, "we never thought that to begin with—"

He ceased speaking as Haniel brought bowls of chicken chili to the table. She then dropped herself in front of her own bowl.

"Please eat. I know that we still have a lot to talk about, but a teacher's schedule can leave one quite famished. You'll just have to wait."

Neither Jonah, Terrence, nor Reena touched it. One too many experiences with duplicity wouldn't allow them to.

"Why should we trust you?" asked Jonah flatly.

"Because I have nothing to gain by hurting you."

"How come you are so trusting of us?" Terrence this time. "It's a little naïve of you, I hate to say."

Haniel snorted. "You don't strike me as vicious or violent people. I'm a pretty decent judge of character. Besides that, help is within arm's reach. My brother Mayce and my best friend Josephine are out front, just in case I'm wrong. Moreover, I'm confident enough in my ethereality to give a good accounting of myself. But I've already told you, I don't want to fight."

Automatically, Jonah and Terrence looked at Reena. She sneered at Haniel.

"Why can't I read your essence?"

Haniel sighed. "I'm going to eat now. I'll speak more when I'm sated. Now, unless you want it to get cold, I suggest you do the same."

She began to eat. Reluctantly, Jonah, Terrence, and Reena followed suit. Jonah had to admit that the chicken chili was excellent stuff. He'd never had it before, so he could only assume that Terrence's tip about the cumin was on the level. Even Reena couldn't vilify the dish; there were just as many lentils in it as chicken. It was very filling and didn't even require bread.

Haniel wiped her mouth and pushed the bowl to the side. "Now then, I'm well aware that you have many questions for me, but Terrence asked what my job was. I am an ESL teacher, that's my day job. But beyond that, I have other responsibilities as well. We're all Elevenths here, so thankfully, that's no revelation. But ... well, let's just say that if this were football, I'd be a part of the defensive line. You come into our zone, and I have to stop you and find out why you're there. Nothing personal. It's what I have to do."

"Okay, I'll bite." Jonah pushed the bowl away. "You're part of a defensive line. Whatever. How many are on said line with you?"

"Enough," evaded Haniel. "Surely, you can understand the value of information, what it could mean if that was given out freely."

"Thought you could trust us." Reena had gone from angry to shrewd. "Thought we were no threat."

"I never said that, Reena. I never once said that you weren't a threat. I said you didn't seem violent or vicious. I said that I was a decent judge of character. But that doesn't mean I can't be wrong."

Reena regarded her and nodded. "That's fair. I don't need essence reading to know that you're genuine. Enough, anyway. But I could be wrong, too."

"And that's why we're getting to know each other better." Haniel spread her hands in a welcoming gesture. "By no means is this an interrogation. It's a conversation."

Jonah glanced at his brother and sister. Unless he was very much mistaken, Haniel was on the level. At the very least, she knew he was Jonah Rowe and hadn't called in Creyton or whoever else. "Alright, Haniel. We'll meet you where you are. If you're part of the defensive line, what are you defending?"

Haniel shook her head. "Again, you have to understand the value of information. Let me ask you something: why are *you* here?"

"We were looking for a place." Jonah could play the vague game, too. How were we to know that we happened into your 'zone'?"

"I'd been tracking your progress for about fifteen miles. Whatever you were doing, you were focused as all get-out. But it was also clear that you knew you were in a place where you had to be watchful and on your toes."

"Do you blink and knock out everyone who encroaches your zone?" asked Terrence, an edge in his voice.

Haniel looked away. "I'm sorry. You should be aggravated, or even ticked off. I thought that you might be Deadfallen disciples, and I had taken one of my personal leave days to catch up on project plans for my students. Being alerted that someone had come into my zone—someone I had to watch and track—was a bit irritating because it took away from my time to plan my schoolwork. I was a little rougher than I needed to be. I apologize."

"You're lying," said Jonah. "You didn't think we were Deadfallen disciples. First of all, one of Creyton's disciples wouldn't have helped you cart your supplies. And why would you have your supplies at a rest stop on a personal day?"

"Trap for us." Terrence snorted. "Duh."

"Anyway," Jonah went on, "you also knew we weren't Deadfallen disciples because before I blacked out, you told my name to whoever you had on the phone. I heard all that. If you knew who I was, then you know I'd never be on Creyton's side."

"You're right, Jonah." Haniel nodded. "Had I recognized you immediately, I wouldn't have assumed you were one of Creyton's. But I didn't recognize you until I was up in your face, right before you fell. I've only ever seen you once, you see, and that time, you had a beard."

"Huh? You've seen me before? When was this?"

"A day in the Phasmastis Curaie's Median." Haniel's expression darkened again. "You were there to meet with them, or something. You reduced that sweet Gate Linker to tears because she didn't return your belongings to you fast enough."

Jonah grimaced. Now it made sense why Haniel's eyes dimmed when she said his name when they first stepped in the kitchen. He'd been in a different frame of mind back then. The world seemed to be against him at the time, and he didn't have a firm grasp on his temper due to Creyton's mind games. He took his frustration out on everyone in sight. He hadn't given those times much thought since then. Then again, he didn't think he'd meet someone down the line who'd seen how he'd acted that day and never forgot the impression. "I had a lot going in my life at that time and, admittedly, was a jackass to a lot of people. But I have matured since then. Progressed in how I handle bullshit. And that woman whose feelings I hurt that day? We have since mended those misunderstandings and are now good friends. I even set her up with her boyfriend."

"That so?" Haniel was surprised. "Nice. Classy, even. But that was my first impression of you, Jonah. And it wasn't a great one. If you've matured into a better man since that time, then I applaud you, but I didn't see that maturation. I saw the cantankerous asshole who tore down a sweet woman because he was having a bad day."

Jonah winced. Man, this was just beautiful. Freaking *beautiful.*

At that moment, one of his grandmother's most frequent bits of advice floated to the forefront of his mind: *You got to be nice to people, Jonah,* she always said. *You never, ever know who's watching.*

Nana was a smart woman. She'd been on the money with that one.

"Why were you in the Median?" he decided to ask.

"Reasons. Now, what are you looking for? What place?"

By Haniel's tone, they'd reached the meat of this conversation. Jonah looked at Terrence and Reena and saw that they were in agreement. Honesty was the best policy. He had no desire to trade on his status as the Light Blue Aura. He wasn't that arrogant. Plus, Haniel already knew who he was and had, unfortunately, seen him on one of the foulest days of his life. However, he did have a card to play. It was all about timing.

"Here is the truth, Haniel. We're looking for a place populated only by ethereal humans that we thought was named Spairitin Cousland, but that turned out to be a pseudonym for its real name, Spirit Land. We've been following some directions that were supposed to make sense once we were within a hundred miles of the place. But we messed up somewhere. They made sense, but we wound up here, in Emerald Lakes."

He waited. For the first time, Haniel's eyes darted to the door, where her brother and friend must have been waiting. When she proceeded, it was very carefully. "What exactly is Spirit Land?"

Now it was Jonah who had apprehension. He had had this conversation several times with Terrence and Reena. The residents of Spirit Land guarded themselves quite painstakingly for a reason. They certainly wouldn't want people spouting information. Had he made a mistake? Had he read Haniel wrong? "We don't actually know what to expect when we find it." That was the truth. "Like I said, up to this point, all we've done is follow the directions."

"Where did you get these directions? May I see them?"

Jonah decided to go with his gut. He didn't really know what to make of Haniel, but she just didn't give off the vibes that an evil person would. Here was the time to play his card. "We inherited them from our former mentor, and Overseer of our home. He was vanquished by a War Haunt sent by Creyton. His name was Jonathan."

Jonah knew that he was on the right track when he said that they'd inherited the directions. It made them seem less opportunistic. Mentioning the vanquishing let Haniel know they were still mourning and did this as someone's final wish. But dropping Jonathan's name at the very end? Icing on the cake.

Haniel's eyes widened somewhat when Jonah began his answer, but when he said Jonathan's name, she looked at them with what appeared to be confusion. Reena's eyes narrowed at that reaction as she slid the directions Haniel's way. When Haniel looked them over, she took a deep breath. Jonah didn't understand her reactions, but now he was sure that she wasn't about to betray them.

"I need to know something." Unless Jonah was mistaken, there was a hint of a plea in her voice. "This place you're looking for. Are you looking to find resources for Omega?"

Jonah was taken aback by that. "I don't understand the question."

Haniel waved the directions impatiently. "Are you looking for this place for personal gain or acquiring knowledge?"

Why was that important to her? If she was just a part of some random ethereal neighborhood watch they'd happened across, what did she care? Did she think he'd screw other Elevenths just because? "Personal gain is not a part of the equation. I'd be lying if I said that we didn't want resources for Omega, but not to take them outright. It's more important to get the people's help with all of that. My friends and I also believe that Creyton is trying to find Spirit Land. We want to get there first, give them advance notice. Maybe we can work together. But Haniel, I'm sorry that we stumbled into your zone. We mean no harm to anyone in Emerald Lakes. We don't even plan to stay here. I'm no longer the ... the overemotional dickhead that you saw back in the Median that day. And we have no plans to exploit the people there once we find them. That's what Creyton would do. Not us."

Haniel looked at the three of them once again. It seemed to Jonah that she was trying hard to gauge him, more so than Terrence or Reena. Then she rose.

"Come with me."

She walked through the back door without waiting for them. Jonah frowned. Terrence broke the silence.

"What do you think is going on here? We're just passing through this place. What's her deal?"

"We won't find out by sitting in this kitchen," replied Jonah.

He rose and headed toward the door but paused a few

inches short and looked at Reena. "You can't read anything at all off of this woman? I don't believe she is full of shit, but she is still a stranger."

"From an ethereal standpoint, no, I can't read anything. I don't know what she is doing to block me, but it's effective. But like I said before, I don't particularly need my ethereality."

Reena let that hang there. Jonah raised his eyebrows as well as his hands.

"And?"

Reena shook her head. "Need to learn more. See more."

"Wow, Reena." Terrence briefly palmed his face. "You have no idea how helpful that is."

Before an argument could erupt, Jonah exited the house to see Haniel in hushed conversations with a bearded man who looked younger than him and a stocky blonde woman whose frizzy hair would rival Maxine's. It wasn't a surprise that the conversation ended when he stepped out of the door. He felt Terrence and Reena behind him, so the jabs hadn't commenced. Good.

Haniel turned to face them. "Jonah, Terrence, Reena, this is my brother Mayce, and my best friend, Josephine Dunning. You're going somewhere with us." She pointed to a bluish-green van. "But first, we have some things to return to you."

Mayce regarded his sister rather doubtfully, but she jerked her head their way. He walked up to Reena and dropped her wallet and socket wrench into her hands. Josephine gave Jonah back his batons, and Haniel returned Terrence's steel knuckles.

"Who is that woman in your pics?" the Mayce guy asked Reena bluntly.

"*Mayce!*" hissed Haniel.

"What?" Mayce was undeterred. "I want to know. If I didn't know better, I'd say she was your girlfriend."

Reena's eyes flashed with irritation. "She is not my girl-friend. She is my fiancée, not that it's any of your business."

Mayce's eyes widened. "So, you're—?"

"Gay, yes."

Either Mayce expected Reena to be evasive, or expected her to be sheepish.

"Wow, you're really br—"

"Don't call me brave, little boy. It's not a compliment at all. If anything, it accentuates your ignorance. It's no better than when someone calls people of color *articulate* or *surprisingly intelligent* or when someone refers to a woman who is heavier than a damn size two as *confident*. You need to check that, and check it soon. If you want to call me something, call me Reena, seeing as it's my name and all."

Mayce looked dumbfounded. Jonah and Terrence snorted at each other. Even Haniel looked amused.

Reena paid no attention to any of their reactions as she climbed into the van. Everyone followed her lead. When Haniel seated herself in the front passenger seat, Terrence placed a hand on her shoulder.

"You said you were working on project plans for your students. Is this excursion keeping you from that?"

"You're sweet for thinking of that." Haniel grinned. "But I knocked those out while you guys were unconscious. All I have left are some plans for guided reading, but I welcome any inter-ruption from that. Believe me."

Terrence nodded and slid shut the van door. Josephine cranked up the van and they were on their way.

Jonah spent a couple of minutes staring out, trying to see sights of Emerald Lakes, but there wasn't much to see apart from a collection of houses and foliage. Then he realized that some of these things were familiar.

With a jolt, it hit him. He knew the road from earlier. They were on their way to the city limits. They'd be dumped out and warned not to return.

Son of a bitch.

He had to admit that it was refreshing for Haniel and her crew to be so nice about it. It was also refreshing not to have to fight for his physical life against these very crafty Elevenths. But that was where the positivity stopped. Another dead end.

"Terrence, according to your driver's license, your last name is Aldercy." Josephine spoke for the first time. "Are you related to Lloyd Aldercy?"

"Yep, that's my brother."

"Oh, man." Josephine was giddy. "That's got to be awesome!"

Terrence smiled. "That's definitely a word that qualifies."

"Where are you taking us?" Jonah tried very hard to keep the coolness out of his voice. He needed to interrupt that right now; they weren't about to insult them with niceties and banter.

"Town limits," answered Haniel.

"Thought so." Jonah was already aware of that, but he rolled his eyes anyway. After the dinner and all the dramatics, this shit was beyond irritating. "If you'd be so kind, could you at least drop us off at the Jeep back at the rest stop?"

Haniel looked back at him. "So, you say you've changed, was that right? That your temper wasn't so close to the surface anymore? Doesn't seem like that's true."

Jonah's eyes narrowed. He was ready to give this woman respect and here she was, judging him.

"But anyway," Haniel turned her eyes back to the road, "that would be hard to accomplish. Your Jeep is parked at my house."

"What? You—"

"Jonah." Reena's in a tone that was two parts bossy and two parts warning. "Stop talking."

Jonah took a deep breath but fell silent. He'd have more to say when they got kicked out of the van.

After about six more miles of silence, they stopped right by the town sign. She pulled over and Mayce slid open the door.

"Get out, please."

Jonah breathed heavily through his nostrils and hopped out of the van, followed by everyone else.

"Now, what?"

"Look at the sign," said Haniel.

Exasperated, Jonah did so. *EMERALD LAKES WELCOMES YOU* was what met his gaze once again. He was about as thrilled to see it now as he had been earlier that day.

"Oo-kay." Terrence had little to no patience for the dramatics either it seemed. "Pretty sign. It's burnt orange, just like my aura."

Mayce rolled his eyes. "Go into Spectral Sight. Duh."

Jonah's annoyance was colored by curiosity. Why did he want them to do that?

He closed his eyes, took a deep breath, and willed the curtain to rise and the actors to perform. When he opened his eyes and looked at the sign again, his jaw dropped. What it had said before was nowhere in sight.

The arch didn't look wooden anymore. It was steel.

Ethereal steel.

And it bore these words:

Spirit Land
Quod omne vitae sit

Jonah's irritation and anger faded instantly. He was in awe. Not just at what he saw, but the meaning of the Latin words.

Because of Malcolm, he could read them. But because of Jonathan, he understood them.

"Life is all there is."

"See what happens when you exhibit a little patience?" said Haniel coolly.

Jonah blinked and looked her way. She still had the ethereal inversion band, so she still had Reena's powers. She'd probably read Jonah's essence this whole time.

Oops.

"We weren't kicking you out. We needed to show that your directions weren't wrong. They led you exactly to what you were looking for."

16
A MOST UNPLEASANT SURPRISE

Jonah glanced up at the sign once again. He had to admit that he was at a bit of a loss. After all the planning and searching, he'd half-expected to walk into Spirit Land, head held high, and tell his story. When the directions started to make sense in Henderson, the anticipation and nerves blocked out any extreme planning. Then they got intercepted by Haniel, fed, and driven to the city limits. After numerous weeks of wondering what to say, he was at a loss. That was simply the truth of it.

He looked over at Reena, who didn't look the slightest bit surprised.

"Don't tell me you'd figured it out already."

Reena snorted. "It was pretty obvious after about two minutes of conversation with Haniel, Jonah. I'm surprised you didn't realize where we were!"

"Well, I didn't!" Jonah had no shame. "I didn't think this was Spirit Land! I thought Haniel, especially after she revealed that she had a salty opinion of me, wanted to try to protect them from me; didn't even want us to find them! I thought they drove us here to throw us out of Emerald Lakes and tell us good riddance."

"I considered it," admitted Haniel. "But I decided to be objective and open on this."

"And it was only obvious to yourself, Reena," said Terrence. "Not everybody in the world has the mind you do."

"Yet you were just in Haniel's kitchen batting a thousand, Terrence," countered Reena. "Explain that one."

"That was,"—Terrence looked rather disarmed—"that was ... that was different, okay?"

"If the banter is quite over," said Haniel, "please get back into the van. We aren't done."

For some reason, there was an edge in Haniel's voice. Jonah knew that she wasn't fond of him and despite himself, wanted to stay on her good side. Last thing he wanted was to be blinked at again.

They piled back into the van and Josephine drove off. After several miles, they were on a street full of small businesses and restaurants. Jonah saw what appeared to be a healing haven of some kind, which had the name "Big Top". Jonah's look of curiosity wasn't missed by Haniel.

"Yeah, it's called Big Top. And yes, it's like the circus."

"What, does the circus have a special place in people's hearts in Spirit Land?"

"Yes indeedy!" said Mayce, the excitement of a child in his voice.

"Circuses are over and done with," noted Jonah. "May I ask why it's so special to you?"

"So, because Ringling Brothers ended, you assume that all the circuses on Earthplane ended at the same time?" Josephine sighed. "Close-minded, much?"

Jonah inhaled slowly. Jesus, this was an easily irritated bunch!

"We're almost there," announced Haniel as Josephine rolled up a steep incline. She made a soft right turn into a picnic area and pulled to a stop. Haniel took a deep breath and raised her right hand, fingers splayed. The tips began to glow a pleasant, rosy red. Jonah glanced Terrence's way, and he kind of shrugged. Reena looked more intrigued than anything else. It was at that moment that Haniel spoke again.

"Bear with me for a few moments. Your essences are practically buzzing at me right now."

Reena's eyes flashed and she glanced at her wrist. Jonah knew that she had already tired of the inversion device that enabled Haniel to use her essence reading. She enjoyed wearing her dampener to silence people's essences of her own volition. But since they'd been traveling, and searching for Spirit Land, she'd had her essence reading blocked twice...first by the Deadfallen disciple posing as a deputy, and now by Haniel.

He wondered which of them would lose it first: Reena or himself. The only thing keeping those emotions at bay was the thirst for knowledge.

"We're good." The rosy-red gleam faded from Haniel's fingers. "They're on the way."

"Wait, what?" demanded Reena. "Who is coming? What did you just do?"

Haniel turned to face them. All the while, people stepped through the *Astralimes* around the van. It didn't take long for the van to be surrounded and they all looked as wary as Jonah, Terrence, and Reena did right now.

"No one out here is going to hurt you," Haniel promised. "Unless of course, you do something stupid. This isn't a trap; it's standard protocol for when strangers come into Spirit Land. Drifters are never left unchecked, particularly ethereal ones—"

"But we ain't drifters—"

Haniel silenced Terrence with a finger, wincing as she did so.

"Please don't interrupt me, Terrence. And for the love of Earthplane, would you stop saying *ain't?*"

Terrence grunted, but obliged her. Haniel carried on.

"Somebody is always on zone patrol on the outskirts of town. The city-limits sign has a sensor for ethereality on it, which allows us to keep watch even if people aren't present. When I rendered you unconscious this afternoon, I had to alert the whole town of your presence. Now, you will introduce yourselves."

"The whole town is out there right now?" asked Jonah, incredulous.

"Were that the case, I wouldn't be likely to tell you, would I? Again, the value of information."

"So, why do we need to do this?" asked Reena. "Do you want us to go out there and mingle it up? If so, why are we still cooped up in the van?"

"Because there are some things that you need to know beforehand."

"It's a good thing you ran into Haniel first," Mayce told them. "Had you run into Mark's or Consuela's patrol, they'd have probably made you duel them to earn the right to get into town."

"And if you'd run into Sathvi, you'd have probably had to answer riddles or something," added Josephine. "Complicated as hell."

"But you ran into me." Haniel said it as though there had been no interruption. "And I believe that you are on the level, for the most part." She threw a glance Jonah's way. "But that's me."

"What is that supposed to mean?"

Haniel ignored Jonah's question. "First and foremost, do

not mention that you want assistance for Omega. It has to be offered. If you ask outright, you'll seem like nothing more than opportunistic, crafty people who pilfer and give no thought to who you use. You do not want to foster that assumption."

"Especially *you,* Rowe," added Mayce.

Jonah stared. Haniel continued speaking.

"Jonah, do not trade on being the Light Blue Aura. You need to earn that respect. It will be a challenge, but it can be done."

"That was never my plan!" Jonah threw up his hands in aggravation. "You can ask Terrence and Reena; we've discussed my desire not to do anything like that! What were you expecting? Me to be some entitled diva who presumed everyone would love him?"

"Well—" began Josephine in a tone that denoted that assumption to be affirmative, but Haniel gave her a quelling look.

Jonah was thoroughly rankled by all of this. He felt like they viewed him as some reckless thrill-seeking child who just chomped at the bit to cause mayhem. He had to speak. If he stewed in frustration, it would only spill out at more inopportune time. "Okay, I have told you already that I had no plans to come here for personal gain. I said as much at your kitchen table. I'm not like that. However, since you have warned me against asking outright for aid, when and how do I do so, Haniel? With all due respect, I don't think Jonathan wanted us to join in fellowship with you guys just for our health. I'm pretty certain of that."

"You said, more or less, that you wanted to earn that right, Jonah. That is a wise plan. I'm certain that your plan wasn't to come here, wrangle up information or ethereality that wasn't known to you, and just go on your way. Stay here for a little while; let people get a feel for you. If you're genuine, it won't take long."

"Why do you question our genuineness?" Jonah wanted to know. "Haven't you been reading our essence all this time?"

"I have, but that can be faulty. That could just be your essence at this particular moment. Intention can change, after all."

"Haniel, no disrespect, but time is not something we have a lot of right now."

"She makes a valid point, Jonah." Terrence's words prompted Jonah to look at him in surprise. "Jonathan would never have approved of us taking goods and services from people whose trust we barely earned. It took a while to find this place and after all we've gone through, establishing a rapport with the citizens of Spirit Land is just another task to achieve. Nothin' wrong with that."

Jonah couldn't say anything to that. Terrence made a good point. Hell, if the shoe was on the other foot, he certainly wouldn't want to move heaven and earth for someone he barely knew. "Okay, that's cool. We hang out here for a while. Fine. Anything else, Haniel?"

"Yes." Haniel looked at the three of them. "Under no circumstances do you badmouth the circus."

Jonah stared at her again. "That was a bit random."

"Not really," said Mayce shortly. "I heard the disdain in your voice earlier. Do you have something against the circus?"

"Nothing more than being called to volunteer once by a drunk ringmaster and sliding in an elephant's shit the minute I got in front of my fourth-grade class." To this day, Jonah hated bringing that up. "As well as the other four-hundred people who saw it happen."

Josephine winced. Terrence looked sympathetic.

"You never shared that one, man."

"Can't imagine why."

Mayce was unmoved. "You had one crap experience at one circus, and then you hate them all forevermore? That's how you work? I hate to think how you react when you have crap experiences with Terrence and Reena here. Would you hate them eternally, too?"

Jonah ran his tongue across his teeth. This boy Mayce looked to be around the same age as Spader. He wasn't about to take a lecture from him. It wasn't like it was going to change his opinion about the circus, after all. "Alright, out of this van! And let's get this show on the road."

He then noticed that Haniel wasn't looking at him anymore.

"You've been very quiet, Reena," she observed. "Your essence isn't giving anything away, either. What's going on in your mind?"

Reena half-smiled. "Just because my mouth isn't going doesn't mean that my brain isn't working. I'm just taking things in."

Haniel smiled. It was clear that Reena went up more and more in her eyes each time she spoke. "Tell you what. How about a show of good faith?"

She gave the inversion band on her wrist a tug. Reena blinked and took a breath. She must have been able to read Haniel's essence.

"Now you can read that I am legit. I promise you that the rest of us are as well."

Reena nodded once. "We're good. There is no further point in delaying the inevitable. Let's get this rolling."

"Absolutely."

Haniel she opened the passenger door and got out of the van. On the driver's side, Josephine did the same. Jonah paused, in thought.

So Reena was earning their respect. Terrence had earned points, too. But he was the one who was warned not to do anything except breathe. What the hell was that about? Was all of that because of the negative first impression that Haniel got of him some years back, and she'd shared it with Mayce and Josephine and whoever else?

No. That was only a small part. There was more to the story. He didn't know how he knew, but he did. His gut told him as much.

"Um, Rowe?" Mayce broke him free from his thoughts. "You need to focus, man."

He reached past Terrence and slid open the van door. They all exited.

In addition to Haniel and Mayce, there was quite a crowd around the van. Men, women, children, cats, dogs, you name it. Although Jonah didn't see any weapons, he knew it'd be foolish to try anything rash. Besides, he was forbidden to do anything of the sort.

He scanned some of the faces to get a good bead on things, if that were possible. Some people looked curious, others wary, and a few looked at Jonah as though he were trouble. Part of him could understand that. He and his friends were strangers. The other part of him felt pretty salty about their gazes. They didn't even know him.

He was suddenly acutely aware of their appearances and was very thankful that he'd cut his hair and shaved.

A man who looked to be in his late forties stepped forward. It was clear that this man was the leader by the way everyone regarded him, but Jonah gleaned no fear or apprehension from the people. Good sign. He was Jonah's height, slightly thinner, and balding. His eyes showed caution as he surveyed him, Terrence, and Reena. Also, expected. But at the same time, Jonah felt like he was about to do a recital or something.

"Excellent work, Haniel. And I greatly appreciate you using your day off from school to watch the Emerald Zone."

"It was no problem, Mr. Harrington. But none of them tried any violence. I have to admit that they were all totally cooperative."

Says the woman who blinked us unconscious, thought Jonah, but he kept all emotions from his face.

Harrington nodded and walked closer to Jonah, Terrence, and Reena.

"I'm Clay Harrington. I'm the Overseer of the town; I suppose Tenths would simply say I'm the mayor. I would greatly appreciate it if you'd introduce yourself to us all. Ladies first."

Reena's mouth twitched but she didn't scowl. "I'm Reena Katoa. I'm an artist and a Yellow Aura."

A few people murmured greetings, and then Harrington turned to Terrence.

"Terrence Aldercy." Jonah thought Terrence was probably as glad as he was that he'd made himself presentable. "Being a janitor is what pays the bills, but I'm an auto mechanic on the side, as well as a pretty damn good cook. Aura is burnt orange."

Terrence got the same sort of greetings as Reena. Now, it was Jonah's turn. He made his voice slightly dull and flat, remembering Haniel's warning. It wasn't like he wanted to treat himself like a big deal, anyway.

"I'm Jonah Rowe. I'm a former accountant, but I'm a writer, and love doing anything that involves books. I'm the—um, sorry —I'm *a* Blue Aura."

People's reactions were vastly different from the ones given Terrence and Reena. He was regarded with suspicion and something that looked like—concern? A couple of people even took steps back.

The reactions puzzled Jonah. And aggravated him some

more. *What* was the deal? He hadn't done anything! These people treated him the way he expected to be treated by the idiots from Sanctum Arcist!

A man near Josephine spoke up. "You're the Overseer of the Grannison-Morris estate?"

"Mmm-hmm." Jonah still attempted to sound non-boastful.

"You carry Jonathan's Vitasphera?" the same man asked.

"I do. It's very dark and unclear now, but we hope to restore it to its original state soon."

The man's eyes narrowed, but he said nothing further. Another person, a woman this time, spoke up.

"How did you find Spirit Land?"

Jonah glanced at Haniel, whose expression didn't change. But then, plain as day, a string of thoughts fell into his head.

Tell them the truth, but volunteer nothing.

That was it. No voice. Just words. Where did that come from?

He filed the confusion away and followed the advice. "We inherited the directions from Jonathan."

"Jonathan wrote out directions for all the world to see?" Harrington looked aghast. "He would never be so careless!"

"Jonathan was never careless," said Reena at once. "The pages were done in the Language of Spirit, and the directions were under heavy ethereality. I deciphered it."

Her words elicited interest from many people, especially Mayce.

"How long did it take you to decipher it?"

"A week and a half."

Haniel looked impressed. Mayce laughed to himself.

"Dang. Woman is badass."

Harrington's eyes were on Jonah again. "Why did you come here?"

That inevitable question was in Jonah's head since he'd

heard Haniel's warnings in the van. So, when the time came to answer it, the response was already formed in his mind. "It's our belief that Jonathan believed Creyton is searching for this place, too. We also think that he wanted us to give you advance notice of that."

Harrington's eyes flashed and he looked at some of his citizenry. He took a deep breath and spoke in a louder tone. "As guests of Spirit Land, I officially grant you haven. You are welcome here until such time as you depart or violate the terms of said haven. Although Haniel has spoken of your cooperation, I cannot allow you to be lodged together. This is not to say that you can't meet up or whatever, but you cannot be lodged together. Security purposes. I hope you understand."

Jonah could tell by Terrence's and Reena's expressions that they, like him, weren't thrilled about that. But, unfortunately, they had to play ball.

"Someone will have to sponsor you," Harrington continued. "All three of you. Starting with Mr. Aldercy."

"I will." Haniel said it so fast that it was like she eagerly awaited the moment. "Mayce and I will."

Mayce nodded and patted Terrence on the back.

"Very good," said Harrington. "Miss Katoa?"

"She can stay with my family." It was the man who'd asked Jonah about the Vitasphera. "We will sponsor her."

"Sweet." Josephine flashed that grin again. "You're coming home with me, Reena!"

"Great." Harrington eyed the crowd. "And Mr. Rowe?"

Silence. Dead silence. Some people even looked away.

Ripples of anger traveled through Jonah's body because of that. Terrence and Reena had no problems, once again. *He* got to be the kid picked last for the kickball team. His brother and sister looked angry, but there was nothing they could do.

He was about to request using the *Astralimes* to Terrence's

Jeep when a tall stoic-looking man came forward. He wore slightly thicker glasses and had stubble that looked as stubborn as Jonah's. For whatever reason, the man made Jonah's mind go to Mr. Steverson. A surge of emotion streamed through him, forcing him to keep his face even more impassive.

The man said nothing but signed with his hands. Harrington was surprised.

"You will vouch for him, Abner?" he asked as he signed the words with his hands.

The man—Abner—nodded. Harrington looked at Jonah with a frown.

"Staying with Abner may be a little challenging if you don't speak ASL—"

"That's no problem." Jonah waved a hand at Harrington. "I speak ASL."

He looked at Abner and signed, *Thank you, sir. I appreciate the hospitality.*

Abner looked pleasantly surprised and pleased. Harrington's doubtful look turned to shock. Jonah took great pleasure in making the man look foolish after all the less-than-savory attitudes toward him. Many people looked stunned, but none were more floored than Terrence and Reena.

"You speak American Sign Language, Jonah?" Reena demanded.

"Yep."

"You never told us that!" cried Terrence.

"I never had any need to use it around you guys, Terrence. But we have all shown things we never knew we could do. Reena siphoned poison from my wound. You practically rebuilt a jalopy, brought it back from nothing. And I happen to speak sign language."

Terrence looked dumbfounded. Reena shook her head.

"That's damn impressive, Jonah."

"Thank you, Reena." Jonah was happy to have another emotion besides suspicion thrown at him. "I appreciate that."

Harrington remastered his composure and cleared his throat. "Looks like we're good here. Welcome, guests, and good night to everyone."

The crowd gave them more curious looks, the usual reactions you'd expect from people when meeting others for the first time. Except Jonah, of course. He still got stink eyes and leers. But everyone dispersed. Terrence grabbed Jonah's shoulder.

"See you in the morning, brother. We can, I don't know, we can all meet up and do a bodyweight workout, or something."

"That'd be excellent." Reena that time. "Set a 7:30 alarm, Jonah."

Jonah heaved a sigh and nodded. At the same moment, Harrington beckoned to him.

"Jonah? Will you join me, please?"

Jonah tried very hard not to roll his eyes and walked forward as Harrington signed to Abner that this would take a minute. Jonah joined the Overseer of Spirit Land at some hedges and froze.

He hadn't noticed it before because of the crowd that had circled the van. The picnic spot that Josephine drove them to was also an overlook for the town. Jonah could see all of Spirit Land from his spot. It was a beautiful sight. Not particularly sprawling, but far from the one-traffic-light armpit towns they used as stopovers in the horror movies.

Harrington observed Jonah's amazement for several seconds, and then removed his glasses to clean them. It was at that moment that he chose to speak, his voice low and careful.

"I'm glad you appreciate what we have here. Spirit Land has been here for nearly four-hundred years, Rowe. My family roots are here, and I've been here my entire life. I've been the

Overseer for fifteen years and it's been a wonderful time, despite things that may happen elsewhere. The rest of the world may be a moldable piece of clay, bending this way and that with the times, but Spirit Land remains strong and undeterred. Creyton has yet to find us, and we do everything in our power to make sure it stays that way. And now you come along and say that he is searching for us. The stories about you are many, Jonah Rowe, Light Blue Aura. And to tell you the truth, I'm not particularly certain that you aren't a danger. So, I give you fair warning boy, here and now. If the sanctity of my town is violated in any way because of your presence, you and I will have a problem. Understood?"

Jonah looked the older Eleventh right in the eye. He didn't know why the guy had a beef with him, or why everyone was especially leery of him. But this was something that Jonathan desired to happen. He owed it to his mentor's memory to make it work. As such, he bit back his consternation.

"Understood, Mr. Harrington. We're good."

Harrington nodded curtly and stepped backwards through the *Astralimes*. It was just Jonah and Abner now.

Thank you, Jonah signed, *for taking a chance on me, and not treating me like your enemy.*

You needn't worry about me, son, signed Abner in return. *My policy is to treat people the way they treat you, not the way you heard they treated someone else.*

Jonah frowned. *You've heard things about me? What have you heard?*

Abner smirked. *I haven't heard anything, son. I'm deaf, see.*

* * *

Over the next several days, Jonah, Terrence, and Reena didn't get to see much of each other. The bodyweight workout happened the next morning as planned, but beyond that, a close eye was on them all. Through texting, though, they all figured out what that was about: Harrington wanted to make absolutely sure that they had no ulterior motives. While that was understandable, Jonah still saw a flaw in it. If the three of them actually had ulterior motives, then what good would separating them do?

Reena's rapport with Josephine's family was established almost overnight. In Jonah's mind, it was almost laughable because Reena swore up and down that she wasn't a people person, yet it was no trouble at all for her to win people over with her intelligence, approachability, and improvisational prowess. People loved to pick her brain and converse with her whenever there was a chance, especially Sathvi Chadvaram, a theoretical physicist who also patrolled the Emerald Zone like Haniel.

Terrence...God, where to start with him? He was a completely different man from the second that he'd set foot into town. Jonah never really believed in one-eighties, but if there were such a thing, Terrence had done one. Mayce liked him from the beginning and Terrence gave him...along with anyone else who was interested...pointers on car maintenance. The residents of Spirit Land relied a great deal on ethereal travel, which wasn't a problem, but it made things like auto repair a mostly unknown art. With all that he'd learned from Mr. Decessio, Terrence was a ready-made teacher and people ate it up. He'd even pointed out issues with the van they'd used to transport them simply from listening to it as it ran. The mixture of his auto prowess, as well as his usual nature to be comic relief, mixed in marvelously well. He was a hit with everyone.

Which brought things to Jonah.

Damn.

If Terrence and Reena were the favorite children, Jonah

was the step-cousin thrice removed, whom people avoided because he might have a contagious disease. He spent the first several days fielding questions about whether he'd brought trouble in his wake. Harrington did *not* trust him; he made that clear during their first meeting and reiterated the point every time. The only person who seemed halfway interested in getting to know him was Abner, the guy who'd vouched for him and welcomed him into his home.

Jonah liked the man off the bat. Maybe it was because he reminded him of Mr. Steverson, or because he was a decent guy in his own right. The man's home was small, but he lived alone, so that was fine. Jonah had no issue either way, and even if he did, he wouldn't complain. Where else would he stay? The old Jeep that Terrence had restored?

Abner was a creature of habit, and Jonah's presence didn't alter that at all. He had a morning ritual of sixty laps in the community pool. Apparently, he never skipped a day. Jonah went with him because it allowed him to get out of his head. They would usually converse by sign language after that, which Jonah enjoyed. He was only a bit rusty, but that faded after a day or so. When Jonah asked why people acted the way they did toward him, Abner always looked hesitant. Without fail.

Just earn their respect, and give it time, he would always sign to Jonah. *If you're a good man, it will certainly show. Just let them see.*

Jonah didn't understand that at all. But Abner would always change the subject when he wanted to ask further questions.

Jonah didn't care if people disliked him. That wasn't a problem. He just wanted, more than anything, to know *why* he was so disliked. As he'd already deduced, Haniel's first impression of him couldn't be the only thing. This was as if he'd shot somebody and tried to get away with it. But he couldn't ascertain why they treated him this way. He was respectful, tactful, and as approachable as humanly possible. He followed Haniel's instructions to the letter. It made no difference. It wasn't everybody—it was never *everybody*—but it was the lion's share of citizenry.

He found himself occasionally pissed at Jonathan. Why the hell had he sent them here? And had it ever occurred to him that the populace would hate him for some nameless reason?

But Jonah got over that quickly. Jonathan hadn't been all-knowing. He probably believed that Jonah could overcome anything, given his way with words.

But he didn't have a chance.

When Jonah was a kid experiencing bullying and ostracism, he'd vanish into books for hours, allowing his imagination to take him away, or write. He'd done both. He would have loved to go to the library, but Reena was there all the time with people who loved conversing with her. He didn't want to ruin that for her.

So, he did the other thing he had done back in the old days.

He took walks with headphones on.

Terrence and Reena were more than willing to keep him company, but Jonah wasn't angry with them for being well-liked. How could he be? They were the ones forging the bonds, perhaps they could learn the things that Jonathan wanted them to find out.

Besides, when one walked around town, one could learn a great many things.

Jonah learned quickly that Spirit Land wasn't much different from Tenth towns. There was commerce, law offices and businesses, and quaint shops wherever you looked. Jonah's favorite of them was Ace & Ice, a dessert shop run by Horace Mills and his husband, Maurice. They had red velvet cake that was just about the best thing in the world; Jonah put it one step underneath his grandmother's gingerbread. Horace and Maurice didn't give Jonah much grief like other people in Spirit Land, partly because they were such easygoing people, and partly because he was a paying customer. A win-win.

It was things such as those that made things in Spirit Land very much like the rest of the world. Even the conversations he picked up here and there revealed that people fussed and concerned themselves with the same things Tenths did: prices, weather, gossip, etc. Not very different at all.

But the similarities with the Tenth world stopped there.

This was an ethereal town.

The first thing that got Jonah's attention was the weather. The sky was always sunny and mostly cloudless. The temperature always remained pleasant; the evenings got no cooler than the high sixties. When Jonah inquired as to how the plants and things grew without rain, Abner just smiled and headed off to swim.

More than once, Jonah saw people use a combination of air and concentration to levitate groceries down the block—one person explained that it assisted with back issues. It wasn't strange to see the wind pick up and people step out of the *Astralimes* to jog in the park, take their kids to school, get groceries, or just go about their normal routines. He saw children playing very interesting and clever hide-and-seek and tag games that required using the *Astralimes,* but they could only be done with adult supervision. People remained in Spectral Sight all of the time and would be seated in the park having full on conversations with spirits, spiritesses, and heralds. And the spirits and spiritesses were all happy and content. It was like they were in a different world from the spirits and spiritesses beyond the city limits. Which, in all honesty, they were.

Ethereality was mundane here.

And then there was the deeply rooted appreciation of the

circus. Everywhere Jonah looked, streets signs, stores, parks, and landmarks bore names that were from carny lingo. Ballyhoo Road. Cyr Wheel Drive. First of May Bicentennial Garden. Things such as that. In parks all over town, people would do all kinds of activities that mimicked the circus.

Mayce took great pleasure in wowing people. He was clearly a competitive guy, and a bit of a showoff. He was the only person that Jonah had ever seen in his life, not counting television, who could perform a *quadruple* somersault. And he was absolutely fearless. In another life, he'd probably be best friends with Bobby. The elementary school where Haniel taught (which was far larger than Jonah's elementary school in Radner) had a bunch of children who mimicked trapeze artists and lion tamers on the playgrounds. Jonah didn't know whether it was a fascination, or an obsession. Didn't matter either way. They were obsessed with the circus here.

All in all, it was about eleven or twelve days before he, Terrence, and Reena were able to sit together for a period of time that wasn't fleeting. Through their texts, they'd agreed on the overlook as a great meeting spot. Terrence had fire in his eyes that Jonah hadn't seen since before the exodus, and he was happy to see it. It almost made the weeks and weeks of self-doubt immaterial. Reena, on the other hand, looked at Jonah with genuine concern in her eyes once they were all seated.

"Jonah, I know that you said that you don't care, but this has got to stop. These people treat you like a leper, and we still don't know why—"

"Don't worry about it," muttered Jonah. "Just use your access that you've earned. A few people here are openminded concerning me. Abner is cool, and Horace and Maurice are awesome. This time has allowed me to work my own mind, like you said you did the first night. I have walked around town, learned some things here and there ... it's been interesting."

"What have you learned?"

"Not important to this conversation, Reena. What have you found out?"

Reena looked at Jonah a few seconds more, fingering her dampener. Instead of removing it, she decided to speak. "Josephine's family let me in on some things. That zone patrol has been almost airtight since Creyton achieved Praeterletum. They're afraid of the fact that, since he returned from the grave, he's more powerful and less human. Their boundaries have been fortified ten times over, and drifters deal with restrictions, much like we did."

"Hmm. So, have they been letting anyone in at all?"

"I asked that same question. Not really. Not for a couple years. Those were Josephine's exact words."

Jonah eyed Reena, and she nodded.

"I know that there may be secrets there. But I suppose that's to be expected, since we're new."

"Can't argue that," said Jonah reluctantly. "How about you, Terrence? Find out anything from all the folks that love you?"

Jonah heard the bitterness in his voice and instantly regretted it. Didn't seem to matter though; Terrence hopped right to it.

"Haniel and I talk a lot about the ethereality that they use around here. She said that there are Green Auras here that can heal with a touch, no tonics or salves. But it takes a *huge* amount of concentration and effort; it's like running a marathon. They are also well aware that the spirits and spiritesses didn't want to have their essences split by endowments, but the spirits and spiritesses didn't want to leave them hanging. So, they put some work in and mutually aided each other."

"How?"

"The spirits and spiritesses found ways to encase reasonable amounts of their endowments into these amulet thingamabobs—"

"You mean phylacteries?" questioned Reena, wide-eyed.

"Yeah, yeah! Everyone in town, 'cept the kids of course, have one of those in some way, shape, or form. Nothing big or gaudy...some of the women have them in their earrings. Haniel has hers on her teaching lanyard."

"Wow," said Reena. "Josephine and her family hadn't mentioned that, but I imagine that's something you'd want to keep close to the chest—Jonah?"

She'd taken note of the expression on Jonah's face. He'd tried and failed to empty the emotions from it, but it didn't work this time. He shook his head. "I don't know how I feel about that. It ... it doesn't seem right."

"Dude, are you joking?" asked Terrence, surprised. "The whole thing is awesome! It's quick and efficient!"

"And impersonal, Terrence. Imagine you donated blood to one person, and then discovered later on that everyone and their mother has dipped into it, too! There is an honor, a respect, in asking a spirit or spiritess for permission to take an endowment. But to bottle it up like date-night perfume seems a little soulless. I'll take the old-school way any day."

Reena looked pensive after Jonah's words, but Terrence shrugged.

"Want to be a prude? Be my guest. I think it's infallible."

Jonah fastened onto that. "Prude, huh? Does that mean this phylactery thing is a recent thing?"

"Within the past several months or so. The well-being of the spirits who endow us has been a huge concern, man, and that was way before the exodus. Haniel described it and truly thinks that it's a great idea. I do, too."

Jonah felt his face pull almost independently of himself.

"Haniel thought that, did she? It's like that? What Haniel says goes?"

Terrence froze instantly. He gave Jonah an expression so venomous that Jonah's eyes widened in alarm.

"I'm only gonna say this once, Jonah. Do not throw shade at me for respecting Haniel. She is a *boss* Eleventh, and an awesome teacher. Teachers do not get enough respect, 'specially in *this* state. They are expected to make miracles out of the shitty budget that the state begrudgingly gives them, and that expectation is repeated every single year. She does it like it's nothing. And did you know that the school here in Spirit Land isn't the only school where she teaches ESL? It's just her 'A' school. Her 'B' school is two hours away. Not a problem with the *Astralimes,* but the people think she commutes those two days. You understand what I'm saying to you? She makes cuisine out of scraps day in, day out. You should see her lesson plans. She is a great woman, full of ideas. So don't go hating on her, got it?"

Jonah blinked, stunned. Reena was taken aback by Terrence's outburst. Where in the hell of hells had that come from? "Whatever, man. Fine."

Seconds later, the wind picked up, and Haniel stepped out of thin air, eyes on Terrence.

"Hey, Reena, Jonah. Terrence, I've been looking for you. You seem to be so cognizant concerning food, so I've got a challenge for you."

"Great." Terrence stood. "I like challenges. Whatcha got?"

Jonah frowned Reena's way. Since when did Terrence like a challenge?

"There is a dinner tonight in the community room at the town hall. Two of the women who were cooking with me had to back out. One went into labor ten minutes ago and the other got a bad case of vertigo in the library and needs to spend some hours in the healing haven. I need you. You've got nine hours to cook for a boatload of people."

Terrence regarded her, looking almost insulted. "Haniel, what's the challenge?"

Haniel frowned. "I just said it. You have nine hours to cook for dozens of people."

Terrence stared. "What's the *challenge?*"

Haniel looked at Jonah and Reena, both holding back snorts. "I just gave you a request on short notice to cook for a number of people that is about the same size as the group you saw when you first got here. Are you not getting me?"

Terrence patted Haniel's shoulder with mirth in his eyes. "Okay, Haniel. No problem. I got it."

With a nod to Jonah and Reena, he stepped into nothingness. Jonah ignored his sister, who snickered, and focused on Haniel.

"What's this event?"

"One of Mr. Harrington's best friends is coming back into town." Haniel still looked baffled by Terrence's reaction to her "daunting" task for him. "He's had haven here for a bit, but he travels all over, and he's been a blessing to this town. Today is his birthday, and Mr. Harrington wanted to give him a surprise party."

"Really?" asked Reena. "So, some people do leave here and come back as they please?"

"Of course, Reena. Spirit Land is not a prison. I myself leave here all the time—I do have a life beyond teaching. Residents leaving isn't the problem. It's the strangers coming and going that we worry about."

"Uh-huh," said Jonah. "What's this guy's name?"

"L.C. Pilcher. You'll meet him tonight. I'm sure Mr. Harrington will want him to know about the three of you guys."

* * *

Hours later, Jonah and Reena were among the throng of people in the town hall. People chatted excitedly, used unbridled ethereality, and eagerly anticipated L.C. Pilcher's arrival. Terrence, as he'd always done back at the estate, made the cooking look easy. People were in awe when they discovered that he'd just found out that day that he'd have to cook like that. Jonah had long since been impressed by Terrence's culinary prowess, but to people who hadn't experienced it, such a thing was magnificent. Terrence looked tremendously pleased with himself and with the attention he received. Jonah smiled. Good for him. Terrence deserved praise. He didn't get it often enough.

He and Reena were at a table with Haniel, Mayce, Sathvi, and Josephine. Harrington, his wife, their daughter Kimberly, and son Jackson were at the table right next to them. Harrington looked as excited as a kid, far removed from the stern, suspicious man he was when he looked at Jonah. His son was as well, but Kimberly looked as if she'd rather be any other place but here. Jonah smirked at her, and then tapped Mayce's shoulder.

"What's the deal with this Pilcher guy?" he wanted to know.

"He was an outsider and stranger at first, just like you guys were. We didn't know what to think of him, and then Jackson got sick. Like, horribly sick; the Greens hadn't ever seen anything like it. Pilcher, like Reena, did some improvised healing. He fixed Jackson up like it was nothing, and he's been cool by us ever since."

Jonah sat back in his chair. This L.C. guy got the chance to be a hero. He didn't meander into town with an already shitty rep. Lucky guy.

He excused himself with a look at Reena, and she rose to

join him. They walked over to Terrence, who assisted with refreshments and appetizers.

"You've wowed them again, brother. First car maintenance, now food. You're a darling!"

"You know I wasn't trying to impress anyone, man. Cooking for a whole bunch of people wasn't a damn challenge … it's what I do."

"I have to admit, I'm curious to meet this Pilcher guy," Reena told them. "If these guys love him this much, he must be a great guy. We might even be able to forge another alliance. A kindred spirit, a person who knows what it's like to be an outsider here. Might get us an in with Harrington for help with Omega."

"You're too modest, Reena." Again, Jonah didn't hide sarcasm. "A couple more days, and you and Terrence could both be full-fledged citizens here."

Reena surveyed the crowd, annoyance in her features. "I also want very much to know why they have such disdain for you, Jonah. It's all I can do to keep a level head. Josephine doesn't talk about it."

"Haniel and Mayce don't either." Some of the light dimmed in Terrence's eyes. "I've tried very hard to glean things. No luck."

"It is what is." Jonah tried to sound nonchalant. "I wouldn't really want to live here, anyway. All this freedom with the ethe-reality has made the citizens rely on it far too heavily. Remember what Felix said about that some years back? Makes me glad Jonathan trained us for all scenarios. These people may be powerful, and well-versed in ethereality, but I'd hate to see them in a situation where they had to adapt—"

Someone hurried into the hall, grinning.

"Pilcher's on the way! Julia and Jerry are guiding him here, with a bag on his head."

Everyone got quiet, buzzing with anticipation. Jonah fixed his eyes on the doors.

Maybe two minutes later, the doors opened slowly and carefully. Two teenagers who looked like siblings guided a man inside, gingerly shuffling forward due to the bag on his head that obscured his vision. Once inside, they ripped off the bag, and a synchronized *Surprise!* practically shook the room, followed by cheers and applause.

Jonah, Terrence, and Reena were not among them.

Terrence dropped the appetizer headed for his mouth. Reena gasped so starkly that it was a miracle she didn't get lightheaded. Jonah felt as if all the blood in his face had turned to ice. God only knew how pale his face was.

Unbeknownst to the elated people of Spirit Land, this man in their midst was not named L.C. Pilcher.

His name was Laban Cooper.

17

DEADFALL

Jonah instantly tried to convince himself that it was a lie. A bad dream. It was yet another moment where he waited to hear the laugh track, but none came.

Laban Cooper was the guest of honor. This vile, opportunistic ex-Deadfallen disciple was beloved in the town of Spirit Land.

And Jonah, who wanted to be in their good graces and follow Jonathan's directives, was not.

One would think that God would have a sense of humor if any part of this situation were funny.

It was at that moment that Jonah realized that his legs could move again. He had half a mind to find a secluded spot and reorganize his thoughts, but he couldn't leave Terrence and Reena. He about-faced as fast as he could. He didn't want Laban to see him.

"My God." Reena sounded genuinely scared. "What's *he* doing here?"

"And he's *popular?*" demanded Terrence. "What the hell is this—the Twilight Zone?"

"We need to get out of here." Jonah tossed his plate in the trash. "Spirit Land is officially a bust."

"Where are we gonna go, Jonah?" Terrence actually sounded more curious than sarcastic. "Jonathan sent us here! And we can't bail out; the whole town knows we're here."

"Let's just step out for a few minutes then. Figure out some kind of plan—"

"Too late." Reena's eyes somewhere behind Jonah's back.

Cursing, Jonah attempted to manufacture a smile as he turned. Didn't happen.

Laban was in front of him, Harrington to Laban's right. The surprise in Laban's eyes was fleeting, and then there was mirth. Manic, savage mirth. Jonah couldn't believe it. Only Laban could make laughter in someone's eyes look evil.

"L.C., these are the guests I mentioned," said Harrington, some of the jubilance exiting his face when he looked at Jonah. "Terrence Aldercy, Reena Katoa, and Jonah Rowe."

For some reason, a look passed between Harrington and Laban. Not only that, but other people did the same thing, as if there was some sort of open secret or something. But then Laban just smiled at Jonah and extended his hand.

"It's a great pleasure to meet you, friends. I feel as if I know you already!"

Jonah looked at his hand and fought the desire to recoil. "I, um, was handling some greasy food earlier. I'm not comfortable shaking your hand for that reason."

"Oh, nonsense." Laban grabbed Jonah's hand.

Jonah was nearly lightheaded. Knowing who this man was and what he had done ... and now they shook hands like old friends. He fought the urge to throw up.

After what felt like years, Laban released his hand, nodded at Terrence and Reena, and went back to mingling. There were more people in the line for food, which forced Terrence to return to his task. It must have been pure torture for him to power through the emotions he must have felt. Jonah and Reena took plates of food that they had no intention of eating, and reluctantly left Terrence for seats.

"Reena, I truly do not know how to play this. I feel like a cornered rat. Anything I say will be my word against his, and of course they'll take his side—"

"I think I've got something," Reena told him. "I just need to check something."

She looked over at Haniel, who was conversing over a cup of punch with a man Jonah didn't know.

"What are you—?"

"Perfect." Reena fidgeted with her sleeve.

"What is *perfect*?"

"Haniel is wearing her inversion band. I'm going to do something to her, and she won't love it."

"Huh?"

Reena lifted her sleeve, which revealed that her band was still there. Clasping it with her thumb and forefinger, she gave a hard tug.

"Watch this.".

Jonah wondered what she intended to do but complied.

For several more seconds, Haniel had a grin on her face. Then the humor faded, and the smile slid away. She shook her head a little, as though she had cobwebs to clear, and looked at her wrist, then at Jonah and Reena. Slowly, she turned her gaze to Laban, who was chowing down on birthday cake. Her eyes widened in shock and horror. She wrestled the inversion band off her wrist and threw it to the floor.

"That's right, Miss Teacher." Reena looked smug. "*My* class is in session now."

Jonah marveled at Reena's tactic when Haniel staggered to

their table and stumbled into a chair. "R-Reena, wh-what did you do?"

"Those little bands of yours are quite the contraptions. I figured if I was to be subjected to them, I'd learn how they worked. Once I figured out the essence ratio necessary to invert ethereality, it was a simple matter to cause an imbalance. In other words, I flipped the receiver."

Haniel gaped at her. "You flipped the receiver? How in hell did you unbalance the ratio?"

"Never mind that. You read that bastard's essence, didn't you?"

Haniel nodded, looking shell-shocked. Jonah got in close. Yes, it was a loud party, but speaking too loudly was always a risk.

"His name isn't Pilcher. It's Cooper. Laban Cooper. And I'm curious—what, pray tell, did you read?"

Haniel placed her fingers at her temples. "Evil. Oh my God ... I have never felt anything like that. Was I also correct in reading you guys' familiarity with him? You already know him well?"

"Yes," answered Jonah through clenched teeth. "Quite well."

Haniel looked at them with desperation. "Who is this monster? How do you know him?"

Jonah glanced at Reena, who nodded. They were on the same page. "Haniel, you get nothing until we get information, too. You're an honest woman. We figured that out for ourselves. But anybody with a fully functional brain knows you've been holding out on us. This is give-and-get. Nonnegotiable."

Haniel looked at him, and then nodded. "We can't talk here. I'm leaving in about thirty minutes; I'll think up an excuse. Wait for a few, and then you leave, too. Use the *Astral-*

imes to my house and make absolutely sure no one sees you. I'll get Mayce and Terrence—wait. Does Terrence—?"

"Yep, he's in the know. Why thirty minutes?"

"That's when the liquor will start flowing. No one will notice we're gone when they're lit."

* * *

A little over an hour later, Jonah, Terrence, Reena, Haniel, and Mayce were in Haniel's kitchen, like that very first night. Haniel was about to speak, but Reena raised a hand to stop her. She pulled out her notepad, wrote something very quickly, and turned it to Haniel. It read:

USE YOUR ENDOWMENT. CHECK FOR SONARUSIS.

Jonah frowned, then remembered. Sonarusis was an ethereal auditory tactic used to spy on potential threats. Nearly two years prior, the Curaie had Spectral Law Practitioners using it to spy on the estate.

Haniel contemplated Reena, then grabbed hold of her teacher's ID on the countertop. She pressed her skin to her phylactery and spiritually endowed herself. She then raised her left hand, spread her fingers wide, and closed her eyes. A second later, she opened them, looking frightened. Reena's suspicion was true. She wrote another message on the notepad, and held it up for all to see:

STAY CALM. IT'S EFFECTIVE, BUT LIMITED. WALK UPSTAIRS. IT CAN'T DETECT SOUNDS ON A HIGHER LEVEL.

Haniel nodded. They all rose, walked to the second floor,

and into the same bedroom that Jonah, Terrence, and Reena woke up in almost two weeks prior. The minute that Haniel closed the door, she rounded on the three of them.

"What in God's name is going on in our town?"

"That guy whose ass all of you are kissing?" Jonah sniffed. "He's a former Deadfallen disciple. He was in Creyton's inner circle until he betrayed him, then he ran."

Haniel and Mayce looked at each other. Jonah hated to spill it to them like that, but it was what it was.

"Are you sure about this, Jonah?" asked Mayce. "Are you sure you don't have him confused with another guy?"

"It's him, Mayce. Now, listen to me very carefully."

Jonah told the siblings everything. His initial meeting with Laban on The Plane with No Name. The arrangements that were made at the estate with the underground cell. The months of mind games. Of course, the events of the Six. He accentuated the fact that vanquishing Jonathan was Five and the Splinter at the estate was Six. Haniel and Mayce listened, shock on their faces the entire time, but when Jonah reached Five and Six, they looked at each other again, as though a stark realization had occurred. Reena jumped on it before Jonah got the chance.

"What was that? Give-and-get, Haniel, remember?"

Haniel sighed. "We were told that over seventy percent of the Grannison-Morris estate residents abandoned the place days after Jonah became Overseer. Something about Jonah beating an unarmed man who'd lived there for almost twenty years to within an inch of his physical life. Clearly, there was more to it than that."

Jonah's eyes bulged, but something within him calmed. Could have been his balancing power; he didn't know. "Haniel, there is a disconnect in the communication some-where. We have told you a great deal. Now, it's yours and

Mayce's turn, starting with why almost everyone here hates me."

Haniel looked down at her hands, breathing through her nostrils. It was clear that she was angry, but for once, the negativity wasn't toward Jonah. "There are a couple reasons, but the main one is L.C. Or Laban, or whatever. He said that Jonathan's vanquishing was entirely because of you."

Jonah's mouth fell open in shock and fury. Terrence closed his eyes tightly, gritting his teeth. Reena rose and turned away, murmuring, "Lying motherfucker."

"That was enough to instantly turn people against you, man," said Mayce. "He said Jonathan told you to hide and you bucked on his order ... and got him vanquished by a War Haunt as a result."

"He's a goddamned liar!" snarled Jonah. "Jonathan didn't tell me to hide; he had me ethereally grounded and told me to find Terrence and Reena. I tried to, which is the honest truth. But then I realized that the attacking Deadfallen disciples were trying to maneuver us away from the estate, which would leave Jonathan completely alone. I went to help, but Jonathan immobilized me. He sacrificed himself, took that War Haunt with him. He knew his end was coming—knew he was the Cut. He didn't want them to gun for me."

Haniel sniffed. "Laban said that you were opportunistic, perpetually defiant, and loved being a big deal. He said that when you became Overseer of the estate, you didn't tell anyone for days, trying to wait for the most dramatic time you could before announcing it."

"That's bullshit, too." Jonah almost choked on fury. "But it made something else make sense. That's why you warned me not to trade on being the Light Blue Aura that night. You were trying to protect me."

Haniel nodded but said nothing. The exposure of Laban's lies was a lot to take in. Mayce finished it up for her.

"I think that the thing that sealed it for you was that Laban predicted you'd stumble across Spirit Land eventually, with plans to pilfer and rob us blind so that you could try to be Omega's ultimate hero."

Jonah rose to his feet. The messed-up thing about being in someone else's house was the fact that he couldn't pick up anything and throw it. "I never had a chance. Laban was smart enough to know that if there was a place filled with nothing but Elevenths, Jonathan would know about it and inform me. I'll bet you every dollar I've got to my name that he set out to find this place first, and he couldn't very well have me come along and expose him, could he? So, he slanders me, drags my name through the shit. And then, when we did show up, I already had a bad rap."

"Question." Terrence drummed his fingers due to nerves. "How exactly did Laban get here? How did you guys link up with him?"

"Remember when I warned you about bad-mouthing the circus? It's dear to everyone in Spirit Land for two reasons. First, it's a magnificent art form and probably the funnest thing on earth. That's the reason why everything around here is named after circus terms. Second, circus troupes and magic shows are how we make forays into the world, staying abreast of things."

"Really? You're serious?"

"Just think, Terrence," said Mayce. "What other platform is there where ethereal humans can be who they truly are, and people write it off as part of a show or an act?"

Terrence thought about it. "Point."

"The circus has allowed us a great deal," said Haniel. "The troupes are also, well, spies. But mainly, we find out things, so we are aware of the rest of the world. We never really used animals or anything like that, but everything else was involved. And using our ethereality and have people applaud? That was always such a clever and fun touch. I was in it myself for several years, but I wanted to do something more for children than just make them laugh."

"Really?" Terrence looked at her, intrigued. "What was your shtick?"

Haniel grinned. "My ethereality allows me to be a mockingbird. I can mimic the powers of other Elevenths. People thought that was the neatest thing, when I copied the gifts of other people in the troupe. Look."

She lifted her sleeve up to her shoulder, revealing a tattoo that said *Mistress Mockingbird.* Jonah, Terrence, and Reena looked at it, mystified. That was an interesting ethereal power, after all.

"You can really mimic any power of any Eleventh?" asked Jonah.

"All except one. I can't mimic yours. The Blue Aura ethereality is impossible."

Jonah suppressed a smirk. For some reason, he appreciated that fact. But Reena looked at the bands on the table.

"What's the point of these things?"

"It allows me to focus on other things while using my endowment," Haniel explained. "It also prevents too many ethereal attributes from crowding my consciousness at once; can you imagine what it would be like to heal, have enhanced strength, and then top it off with essence reading and speed manipulation? I'd lose my mind. But I try very hard not to use it incessantly."

"Really?" asked Terrence. "Why's that? It's cool as hell."

"It's the price of being a mockingbird," answered Haniel.

"If you spend too much time copying others you run the risk of forgetting who *you* are."

Jonah sympathized with that part. But he'd had enough. His thimbleful of patience for the side story had long since emptied. "That was great information, and I mean that, but what does this have to do with Terrence's first question about Laban?"

"The circus was how we met Laban," Mayce replied. "He stowed away in one of the vans during a foray a while back. The one where we learned about Jonathan's vanquishing. When we came back into Spirit Land, Haniel and some other patrollers of the Emerald Zone went through our stuff and discovered that he was there."

Jonah frowned and remarked, "If ever there was a cause to blink someone unconscious, that would be it."

"I wanted to," admitted Haniel. "But he was so damn persuasive. He mentioned something about being held against his will underground, and that he needed assistance. He said he stowed away because he didn't know who to trust."

"I'll be damned." Jonah scowled. "The bastard used the truth to tell a lie."

"He was kept at arm's length for a long while," said Haniel, "but then Jackson got sick. Laban cured him. It was such a self-less and noble act that we warmed to him. Harrington's loved him ever since."

"Yeah, Mayce told us So, he snuck in, weaseled his way into everyone's hearts, and then spread lies about me. Bitch."

"What *was* the truth, Jonah?" Haniel asked him. "Did seventy percent of the estate residents really leave after you became Overseer?"

Jonah gritted his teeth. "Yes. But that was only because of another resident who's hated my guts since I got to the estate. And before you ask the next question, no, I wasn't waiting for a grand time to announce that I was Overseer. I was silent for days because I was scared. But that night, I got my nerve up. The bastard who started it—Trip's his name—was pissed Jonathan chose me and staged an insurrection. He attacked me first. There was a big fight between my friends and his. I was unendowed and completely caught off guard."

"You were *unendowed?*" Mayce was amazed. "How did you beat him?"

"There is a line that you just don't cross, and he crossed it. He made comments about my late grandmother, and I lost it. When that happened, his spiritual endowment no longer mattered."

Haniel nodded. "I get that. I can't say that I wouldn't have done the same thing if someone made insensitive comments about our parents."

"Your parents are in Spirit?" asked Reena.

"Yes. Eight years."

There was an understandable moment of silence, which for some reason triggered a memory in Jonah.

"Haniel, I just remembered something. The first night we all spoke, you grilled me about whether or not I planned to just seek information and blaze. Now I know why. But when you found out that Jonathan handed down the directions, you looked really confused about it. Why?"

Very slowly, Haniel looked at Jonah. "Jonah, my first impression of you wasn't a great one. So when Laban came here, talking about you like that, I found it easy to believe. But when I saw you again that day after I corralled you guys ... it just didn't make sense. Despite my first impression of you ... despite Laban's words ... you just didn't seem to have darkness in you. And when I had access to Reena's essence reading, it was there again. No darkness in you. In any of you."

Jonah noticed Haniel's glance at Terrence as she said that last part but continued.

"Another thing was the fact that all the months we've known Laban, he has been *vicious* about you. If he had spoken his piece and moved on, that'd have been one thing. But he just continued to lay into you, just kept throwing massive shade—how you were this, that …"

"Truth be told," threw in Mayce, "he made you sound like Creyton."

"Which, like I said, made no sense," continued Haniel. "At first, I bought it. But when it continued, I started to wonder. I apologize for how I've treated you, Jonah. I truly do. Whatever anger or frustration issues you had in the past, you're not the man that Laban has painted you to be. I apologize for ever thinking so."

Jonah just nodded. That was all he could do. Things were looking up. In this particular regard, anyway.

"You want to know something ironic, Haniel?" Terrence spoke up. "Everything that Laban told you guys that Jonah was, he is. In spades."

"Damn straight," said Reena.

"So, the sixty-four-thousand-dollar question," said Mayce. "Now that we know the truth about this scum prick, what are we supposed to do about him?"

Jonah was ready for that. "Wait for him to slip."

"Jonah, he's been in and out of Spirit Land for months, and he hasn't slipped yet," Reena pointed out. "And the man is beloved. One would think he'd be careful with every step."

"Then I'll apply pressure." Jonah cracked his knuckles. "Might panic him into doing something stupid."

Mayce whistled. "Forgive me, Reena, but I think that Jonah is the one I should be calling brave."

"This isn't a joke, Mayce." Haniel looked worried. "That man has had dinner in our home. A lot of people's homes!"

"He's probably got Sonarusis set up on them, too," said Terrence.

"It's almost like Spirit Land is contaminated due to his presence," said Haniel as if there'd been no interruption. "God only knows what his true motives are."

Jonah felt fear when he saw Laban in that town hall. After he discovered that he was the reason that his name was mud in Spirit Land, the fear had dulled somewhat. At the very least, he now had something to do in Spirit Land besides walks the streets and steel himself against glares and leers.

"Don't worry, Haniel. Laban will slip up. Those types always do."

* * *

Jonah was on his way back to Abner's house by foot. He couldn't risk use of the *Astralimes because* he might run into someone who didn't like him. And the last thing he needed was a fight.

His mind swam with the conversation he'd just had. Laban had been here long enough to be a darling. The only people who would hear a word against him had to be convinced via ethereal means before they would listen. Aware that Laban was somewhere around here, scot-free, and loved and adored to boot, made this November evening feel chilly to Jonah, despite the ethereal control over the weather.

He turned left on Main Street and began the trek up Abner's walk when—

"Fancy seeing you here, Boy Blue!"

Jonah barely had enough time to react when a strong arm ringed his torso and he was forced through the *Astralimes.* The trip took just a second and then he was thrown to the ground, near the overlook. He was seconds away from scrambling to his feet when Laban reached into thin air and produced the largest hunting knife he'd ever seen, with serrated edges on one side and a filet blade on the other. Jonah looked at the open space where Laban retrieved the blade in alarm, which prompted Laban to chuckle.

"Didn't know you could store weapons on the Astral Plane and retrieve them at your leisure? Oh yeah. That was how Creyton had us stash weapons when we attacked places that had ethereal inspection measures. I don't have to be Deadfallen to still partake in the benefits. Now, don't make me use this."

Jonah's eyes ran over the knife dubiously. "What are you going to do, Superstar?" Gut me? An unendowed guest? That'd be bad for your rep, don't you think?"

Laban tilted his head to the side. "I'd think of something. I always do."

Jonah rose to his feet, unconsciously reaching for his pocket. Then he thought against it. Although freedom agreed with Laban, with his full features, trimmed moustache, and crisp clothing, Jonah was well aware of the monster under the wrapper. That same monster was the one Jonah didn't trust to keep the blade away.

"Why did you bring me up here? What do you have to say that can't be said down there, where everybody's lips are glued to your ass? They hate me anyway, compliments of you. So why the secrecy?"

Laban laughed. "That was a nice touch, wouldn't you agree? Surely, you weren't expecting the wonderful people of Spirit Land to just hand you goodies because you were a special shade of blue, did you?"

"It was never my plan to screw anybody over!" shouted Jonah. "We were going to work with them!"

Laban's eyes flashed. There he was again. Mr. Changeable. "Don't act like you're any better than me, boy. We're both using the idiots of this town to get what we want."

"I'm nothing like you!" Jonah shot back. "No matter what the situation, you only think about yourself!"

"Guilty." Laban was calm again. "Whether you agree or not doesn't really matter to me. Self-preservation has helped me, every time I have used it. Why do you think I'm golfing with Harrington on select weekends?"

"Because you saved his son, duh." Jonah was tired of the story already.

"Yes, but only *after* he got sick. Didn't you find it a tad bit odd that Harrington's brat got sick with something the healing havens here couldn't fix?"

"What?"

"They didn't trust me, dumbass. Couldn't have that ... fucked with my plans. But trust and respect flow fluidly in a situation where you play White Knight. So, Jackson's illness was arranged."

Jonah was horrified. "What did you just say to me?"

Laban shook his head. "You are just as stupid as you look, boy. I engineered a very weak strain of Creyton's so-called Mindscope Illness and made the little prick ill. I sat back and watched people flail around in despair and hopelessness for about a week, and then swooped in and administered the cure, and boom. The rest is history."

Jonah felt nauseous again. "You're frickin' sick."

"No, actually, it was Harrington's kid that was sick. Now, what exactly did you tell Haniel and her kid brother about me?"

"I don't know what you're talking about," said Jonah. It was better than *Huh?*

"Oh, do you think I'm a fool? You and your little friends

left my party early and went to Rainey's house. You were there for a good little while, yet I heard nothing. Which means that you figured out I was surveilling you with Sonarusis. Was it Katoa who figured it out? Now out with it. What did you tell them?"

Jonah said nothing, which clearly made Laban angry. *That's right, Changeable One,* he thought, *lose it ... show who you really are.*

Laban forcibly brought himself back to center, or so it seemed. He even smiled. "It doesn't matter. At best, you've converted two measly people to your cause. Have fun trying it with the rest of Spirit Land. I truly bid you good luck. I'm hiding comfortably in plain sight, right there." He pointed in the direction of the rolling hills, toward the town. "The little cottage on the corner of Essex and Mercier. I've worked too hard for this to come to fruition, and nothing can stop it now, least of all, you."

"What?" demanded Jonah. "What have you done?"

"Never you mind, Rowe," said Laban with a smile.

Jonah hated that smile. It signified that Laban was back in control, and he knew it.

"I brought you up here because I truly missed our talks from the underground hole when I was in that Hilton of a prison cell. Shame it has to end."

"What did you do, man?"

"We aren't going to speak too much after this, Rowe." Laban manufactured wistfulness. "I estimate that we'll have one, maybe two more conversations after tonight."

Once again, Jonah was sick and tired of the dramatics. Laban had played all his old mind games, only this time, there was no Jonathan to rationalize the situation. "I don't know what the hell you've done, Laban. But I'll stop you."

"No, Rowe. You won't." Laban chuckled, as though he

found that cute. He even shoved the knife back into thin air. It vanished. "But I will tell you what you will do, very soon."

"Yeah? Do enlighten me."

"It's very nearly time for you to pay what you owe me, Rowe," said Laban. "For sparing your friend's lives the night Jonathan bought it. Not to mention paying me back for being the son of the Ungifted filth who died before repaying his debts. All in good time though. All in good time. Nighty night."

He produced a twig and dematerialized before Jonah could speak another word.

1 8

THE TOOL OF OMEGA

"So, he made the Overseer's son sick," said Terrence. "Why am I not surprised?"

Jonah told Terrence and Reena everything the next day, which happened to be the day before Thanksgiving. He didn't say a word until they reached the overlook. It was the highest point in town, and there was no possible way that Sonarusis would work up there. Haniel and Mayce were up at the school, helping with some type of spirit meditation that was held every week. Jonah would tell them later, but he had to be leery of Laban's surveillance. God only knew how many people he'd "bugged".

"The thing that gets me is how he knew what particular circus troupe would lead to Spirit Land," said Reena. "It isn't like these guys would've been stupid enough not to check for a stowaway."

"Remember, Deadfallen disciples can shape-shift into crows," Jonah reminded her. "It's not that far of a stretch to think that former ones still can as well. I'm sure stowing away was the easiest thing Laban did during that time."

Reena rolled her eyes. "Of course."

"And did you say that he pulled a knife on you, out of thin air, Jonah?"

"Hell yeah he did, Terrence. It was like he had an invisible drawer or something. He said that it was an old Deadfallen method for having weapons at hand when they had to siege places that might have security checks."

"My God," said Reena. "Do you have any idea how dangerous that makes them? Having the ability to just grab weapons off of the Astral Plane?"

"It gets worse, Reena. Laban knew that you figured out he had Haniel's house under Sonarusis. He grilled me about what I told her."

"Did he now?" Reena looked at Jonah. "What did you say?"

"Didn't say a word. But then, things got worrisome. He got really angry when I held out, but then his mood flip-flopped again, and he said it didn't matter because 'converting two people' meant nothing since no one else would believe me. And he also said his plan was irreversible."

"Plan? Terrence looked alarmed. "What the hell could he possibly do? Spirit Land has been here for centuries, and they have defenses and blanket protection. The ethereality here is top notch, really—"

"And they rely on it too much, I've already said that. Laban needs to slip up. He's smart, but not infallible. I just wish I had a clue what he was doing."

"But Terrence is right," said Reena. "What could he do? I've been going over that in my head even before you told us these things, because Laban is Laban, and he was bound to be up to something. He can't pilfer them and bail, because there is no exit strategy that isn't monitored by zone patrol. He can't possibly leak information to the Deadfallen disciples—they'd terminate him on sight before he uttered a single word. Still, I'm worried. They have top-of-the-line ethereality here, but the only weapons I've seen are no different from the ones we've practiced with at the estate for years. In every scenario I've thought of, I can find no logical end play that would satisfy that bastard."

"Well, he's got one," said Jonah. "Maybe Haniel and Mayce could help us figure it out."

It was late evening before they saw Haniel and Mayce, and Jonah didn't hesitate to tell them everything that had transpired. When he posed the question about what Spirit Land might have that could exert a pull on the ambitious, Haniel looked over at Mayce. They both looked frightened as hell. That made Jonah feel better. It meant they were finally getting somewhere.

It only took forever and a day.

Strangely, Haniel looked at Reena and raised her wrist, revealing the inversion band. "Reena, will you humor me, please?"

Reena frowned. "Seriously, Haniel? You know by now that you can trust us—"

"I know, I know." There was a note of supplication in Haniel voice. "I just have to have reassurance."

Reena appeared to swallow down the irritation that Jonah knew she felt, then she nodded. Haniel tugged the band, closed her eyes, and then nodded herself.

"Before you tell us anything, Haniel," said Terrence, "shouldn't we all go upstairs first? For obvious reasons?"

"No worries, Terrence." Haniel pointed to a set of items that looked like railroad spikes, one near the kitchen door and one near the stove. "Those pegs nullify ethereal surveillance. I got a pair made at the steel mill the day after I discovered my home was bugged. I'll be damned if I can't speak where I want in my own home."

They all sat down at the kitchen table, except for Haniel. She poured herself a glass of bourbon and sipped it.

"Now, Jonah, when it comes to what we have here, you know a great deal already. I'm aware of all the sightseeing walks you've been taking the whole time you've been in Spirit Land."

"I assumed you were," Jonah replied with no awkwardness or alarm. "Sathvi's seen me on more than one occasion when she's out running. I figured she wasn't actually exercising."

"Oh, she was, but she was also being observant, just like yourself. Anyway, our ethereality is our bread and butter. But ..." she sighed. "But there is one thing you haven't seen."

Jonah zeroed in on Haniel, rapt. "Please, go on."

"It's something we call the Tool of Omega."

Jonah regarded her, then Terrence and Reena. "The Tool of Omega. Sounds a little heavy, don't you think?"

"Oh, it isn't the technical term for it, I'm sure," said Mayce hastily. "It's just what people 'round here started calling it when it became clear that Creyton was going forward with Omega."

"So, what is this ... tool?"

"Pull out your baton," said Haniel.

Jonah removed the baton, along with the apparatus he'd carried for several months. Mayce looked it over.

"I know a bayonet apparatus when I see one, Jonah. Who are you planning to kill? Is that for Creyton?"

"No," was all Jonah said as he looked at Haniel. "Why do you need to see this?"

"Visual reference. It's kind of like your baton, but it has a hilt, like a short sword. The tip is pointed, but it's not quite a blade either. I suppose its purpose is a hybrid between blunt force and stabbing. It can only be handled by a Blue Aura, so they say."

"Why is that?" Jonah asked. "How did it come to be here?"

"To answer your first question, a Blue Aura created it," answered Mayce. "And it was put here by that same Blue, who also founded Spirit Land. The last Blue Aura before Creyton showed up."

"The guy founded Spirit Land?" asked Terrence, amazed.

"The seventh Blue Aura was a *woman*, Terrence," Haniel corrected him. "Charis Rayburn."

Terrence's eyebrows arched. Jonah was more interested in knowing the name of the Blue Aura. He'd only heard of himself and Creyton. But Reena rolled her eyes at Terrence.

"I knew Charis Rayburns's name. I just didn't know she founded Spirit Land."

"That was done by design," said Haniel. "She founded the settlement during the witch trials. They weren't just done in Salem. The women during that time that were branded witches—"

"Were actually Eleventh Percenters," finished Jonah. "We know."

Haniel looked at Jonah in amazement, but Jonah didn't feel the need to gloat over knowing the information. He didn't enjoy how he'd learned it. The Creyton-in-disguise incident was one he'd just as soon forget. Haniel went on.

"Rayburn founded this settlement with a bunch of women that fled the witch trials, along with several male Elevenths who tried to protect them. This was a place where ethereal humans could be free of puritanical persecution. The Puritans used God and their Bible to justify what they were doing to us. That's one of the reasons why you don't see much organized religion around here. Most distrust of Tenths stems from that, and outside ethereals as well."

"Let me guess." Terrence's upper lip curled. "There were Elevenths out there willing to out other Elevenths to save their scrawny asses, right?"

"Pretty much. But Rayburn made a weapon that would protect the settlement of Spirit Land at all costs."

Jonah sniffed. That sounded a little hardcore. "What's the big deal about this weapon?"

Haniel swallowed and glanced over at Mayce. The latter actually had perspiration on his forehead. "It's said that the Tool of Omega is a weapon—the only one in the world—that can cause death."

There was silence. Jonah couldn't believe that those words had escaped the lips of an Eleventh Percenter not branded Deadfallen. "Th—that can't be. Death isn't real."

"In all other instances, that's true," Haniel told him. "But with this weapon, we all believe that it's real. Charis Rayburn somehow forged an ethereal weapon that can neutralize physical *and* spiritual life. Obviously, none of us were there, but there are spirits and spiritesses around here that were. Even they don't have all of the information. The most that we put together is that Rayburn was pissed about the witch trials and was ready to eliminate anyone who threatened her or family and friends. It's also been said that she came to regret making it and wanted no part of it later on."

"Why didn't she just destroy it?" asked Reena.

"No idea," said Haniel. "All we know is that she didn't want any other Blue Auras near it. She supposedly made a decree before she passed into Spirit that if any other Blue Auras were born into the world and crossed the borders of Spirit Land, they were not to come near it. Nonnegotiable."

Terrence chuckled nervously. Reena sat back in the chair and whispered, "Damn."

"So, that's the main reason why you guys are leery of me,"

said Jonah. "You're leery of all blue Auras. You guys probably never expected for there to be two in the world at once. And Haniel, allow me to apologize to you now."

"Really?" Haniel was puzzled. "Why?"

"I thought you grilled me just because of Laban's slander. I thought you had it in for me. But you were trying to make sure that I wasn't searching for the Tool of Omega."

Haniel nodded. "Apology accepted. And I hope that you will accept my apologies for not trusting you at first. As well as my desire not to tell you where to find it."

"I can respect that," said Jonah, even though he didn't feel that way one-hundred percent.

"But I'm confused." Terrence again. "How would this weapon help Laban? Never actually knew his aura color, but it damn sure ain't blue."

"Again with that *ain't*," said Haniel wearily.

"My bad, Haniel. But Jonah, did you catch the aura color last night?"

"Nah." Jonah shook his head. "He was unendowed at the time. But whatever he is going to do—and I still don't know how the Omega weapon comes into play—it will happen tomorrow night. I feel it with every fiber of my being."

"Jonah, it makes no sense," said Terrence. "Laban can't betray the whereabouts of the Tool to Creyton because he doesn't know where it is himself. Besides, he burned that bridge. Napalmed it. Creyton'll tear his head off the second he sees him. The thing is of no value to him."

What Terrence said made sense, but he didn't know Laban like Jonah did. He didn't converse with him regularly or see how psycho he was. Sure, he'd told him and Reena everything that Laban told him, but somehow, third-party information didn't quite convey the man's evil.

"You make a very valid point, Terrence," Reena acknowledged, "but I think that Jonah might be right as well. I wouldn't put it past Laban to try something when the majority of the town is in one place. Haniel, do you have guards and sentries for events?"

"Some," said Haniel. "But it's lax. Spirit Land is a quiet, serene place. The true guards are people like us who do zone patrol. And of course, the ones who keep watch over the Tool of Omega."

A very unsettling feeling formed in Jonah whenever he heard that name. Was it possible for something to sound epic *and* frightening at the same time? "I volunteer myself. I'll patrol around the holiday gathering. I can't speak for Reena—"

"You think I'd be anywhere else?"

"Hey, man," said Terrence, indignant. "Why did you leave me out?"

"Because you volunteered to cook, remember?"

Terrence's face slackened. "Oh, yeah. Right."

"But that doesn't mean that you can't still be watchful after all the food has been doled out."

Terrence smirked at that. "Damn straight."

Jonah rose. Since Omega had begun, he'd come to view everyday as a gift. Since he, Terrence, and Reena had been on the hunt for Spirit Land, he'd viewed each day as a blessing. So far, Spirit Land hadn't actually gone as planned. Laban had screwed things up for Jonah with his lies and because of that, only five citizens in the whole town even bothered with him. That thought alone pushed away most of his nerves.

But not all of them. And that Tool of Omega ...

"Mayce, just ... hypothetically speaking, how does the Tool work? Is it a worthiness thing? Does it recognize good and evil, or something?"

Mayce laughed aloud. "What the hell do you think this is, Jonah? Thor? Worthiness, good and evil—that crap doesn't play a part at all. I'm pretty sure that the first Blue Aura that touches it is the one who gets to use it."

Jonah looked away. "That's what I was afraid of."

* * *

Thanksgiving dinner began at 5:45 P.M. Big Top Road was closed and tables with comfortable plastic chairs were set up right there on the street. Food was made by Terrence and several other Spirit Land citizens. Due to the ethereal control on the weather, the November evening felt like spring. Many attended the dinner, but several other people remained home. Everyone was fine, either way.

Jonah thought all those things were cool but paid them no mind. He'd learned the layout of the town fairly quickly and walked a wide circuit around the festivities as he munched a turkey sandwich. Reena, who had a plate of turkey without bread and a small portion of potato salad, made a circuit in the opposite direction. Although he didn't see him, he knew that Terrence was doing the best he could to be mindful of surroundings between piling up plates and smiling at people that were appreciative of his cooking.

Haniel offered Jonah a phylactery, but he declined, preferring to summon a spiritess and make an official request for a spiritual endowment. In his mind, those phylacteries were like sweet tea that wasn't served cold. It just wasn't natural.

The party was easy enough to tune out. It wasn't like anyone had anything to say to Jonah, anyway. Abner signed to him that he didn't need to take the night so seriously. Jonah signed back that he was entitled to his opinion. Before they went to the party, Horace and Maurice were kind enough to give Jonah a slice of sweet potato pie and a square of apple crisp. Those dudes were by far some of the best people he'd ever met. If only those delicious desserts were enough to assuage his bad feeling. Even so, he was glad when Abner headed to the local fitness spa (where he could have the swimming pools to himself while everyone else partied), and Horace and Maurice went to the party. It kept his mind clear. Less conversation meant more focus.

On his fourth circuit, he bumped into Kimberly, Harrington's daughter.

"What the hell are you doing here?" she demanded.

"I can ask you the same question, Sweet Pea. Where are you going in the skimpy outfit?"

"Me and this *skimpy outfit* are minding our business. If you know what's good for you, you'll leave me be, Rowe. No one here likes or trusts you, especially Daddy."

"This is true," said Jonah, "but I'm certain that Daddy would dislike the fact that his daughter slips off to the overlook to smoke weed and get banged by her boyfriend."

Kimberly froze.

"What's his name again? Shade, right?" Jonah gave her a pensive look. "What the hell kind of name is Shade? Harrington hates *him* almost as much as he hates me. Then again, I've seen that boy, and your father might actually be right about him."

"How do you know about that?"

"You see very interesting things when you keep your eyes open and your mouth shut," was all Jonah told her.

Kimberly paled. "Jonah, please—"

"Oh, I'm *Jonah* now." He could've laughed. "What happened to your icy regard of me?"

"J-Jonah, wait." Kimberly looked petrified. "I'll do anything—"

"Oh, shut up." Jonah tired of the supplication quickly. "Tell me something I don't know about this town, and I'll forget I ever saw you."

"The rock quarry!" Kimberly burst out so readily that Jonah took a step back. "There is a spot in the rock quarry that no one's allowed to go. Not even the miners."

"Thank you," said Jonah. "We're good. Now, go on. Get."

Kimberly hurried off and Jonah breathed with relief. He'd kept his expression annoyed after she'd said what she said, but all his senses were on alert. The place in the rock quarry had to be where they kept the Tool of Omega. Damn. Jonah believed with everything in him that Haniel and the rest of her patrol worked ardently to maintain their secrets. So, if Harrington's nosy daughter knew that there was a place that no one was allowed to go, then she found out about it because she was snooping around, getting high and laid with that Shade boy. Laban had Harrington's house under surveillance; Jonah had no doubts about that. Could Kimberly have told Shade something that Laban had overheard?

Jonah had half a mind to head to the rock quarry himself when he realized something.

Laban. He hadn't seen him when he'd made the circuits around the party.

Where was the bastard? Shouldn't he have been right there in the midst of the party, hamming it up, and playing his façade? Didn't his adoring public find his absence odd? Sure, several people remained in their homes, but Laban would have been out there, kissing babies and glad-handing citizens. Anything to maintain his rep.

So, where was he?

He was about to text Reena about this along with the rock quarry when an uncertain voice said, "Mr. Rowe?"

He turned. It was Julia, one of the teenagers who'd helped guide Laban to his birthday party. Jonah bit down on his lip to keep the scowl from his face because Julia looked like she was frightened that he might mug her or something.

"Yes?" he tried to remain as friendly as possible. "What is it?"

"Mr. Harrington was wondering why you were making circles around the party—"

"Don't like holidays; they're too commercial," Jonah lied easily. "Say, where is La—Pilcher? Mr. Pilcher?"

"He said he wanted to remain home," answered Julia. "He said he wanted to be introspective about his blessings."

"Oh. Well, isn't that lovely? Well, you can tell Harrington that I'm not doing anything wrong. Later, Jules."

He turned his back on her, careful not to look to suspicious or anxious. Last thing he wanted was Julia's mouth running rampant. He yanked out his phone and debated texting Reena, but if he did that, no one else would have eyes out. He didn't have the greatest faith in the zone patrol for the simple fact that Haniel had freely admitted that everyone was lax and festive at times like these. And poor Terrence was too busy playing Chef Emeril to be of much help at the moment.

So, he put the phone back in his pocket. This one was on him.

Jonah decided to go to Laban's cottage. Introspective? Bull-shit. But he wouldn't be caught unawares this time. He was spiritually endowed.

To reiterate the fact, he willed his entire body to sting. Electrical current buzzed right underneath his skin. *See that bastard try to grab me now.*

* * *

Jonah was on Laban's property faster than he wanted to be. Maybe it was his imagination, or maybe it was his experiences.

But this cozy, homey little cottage seemed like a little piece of hell right now.

He gloved his hands and removed his batons. Then he frowned.

No one was there. The lights were off. The front door was actually ajar. Where the hell was Laban? Had he gone off to the rock quarry? Were the people who guarded that damned dinner party even cognizant at this point?

He gritted his teeth. Go to the rock quarry, face a known threat and an unknown ethereal weapon? Or inspect Laban's cottage, see if there was anything that could be used against him? Even the cleverest and craftiest slipped up. Jonah chose the latter. This was too good an opportunity to pass up. See if Mr. Slander had any proof of the true serpent that he was.

He paused at the threshold and inspected it. It'd already been slashed. So, Laban hadn't left himself vulnerable in that regard. With a steeling breath, he stepped inside.

"I was wondering when you'd get here."

Jonah whirled around. No one was there.

And then, Laban was.

The dark house suddenly lit up; the slightly ajar door slammed. The entire façade slid from the walls like water, straight into Laban's palm.

"What!" said Jonah, aghast. "How the hell do you know how to do a Spectral Illusion?"

"Does it matter?" Laban grinned. "You took your ever-loving time walking in here. What, did you think that I'd gone to the rock quarry?"

Jonah stared. Laban's eyes gleamed.

"Yes, I heard your conversation. But if it helps anything, I knew about the off-limits zone at the quarry months ago. That little skank went there all the time with her boyfriend to smoke pot and fuck each other stupid. They abandoned it because they thought the overlook was more romantic. A romantic setting for cannabis and fornication ... my dear God."

"I don't want to talk about stupid teenagers, Laban," Jonah snapped. "And if you try anything, I'm ready for you."

"Yes, I believe you are." Laban's tone was lazy. "But I have zero plans to hurt you."

Now that room was illuminated, Jonah could see more. Laban lived a meager existence while he was here. Besides a camp table, lawn chairs, and a welcome mat, he had no furniture. The taupe walls boasted no pictures. The small kitchen could be seen from the living room, and nothing was there except a refrigerator. "Not that I care, but this is all you've got?"

Laban seated himself in the lawn chair furthest from Jonah, located in front of the window. "I have little need for material possessions. The Plane With No Name cured me of my need to fill my life up with stuff."

Laban grabbed a mug from the floor and began to sip from it. He was quite serene and relaxed. Jonah snarled and got in his face. The mock serenity was infuriating.

"I am done with this bullshit, Laban! What is your game? I know you've got one! Just spare me all the crap and spill it!"

Laban looked at him, and then threw the mug across the room. It shattered to bits against the bare wall. "God help me, I'm sick of this façade, too. Haven't done this in years, but hey—necessary is necessary."

Then Laban did the unthinkable.

He tapped his throat twice and chanted, "*Per mortem, vitam.*"

Jonah looked at him in utter horror. "What have you done?!"

"One tap is for Deadfallen support, two taps are for Creyton," said Laban casually. "Protocol never changes."

"Creyton took you back? After all you've done?"

"Hell no," scoffed Laban. "Nor do I want to go back. Despite whatever happens, I only ever look out for Number One."

Then the screaming started. Two streets over, Jonah could hear it.

"No!"

Jonah raced for the front door and tugged with enough force to rip it off—but it didn't budge. Laban cackled.

"It won't open, Jonah. Nothing you can do will open that door or break the windows. I've been on the run from Creyton for years. Best believe that I mastered impenetrable ethereal shielding."

Jonah ignored him as he viciously bashed against the door with his batons. No effect. "You son of a bitch! You should have left these people in peace! My friends are still out there!"

Laban shrugged. "I did warn you about connections."

The door wouldn't open. The glass wouldn't break. Jonah rounded on Laban.

"What the hell is this, man?" His question was somewhere between a demand and a plea. "Creyton will kill you!"

"Ah." Laban rose from the chair and placed his hands behind his back. "Therein lies my game."

Laban turned to face the window again and closed his eyes as though the dreadful screams enraptured him. "As I said, I've known the location of the Tool of Omega for months. But there isn't a damn thing I can do with it. I'm no Blue Aura. So, after I got everyone in the town under surveillance, learned them ... studied them ... I came to realize that they rely too heavily— almost exclusively—on their ethereality. That is a horribly inept way to live. It's a miracle these fools haven't been waylaid before."

Jonah closed his eyes in disgust. He'd said the exact same thing more than once since they got there. Damn it all.

"This is you paying what you owe Jonah," Laban went on. "I told you that you would pay double for your filthy excuse of a father. Your debt for Luther was coming into Spirit Land with the foulest reputation I could spin. You probably hoped for a red carpet and got just the opposite. That was fun. I have no other word for it. It was fun. The second and final part of your debt is—well, you being right here, conveniently placed to be blamed for all that is happening out there. The blame will be posthumous, of course."

Jonah's eyes widened. *No.*

"Creyton is on his way. And you're right—he wants to kill me. However, I did something wonderful. Something even he couldn't do. Apprehend you. And the cherries on top? I've also given him Spirit Land! You probably thought I wanted to pilfer the place. I don't give a damn about anything here. Harrington, his brat son, or his loose daughter—none of them. Creyton can do whatever he wants with this place. He can even take the Tool of Omega and figure out how to work it."

Jonah didn't even bother to ask what that last part meant. He was scared for himself, Scared for Terrence and Reena. If he could only get through this damn door—

"The Light Blue Aura, Spirit Land, and the Tool of Omega." Laban's smile was blissful. "I think I've earned more than immunity from Creyton's wrath for finding you. I think that's enough to earn me a golden parachute right there! A retirement from all this crap and the promise to never see him again!" Laban laughed. "Won't that be the biggest flick-off to Creyton, knowing that I've bought my way from him?"

"Are you serious?" demanded Jonah. "You can't possibly ..."

Suddenly, the temperature dipped at least thirty degrees. Jonah fell silent, wanting to fool himself into believing that Reena had done a cold spot to help someone out. But he knew the reason that the world chilled.

"Speak of the devil!" said Laban with jubilance.

Jonah turned and saw Creyton.

He looked every bit as evil and cold as he remembered. The longer hair and beard made those attributes even more pronounced. Jonah wasn't even in a position to fight him. He was stuck in this damned house.

He didn't know what was more prevalent in his consciousness: fear of Creyton or hatred of Laban.

Laban waved from the window, smugness and triumph on every inch of his face. "He's in here! I think you've been paid in spades! Now, be a good little Transcendent and honor your word of immunity!"

Creyton smirked ... then lifted his staff and pressed the head of the crow at the tip. With a sound like a nail gun, something flew from the bottom of the staff, and penetrated Laban's supposedly impenetrable window.

And it flew clear through Laban, into the wall behind him.

Laban gasped in surprise, flying back into his lawn chair. The force of his impact cracked the plastic and he fell to the floor. Lifeblood flowed liberally from his newly made wound.

"You fucking idiot!" cried Jonah. "Didn't you remember that Creyton wasn't impressed by ambition? You *truly* didn't see that coming?"

For the first time in a long time, Jonah felt the painful buzz in the back of his skull. Clutching his head with a growl of pain, he heard cold, harsh words in his mind:

You will survive this, Rowe, because your death will come on my terms, and my terms exclusively. This will not end because of this traitor's ambition and hubris. See you soon.

Creyton vanished. Jonah stared at the space where he stood, stunned. Was he serious?

"Deceitful piece of shit!" Laban gasped out.

Jonah turned his way. Deluded fool. He thought he was so clever, had the perfect plan. A gamble.

And that gamble cost him.

But something Creyton said struck a chord in Jonah. Jonah's death would come on his terms.

He dropped next to Laban and grabbed his bloody shirt. "Laban, what is Creyton's endgame for Omega? How is this supposed to end? I know you know!"

Laban's watery eyes darted here and there. "Be-be-betrayed me. F-foo-foolproof plan, and he b-betrays *me?*"

"Laban, listen to me!" snapped Jonah. "What's Creyton going to do? What's his plan to end Omega?"

Between heaving gasps, Laban's eyes slid Jonah's way. Even now, they showed scorn. "You ... you we-were supposed to be my t-ticket—"

"Laban," said Jonah, "tell me Creyton's plan, and I promise you that he won't get away with this."

The scorn in Laban's eyes faded. Or maybe that was him fading. "The Final Destination. It's ... it's all that matters."

"What? What's that mean?"

A red bubble formed in Laban's mouth and burst. With a final wheeze, his head turned to the side, and he was gone.

19

TRUTH AND CONSEQUENCES

Jonah didn't know what to do about anything.

All he knew was that he was in a very shitty position at that moment.

He was in an inescapable house, which had only been penetrated by Creyton's weapon. The one that pierced both the window and Laban.

Jonah knew what had happened. He'd witnessed it.

But what truly happened and what it had looked like were two different things.

He remembered when Doug was discovered with the blood of Gamaliel Kaine all over himself, which resulted in the entirety of Sanctum Arcist believing he was a murderer. He'd have done anything necessary to prove Doug's innocence but, at the same time, didn't envy his position.

Fast forward to now. He was in the exact same position.

He stood and attempted to push Laban's physically lifeless body to the back of his mind. He tried the door again, didn't budge ... until someone saw his movements and approached the front door. The door instantly relented and yielded to his grasp.

"Ain't this a bitch," muttered Jonah in alarm. "*Now* you open? When someone is coming?"

As the person got nearer, Jonah swore aloud. It was the absolute last person that he wanted to see right now. Even with a bloody nose, blackened eyes, and two teeth missing, he was easily recognizable.

Mr. Harrington.

He pushed through Laban's front door. His eyes were on Laban's body within a nanosecond. He then looked at Jonah, with blind rage all over his battered face.

"Harrington, you don't understand," said Jonah, immediately on the defensive. "I didn't do this. If you look at the window—"

"Murderer!" Harrington roared, having not registered a single word. "You!"

Harrington lunged for Jonah, and Jonah easily backed out of the way. Before the man had even fully regained his balance, he was back on Jonah, attempting to grab his throat.

"Heartless ... murderous ... beast—"

"Get ... off ... me," gasped Jonah, "you don't understand—"

The man wouldn't listen to reason. He had one goal only and it was to throttle Jonah. Once Jonah realized that, the next part was easy.

He grabbed the man's wrist and twisted, then knocked him back. Harrington landed on his back rather hard. Jonah couldn't have cared less.

"I told you to get off of me," he rasped. "If you would pull your head out of your ass, maybe I could explain things!"

"I don't want to hear anything from you! You killed L.C.! You brought Creyton and his Deadfallen to our home!"

"Goddamn it, shut up!" Jonah snarled. "Look!"

He jabbed his index finger at Laban's wall. Creyton's

metallic nail was still visible there. Still dripped with Laban's blood.

"*That* is what killed him! Not me! Creyton stood in the front yard and shot that nail thing from his crow staff! It came through the window right there."

Jonah pointed at the hole in the glass.

Harrington looked at the evidence right in his face and, try as he might, he couldn't dispute it. Jonah had proof of that part, anyway. The bloody man changed tack.

"What were you doing in this house then? Why didn't Creyton kill you, too?"

Jonah headed for the door. "Fuck you, man. I have to find my friends."

He left a seething Harrington on the floor and walked into Laban's yard.

Chaos reigned across the entire town. Jonah counted twenty-two fires, and those were the ones that he bothered to count. But the fire at the health spa sent a shock wave of fear through him. Abner had been swimming when all this had begun. He wouldn't have heard the screams or explosions.

Oh, shit ...

He tore off for the place, trying hard to compartmentalize his worry for Terrence and Reena. When he reached the spa, he noticed that half the roof was caved in. The fire there seemed to be spreading somewhat. But Jonah worked his way through the ruined door anyway.

He searched here and there, frustration and fear building in him. It wasn't as if he could shout out to Abner, after all.

Then he reached the pool area, which was located just underneath where the roof had caved in. A chunk of it had fallen into the pool.

Abner was pinned beneath it, eyes closed.

"*No!*"

Jonah jumped into the dirty, debris-laden water and conjured ethereal mist to cover his hands, thereby augmenting his strength. He hauled the roof debris off Abner, and drug him out of the pool. He was still non-responsive.

"No," gasped Jonah as he frantically began CPR. "Come back, man. I need you to come back ..."

He performed rescue breaths, and then began chest compressions. A part of him wanted to remain frantic, but he also remained considerate. Though durable, Abner was an older man. The last thing Jonah wanted was to fracture his ribcage ...

"Come on, man," cried Jonah. "You've got more to do!"

Then, after what seemed like ten lifetimes, Abner frowned and spat out water. Jonah backed away, relieved, but barely. He still didn't know where Terrence and Reena were.

Abner gagged for several seconds, and then regarded Jonah with gratitude.

You doing alright, sir? he signed. *"That stone block didn't break anything, did it?"*

Don't think so, Abner slowly signed back. *Do you know what happened? Was it an earthquake?*

Jonah grimaced. *No. Something much worse. But we have to get to Big Top Road. I need to find Terrence and Reena.*

He helped Abner to his feet, and they left the destroyed spa. Abner was still barefoot and in his swim shorts. Jonah contemplated telling him to at least put on his shoes, but they didn't have time for that.

He and Abner ran the entire way. Fear mounted higher and higher for Jonah as each passing step revealed more destroyed structures, overturned cars, and bodies...

"Jonah! Help me! Please!"

Jonah's head shot in that direction. It was Josephine. She was pinned underneath broken boards, which covered her torso and legs. He ran to her without hesitation, manipulating the winds as he went.

"Josephine, whatever you do, do not move."

He continued focusing on the winds until they became mildly visible. He then used them to move heavier debris, while Abner moved the lighter ones. Finally, he reached the biggest piece, the one that had Josephine pinned down. He used the winds to lift it to a reasonable height and Abner, quick on the uptake, pushed it away. Josephine attempted to move and yelped when she moved her left leg. It was broken. She needed further medical attention. But Jonah needed to find Terrence and Reena.

Still, there was no way in hell he could leave Josephine there.

"Josephine, I won't abandon you. But ... but I'm afraid to pick you up. It might screw with your leg—"

Abner whacked him on the shoulder. Jonah turned his way.

Use your wind ethereality, he suggested. *Lift her up to your arms.*

"Huh." Abner must have read his lips while he was explaining things to Josephine. "That's not a bad idea at all."

Jonah intensified his focus, and Josephine began to rise to him, as though through levitation. When she was about waist height, Jonah caught her up in his arms.

"Thank you," Josephine sobbed. "I couldn't stay here. I couldn't. I've never seen bodies before."

"Stay calm." Jonah wasn't even sure that he could do that himself. "We need to get to Big Top Road."

As Jonah had Josephine in his arms, he couldn't jog anymore. He looked at Abner and jerked his head, giving him free reign to head on without them. But Abner affixed a steely gaze on Jonah, and didn't move a muscle. Jonah shrugged but appreciated the gesture nonetheless. Abner walked at Jonah's side, looking neither impatient nor frustrated.

"Josephine, when we get to where we're going, I'm going to have to set you down somewhere. Please don't think bad of me, but—"

"I understand," said Josephine. "The fact that you've done this much for me means a lot. I'm worried about Haniel, too."

When they finally reached Big Top Road, Jonah's heart fell.

Carnage. That was what Creyton and the Deadfallen disciples left in their wake.

The dinner setting that Jonah had ignored earlier was now a disaster area. Broken chairs, overturned tables, food debris, decorations, blood ... they littered the entire road.

Then, there were more bodies. Abner looked around in horror, and Jonah noticed the bodies a few seconds before Josephine, who blanched.

"Oh, Jesus." She gasped and burying her face in Jonah's chest.

Jonah walked her to an upright chair that had somehow survived the hell, and carefully sat her down. "Pick a point and focus on it, Josephine," he instructed her. "Focus on it like it's the only thing that matters in this world. Don't let your eyes wander. I'll be back, I swear on my physical life."

He turned from the poor girl, finally able to pay attention to things, like the few people who stirred or moved around. A movement caught his eyes and he saw Terrence lifting a huge slab of concrete, which allowed a bunch of children to exit from some underground stairs.

"Terrence!"

He saw his brother's body relax somewhat. "Jonah! I'd greet you properly, but, as you can see—"

"Understood. What happened to you? When did Creyton and all of them show up?"

"I didn't even try to fight too much, man," responded Terrence. "I was just trying to round up the kids and get them to safety. Bastards didn't care who was in their way; they were just destroying, laughing, killing ... causing chaos was all they cared about."

Jonah gritted his teeth. "So, what's the story with this platform? Where's Reena?"

"A bunch of people thought they could go down into this storm shelter and just ride out the siege. Damn Deadfallen disciples decided to level the café next door to it, and half of the place fell on top of the door and trapped them all. Luckily, Reena read their essences. God only knows when we might have found them otherwise. I got an endowment—good thing not all the spirits and spiritesses fled Creyton and his pack of fools—and lifted most of the stuff off the door. This big one here was the last piece, and all I can do is hold it up. Can't push it to the side. "Now, they're getting the people out."

"They?" asked Jonah.

"Reena and Haniel," said Terrence.

"Oh, right. Let me give you a hand with that, man."

He manipulated the wind once more, which elevated the other end of the slab. The action allowed Terrence to push it away entirely. Abner moved away from them, checking on people who stirred and moved around here and there on the ground. Some distance away, Jonah saw Horace helping Maurice to his feet. His husband's foot stuck out at an odd angle, but other than that, he looked more or less whole.

Now free of his burden, Terrence grimaced. "I wish that everybody had made it to the shelter. Like I said, some people got killed outright. Once Creyton and the Deadfallen disciples left, Kim and Shade showed up from somewhere—they weren't even hurt."

"That's because they were smoking weed and screwing up

at the overlook. Their being idiot kids actually saved their physical lives."

Terrence shook his head. "And Josephine ran off to try to round up whoever might have been left out there. I don't know where she went."

"She's over there." Jonah pointed. "She's got a broken leg but seeing all this has really messed her up. I saw a bunch of other people who ... who didn't ..."

Jonah didn't finish, preferring to allow himself to be distracted by the people walking up out of the storm shelter, the entrance of which was now completely unencumbered. Reena led a group, closely followed by Haniel, who carried a child on each arm and one on her back. Jonah frowned.

"Somebody's been eating her spinach," he observed.

"Not quite." Despite the situation, Terrence snorted. "She's piggybacking off my endowment. You know my ethereality can make me stronger."

"Oh, right."

Reena saw them and hurried over.

"Thank God," she said when she reached Jonah. "We didn't know what happened to you. Jonah, we didn't see Laban out here when all hell broke loose—"

"He's in Spirit," grunted Jonah. "I wanted us to all be together before I said anything. I went to that house of his and it turned out to be a trap. He wanted to have me there, so he could alert Creyton of my whereabouts. His plan was to set me up and turn me over to Creyton. He thought that Creyton would honor his word of immunity. He actually tried to play Creyton. Creyton shot him down with that crow staff. Literally."

Terrence and Reena looked stunned. Jonah couldn't blame them. How were any of them supposed to feel? Laban had been a thorn in their side for a good little while, and now he was gone. Game over.

But it wasn't quite that.

"Terrence, Reena, there is more. Creyton let me live. I couldn't believe it, but then he said via a Mindscope, *your death will come on my terms, and my terms exclusively.* Those were his exact words. I guess his ego wouldn't allow him to take advantage of a trap that Laban set. Anyway, before Laban passed into Spirit, I asked him what Creyton meant by that. And he told me—"

"Grab that man," said Harrington in a cold voice.

Before Jonah could turn, some extremely strong arms seized him.

"Watch his hands," warned Harrington. "He enjoys shock treatment."

"What the hell is this?" snarled Jonah.

Harrington walked around to face Jonah. "You were found, by me, no less, in the home of—and next to the body of—one of my friends. Not to mention that my town was besieged by Creyton and his followers while you were conveniently in said house. Then you assault me, and simply walk out of the front door? Surely, you didn't believe that I would let any of that stand?"

"What the—?" began Reena viciously as she abandoned an injured person to assist Jonah. Unfortunately, she was blocked by another man.

"Stay back," he murmured. "This isn't about you."

Before Reena could react, no doubt violently, Terrence was at her side, eyeing the man intently.

"Leary, look around, dude. With all that has happened, do we need any more violence?"

The man looked around at the evidence of the massacre

that had occurred, shook his head with sadness, and backed off. His eyes remained on Reena.

"You're lucky, woman," he told her.

"He didn't do that for *my* sake, Leary. He did that for yours."

"She's right, bro," agreed Terrence.

It took Jonah that long to refocus his ethereality up through his arms to the places where the men held him. Nothing extreme, just pin pricks. The men immediately released him and when they tried to return, he raised his hands to bar their path.

"We're fine," he told them. "It's not necessary to hold me. But if you come at me again, the pain will be worse." He looked at Harrington. "We can get all this bad blood out, but before we do, I have to do something. I swore that I would, and I keep my word."

He walked away from them and returned to Josephine. Through all of this, the girl hadn't moved.

"Please don't tell me it will be okay." Her voice was dead. Hollow. "I—I can't reconcile all this stuff I've seen. I've been over here trying. And ... I just can't."

Jonah knelt in front of her. "Josephine," he said in a voice much calmer than the one he'd had with Harrington, "look into my eyes."

She did so and Jonah could see, and sense, that she wasn't lying. She was holding it together by fibers, maybe even less. There was an undiluted horror, a silent scream in her eyes. And it took every iota of her being to control it. She was not succeeding.

Christ, she reminded him of Vera when she'd first found out about the ethereal world. She thought she lived in a bad dream, but he'd successfully convinced her otherwise ...

He filed those thoughts away. *Task at hand, Jonah.*

He focused his mind, concentrating entirely on balance and centering on the erratic state in Josephine's consciousness. His fingers began to gleam blue as the craziness in her mind dulled. All the while, the horror in her eyes dwindled. After several more moments, he released her hands, and regarded her.

"Better?"

Josephine blinked. "Yeah." She seemed surprised at how she felt. "What did you do? Did you take the pain away, or something?"

"I'm not that powerful," replied Jonah. "I can't erase the crap that you just experienced. I just ... helped you reclaim your grip. Made it bearable."

The gratitude in Josephine's expression was absolute. "You're awesome, Jonah."

Jonah let that pass and he carefully lifted Josephine in his arms once more. He brought her to Haniel. The gathered crowd, who'd watched their entire exchange, regarded Jonah with surprise and confusion. Even Harrington looked awkward. Jonah saw the reactions and met them with a scowl.

"Yeah," he sneered. "That wasn't the behavior of a selfish, opportunistic asshole, was it? But I'm not surprised that I just shocked you all. I have no intention of being rude by saying this, but all of your eyes have been glued shut for a while now. There are some things you need to know. I'll talk, you listen." Jonah took a deep breath. As wronged as he felt, tearing asunder people's illusions was a tough and tricky business. "The man that you knew as L.C. Pilcher was actually named Laban Cooper. For many years, he was one of Creyton's most trusted Deadfallen disciples."

The remaining Spirit Land residents look at each other in disbelief. Jonah went on.

"He had a falling out with Creyton, due to a bold move on

his part to try to convince Creyton that he wasn't expendable. Further details aren't important. When Creyton sent disciples to kill him, he used the *Astralimes* to the Median and turned himself in. He spent a bunch of years on The Plane with No Name, hiding from Creyton's wrath.

"Last summer, Jonathan pulled some strings, and got Laban off the Plane, so as to obtain information on Creyton after he decided to proceed with Omega. I will spare you the details of the mind games that he put everyone through, especially me, but he escaped months later."

"You're leaving something out," said Harrington. "You failed to mention that he escaped after you got Jonathan vanquished."

Jonah employed the diaphragmatic breathing that Felix taught him. It was still very beneficial. "I did *not* get Jonathan vanquished. Despite being unendowed, I was trying to protect Jonathan that night. When the War Haunt came through the twig portal, I tried to defend Jonathan, but he put a protection over me, and threw the Vitasphera my way. It knocked me out of the window. There was nothing I could do for him."

Now, people were even more confused. Clearly, that wasn't the way they'd heard it. Laban must have spun the worst tale imaginable.

"You're lying." Harrington still looked determined to throw Jonah under the bus. "L.C. always said that you had a way with words—"

"Yeah," interrupted Jonah, "and *Laban* probably also said that those phylacteries were meant to be a blessing. That was a lie."

He pulled the one that Laban had had out of his pocket, regarding it the way one might regard feces on the bottom of their shoe.

"They were a trap," he revealed to them. "Laban made the

crystal with the same kind of inverted scuting that the Dead-fallen disciples' code words have. It enabled him to sap all the spirits and spiritesses' essences when Creyton and his fools showed up. Didn't you wonder why you didn't have access to spiritual endowments when all hell broke loose? The only spirits that were safe were the ones who didn't participate in the phylactery share. I got a spiritual endowment from one prior to the party, as did Terrence and Reena."

Nobody had anything to say. Some people looked at their empty crystals in doubt. Rather timidly, Haniel spoke up.

"If he sapped spirits and spiritesses' essences to that crystal you're holding, are they still in there now?"

Once again, Jonah was disgusted, but not with Haniel. "Creyton usurped them the second he sensed them. I watched the crystal's luster dull to nothing while I was trapped in Laban's house."

"Explain *that!*" snapped Harrington. "Explain how you came to be there, with his lifeless body!"

"I'd be happy to, if you'd shut up," Jonah threw back at him. "During your Thanksgiving dinner, I was circling the block so as to make sure that nothing suspicious occurred."

"Same," said Reena.

Jonah waved a hand at her. "Reena, I'm the one they hate. All this heat is on me—"

"Shut up, Jonah. That's not the way this is going to work." Reena turned to the crowd. "Jonah was doing one circuit and I was doing another."

Jonah closed his eyes. If nothing else, Reena would always be who she was. Unswervingly loyal to her family. "Yeah," he conceded. "That's right. The minute that I realized that Laban wasn't out there with you all, I went to check out his cottage. I ran into Kim, and she was kind enough to point me in the right direction."

Kim's eyes widened. Jonah ignored her and continued.

"I went to the cottage, only to find out what he was planning. He trapped me in there with ethereality that I've never encountered before, and therefore cannot explain. He told me to my face that he didn't give a damn about Spirit Land, or anyone here. He made Jackson sick with ethereal plague, and then cured him, just so you all would trust him. He gave you those phylacteries, helped with zone defenses ... all traps. He was waiting for us to show up, which is why he turned you all against me, made sure that you didn't trust me.

"He trapped me in his house to make it look like I had something to do with the deadfall. He betrayed you, tried to wrap it around my neck, all to take advantage of Creyton's immunity. He failed. Creyton killed him the minute he saw him, and then told me, and I quote, 'You will survive this because your death will come on my terms'. I asked Laban what that meant before he passed into Spirit. His last words included something about a place he called The Final Destination. He said that it was all that matters."

Terrence and Reena looked at him in awe. A great deal of what he'd just said was as much a revelation to them as it was to everyone else. Harrington was speechless. He walked a little ways away from the crowd and cast somber eyes across the extensive damage Creyton had caused to Spirit Land. It was in that moment that Jonah took a measure of pity on him. He'd put his heart and soul into running the town, and it'd been ransacked. Then again, he was blind and dumb enough to believe everything that Laban fed him.

Oh, complexities.

"With all that has happened," Harrington whispered at last, "there can be no question at all that this all boils down,"—he turned his face back to Jonah, and Jonah saw that the solemness had turned to rage—"to *you*."

"Say what?"

"This is all your fault, Rowe! You are the one who wrought this hell on us!"

"How in the hell can you say that?" demanded Jonah. "It was Laban! Did you hear a word I just said? *He* brought Creyton here! He was the one who played you, played us all—"

"In some asinine scheme to get to *you!* He came here, knowing Jonathan would have illuminated the way for you! We were all pawns in an evil scheme, but all of it wouldn't have come to fruition had you never shown your face here!"

"*Are you fucking crazy?*" shouted Jonah. "Are you truly deluded enough to believe that if we had never shown up, Laban would have just sat here, drinking sweet tea and fizzy lemonades, while you created ethereal sweaters on your front porches?"

"You watch it, Rowe," said Leary coldly. "We are not now, nor have we ever been, stupid little yokels."

"I never said you were! Not once! Laban took advantage of you, very easily! That did not translate to you being stupid, it expanded upon the fact that he was evil! *He* was the one, not me!"

"We can't be faulted for being unaware of his duplicity," said a woman desperately. "We have essence readers, but none as powerful as Reena—"

"That is my point!" snapped Jonah. "You didn't realize that he was evil because you didn't have access to a powerful enough essence reader? Seriously? What about intuition? What about that prickle on the back of your neck when something isn't right? A perfect example of that is Haniel. She heard every lie that Laban said about me, just like the rest of you. Upon meeting me, however, she acknowledged that none of it matched up! Simple, old-fashioned discretion! Spirit Land is too dependent on ethereality, and too dependent on powers. Because of that, you missed vital clues!"

Harrington came closer to Jonah. If he expected Jonah to back down, it wouldn't happen in a million lifetimes. Jonah didn't give an inch. "You come into my town. I granted you haven. You brought all of your trouble to our doorstep ... all of your baggage. And now, you criticize our culture?"

"Now, you're twisting my words. Why am I not surprised? But you know what? It doesn't matter. The past doesn't matter because it can't be undone. We need to work together. Jonathan wanted us to find you guys for a reason. You have seen what Creyton and the Deadfallen disciples can do. You've seen the costly losses that can be sustained when you are caught unawares. If we can put these differences aside, Omega might have a much better ending for all of us."

At that second, Mayce came running up to them. It was in that moment that Jonah realized that he hadn't actually noticed that he hadn't been there. There was terror in the boy's eyes.

"Mr. Harrington, everybody, the Tool of Omega is gone."

There were cries of horror. The words even broke through Harrington's rage. Jonah looked at Terrence and Reena. He made eye contact with Haniel. The mere thought of Creyton having that thing terrified her; it was written all over her face.

Harrington's features hardened once more. "Creyton will never get it out of the Impossible Box."

"Impossible Box?" said Jonah, distracted.

"Charis Rayburn enclosed the Tool inside some kind of puzzle box," Haniel told him. "According to lore, not even having it under lock and key was enough for her. She entombed it in that box and took the knowledge of how to open it with her to the grave."

Jonah was unimpressed. "Creyton will get into that box. He'll nuke the damn thing if he has to."

"Not possible," said Jackson, breaking his silence for the first time. "No one but Charis Rayburn knew how to open that box, and she's been in Spirit for centuries."

"Not possible." Jonah gave the young man a look of pity. "I watched Creyton achieve Praeterletum and come back from the grave. My perspective of what is *not possible* is a little different from yours, kid."

Jackson looked disarmed. His father did not.

"This shows that, under no circumstances, can Blue Auras be trusted."

"Excuse me?" said Reena. "Now, you're putting the blame on Blue Auras? Your town was founded by a Blue Aura—"

"Who made an unwise decision in fashioning that Tool," interrupted Harrington. "Jonah, I have no choice but to terminate your haven and banish you. Get out of my town."

Jonah's eyes bulged. Several other people, including Haniel, Mayce, and Josephine, looked stunned as well. Abner must have read Harrington's lips, because he looked appalled.

"Nah man, that's not right. You can't make me go away. What about Jonathan's wishes?"

"Jonathan isn't here. He's in a place where he doesn't have to make hard choices anymore. I, on the other hand, still do. Leave."

"Harrington, listen. Sanctum. Here. My family at the estate. We can't function like little fiefdoms. Creyton will wipe us all off of the map. We have to be united—"

"And I do stand united," interrupted Harrington. "With my family, and my people. Some people are currently homeless, and we have to attend to them. We are rebuilding. We have work on top of work, on both physical and spiritual levels, to repair things here. And, most importantly, we have memorials to arrange. They will be simpler to achieve without your poisonous presence, Rowe. Terrence, Reena, you are welcome to remain. But Rowe, you must depart. Post haste."

"Mr. Harrington, this is wrong," said Josephine, who hadn't spoken in a long while. "Jonah isn't the man L.C., or Laban, or whoever he was, told us that he was. He just saved my sanity—"

"One good deed changes nothing," said Harrington, undeterred.

"And one stupid deed can change everything," countered Jonah. "You want me gone? Fuck it. Fine."

He straightened. Reena popped her neck muscles and stood by his side, eying Harrington with the gaze of Medusa.

"Harrington, if you think I'm abandoning my brother, you're just as stupid as you are stubborn."

Jonah was touched by the loyalty. Truly, he was. "Thanks, Reena. Let's get out of here. Terrence, ready to drive stick again?"

He turned, expecting Terrence to be where he always was. Frowning, he turned to see him next to Haniel and Mayce.

"What's up, man?"

Terrence had his eyes on his feet. "I can't go."

Jonah leaned forward. "Huh? What?"

Terrence slowly raised his head. "I can't go with you guys."

Jonah made to repeat his question, but there was no point. He heard what Terrence said. It wasn't like he hadn't heard him say it twice already. "Are ... are you joking?"

"He isn't joking, Jonah," Reena. "He's serious as suicide."

"You didn't have to read my essence, Reena." Irritation passed over Terrence's face. "I'd have told you that I meant it with my own mouth."

Jonah was incredulous. He couldn't believe this at all. "Why can't you come with us, exactly?" he asked slowly.

"Look around, Jonah," said Terrence. "Spirit Land needs help. They need all the hands they can get. Our fight got dumped in their lap. It'd be kinda foul to leave them hangin', don't you think?"

Jonah's mind couldn't compute this. It was so left-field he'd have said it was a dream, were it not live and in color. He flashed a look at Harrington.

"We, as in the three of us, need to converse in private. We'll go into the general store if you don't mind. Hell, we're going even if you *do* mind."

He turned his back before Harrington could give a disparaging remark, and the three of them walked into the store. All the aisles had been destroyed, all glass broken, surfaces overturned. Jonah barely noticed.

Terrence raised a hand before he or Reena could say anything.

"I know what you're gonna say. But my mind is made up. I'm helping these people. I know what it's like to be down to nothing, wondering if I'd have a place to rest my head. So many people out there are facing that at this very moment. I want to do what I can to ensure that that feeling is not indefinite for them."

"Terrence," said Reena in confusion, "what brought this on?"

"Don't know." Terrence shrugged. "I don't know, okay? Maybe it was the part about everyone relying on ethereality, and not their common sense. Maybe it was hearing Harrington say something about homelessness. You know that was me once. They are really facing an uphill battle right now, and I need to help them."

"Battle!" Jonah latched onto that word. "Remember that, Terrence? This big, damn war we've got? Omega? Ring a bell?"

Terrence looked Jonah in the eye. "Let me tell you something, Jonah. You're my brother. No doubt about that. But there is a disconnect."

"I beg your pardon?"

"The whole time we've been family," said Terrence with an infinitesimal trace of bitterness in his voice. "Everything we've done, everything we've been through. You two have always been here,"—he lifted his left hand—"and I've been here." He put his right hand numerous inches below the left. Jonah looked at the discrepancy, feeling scandalized. Reena looked stunned as well. Terrence spoke again.

"I ain't blaming either one of you for it. But that's how it's been. Jonah, you're the Blue one, the brave one, the crafty, resourceful writer. Reena, you're the smart one, the brave one, the painter/athlete with the sharp mind and the essence reading. Let's not forget the speed and the cold spots. Me? I'm the one who cooks, fixes cars, and the one whose strength ethereality is no different from about a thousand other Elevenths. How many times have I screwed up since we've been on the road? How many times have I been the low man on the totem pole, from an ethereal standpoint? Then we get here. Not once have I been dismissed, not once have I been shot down, not once have I been singled out, and not once have I felt like a weak link. It's been like a shot in the arm."

"A shot in the arm!" cried Jonah. "Terrence, are you in there? You can't just stay here and play savior to these people! What about your parents? Your brothers? Your estate family?"

Terrence looked at Jonah for a second. Two seconds. Three, Four, Five. Then—

"*Play* savior? You are the only one who can help people now, Jonah? Forgive me for not being able to balance people's minds, but we ain't all as perfect as you are—"

"*Perfect?*" roared Jonah, but Reena stopped him.

"Elevation of tone will send this way in the wrong direction, Jonah. Now, Terrence, listen to me, and answer me honestly. Those things you've just said? They were in your heart and mind already. Long before we got to Spirit Land. What else has been stewing in you?"

Terrence shook his head, seemingly frustrated. "This isn't about stewing, Reena! It's about making decisions for *me!* Terrence! All those folks you just named, Jonah? Ma? Dad? My brothers? The estate? I love 'em, and I will till my last day. But they are all making decisions for themselves. Now, I'm doing the same."

Terrence had made that particular point rather animatedly. When he moved to the side a bit as he spoke, Jonah caught a glimpse of Haniel beyond the storefront glass, which was, remarkably the only glass unbroken. She was trying very, very hard to keep emotion out of her face. But it was clear that she was glad Terrence wanted to stay. Jonah's eyes narrowed.

"Ah. That's it."

Terrence frowned. "What?"

"You know damn well what," said Jonah. "Really, Terrence? Has the old infatuation been snuffed out so easily, just to make room for the new one?"

Terrence looked genuinely confused, but then figured out what Jonah meant. Now he looked furious and jabbed a hand in his pocket, where Jonah knew his steel knuckles were. Wasting no time, he raised a baton, not even registering the blaze of blue that gleamed there.

Reena got between them so fast she almost created a breeze. Her eyes were blazing.

"Oh hell no. Down boys, *now.*"

Jonah wavered. Even Terrence's fury ebbed. Only Reena had that effect.

Terrence screwed up his face, as though he was shoving down his negative feelings. When he spoke, his voice was normal and calm.

"Look, I've made my choice, and I ain't changing it. But I

don't want there to be any bad blood. We're family. You two will be just fine without me, I'm sure of it. But I'm staying to help these folks get back on their feet. However long that takes. And no, Jonah, there is no ulterior motive. We're cool."

He extended his hand. Jonah contemplated it. Then he pocketed the baton and shook Terrence's hand. He chose not to say anything.

"Alright then," nodded Terrence. "See ya."

He backed out of the door. After a few seconds, Jonah and Reena stepped through the *Astralimes* and returned to the rest area where the entire Spirit Land saga had begun. Kimberly was there; she'd dropped off their bags. Jonah didn't question it. He just snatched his up and slung it over his back. When he noticed that Kim's eyes were still on him, he glared at her.

"What?"

Kim shook her head. "You didn't snitch on me. You could have sold me out to my father, but you didn't."

Jonah rolled his eyes. "I'm a lot of things, but a stool pigeon isn't one of them."

He turned his back on her and headed away. Reena fell in step with him.

"He and I aren't cool, Reena."

Reena sighed and picked up her bag more slowly. "I know, Jonah. I know."

20

CRITICAL MASS

Jonah and Reena were back in Henderson, back in the same motel they'd been in when the Spairitin Cousland directions had begun to make sense. They both wanted to put as much space between themselves and Spirit Land as possible, but they were so exhausted that a concession was made. Reena resumed her juice fast, and Jonah decided not to make waves about it.

After both their guts were full of smoothies, Jonah and Reena were both prone on the twin beds. Probably not the most advisable thing to do immediately after a smoothie, but things such as dietary guidelines were so far beside the point at that moment, it wasn't even funny.

After three hours of seemingly awkward silence, Jonah decided to attempt talking.

"Do you want to tal—?"

"No," was all Reena said. Jonah blinked.

"Oo-kay. Resuming silence now."

And the silence persisted.

And persisted some more.

That quiet night became a week, and another week, and

another week. Even running into some more opportunistic Eleventh Percenters didn't prompt Reena to speak. Three weeks and three towns later, she still hadn't said one word. The problem with silence, at least for Jonah, was that the absence of talking made way for lots of thinking. And, of course, it was about Terrence.

Once he started to move past his anger and borderline feelings of betrayal, he began to wonder whether he had any part in Terrence's choice to remain in Spirit Land. He wondered if that was selfish, making it partly about himself. He did not need his brother's permission or anything; he was a grown man. Hell, Terrence was even older than Jonah!

Nevertheless, the thing that seemed superimposed on his thoughts was what Terrence had said: *The whole time we've been family, with everything we've been through, you guys have been here, and I have been here.* Terrence said he didn't blame him and Reena for that distinction, yet Jonah couldn't help but wonder if he'd ever endorsed it in some way, without knowing. Problem was, the three of them had been through a whole hell of a lot over the years, so a mental audit of every situation just wasn't possible.

Then, there was Haniel Rainey.

Jonah didn't give a damn what Terrence said. Hell, it might have even been true for the most part, but his staying there had something to do with her. The crush just seemed strange to Jonah. Terrence's previous unrequited crush, Rheadne Cage, was the one Jonah could understand. She was gorgeous, adventurous, fearless, voluptuous, highly sexual ... you name it. For Terrence to go from having a crush on a badass woman like that to one who was a schoolteacher with a past as an acrobat and carny? Strange. However, those weren't the only thoughts the silence brought into focus.

Spirit Land was a complete and utter bust. The thing that

made it more infuriating was the fact that Jonah hadn't even had a fair shake. Laban had swooped in, planted all those lies in those people's heads about him, and they had no trouble taking root because of the citizen's misgivings about Blue Auras. When Jonathan left those directions for Reena to decipher, he had no idea. He hadn't planned on Laban screwing things up.

It made him so angry, wondering what alliances could have actually been forged had it not been for Laban. Who was killed by his own ego. Jonah didn't feel the least bit sorry for him. He made his bed. More accurately, he dug his grave.

Jonah and his family went to that damn place looking to grow. They'd left having not only lost that opportunity, they'd lost Terrence as well.

That was where Jonah's mind kept going. He couldn't help it. Terrence was beginning to seem more and more like a loss of Omega. Like Barisford Charles. Like Naphtali. Like Felix. Like so many others. He wondered what Jonathan would think if he could see the track record of the man he'd chosen to pass the torch to.

No.

The self-deprecating thoughts had to go. There were far more pressing things to occupy his mind.

Like Laban's last words: *The Final Destination ... it's all that matters.*

Something about those words stuck with Jonah. He simply couldn't let it go. He knew it meant something specific, and something was telling him that it should be obvious. Although his mind wasn't working properly due to Terrence's absence, an idea slowly crept into his consciousness. Crazy and dangerous? Yep, of course it was. Nevertheless, it might be something that would yield beneficial results, and take his mind off that Tool of Omega. He just had to figure out how to pitch it to Reena.

They were at an old motel in Beaufort County when he'd

gathered up enough courage to tell Reena his idea. If the past three weeks had taught him anything, it was that Reena was adamant about not wanting to talk. He hoped a proper spin would prevent her from blowing her stack.

"Reena, I've had an idea."

"Promise me I'll see you again," Reena said softly.

Jonah looked at her, puzzled. "Um, huh?"

"That's what Tempie said when our mom kicked me out," said Reena. "The whole thing was this: *I don't care if Mama says you're strange. I love you, Reena. Promise me I'll see you again.*"

Jonah didn't know what to say to that other than, "Oh."

Reena was still staring at the wall. "I didn't keep that promise, Jonah. And it wasn't my fault. My mom changed the numbers and moved. My dad went along with it. Kai and Myleah went along with it. But Tempie still loved me. And she was gone, out of my reach."

Jonah didn't know where this was going, but suddenly he had the urge to step back. Reena didn't notice.

"I've always been strong, Jonah. You don't go through the things I have and not get stronger. I pride myself on it. And, in turn, I've been strong for other people. The problem? The times I've been strong for others far outnumber the times people have been strong for me."

Jonah was at a loss. He truly was.

"Jonathan never treated me like a disturbance, or an abomination. He always treated me like one of the pack. Always. Now, he's gone. Kendall ... Jonah, you don't know what it's like to know you have the one who makes you whole. That one that makes everyone else second-best. You remember when you first came to the estate and asked to see my paintings, and I showed *The Impressionable Heart*?"

"Yeah, Reena, of course I do."

"Do you remember the fourth part?"

"Easily," Jonah replied. "That was the you that *you* wanted to be. Fit, athletic, and with the woman who was as sure of herself as you were."

Reena looked touched that Jonah remembered. "Kendall is it, Jonah. She makes me whole. And now, she's gone."

"Reena, Kendall isn't in Spirit, or anything. She's safe. She's in Tullamore— "

"I don't want her in Tullamore!" Reena bellowed. "I want her in my arms! I want to feel her, touch her, and kiss her! I don't want us to be scattered, with the need to move every few days because either Deadfallen or misguided ethereal humans want to hurt us! Jonah, I'm tired of this. I am. I want the danger to end, and I don't know when it will. I'm tired of being a target, and having people scatter and hide like bugs. And most of all, I am tired of people I care about, through extraneous circumstances, being away from me!"

With that, the unthinkable happened. Reena flung her arms around Jonah and wept uncontrollably.

Jonah didn't know Reena had all of this in her. Her wall was always pretty solid. He'd seen her on those nights that she missed Kendall, wiping a stray tear, but he thought that was it. Reena was too proud to lose herself to raw emotion.

She wasn't too proud now.

Jonah had nothing to say, but maybe Reena didn't need talking to. She just needed someone to be strong for her. He could do it. Whatever. It didn't change how he viewed Reena; whoever said the hardcore never needed their moments here and there?

"And don't you dare try to balance me, Jonah." Reena's voice was stern despite her emotion. "If I'm going to get through this, I have to let it all out, unencumbered. Didn't you just accuse the citizens of Spirit Land, and rightfully so, for relying too much on ethereality?"

Jonah snorted."That's the old Reena."

Reena snorted herself and then pulled away from him, completely serious. "Jonah, I want to go home."

He raised his eyebrows. "Y-you mean Rome?"

"Hell yes, I mean Rome."

"But Reena, that place is no man's land for us right now! You can't be serious about staying—"

"I don't mean staying," she interrupted. "I know all of our family are elsewhere. I know it's dangerous, but not if we plan it out properly. I just want to spend a day or two seeing old sights, and ... and just being back in Rome. I swear, Jonah, I only need one or two days. But if I don't have the chance to go back to where my life made sense, just for a little while, it will be bad."

Jonah let it sink in. Reena had reached critical mass, Terrence staying in Spirit Land had made him, Jonah, lose confidence and focus, not to mention the abysmal failure the trip had been. Would a brief return to Rome cure some ills? Or staunch the proverbial bleeding both he and Reena were experiencing, at the very least?

"Few days, Reena. Two, three days max," he insisted. "We can go right before the Auld Lang Syne parade. After that, we get back to trying to figure something out for Omega. That cool for you?"

Reena looked away for a few seconds, and then faced him again. "That's cool. I'm on board."

21

GHOSTS OF ROME

Jonah and Reena spent the next several days plotting and planning on how to navigate Rome and be subtle about it while doing so. Jonah managed to file Terrence's absence away—enough, anyway—and Reena had, as well.

Then again, Jonah wondered why he was lying to himself. He hadn't filed anything away. Terrence's absence was a gaping hole, and it hurt.

That hurt would just have to be prioritized at a later time.

They decided that the Auld Lang Syne Festival was a great time to blend in. It was traditionally held about a week and a half into the New Year, which the townsfolk looked upon as hilarious because it coincided with the end of most people's resolutions. It was a three-day event that included a pig-picking, a New Year's pageant, and culminated with a parade. People from major metropolitan areas might have thought that a population of six-thousand, eight-hundred and sixty-two people was small, but for what Jonah and Reena had planned, that amount of people was perfect.

Once they had their plan in place, complete with a Plan B

they didn't think they'd actually need, they put their minds back on the present. They were too mentally taxed to notice Christmas, but Jonah suggested that they spend the heaviest Christmas days—the 24th, 25th and the 26th—in the Outer Banks. So, they used the *Astralimes* to Coastal Shores. Most folks were out of town or visiting relatives for the holidays, and since it was the off-season, the hotel rates were excellent. Jonah didn't get Reena any presents, but she spent several mornings running along the beach. He felt like that alone time was the greatest gift she could have at that time.

Several days after Christmas, Jonah had an unexpected, and unwanted, dream about the last Christmas everyone had shared at the Grannison-Morris estate. Themis had awakened everyone to show off the guitar that she and Malcolm made for Nella. There was the great Christmas breakfast and dinner, both overseen by Terrence. There was the gift-giving. Jonah raked in a sweet haul that Christmas, which had ended in Vera returning his class ring to him ...

Jonah awoke instantly. With everything in him, he wanted to resent the feelings of yearning that he had for family and familiarity. But he didn't resent thinking about Vera.

As if entranced, he reached for his cell phone. He scrolled to her name and sent a simple, *Are you O.K.?*

Not even a minute later, he received a response.

Fine. Hoping you are.

Jonah grinned. The brief moment of relief was welcome.

But it was time to get moving.

The day before he and Reena were set to go to Rome, they went to grab something to throw in the blender when they passed a vehicle at the community center.

A very familiar vehicle ...

Jonah tapped Reena's arm. "Reena," he said quietly, "doesn't that look like the mobile bunker?"

She inspected the SUV and her eyes widened. "It *is*. Of all the towns in the world, why is Felix here?"

Jonah threw his hood on his head, thankful that his beard had grown out once more. "Only one way to find out."

Reena undid her hair tie, which allowed her black and scarlet hair to fall and obscure her face. They walked inside the place.

It was a group of people sitting stadium style, facing a podium. Jonah and Reena tucked themselves in the back, wondering what this was all about. As luck would have it, Felix was the first one at the podium.

He looked a bit downtrodden and was attired in a denim jacket and baseball cap. He'd let his beard grow out as well, but he didn't look scruffy or like a bum. He also didn't have that wild, feral look in his eyes that he'd had a few months ago. He seemed calmer, humbler. He gripped the podium, took a deep breath, and spoke.

"My name is Felix Betran Duscere, and I am an alcoholic."

"Hi, Felix," all the occupants responded.

"Three-thousand, two-hundred and eighty-five," he said after a sigh. "That was the number of days I had before I made a conscious choice to wash them away in bottles of Distinguished Vintage and vodka."

Some people nodded slowly. Some people's mouths twisted, as though they could relate. Felix shook his head.

"I kept a bottle with me for nine years," he confessed. "Hadn't cracked the seal or anything, but still ... I thought I had it figured out. Thought I was so clever. I had gotten it in my mind that if I carried it around with me, I would always have a reminder of why I got sober. I was wrong. Why? Because my resolve was broken, due to being haunted by ghosts."

Many people looked around, befuddled. Jonah and Reena

looked at each other. Her apprehension mirrored his own. What was Felix about to say?

"Yeah," said Felix, unperturbed. "I said haunted by ghosts. We're all haunted by ghosts, especially us addicts. My ghosts are guilt, loss, regret, and grief."

There was an almost collective sigh of relief and understanding. Jonah smiled with relief himself. Felix used one truth to touch another. As a writer, Jonah had done that many times.

"There are ghosts all over the place. Those particular ones are mine. I thought that when I got sober, the ghosts would stop haunting me. The minute that I lost sight of that, I picked up the bottle again. Although I blamed those ghosts, I made the choice to drink again. All the reasons that I made that choice became irrelevant against every friend, ally, and confidante that I betrayed. Three of those friends discovered that I was drinking again. Seeing the look in their eyes ... man, it felt like I had just shouted from the highest mountain that I had broken every promise that I'd made."

A woman seated near Jonah shook her head. "He's telling my story," she murmured. "He's telling my story."

"They threw me out of my own place." Felix chuckled derisively. "And I deserved it. What did I do to try to get their forgiveness? I tried to bribe them."

There were incredulous laughs. Felix joined in, very briefly. But then he was serious once more.

"One of them said that he didn't know who I was anymore. And it pissed me off at first, but then I had to wonder about the answer. Who am I? I didn't know the answer to that then, and I am still trying to figure it out now. Maybe that's yet another thing that I'll have to figure out, one day at a time."

With a half-shrug, he left the podium. People patted him on the back as another speaker took the podium. Jonah and

Reena rose, careful to not bring attention to themselves, or their exit. Once they were out, Reena chuckled to herself.

"Who would have thought, Jonah?"

Jonah was mystified. "I'm glad he's holding himself accountable. I'm also glad that we didn't take that money. But why is he attending meetings in North Carolina? He's loaded. He could have gone to one of those upper echelon clinics in Malibu or someplace."

"Jonah, Felix has never thrown his money around like that. He wasn't likely to do that, even for AA meetings."

Jonah nodded. "Point."

"Do you think he'll be ready to help us with Omega?" asked Reena.

"Don't know. But that's completely fine. So long as he is getting himself back together."

Reena nodded. "Well, Rome's tomorrow. Are you ready for that?"

Jonah looked down the quiet beach street, turning the question over in his mind. "As ready as I'll ever be," he replied.

* * *

The next day, Jonah and Reena used the *Astralimes* to Rome at 6:00 P.M. Jonah knew that the pig-picking was near its end. He wondered how the barbecue was that year. One bite of it and Terrence could have told him who made it, what they put in the slaw, how the meat had been prepared, and how long it had cooked.

But Terrence wasn't here.

They hadn't seen or heard anything from him for almost forty days.

Jonah filed that away. Task at hand.

"Reena, I think the Meadow Road Inn would be a decent

place to crash while we're in this area. It's out of the way, quaint, but always clean, and real cheap."

Reena nodded. "Sounds good. Have you ever stayed there? You know that from experience?"

"Sure do. It's where ... it's where I spent a little time hiding out when Trip wanted my head for supposedly putting you in the infirmary after that whole tainted dampener drama."

Reena had on that very dampener at the moment and wasn't able to read his essence. Still, her eyes narrowed. "Jonah, I already told you back in Spirit Land that I didn't need ethereality to read people. Terrence. That's his name. After all these years, he won't be relegated to a nameless citizen."

Jonah shrugged. "Okay, fine. It was the motel that *Terrence* took us to when the dampener mishap occurred. Bast was there, too."

Reena looked slightly wistful but remained composed. "Meadow Road Inn. I'm cool with that. Now, I'm off to get a look at my old colleagues; see how they're doing. Meet you back here in an hour?"

"Yep," said Jonah. "You know I'm doing the same."

They parted. It was another thing they'd agreed on. Since they couldn't check on their scattered friends, they'd compromise by checking on the Tenth friends they had. Before they'd left Rome, they'd placed ethereality zone protections over as many neighborhoods as they could. They could only do so many; too much ethereality on their parts would have alerted the wrong parties. So, one of the first people he checked on was Mrs. Ernestine, his former colleague at the library, who had retired. She lived in one of the neighborhoods that didn't get zone protection.

Her home was in Historic Rome. Jonah went into Spectral Sight and saw a low spirit and spiritess count. It stirred feelings or irritation within him, but he focused on his friend. She had a big family, and not all of them had left from the holiday visits yet. Jonah kept his distance, not wanting to look creepy or anything, but looked in her window. She was washing dishes with one of her sons while her husband put away leftovers. She looked happy, serene, and content ... all the things that her retired life should be. And no one had screwed with her. So much the better. Jonah smiled.

"Looks good here," he said quietly. "Keep up the awesomeness, Mrs. Ernestine."

He walked to the start of the tree-lined street and looked both ways, as though traffic might be en route. He then knelt, murmured the words he'd learned from Daniel, and put a zone protection over her neighborhood. It didn't matter to him if there were consequences. The Curiae were the ones who wanted to be butt-hurt over them using excessive ethereality. But the Curaie lay in ruins at the moment.

Therefore, his friend got protection.

He checked on some of his other colleagues from the library, even Paula, the judgmental bitch. All of them were fine. He checked on Lola's house. As she was in the United Kingdom now, she didn't live there anymore, but he checked on the new people, anyway. They weren't in when he passed through but given the state of the house and the garden, they were alright as well.

He was about to return to his and Reena's rendezvous point when Reena found him. She looked irritated and tense.

"Reena, what's wrong?" he asked.

"I was checking on my former supervisor on the other end of town."

"What about him?" inquired Jonah, worried. "Is he alright?"

"*He's* fine," said Reena, "but his first cousin in Pearce, the next town over ..."

Her voice trailed off. Jonah filled in the blanks.

"Oh, no," he murmured. "How did you find out?"

"They were talking about it," said Reena. "His whole family, a household of six. Gone. They said that the sheriff's department and coroner were at their wit's end. All they could figure was that it looked like their insides had been cut, even though they had no visible wounds."

Jonah closed his eyes. "Bloodless Severs. The Deadfallen disciples slaughtered an entire family, just because?"

Reena nodded. "Motherfuckers. You *know* the only reason they did it was for their fun. And his cousin and his family ... I've met them all before. Christmas parties and what have you. Good people, all of them. Just gone."

Jonah inhaled slowly. His heart went out for those people, even though he didn't know them. The *shit* that Creyton and his pack of dogs were doing to innocent people ... "I want to use the *Astralimes* to Katarina's house."

Reena's eyes widened slightly. "You think she is next?"

"*Anyone* could be next. But innocent people getting killed —it just made me think about Phoebe, her successor. What they did to her. Man, I read Patience's report. I still have dreams about it. Let's check her out, and then we can hunker down for the night. Pageant is tomorrow and I've got no interest in that. The parade is the last night. I haven't missed that for the past several years; I ain't about to now."

Reena nodded and they used the *Astralimes* to Katarina's home, about three hours away. They hid behind a collection of trees. The second they did, Reena made a sound of approval. Jonah looked her way.

"What?"

"Katarina has laced this place with ethereal security. I can feel the resonance of it. Almost seems like no one short of God herself is getting in there."

Jonah raised an eyebrow. "Reena, you just said God *herself*."

"I know what I said."

Jonah snorted, deciding not to push the issue. "And look. Doug's car is there. It's got to be him; Katarina doesn't drive."

"Did you think that he'd be anywhere else?"

"I take it that Doug probably doesn't spend much time at his grandmother's house anymore," said Jonah.

"Not any more than he has to. Katarina is probably the freshest breath of air in his entire life. He told me once that growing up with two significantly older sisters was almost like having three mothers. Four, counting his grandmother. He probably finds Katarina so irresistible because he has finally met a woman that isn't an overbearing bully."

Jonah grinned. "Not to sound crude, but Doug never told us what it was like taking her virginity."

"That's because he didn't. Katarina took his."

"What? Are you serious?"

"Of course I'm serious, Jonah. Katarina started confiding in Liz, Magdalena, Maxine, and me once she started trusting us. She hasn't been a virgin for a while. She almost got married three years ago. But that guy was just a fucking idiot. Anyway, *she* made Doug a man. She told Liz and me that she might have started an addiction for him, but she was pleased with that."

Jonah blinked and looked at the house again. "Son of a bitch."

Reena punched him.

"Ouch! What the hell was that for?"

"For being a sexist ass, and assuming that the *man* is always the one who makes dreams come true."

Jonah's eyes narrowed. "You know, Reena? If you weren't a woman—"

"But I am, so your argument's immaterial."

They looked at each other, and then laughed aloud. That was refreshing as hell.

"Let's get out of here before someone hears us and calls the Tenth police," he said after a few minutes. I'm looking forward to the parade tomorrow."

* * *

Jonah spent the next morning writing while Reena sketched. The idea in his head was like money burning a hole in one's pocket, but he'd made Reena a promise that the larger task would be resumed after they'd left Rome, and not a second sooner. He got details concerning his idea out of his head and onto a bunch of flash cards, but didn't bring anything up. Yet.

That night was the final night of Auld Lang Syne Festival and held the final event, the parade. There'd been light snow flurries that morning, but nothing further than that. Jonah and Reena weren't concerned with being seen. Who'd pay attention to two random Rome citizens among the masses lined up on Main Street?

They used the *Astralimes* to a spot near the local mill. Although it was the middle of winter, the area still smelled of freshly cut cedar. That smell never got old to Jonah.

"Alright, Reena. We split up and enjoy the parade. End of the night, we'll meet up back here. When we do that, we'll figure out our next move. I have some ideas, but they can wait until after everything is done tonight."

Reena nodded once and clapped Jonah on the shoulder. "I greatly appreciate you going along with this, Jonah. And I also apologize for you seeing my damn meltdown the other night. I usually have a good handle on my walls, but –"

"Reena, don't even worry about it. It doesn't change how I view you at all. It just makes you human every once in a while."

Reena regarded him. "You think that I want to cry with every emotion?"

"Not at all," smiled Jonah, "but you got to let it out eventually. Crying here and there beats going postal."

"Oh, shut up," she smirked. "See ya."

"See ya."

The second that Jonah got away from Reena, he pulled out one of the king-sized Snickers bars he'd bought earlier. With those damn juice fasts, Jonah could swear that he'd lost fifteen pounds since they'd been traveling. This time, though? It was time for a treat.

Gnawing on one of the bars with relish, he began to walk through the crowds of people. With his hood on, people paid him no attention. On a winter evening such as this, attire like his didn't attract suspicion or scrutiny.

The parade started a few minutes after he'd found a decent enough spot to stand and, man, if it wasn't a hilarious sight. Some of the floats were admittedly tacky, but Jonah looked past that. It was all fun. He saw some other people he knew throughout the crowd. Like the owner of the Chuck Wagon. Whit Turvinton, who ran the bookstore at L.T.S.U. and Jonah's former supervisor was there with his wife and son. Then, with a mild jolt, Jonah saw an old face.

It was the man that Jonah saw in the town square on the same day that he'd discovered that he was an Eleventh Percenter. At the time, the man had just become a widower, and had three daughters to raise. Jonah had gone into Spectral Sight for the first time in his life and, among the other spirits and spiritesses, saw the man's wife near him, giving him loving words that he couldn't hear. The man's daughters were with him now, a bit older, with the youngest on his shoulders. Though he smiled, grinned at their jokes, and laughed when they did, he was still hurting. Jonah could sense it. He'd made gains, moved on with his life as best he could for his daughters' sake, if no one else's. However, it was clear that the man missed his wife. His best friend that was supposed to be next to him forever. Jonah's heart went out to him. He hadn't ever lost a spouse, but he knew what it was like to lose an anchor in his life.

It made Jonah think about his estate family, scattered all over the place. It was that—the scattering—that was one of the reasons why he had never been entirely on board with the exodus. How was he, the Overseer of the estate, supposed to do his job if everyone was all over the place, and he had no idea where? Overseer of the estate. Oh, there were plenty of people who'd debate that.

And, in this particular moment, he couldn't disagree with them. Especially after what had happened in Spirit Land. Convince people to join the cause? He couldn't even convince Terrence not to jump ship.

He buried his face in his hands. He found himself relating to Reena during her meltdown.

Suddenly, he tensed. A prickle of warning made his eyes fly open.

He was being watched.

Immediately, the logical part of his brain went into gear. How exactly was it possible to watch him? Nobody knew he was here, except for Reena. Besides that, he was in a crowd, with what seemed like the entire town of Rome, and he had on a *hood*.

So, how could he be singled out?

But then another part of his brain kicked in: all his points were valid points. Despite them all, though, he was still being watched.

He knew this feeling. It was a feeling that he'd come to trust back when he first learned that he was an Eleventh

Percenter. Hell, even the hairs on the back of his neck were standing.

Very slowly and inconspicuously, he detached himself from the crowd. Several minutes later, he was back on the train tracks, which had been closed for the parade. The feeling in Jonah was almost at fever pitch. But he still couldn't figure out who was watching him.

Then, plain as day—and despite the noises of the parade— there was a clear and audible sound.

"Jonah."

Jonah froze. It couldn't be. God in Heaven, it couldn't be. But he'd heard it.

He turned slowly around. His ears hadn't betrayed him.

Five feet in front of him and staring at him as intently as he always had, was Jonathan.

22

LIFE'S LITTLE IRONY

Jonah blinked.

But it made no difference.

He blinked a second time.

Jonathan was still there.

"Jonathan?" he whispered. "Is it really you?"

Jonathan smiled and nodded. "Indeed, son, it is I."

Jonah couldn't corral the barrage of emotions that he felt. He couldn't help it. There had been so many things left unsaid. So many things Jonah had never asked. He still held guilt about Jonathan being vanquished in his presence, although there wasn't anything in the world that he could have done about it. Jonathan had refused to endow him, which made *him* a more appealing target. He'd sacrificed himself for two reasons: to save Jonah and because of the knowledge that Francine Mott, the fiancée that he never got the chance to marry, was soon to pass into Spirit.

Despite those things, though, the spirit stood before him, piercing eyes, assuring smile—the whole nine yards.

"It's ... it's not possible."

"And yet, here I am, Jonah."

"But *you* said that once a spirit or spiritess crosses to the Other Side, they cannot return."

Jonathan smiled. "I said many things when I was confined to the Earthplane and the Astral Plane, Jonah. Yet, with all I knew at that time, I know even more now."

Jonah took a quick breath. "So, I take it that you won't be explaining to me how you're here?"

Jonathan shook his head, apologetic. "It's nothing that you could comprehend."

Admittedly, Jonah had a mild trace of suspicion about this. After those words, however, his suspicion faded. Jonah always spoke on what physically alive humans would and wouldn't understand. "Okay, sir. Why are you back? What's the deal?"

Jonathan squared himself. "We must speak, but not here. I'm certain that you don't want to appear as a crazy person, speaking to thin air."

With a frown, Jonah looked around. He'd almost forgotten that he was on the train tracks, away from everyone. Though the crowd remained highly focused on the parade, a few folks gave him questionable looks.

"Right, thanks for that, sir. Where did you have in mind? The estate?"

Jonathan shook his head. "No. I'll not undermine your exodus call. Wise decision, that. Come, I know of a place."

He turned and walked away. Jonah wondered whether he should follow, and hesitated. Should he tell Jonathan to wait and go find Reena? She, after all, had known Jonathan longer. When she'd had her meltdown, she'd mentioned losing Jonathan. She probably needed to see him more than even Jonah did himself.

As he was about to voice this, Jonathan looked back and spoke again.

"My link is with you, Jonah. No one can see me but you."

Jonah frowned. "How did you know what I was thinking?"

"I didn't. It was written on your face."

Jonah rolled his eyes. He *had* to work on that.

Jonathan started walking again. Jonah followed, but at a distance. He had to remain wary in Rome, but that had always been the plan. As such, he put his hood back on his head, just for good measure.

Jonathan led him away from the crowds, away from the tracks. They walked past shops and the local pharmacy. Past Ballowiness, Rome Elementary, the post office, and the duplex that was one-half taxidermy and one-half jewelry shop. Jonah jokingly thought that with all this walking, they'd soon be out of Rome.

That thought worried him a bit. He was quite a ways from the parade now, which meant he was a long way from Reena. They were supposed to rendezvous, but that was going to be a whole hell of a lot harder all the way out here. But Jonah had always trusted Jonathan. Surely, his counsel was important enough to warrant a delay with Reena?

Jonathan ceased walking at the old lumber mill. After a thorough inspection of the area, he turned around and faced Jonah.

"Now, I am assured that we will not be overheard. Now, Jonah, as I'm sure you figured out—if Reena hadn't already— that I left map coordinates to a dwelling comprised entirely of Eleventh Percenters, named Spirit Land. Did you find it?"

Jonah's mouth tightened. "Yes, sir, we did."

"Were you able to speak your piece and obtain backing for Omega?"

That old anger ran over Jonah like water. "Any chance of that happening was ruined by Laban, sir," he said rather ungraciously. "He found the place months before we did. He firmly embedded himself within their good graces and painted me as a villain. Don't make me give you the gory details. All you need to know is that Laban ruined the entire thing. I didn't have a chance."

Jonathan turned away, looking angry, but he composed himself as only he could. "What happened after that?"

Jonah was the one who looked away this time. Didn't he just tell Jonathan that he *wasn't* interested in giving the gory details? "Laban gave Spirit Land up to Creyton. It was all a stupid bid to get Creyton's immunity. He failed, big time. Creyton killed him the second he saw him, and then said that he would kill me on his own terms." Jonah was gripped with inspiration with those words. "Jonathan, before Laban passed into Spirit, I asked him what Creyton meant by his own terms. He said something about the Final Destination and that was all that mattered. Do you have any idea what that means?"

Jonathan didn't answer. It seemed like he was lost in thought. Jonah waited, eager for insight of any kind. Moments later though, he caught himself frowning. Jonathan looked to be pained, not pensive.

"Are you alright, sir?"

"What? Oh yes. Yes, of course." His features smoothed out and he squared his shoulders. "Now, Jonah, I must ask you: did you find out anything about the Tool of Omega?"

Jonah's eyes widened. What about the question that *he* had just asked Jonathan? "Not much. Creyton took it from Spirit Land. But I was told that he'd never be able to use it. It's supposedly in some impenetrable box, or something, and Charis Rayburn, the Blue Aura who created it, took the way to get into it ... with her into Spirit. But Jonathan—"

Jonah's voice ceased. Jonathan looked pained again.

"Jonathan, what's up?"

"Nothing," he insisted. "I assure you, I'm well. So, have you been holding up well since I've been gone?"

Jonah blinked. Random, much? "It's—I'm still standing, Jonathan. You wanted to save me. Plus, you're back with Miss Francine."

"Who?"

Instantly, alarms went off in Jonah's head. "Who *are* you?"

Jonathan looked confused. "What? I didn't hear you—"

"You heard."

Jonathan looked flabbergasted. Maybe even hurt. "Jonah, how could you ask that question? After everything that has happened?"

"I thought you didn't hear me," said Jonah shrewdly.

"That ..." Jonathan frowned. "I didn't say that because I didn't hear you. I said it out of disbelief. I would have never believed that you would doubt me."

"That's where you're wrong," said Jonah, who pulled out his batons. "I never doubted Jonathan. I am doubting *you*."

He pitched the blue-gleaming baton at Jonathan, thankful that he and Reena had taken spiritual endowments from two spiritesses before coming to Rome. The baton hit Jonathan square in the face, knocking him backward. Jonah used the wind to bring his baton back to him, but he barely noticed its return.

Because the apparition that rose to its feet wasn't Jonathan anymore.

It was a Phantasm.

The thing was a pitch-black shadow and had grown in height upon rising; it was now a foot and a half taller than Jonah. It didn't even waste time posturing. It picked up what was easily a hundred-pound piece of lumber and flung it at Jonah.

"*Whoa!*" Jonah threw himself out of the way, his eyes

darting wildly this way and that. The Phantasm's presence meant that a Deadfallen disciple was nearby, controlling it. But he couldn't actually put a lot of effort into looking for the disciple, as the Phantasm began to advance.

Jonah summoned wind ethereality to heave wood of his own, and though it slammed the Phantasm to the ground with enough force to spring up dust, it was unfazed as it had no physical body to injure. It wrested itself free from the wood and proceeded to charge at Jonah. Jonah threw his left baton with accuracy and hit the Phantasm in its chest. Blue current ran the length of the shadow's form, but the only thing that occurred was that shadow staggered backwards. It immediately regained its balance and advanced once more.

Swearing to himself, Jonah turned to run, and desperately looked around. Where the hell was that damn disciple? If he could find him, he could end this.

But the bastard was hidden very well.

Jonah found a hiding place and paused to regroup. But before he could even think, he saw the Phantasm standing ten feet away. He tensed, not knowing what to do, but his batons were ready.

But something was odd.

The Phantasm simply stood there. It didn't come forward; it just stood, stock-still. Jonah was absolutely bewildered, idly noting a crack or snap somewhere—

"Jonah!"

Jonah was tackled from behind, none too gently. A platform of lumber, glass, and steel crashed to the ground where he'd been standing not seconds before. Jonah had been herded into a trap.

But someone had pushed him out of the way.

Who was his savior?

"Come on, man, get up. Time's something we don't have right now."

Jonah's eyes bulged. *"Terrence?"*

"Yeah, it's me! But we can talk later!"

Jonah refocused on the situation and nodded sharply. "We need to find the Deadfallen disciple who is the puppeteer for the Phantasm—"

"No need!" Terrence picked up a large piece of wood and flung it at the Phantasm, knocking it down. "I know where he is! It's Denny, that bitch sazer from Laurinburg. He must've picked up some gifts. Go break his concentration; he's over there, hiding behind the bulldozer!"

Jonah was puzzled. "You want me to actually leave you behind?"

"Yeah. I'll distract the Phantasm while you break the sazer's concentration and make the shadow bastard disappear."

"But, Terrence," said Jonah stubbornly, "don't you remember the last—"

"Not gonna be a problem right now, Jonah! Now, go drop that asshole! I'll be right behind you!"

Something in Terrence's voice let Jonah know that his brother was certain. He had conviction, anyway. But that sazer from Laurinburg, which they'd saved from a hate crime, had ended up joining the very Eleventh Percenters who perpetrated the crime. Now, he was disguising Phantasms as Jonathan. Just to play with Jonah's head.

Jonah pumped his running just a bit and, before he knew it, he'd circled the bulldozer. The sazer was so busy focusing on controlling the Phantasm that he realized Jonah was next to him far too late. He broke his focus and attempted to scramble to his feet. Just the sight of him pissed Jonah off.

"You little shit—"

Jonah didn't even finish his own sentence as he grabbed the

sazer and began to throw repeated knees to his gut and face, and then threw him against the bulldozer. Somewhere in his mind, rational thought remained. He knew that he had to dispatch the sazer before he went into Red Rage.

"Jonah!" called Terrence. "On your left!"

Without thought, Jonah flung the sazer to his left. He looked that way just in time to see Terrence throw a Superman-punch at the bastard. With his spiritual endowment and steel knuckles, that punch probably felt like a bowling ball had crashed into the sazer's face. The sazer crashed to the ground, out like a light.

Jonah stared at Terrence, eyebrows raised. "Let me guess. You got that from Roman Reigns?"

"Yep," muttered Terrence. "Now you see that not all the wrestlers I like are from the Attitude Era."

Jonah struggled with himself for a second. But, in the end, he decided not to shame Terrence for being a Roman Reigns fan. To each their own.

He grabbed some rope from a nearby workbench and bound the sazer. He then augmented that with ethereal fetters. When he was done, he seated himself against a weather-eroded wall near Terrence. After some awkward silence, he spoke.

"Why exactly are you in Rome?" he asked.

Terrence idly scratched his forehead. "Same as you, I imagine. Wanted to check on friends of mine that weren't Elevenths, since my Eleventh friends are scattered. I thought the Auld Lang Syne Festival was the best time to do it."

"Did you see Jonathan?"

"Yeah, I did. I saw you get away from the crowd, and when I saw Jonathan, I didn't know what to think. When you followed him, I did too. When I saw that it was another Phantasm, I tried to locate the person doing it, and I saw the sazer.

But before I could drop him, though, I saw that trap. I had to get you out of the way."

"Thanks for that. Did you know they could disguise Phantasms like that?"

"Naw," said Terrence, "but I'm willing to swear that it's a Deadfallen trick. That's why I assumed that the sazer must have joined up with Creyton since Laurinburg. He must have learned some new things since that time, too."

Jonah nodded. "How were you able to hold your own against the Phantasm?"

Terrence looked at the unconscious sazer with disdain. "The reason why the Phantasms had such a mad-on for me was not because I was the weak link. Phantasms are kinda like Haunts. You know how Haunts are invulnerable so long as you're afraid of them. Well, Phantasms, supposedly, will hound you when you're the weakest. The thing about it, though, is that they pick a certain person as a weak link because the person *believes* they are the weak link. The shadow thing was using power that I gave it with my bullshit beliefs of inferiority. When it didn't have that doubt to zero in on anymore, it no longer had power over me. Haniel helped me out with it."

Jonah nodded and turned away. Awkward silence again. Once again, Jonah was the one to break it.

"We could sit here and have our old-school NBC family moment and say that we both said things that we didn't mean. But the problem with that is—"

"The fact that we meant every word," Terrence finished for him.

"Exactly. So, what do you suggest we do?"

Terrence took a deep inhalation and expelled it deliberately. "Be men enough to admit that we were out of line, apologize, and move on."

He extended his fist. Jonah met it with his own, and that was that.

"Now, we'd better go find Reena—"

"No need. She's right here."

Terrence's head snapped in her direction while Jonah turned more leisurely. Before either of them could say anything, Reena raised a hand.

"I heard you guys make up. Very to the point, and all that. Wonderful. But I can be to the point, too, Terrence. Ready? Well, first and foremost, I get that you're a grown man and you have the right to make your own choices. That's all well and good. Despite that, you springing it on us that you were staying put in Spirit Land ... it was a very unpleasant surprise. *Very.*"

Terrence stared as Reena paused to catch her breath.

"Jonah may have easily moved past it; great for him. I, however, am not at that point just yet. I don't have the ability to just turn off emotions. It is what it is."

Jonah regarded his sister. Did Reena really just say that?

"I'm still upset with you," she went on. "You are my brother and I love you, but that's how I feel. That might come out every now and then, at least until I'm over it. Don't take it personally; it'll just be me working through crap. That's all I've got to say."

When Reena had initially begun to speak, Terrence had had a kind of puzzled defiance. By the end, though, he looked as though he'd resigned himself to the fact that this was Reena, and he was just going to have to roll with it.

"That's cool by me, Reena."

"Good," said Reena. "Now, what happened?"

Jonah told her, including the Jonathan ruse. At that, Reena lowered her eyes. Jonah recalled her meltdown and promised himself that he'd never tell Terrence about it. Terrence threw in how he'd followed Jonah after seeing the ruse, and when he reached the part about the apparition being revealed as a Phantasm, Reena's eyes widened.

"Did it—did it go for you, Terrence?"

"It did," said Terrence, "but only because I baited it. They'll never come after me as the weak link again, though."

Reena gave him an appraising look, approval in her eyes. "So, who was the—"

Her eyes fell on the bound sazer. Her eyebrows knitted.

"The bastard from Laurinburg," she said with quiet rage. "Moved up in the world since we saw him last, huh? Only a fully-fledged Deadfallen disciple would be able to make the spectral ruse for a Phantasm."

"Yep," said Jonah. "That's what we thought, too."

"And it's as good a reason to get away from him," said Terrence, rising to his feet.

"Oh, I've got that." Reena cracked her knuckles. "Little bitch wants to fuck with emotions? Time to pay him back in kind."

Jonah frowned. "What are you about to do ...?"

Reena grabbed the sazer by the collar and disappeared through the *Astralimes*. Jonah and Terrence looked at each other with confusion but a few minutes later, Reena returned, empty-handed. Jonah gave her an obvious look.

"And just what the hell did you do with that little bitch?"

"Oh, just dropped him in an area known for its high vampiric activity. He was stirring, just a bit, which is good. With those cuts on his face, they'll smell his lifeblood soon."

Jonah grinned. Terrence chuckled a bit shakily.

"That's a little dark for you, Reena," he commented.

"I didn't kill him," shrugged Reena. "If he's a sazer worth his mettle, he'll get away. If not, then screw him."

"Fine by me," said Terrence, shrugging as well. "Where are you guys bunking?"

"The Meadow Road Inn," snorted Jonah.

Terrence smirked, remembering their first time there. "Well, let's move on, then. It's freakin' cold out here."

Terrence led the way through the *Astralimes,* and Jonah and Reena shot glances at each other as they followed.

Somebody had authority in their tone.

When they stepped out, they were behind the motel, and Jonah led them to the room. Once there, Terrence walked over to a chair near the window and lowered himself onto it with a grin.

"I haven't been with you guys for forty-something days, and yet, this is just like when we got to Laurinburg. Two beds, and I'm on the chair. Not complaining or anything; I just find it ironic. Life is full of little ironies like that, ain't it? Wait, I'm sorry." He closed his eyes and looked like he was mentally scolding himself. "I meant to say, *isn't* it?"

Jonah glanced at Reena again. Seriously?

"Terrence, I got to ask," said Reena, sitting on one of the beds. "What prompted you to leave Spirit Land? We remember your goal, and all. So, what was it that made you deviate from it?"

Jonah could only shake his head. That was definitely some of that annoyance that Reena had warned them about. Admittedly, though, he was just as curious as Reena about why Terrence was back.

Terrence tilted his head back and closed his eyes. "Before any repairs or rebuilding could be done, it was necessary to toll the losses.I'm not even rehashing that. Believe me, you don't want me to. The repairs and restorations were easy. When you have that many spiritually-endowed Elevenths working all at once, things really get done. It was the rest of the stuff that was slow-going. Creyton and the Deadfallen disciples rendered every security measure they had in Spirit Land useless. Even ethereal defenses that they'd had for decades were pretty much shot. It took a great deal of concentration and ethereality to restart those processes, and many of them still aren't finished.

"They had to double the amount of people who did the zone patrol, just so that manpower could pick up the slack where age-old ethereality couldn't. But they are some resilient people. Even so," Terrence shook his head, "there was a degree of naiveté when it came to not using endowment-powered solutions for every problem. You were right, Jonah. They did rely too much on ethereality. I helped as much as I could, though. I had thirteen years' experience under my belt before I knew anything about the Eleventh Percent. For that reason, I was confident that I could be a huge help.

"And Jonah," he turned to face him. "I also spent a lot of time stressing to people that what Laban fed them about you really was bullshit. Harrington has made up his mind about you. That became a point of contention for us, but whatever. There were a bunch of people that he did not speak for, though. People in Spirit Land have their misgivings about Blue Auras, maybe even more now, after what Creyton did. But even the most rigid of them had to admit that you didn't get a fair shake."

Jonah inhaled. "Well, that's something."

"Haniel and Mayce were on your side, too," continued Terrence. "Kim had nothing but nice things to say about you, but that was because you didn't snitch on her about what she'd been doing with Shade. And Josephine—man, she idolizes you. She said that she would surely have lost a grip on her sanity had it not been for you. She had a part-time job in Harrington's office. She quit because she got tired of him throwing shade at you."

Jonah snorted. "Are you serious?"

Terrence nodded. Then he turned back to Reena. "But I

never actually answered your question. Improvements were coming along, and there was some bit of comfort again. But damn ... I started getting restless. I started thinking about you guys being God-knows-where, fighting God-knows-who, while I'm in Spirit Land, not exactly twiddling my thumbs, but—okay, twiddling my thumbs. After most of the work was done, anyway. I couldn't be there. I had no problem whatsoever helping them put out their fires, but there are bigger fires out in the rest of the ethereal world. So, I told everybody that and even though I became kinda attached to Spirit Land, my place was with my brother and sister. Helping to get our world out of the condition it's in."

Jonah nodded. He could also tell that that reasoning pleased Reena a lot more than she let on, but she still seemed curious about something.

"How, exactly, did you find us?"

Terrence frowned ... or did he look apprehensive? "Reena, I already told Jonah that—"

"I know what you already told Jonah," interrupted Reena. "Or, I've got my own ideas, anyway. But something in your essence lets me know that that's only half the truth. So, what's the deal?"

Now, Terrence actually did look apprehensive. Jonah could tell. What was he hiding?

"Okay, fine. Haniel's little wristband thing. It has a—a kind of storage capability for spiritual-endowment powers. You know how cell phone stuff is backed up in the cloud? It's kind of like that. If she is intrigued by certain Elevenths, she stores some of the power that she'd mimicked."

Reena blinked. "So, she stored my essence reading ability."

"It's only because she was fascinated by it," said Terrence hastily. "She said that you're one of the most powerful essence readers she's ever met. And the minute that she used what she stored, it was depleted, so no blood, no foul."

Jonah couldn't help laughing. The whole thing was hilarious. "You know what they say, Reena. Imitation is the sincerest form of flattery."

"Shut up," said Reena. "So, how did the storage of my power help you find us?"

"Haniel tracked your essence by using the power she'd stored. When she said that you guys were in Rome, I assumed that you showed up for the festival. Which was my plan, too. The fact that we all wound up here together was an added bonus. I figured that I would see at least one of you before the festival was through. And I was right."

Reena relaxed her weight on the bed, still a bit miffed about Haniel storing her ethereality. Jonah had ceased with the laughter and rose, facing away from Terrence and Reena.

The band was back together. It was time to tell them his idea. Lord knows it had been in his head long enough.

"Terrence, Reena, now that we're a unit again, I've got to tell you guys about an idea I've had since Te—since November."

Jonah saw his brother and sister in the mirror. He had their attention.

"I've been thinking about the last thing that Laban told me. He said the Final Destination was all that mattered. I think that he is just about the only person who had any idea what was going to happen."

"You think he knew how Creyton thinks?" asked Terrence.

"There is only one person who knows what goes on in Creyton's head, and that's Creyton," replied Jonah. "But Laban was surprisingly well-informed for a man who was a prisoner for so many years. How? He couldn't exactly keep his ear to the ground, could he? He didn't just burn bridges, he nuked them.

But that thing about The Final Destination ... I keep feeling like he may have been privy to something, even before he betrayed Creyton and everybody else. He may have even had information on it so as to see how he might be able to swing something for himself."

Terrence's reflection showed puzzlement. Reena's, however, did not.

"Jonah, you can't possibly be thinking—"

"I am, Reena," said Jonah, who finally turned to face them. "I'm not thrilled about it, but I am."

Reena looked stupefied. Terrence's eyes narrowed.

"Y'know something? For the first time, I think I'm on the same level with you guys. But Jonah, you are bananas!"

"Probably," agreed Jonah, "but I think I'll find out what The Final Destination is in that little shit shack of Laban's ... on The Plane with No Name."

23

AN UNEXPECTED STOP

Terrence and Reena stared at Jonah. To be honest, there was a part of him that still couldn't believe that he'd said it himself. When Reena spoke again, it was deliberate and calm, almost like she was concerned that Jonah had cracked after having been on the road for so long.

"Jonah, The Plane with No Name is a place that you said you wouldn't even wish on Trip. Besides that, Elijah said that it was dismantled and emptied—"

"I remember what he said. Did you really think that I'd forgotten about that? But Patience said later on that people were being punished by being shot up with Sean Tooles' anti-*Astralimes* concoction, and were sent to what was left of The Plane with No Name. That was what he said. I'm willing to bet that the things that were dismantled were the gates, and the boundaries. The shanty city is probably still there."

Terrence didn't bother hiding his concern. "Um, Jonah? You're willing to risk your life on a *probably*? What are you expecting to find there?"

"I think that Laban knew exactly what Creyton was planning. Laban had the nerve to be surprised that Creyton betrayed him. And it pissed him off. Be that as it may, he wasn't able to help anything. So, he simply mentioned The Final Destination. He dangled just enough, then checked out."

"So, how does the Plane come into it?"

"Laban, like I already said, was well-informed for a prisoner. He probably had some sort of information hidden in that ragged dwelling of his. He was a master manipulator, which probably served him well on The Plane. I wouldn't have put it past him to have had something—a weak point, if you will—on everyone he came in contact with while he was there. It isn't like the man had a photographic memory; he tried too hard to screw people for that. He didn't bring anything with him to that underground prison back at the estate because Jonathan wouldn't have allowed it. And he certainly didn't go back there to get anything. Why would he lug around potentially incriminating evidence? Which means that he left it where it'd be safe."

Reena shook her head. "Jonah, you went to that place one time. Only once. Do you even remember where Laban's—?"

"Eastern district," said Jonah at once. "Dwelling 3034."

Reena looked at him, stunned. "After everything that has happened, you can recall that?"

"Of course. I had no idea that the memory would come in handy, but I retain random information. You know that about me."

Terrence spoke up. It was almost like he was tagging in. "Let me ask you something, brother, and I mean absolutely no harm. But let's just say that we go to The Plane with No Name, and we actually find something where Laban used to be. Something that may pertain to The Final Destination. What exactly do you plan to do with the information?"

Jonah looked at his brother. It was a fair question. "Truth

be told, Terrence, I haven't thought that far ahead. This may seem like a cheap answer, and if you view it that way, so be it. But it seems like Creyton has a counter to just about everything we could plan. He had the Exodus scouted so well that, not only did he lure us into a false sense of security, he had an infiltrator within the Curaie security detail. With the search for Spirit Land, although it couldn't be entirely attributed to Creyton, Laban's lies and schemes led to Creyton pillaging the place. So, I'm thinking leftfield. Being unpredictable. Maybe, just maybe, we can get ahead of *him,* for once."

Terrence said nothing but seemed pleased with that answer. Reena, though, glanced at Terrence as though he appeared a little too easily pleased.

"That made sense, Jonah," she conceded a little begrudgingly. "And here is the million-dollar question: now that you have a plan to go back to The Plane with No Name, how exactly do you plan to do it without Jonathan and Elijah?"

Jonah seated himself. He hadn't thought that far ahead about that one, either. "I'd been thinking about people who would have access to places like the Median and The Plane itself. Median is out of course, but I thought about other people who could greenlight it. The number of those we can trust narrows it down."

"Patience?" suggested Reena.

"Nah. He's already skating on thin ice because of that Tribby bitch. I don't want to screw him out of a job. I thought about Katarina Ocean, but she is nowhere near a fighter, and I didn't want to put Doug in danger, either. Yeah, he's got more of a stomach for it now, not by much, though—Terrence?"

Jonah looked at him, confused. He seemed to have a look in his eyes that denoted that he knew something that they didn't.

"I think I know the perfect person to help. Remember how Haniel said that the Spirit Land circus troupes are also spies?"

Jonah and Reena nodded.

"Well, not only do they keep tabs on the outside world, they keep tabs on the remains of the Curaie. Some Networkers have either been killed or shunted through one of those Median doors. Tribby didn't even step back and organize, because then she would see that the people were running too ragged. She simply promoted several S.P.G. practitioners to Networker status, one of whom might owe us a favor."

"Who are you talking about?" asked Jonah.

Remember the woman those vampires stripped down, so her blood would travel to her heart?"

Realization overtook Jonah. "Amelia Bennett."

Terrence nodded. Jonah was floored.

Amelia Bennett and two of her colleagues had been kidnapped by Deadfallen disciples the previous year. Jonah, Terrence, and Reena rescued them after the Curaie decided to cut their losses. Jonah could not believe that the terrified hostage that he'd wrapped in his jacket that night had gone from junior grade S.P.G. practitioner to a full-fledged Networker.

"She might be inclined to help us," said Terrence, "She owes us and whatnot."

Reena shook her head, not even trying to hide her disbelief. "Jonah, you told me once that Elijah said he didn't really care for the S.P.G. but thought that the Networkers were always polished. If he only knew that the woman whose physical life he worried about is now one of the elite."

"Hey, she might be worth her weight in ethereal steel," said Jonah. "Provided she didn't get the spot because she was kissing Tribby's ass."

"So, when do we track her down?" asked Terrence, rising from his chair.

"In about a month," answered Jonah.

Terrence and Reena looked at him, surprised.

"Why such a delay?" asked Reena.

"Because if Amelia Bennett can show us how to get to where we want to go, then you guys need to be prepared. I'm going to train you, just like Jonathan trained me. We'll start tomorrow."

* * *

Jonah started Terrence and Reena's training the very next morning, right after they left the Meadow Road Inn and went to camp out in the woods. This was exactly what Jonathan had done with Jonah; he'd said that to become attuned to new ethereality, one had to be attuned to nature. Luckily, they'd brought their tents along with them, so it wasn't difficult. Jonah started them with practice of rapid-fire *Astralimes* travels, much like Jonathan had done with him. Jonathan had explained to him that using the *Astralimes* in this manner would build up the necessary momentum from ethereal standpoints. Since The Plane with No Name was such a volatile destination, one had to be as precise as humanly possible when following the steps.

Next, he began to figure out places to use the *Astralimes,* to get to Amelia Bennett's house. Terrence had learned through Mayce and Josephine that people who worked in Spectral Law resided in homes a little more secure than others, which infuriated Reena to no end ("They get to be safer than the people they protect? That's bullshit in its purest form."). After some hemming and hawing on Reena's part, they decided to go from Rome to Seaboard, from Seaboard to Raleigh, from Raleigh to Dunn, and finally, from Dunn to Amelia's home in Boone. Jonathan had had Jonah make three trips to throw off any potential tails, so Jonah threw in a fourth simply for good measure.

When that decision was determined, the next thing they did was find ragged clothing, for when they made it to The Plane. Jonah told Terrence and Reena that they had to find the crappiest, most ruined, most shabby clothes ever. This proved difficult for Reena, who ran into the issue of gleaning some of the essences of the previous owners of the attire. As Jonah didn't want any of them to be distracted or have issues with concentration, he told them of another way things might work.

"Patience told us about how Networkers can do Spectral Illusions. We saw him do them, so we know that they aren't always sinister, like thy were with that Deadfallen sazer. Maybe Amelia will be willing to do one for us. I'll do the best negotiations I can and if it proves difficult, I can use ethereality to try to balance the situation. It's a cheap resort, but all's fair in love and war."

Terrence and Reena agreed with that.

Jonah wasn't surprised that Reena took to his tutelage like a duck to water. What was surprising, though, was Terrence.

He cracked fewer jokes, didn't make as many droll quips about what Jonah made him and Reena do, and most surprising of all, he didn't bicker with Reena about food anymore. After days of salmon and salads, Reena re-employed the smoothie fasts yet again. They had no electricity in the tents, but Jonah's ethereal power over electrical current kept their phones charged and Reena's blender working. Terrence not only raised zero objections, but he sometimes volunteered to make the smoothies. It was as though Spirit Land had changed him, but for the better. Reena had her own ideas about what had changed for Terrence, and gave Jonah knowing looks whenever Terrence made responsible, mature decisions. Jonah wasn't going to pry, though. But a few nights before Jonah's month of training was to end, he snuck to a gas station after Reena was asleep and bought some Little Debbie snacks. Terrence was waiting when he returned, as he expected. With a grin, he tossed him a couple. They snacked in silence for a few minutes, and then Terrence finally spoke.

"Jonah, I want to ask you a random question."

"Sure."

"When Vera moved to Seattle, how long did it take you to file her away?"

Jonah frowned. Terrence had said that it was random, but he still hadn't expected anything that far leftfield. "Uh ... to what is this pertaining?"

"Just a random, curious question from your big brother, man." Terrence's eyes were focused determinedly in the other direction.

Jonah took a breath. "I won't lie to you, man. I never did file her away. I never could."

"Not even when you were having sex with Lola?"

"Nope, not even then. I'm not saying I was thinking about Vera during those times, no. I'm just saying that I was never successful at putting her completely in the back of my mind."

Terrence closed his eyes and exhaled gently. "Damn. You never put her in the back of your mind. Well, thanks, anyway."

"Don't mention it," said Jonah, who had no trouble filing *that* random exchange away.

But he also wasn't an idiot. Despite that, Terrence's business was his own.

Three nights later, it was time to get the ball rolling. Jonah, Terrence, and Reena packed up their things and readied themselves for the *Astralimes*. Jonah was pleased with how prepared his friends now were. He gave one final glance to the campsite that had been their home for the past month, silently hoping that the days on the road were near their end.

"Here is hoping that this search proves more fruitful than the one in Spirit Land," said Reena.

Terrence threw a reproachful look her way, but Jonah voiced something that had been on his mind for the past couple of weeks.

"I don't think that Spirit Land was a complete bust. Not anymore, anyway."

"What?" said Reena.

"Seriously?" asked Terrence. "And why is that?"

"The Tool of Omega. Jonathan had to have known about the caution they had regarding Blue Auras, so he also had to know that they wouldn't just hand it to me or Creyton. When Creyton achieved Praeterletum, Jonathan probably thought that it was desperate measure time, to find a way to eliminate Creyton from ever doing that again. I think that he wanted us to find Spirit Land, not only to forge new bonds, if possible, but to get the Tool back into play."

Reena sniffed and reminded him, "Jonah, Creyton stole the Tool."

"But he can't use it," countered Jonah. "He can't even open the box. Which leads me to believe that Jonathan knew something that I don't. Most importantly, he knew something that Creyton doesn't know, either. With the Tool of Omega, I believe that we are on even footing. But we needed to find Spirit Land to get the Tool back into the game."

Terrence looked fascinated. "You just might be on to something, man."

"Here is hoping so," said Reena gravely.

"Alright then." Jonah was all business. "Ready, set, go."

They stepped onto the Astral Plane to the respective stops, and then into Boone. It all occurred so crisply that it felt to Jonah like they had disappeared and simply reappeared. The second they'd touched ground in Boone though, Reena yanked Jonah and Terrence behind some nearby trees.

"Reena, what the hell—"

"Shut up! Amelia's got company!"

Jonah looked from behind the trees. Amelia lived in a neat little house situated at a point which provided a great view of the mountains every morning. She was in her living room, conversing with a brownish-haired woman, who seemed to be a colleague or pal.

"Well, this changes things a bit," said Terrence with an unpleasant expression. "Now what are we supposed to do?"

Jonah steeled himself. After everything that had happened, not to mention the training that he'd put Terrence and Reena through, regrouping was not an option. "We walk up to her door, knock, speak our piece, and get this done. Answers won't find themselves."

Before either of them could stop him, he crossed the street and rapped on Amelia's door.

It got silent in her home, which didn't surprise Jonah at all. When the door opened, Jonah was met with a crossbow at his face, the arrows of which gleamed the plum color of Amelia's aura. She looked shocked when she saw him.

"Hi, Amelia," said Jonah in a pleasant tone. "Is this how you greet all of your guests?"

"I don't have guests, Jonah." Amelia's crossbow remained raised. "I have ethereality laced all over my home. Only a very, very powerful Eleventh Percenter could just walk right through them."

"Huh," said Jonah with a quick shrug. "Well, I'm not egotistical enough to say that about myself."

"Humility," said Amelia's friend, who had a knife trained in Jonah's direction. "That's refreshing."

Amelia lowered the crossbow, but her friend didn't drop her weapon. Amelia looked her way. "He's a friendly, T. Forgive my colleague, Jonah. She was recently reassigned to our S.P.G. unit from Washington State, but everything went to hell right after that. Trust is a precious commodity nowadays, especially with people she doesn't know."

"Wise policy," commented Jonah and he looked the other woman's way. "I mean you and Amelia no harm, ma'am. We're on good terms; I even saved her life when the Curaie left her to be killed."

The other woman—T, Amelia had called her—lowered her weapon. "Okay. Then, we're cool."

Jonah nodded and returned his gaze to Amelia. "I hear that you're a Networker now." He chose to make his voice slightly apprehensive. "Was that due to you proving your mettle, or was Tribby feeling generous?"

At her superior's name, Amelia's eyes flashed. "That woman's name and generous don't belong in the same sentence. But come on in before someone sees you."

"I've got my friends with me, over there." Jonah pointed behind him. "Can they come, too?"

"I trust them if they're with you. Bring them on in."

Grateful, Jonah beckoned to Terrence and Reena. The three of them walked into Amelia's living room.

The room looked comfortable and cozy, and Amelia didn't appear to own a television. Pictures were plastered all over her walls, with the most prominent one showing her with hair styled in a professional bun, looking resplendent in her plum-colored S.P.G. dress uniform.

"That's a nice picture," observed Terrence. "Are you going to change it now that you've been promoted?"

"No need," answered Amelia. "It's not like my aura color has changed—"

Suddenly, there was a loud clatter. They all looked around, instantly on guard, but it came from Amelia's colleague. She'd dropped her weapon to the floor. She hadn't seemed to notice.

"T, what—"

The woman raised her hand to stall Amelia's startled question. She never took her eyes off Jonah, Terrence, and Reena. Jonah's mind went on all cylinders, thinking that this woman might be someone they couldn't trust after all, like that bastard infiltrator at the exodus.

But then the woman shocked them all.

"Reena?" she whispered.

Now, it was Reena's turn to be shocked. She glanced at Jonah and Terrence, then back at the woman. "Um, that's me. Do I know you?"

The woman began to sob. Jonah didn't know what the hell was going on, but he also didn't know what to say.

"After everything that's happened," the woman finally choked out, "you kept your promise. You kept it."

Reena looked a little frightened. Jonah couldn't blame her. "I'm afraid that you have me at a disadvantage—"

"It's me, Reena," said the woman, her voice ragged from the sobs. "It's Tempie, your sister."

24

ASUNDER

Jonah was dumbstruck. Terrence numbly managed, "Say what?"

But their reactions were nothing compared to Reena's.

Her eyes were in danger of bulging out of their sockets. She truly looked like she was facing a ghost from her past, which was actually half right.

"Tempie? Little Sister, is it really you?"

Trying, and failing, to stem her tears, Tempie nodded. Jonah observed both women in as acutely as he could. Reena had black and red hair with dark features. Tempie was fair featured with bright brown hair. Whereas Reena had a certain hardness in her demeanor, the other woman's seemed curious and slightly uncertain (however, Jonah could easily understand that one; she'd just gotten a promotion and wasn't quite sure what to expect). But it was in their eyes that Jonah could see it. Both sets of eyes were an identical dark brown, piercing, and seemed to regard things with equal parts caution and wonder. The irony of the matter was that it was the little details that he paid almost no attention to with Reena, that served to confirm she was the older sister of Tempie.

Amelia, like Jonah and Terrence, was flummoxed. "Erm, maybe we should give you two some privacy. I think it's safe to assume that you have a great deal to catch up on—"

"No," said both women, although Tempie's eyes were on Amelia and Reena's were on Jonah and Terrence.

Reena took a deep breath. "Let's all just ... let's all just sit down."

Jonah locked eyes with Amelia. She looked as iffy as he felt as she nodded and lowered herself to the couch. Everyone else sat. Reena's and Tempie's eyes never left each other. After nervous, awkward silence that lasted almost two minutes, Tempie finally spoke.

"My relationship with Mom was never the same after she threw you out. She tried to bully us, force us into accepting the fact that she did the right thing. It never worked with me. She couldn't convince me that not having our oldest sister with our family was right for us."

"You didn't buy that shit, and I believe it from you. What about Kai and Myleah?"

Tempie took a slow breath. "Kai ... kind of numbed out. Myleah tried to act like everything was normal. I cried every night for almost a year. It was at that time that my ethereality began to manifest."

Reena nodded. Jonah could see that she was at a sincere loss how to deal with this occurrence. She could have easily taken off her dampener and read Tempie's essence, but it was clear that she wanted to do this on her own. Apparently, Terrence was thinking about essence reading as well, but for a different reason.

"Reena, you had no dampener then, which means that your

essence reading was on full blast. You couldn't read your mother's feelings? Or sense her intentions?"

"Our mother didn't bother to conceal how she felt about me, Terrence." Reena barely looked at him. "The essence reading wasn't needed. That day, she was merely more belligerent than usual."

Tempie just hung her head. Reena looked back at her, asking the obvious question without words. Her younger sister looked up and nodded.

"She's been in Spirit for eight years," she revealed. "In her final moments, she was still convinced that Kai, Myleah, and I were better women without you in our lives."

"And your father?" asked Reena.

"Still in Charlottesville. He came to regret not being braver when Mom kicked you out."

Amelia winced. Jonah sighed, his heart going out to Reena. Terrence put a hand on her shoulder. It was testament to Reena's emotional turmoil that she didn't shrug him off. Then again, he hadn't seen her meltdown like Jonah had.

"I suppose that's something," Reena said at last, her voice hollow. "What about our sisters nowadays?"

"Kai and Myleah moved back to Hawaii and opened a bridal boutique. Myleah is married with three boys. I talk to them during the holidays or whatever. We aren't exactly a close unit; Mom saw to that with how she treated you."

Reena nodded again. "When did you find out about the Eleventh Percent?"

It was crystal clear that Reena was done with the subject of her stepfather and other sisters. She was interested in the bit of family she had left that hadn't betrayed her. At least on the surface, Tempie seemed to be done with the matter too, and happily took her cue from that.

"Like I said, my ethereality began to manifest when I was

ten." There was something like relief in her voice. "But I had no clue what any of those things meant until I came of age."

"Who brought you into the know?" asked Reena.

Tempie smiled and clapped Amelia on the back. "Mellie here has been my best friend for years. She and her family helped me become familiar with things. We got recruited into Spectral Law at the same time and lived together in Nevada before she got reassigned and moved to North Carolina. I was in Tacoma for a bit, got reassigned here, and about ten minutes afterward Creyton wiped out the Curaie."

"The lady we saved in Dexter City was best friends with Reena's sister," marveled Jonah. "Small world."

Tempie looked at Reena once more. "You should know that you were my inspiration to join Spectral Law."

"Is that right?" Reena was surprised.

"It is. After Mom did what she did and, of course, after I learned about the Eleventh Percent, I couldn't help but wonder how many ethereal humans out there might be lost or alone, potentially at risk from Spirit Reapers, vampires, Creyton, or simply Tenths who don't understand them."

Reena gave her a small smile. "Hate to crawl back down in the swamp, but were your father, Kai, or Myleah Elevenths?"

Tempie shook her head. "Just you and me."

She raised her left hand, and her fingers began to shimmer with a silver gleam. With a sly smile, Reena raised her own left hand and her fingers shimmered with the yellow of her aura. Tempie regarded Reena's aura color with a smile, then quickly faded.

"Where is your mind at, big sister? What are you thinking?"

Jonah looked at Reena with some trepidation. She'd insulated herself with friends to replace the family she'd lost. She had only recently revealed to him and Terrence that a member of her immediate family had actually bothered to give a damn about her. Could Reena move past that because Tempie, through either fate or good luck, was now back in her life?

Very slowly, Reena rose. "I'm thinking that I can't forgive you, Tempie."

Tempie's mouth dropped. Reena went on.

"I can't forgive you, because out of all of them, you were the only one that I never had to forgive in the first place."

She opened her arms. Without hesitation, Tempie embraced her sister tightly.

Terrence and Amelia beamed. Jonah felt elated. He thought that *he* had had it rough with stupid relatives, but perspective let him know that he wasn't alone.

But Tempie was here, reunited with Reena after all these years. Reena had grimly told Jonah that she doubted whether Tempie cared about her anymore, thinking that her mother had used that time to turn her to her side. But that hadn't been the case. That embrace, that mending of sisterly bonds, was also the mending of a bridge that neither woman had personally burned.

How often did the truth tear asunder the illusions of negativity?

The sisters parted. Tempie wiped her eyes again and noticed Reena's ring.

"You're married? Where is your wife?"

Reena laughed quietly. "Just engaged. We'll get married when the fires die down. She is currently in Tullamore, where she is safe."

"Really?" Amelia looked impressed. "You must have friends in high places!"

"High isn't actually the best word—" began Terrence, but Jonah raised a hand to stop him.

Reena's reuniting with her sister had filled everyone with

positive feelings, which was a welcome digression, but the reminder of why Kendall was abroad brought his mind back to the task at hand.

"Reena, Tempie," Jonah said apologetically, "I'm sorry to put a damper on the reunion. I swear I am. But we did come here for a reason."

Reena nodded, steeling herself once more. Tempie looked understanding too, and sat next to Amelia, whose curiosity was back on her face.

"What's going on, Jonah? Tell me everything, if you'd be so kind."

Jonah took a deep breath and filled Amelia in on everything. But he was careful not to mention Spirit Land, the Tool of Omega, or the fact that he'd spoken to Patience before the wild adventure had even begun. He felt that if Amelia and Tempie knew that, it would possibly bring trouble to them and Patience, particularly if Evelyn Tribby found out. He kept the story on Creyton and Laban's plotting, and how Laban had hoped that betraying Jonah to Creyton would grant him the immunity that Creyton promised anyone who'd give up Jonah. The where and the how were need-to-know, and Amelia and Tempie *didn't* need to know.

Amelia rose and walked over to her fireplace. She'd looked contemplative the entire time. "Jonah, if I may, what makes you so certain that Laban has information hidden on The Plane with No Name?"

"Easy. Laban was like ... like a leverage connoisseur. He was a son of a bitch, but he had a sharp mind for all things fact and gossip, and he was always well-informed. Too informed for someone who was supposedly just sitting on The Plane with No Name."

Tempie spoke next. "A man who would want to know everything ... simply so that he could use it for his own gain at the right moment. Are you thinking there might be a leak some-where? Besides Riley Judd, of course."

Jonah shook his head, ignoring the flash of rage that Riley's name sparked. "Riley was a leak. But he wouldn't have been of any use to Laban. Laban was a pariah to Creyton, after all. But I am certain that he knew how Creyton wants to end this. And I'm certain that it's in that shack of his."

Amelia looked at her fireplace again. "Why come to me?"

Jonah glanced at Terrence, who nodded. They were of the same mind. There was no need to mention that she owed them a solid when pure gold was on the table. "You aren't a fan of Evelyn Tribby. We know that the entirety of the Curaie, or what remains of it anyway, has sustained heavy losses as well. You got promoted to Networker status. The elite unit. You were one of three, maybe four promotions to their ranks. A dream come true. But not like *this*. A wartime promotion is hasty, disorganized and, dare I say, haphazard. Therefore, you —and Tempie, too—are probably pissed all to hell, because Tribby gave you a promotion that you *did* deserve, but the manner in which you got it—the manner in which she promoted you—did not accentuate your talents and skills. It simply plugged up a hole. That means that your peers in the Networkers are having trouble accepting you. It means that you are working twice as hard to get half the respect. You deserve far better than tactics like that, Amelia. You too, Tempie."

Jonah knew that he was on the right track. He knew that his approach was the best one to take after hearing that Patience and Amelia hated their superior. He had seen a hodgepodge of emotions run across Amelia's face as he spoke: frustration, anger, hurt, annoyance, disappointment, floun-dering ambition. The hasty promotion piece was easy; he'd seen enough office politics and workings to know when promo-tions were done on the fly. The recipients of said promotions had such a rough time of it. And that roughness was written all over Amelia's face. Tempie's too.

"Practices such as those can only be stopped if the situation that caused them in the first place is stymied." He knew that putting the proverbial cherry on top would only make things better. "And being that you are currently going through it, you'd be all the more eager to see if you could aid in getting it corrected. Am I right, or am I right?"

The last part was likely what did it. Amelia glanced at Tempie, who nodded. She then nodded herself.

"You're right, Jonah. My God, you're right. It's been hell. We can *do* this job justice, but Tribby made us all look like she was giving us charity. It makes my blood boil."

"Random question." Terrence spoke up. "These champagne glasses on your table? They weren't for celebration, huh?"

"No," said Amelia. "Nothing to celebrate nowadays."

"Yeah," said Tempie dully. "It helped to calm our nerves. If I'd have known that I would be reunited with my favorite sister, then I would have celebrated. But, as you can see, the glass is empty."

Reena merely smiled. "Alcohol isn't necessary, Tempie. I'm not a drinker, anyway."

Tempie chuckled and shook her head. "After all this time, you're still a health nut."

Amelia seated herself once more, her expression slightly more tense than before. "Okay, Jonah. I'll help you."

"I will, too," said Tempie. "However, I can."

"But first, there are some things that you should know," said Amelia. "The Gates and the boundaries around The Plane with No Name are gone, but the derelict community still stands."

Jonah glanced at Terrence, who looked surprised.

"That's not an issue—"

"Oh hell yes, it is, Jonah," Amelia interrupted. "The derelict city is not empty. "

Jonah gaped at her. "Are you referring to the people that were forcibly exiled there?"

Tempie winced at the mention of those people. "God only knows what has become of those people. But Mellie didn't mean them. There were some prisoners who never left. Even after the Gates, Gatekeepers, boundaries, and all ethereal security measures were gone."

Jonah just stared. Terrence swore softly.

"Why would they stay when they could just up and leave? What logical reason would they have to stay?"

"Is it so surprising, Terrence?" asked Amelia. "The remaining prisoners spurned freedom because The Plane with No Name *is* their home. No other place and no other way of life makes sense to them anymore. I'd pity them if they weren't all sadists and psychos."

"But how are they living?" asked Jonah, incredulous. "How are they surviving?"

"Well, seeing as how no more supplies of any kind are being dropped anymore, my guess is that they are surviving any way they can," answered Tempie gravely. "Which is the reason why I said God knows what happened to the poor people who got exiled there."

Jonah swore under his breath. That changed things. He'd remembered what Patience had said about the exiles, but never in a million lifetimes would he have even imagined that freed prisoners would voluntarily stay behind. Were they that far gone?

He could easily answer that question.

Without supplies, those bastards were probably more

savage and feral than ever. And without food, survival was probably in its most primal state. He tightened his fists.

"It has to be done," he heard himself say.

Amelia and Tempie looked at each other.

"You're serious?" cried Amelia. "You still want to do this?"

"I do. I'm not thrilled about going to an even darker version of The Plane with No Name, but it has to be done. Jonathan trusted me to stop Creyton, and if the information on how to do that lay on that damned Plane, so be it."

The two newest Networkers looked at each other again as Jonah turned to Terrence and Reena.

"I'm more than willing to do it alone," he said sincerely. "I know that I trained you, but knowing that there are still sick bastards there—"

"Changes nothing," interrupted Reena. "I haven't backed out on you before, Jonah. I'm damn sure not going to begin now."

Terrence seemed to struggle with himself upon hearing those words, but only fleetingly. "You think I'd miss this? I'm ready to knuckle up."

Jonah nodded and returned his attention to Amelia and Tempie. Amelia, still in shock, reached a hand to Tempie. Almost as if she were in a trance, Tempie put her Tally in the other woman's hand. Amelia then reached into a box on the mantle and took out two more. She put one of them in each of their hands.

"These will be your tethers to Earthplane," she explained. Jonah knew this already, but let Amelia explain it anyway. It seemed easier. "Tempie, if you would, please place a Spectral Illusion on their clothes."

Jonah waited for Tempie to do the Spectral Illusions on them, the same way Patience had a while back, but she didn't do it that way at all. With two fingers that gleamed silver, she pointed at each of them separately, closed her eyes, and snapped her fingers. Instantly, Jonah, Terrence, and Reena were attired in the most ragged, woebegone clothes ever. They looked filthier than street urchins. It was perfect.

"When you take the steps, focus your mind on the center," said Amelia. "Since there are no more Gates, that will be your best bet."

Jonah nodded and stood. Terrence and Reena did the same. Tempie put a hand on Reena's shoulder, trying very hard to look unconcerned.

"Be careful, Reena. Please come back in one piece."

"We'll be fine," Jonah assured her. Or maybe himself. "Nothing to it. I'm ready."

"That makes two of us," muttered Terrence.

Jonah closed his eyes and murmured a few positive affirmations. He'd been there before, but the stakes were far higher now. Jonathan wasn't here to quarterback this time. Jonah was the one in the hot seat.

Along with Terrence and Reena.

"Alright, people. Here we go."

With no more hesitation, the three of them stepped through the *Astralimes*. For better or worse, they were going to The Plane with No Name.

25

THE FINAL DESTINATION

Thanks to all of Jonah's training, the trip went without a hitch. They'd focused on the center, as Amelia had instructed, and that was precisely where they landed. Jonah had already been here once before. He'd seen all this hell.

Now, it was worse.

As Amelia had told him, the Gates and the boundaries were gone, along with all the ethereal security measures. Their absence made the scene even *more* depressing.

Because they could see all around them, it looked as if the place were nothing more than a collection of miserable dwellings and landscapes, surrounded by endless smog. With so many prisoners now gone, a great many of the shanties had fallen to dust. Furniture was strewn here and there, some still intact, some jerry-rigged to function, but ultimately abandoned. Among the refuse that littered the ground were bones. So many bones. Some had been there a good little while and looked bleached and weathered with time. Others were more recent, and they looked, and smelled, as such.

"Holy—" whispered Terrence, but Jonah stopped him.

"Elijah told me something the first time I was here and now I'm telling you. There is nothing here now—nor has there ever been anything here in the past—that can be associated with the word *holy*. Now, remember what I told you. Don't take deep breaths because the smell will choke you. Since there are still prisoners here, I will tell you something else that Elijah told me: never look like you're walking with urgency. Anyone who sees you might think that you have something valuable and attack you as a result. And under no circumstances do you show ethereality. Now, let's go. We're looking for dwelling 3034. I'll lead the way. Hoods on."

Jonah had no way of knowing exactly where they were. Not in the dead center of the place. They had to walk out to a "road" before they glimpsed a ruined district sign. It read 1118.

Wonderful. This wouldn't be quick at all.

"Alright. We go east. Stop for nothing."

The three of them began to walk. Steadily, but not too hurriedly. Jonah couldn't get over how quiet The Plane was now, but that was tiny comfort.

Actually, it was no comfort at all.

The silence just made it feel that much more sinister.

At section 2010, he raised a hand to stop Terrence and Reena, and jutted his head to the left. They slipped quietly into the shadows between two long abandoned dwellings.

"What's up, Jonah?" asked Reena.

"I saw somebody walking. And let's just say that I'm not in a social mood. So, we'll wait a minute and see what they do."

Sure enough, a man who looked worse than they did showed up two minutes later and plopped down on what was left of a bench. He began to devour whatever was in his hands. Jonah's stomach churned.

"Ten dollars says that whatever he's eating was still alive

when he started eating it." Terrence's try for humor was feeble at best.

"No bet," said Jonah. "I can't bring myself to be curious about what he's eating. Let's go this way. I have a feeling that he won't notice us."

They walked from between the dwelling to a road on the other side and resumed their trek. Jonah was glad Reena wore her dampener. God only knew the essence she'd pick up from this place.

Not long afterward, they came to a structure that Jonah recognized. He laughed with derision.

"Iuris Mason and Knoaxx Cisor held *pankrations* right her. I wonder what became of them."

"Those fools probably got themselves killed," said Reena. "That's probably why they worked so hard to be badasses; they wanted reps, because they feared the day someone found out they used to work for Gamaliel Kaine."

"I am not the expert on being a badass or anything," said Terrence, "but one would think that keeping your head down is the best way to stay out of trouble."

"That's something that makes sense, Terrence," said Jonah. "And if Iuris and Cisor were anything like their fallen Lord and Master, they didn't act sensibly."

After walking a good long time, they avoided another collection of stray prisoners; Jonah could have sworn that one of the prisoners saw them, but then ultimately dismissed them as a figment of his imagination. It was a good thing too, because Jonah wanted his mind as clear as possible.

Especially at this moment.

"We're here, people. Dwelling 3034, AKA Laban's House."

The shanty hadn't changed much, and Jonah couldn't very well say that it looked more rundown, because it was rundown the first time he'd seen it. The roof appeared to be weighed down on its left side and the door still lay smashed from when Jonah had been there last. He couldn't help but chuckle, as he was the one who'd smashed it back then.

He walked into the opening and then made room for Terrence and Reena. The second he got the chance to look around, he noticed something was different. However, it was Terrence who said it.

"It looks like the place has been raided."

Reena's eyes widened, but Jonah shook his head.

"I wouldn't worry about that. People here aren't exactly rational. I'm betting whoever raided this was probably trying to satisfy base-level desires only. And if Laban was dumb enough to leave valuable leverage in a place where it'd be vulnerable, I will be the most surprised person in existence."

Reena nodded. The three of them began to search.

"Be careful," warned Jonah. "Laban was a sick bastard."

Jonah chose a portion of the shack and began to search through Laban's belongings. He hadn't meant for it to be an arduous task, but thinking about Laban filled his mind with all sorts of ghastly traps and deadfalls; he used to be a Deadfallen disciple, after all ...

Broken pots and pans? Nothing.

An old ice chest that probably hadn't seen ice since the dawn of time? Zilch.

A footlocker near a crudely constructed bed? That yielded nothing, as well. The damn thing was empty, a fact that was made even more insulting by the crack in the bottom of it—

Wait.

"Terrence? Reena? Get over here. I think I got something."

They were at his side in seconds. Terrence peered in and snorted.

"It's an empty footlocker, man," he said.

"Duh," said Jonah.

Terrence looked puzzled, but Reena looked shrewd.

"You think it has Auric Shielding?"

"At first, yes. But I remembered my private meeting with Laban atop the overlook, back in Spirit Land. Reena, will you give that ax handle over there, please?"

Reena pressed the item into Jonah's hands. He pointed the blunt end directly at the crack at the bottom of the footlocker. Taking a deep breath, he plunged it there.

The point didn't slam against the bottom. It penetrated it.

"What the hell?" Terrence was wide eyed

"Jonah, how did you know that would happen?" asked Reena.

"That Deadfallen trick that Laban loved using. He would have known that nowhere on The Plane with No Name was safe to stash things due to the raids—hell, he was one of the main ones raiding. But his beef with Creyton was almost as personal as my own beef with him, and he definitely didn't want anyone to find anything that he'd hidden. So, he created an ... astral stash, for lack of a better phrase."

"That can't be. He would have had to have made it—"

"Before he turned himself in," finished Jonah. "You're right, Reena. That's what he did. It's the only thing that makes sense."

"So, what did you need the ax handle for?" asked Terrence.

Jonah pulled the end out of the thin air he'd just stabbed it into. The end was covered in blood. "'Cause I knew Laban. It's booby-trapped."

Terrence looked aghast. "Is that—is that old Lifeblood?"

"It *is*." Reena eyed it warily. "It could be tainted, laced with ethereal viruses ... anything. From a Tenth perspective, there is also the risk of tetanus."

"I'm not understanding why the footlocker is here, though," said Jonah.

"I think I do," said Reena. "Jonah, do you think that you can manipulate wind to work like a vacuum, while shielding at the same time?"

"Piece of cake. Why, though?"

"Just do it."

Shrugging, Jonah used his right hand like it was a blockade. "*Shield me,*" he commanded.

His fingers gleamed blue and the air in front of the footlocker became visible and tangible, thickening into a wall. He then raised his left hand, and focused.

Through the wind wall he'd made, other wind currents began to siphon like a vacuum. After nearly two minutes, a ragged pile of objects flew up from thin air: nails, spikes, shanks, glass, and something that looked suspiciously like piano wire. It slammed into Jonah's wind wall, and then fell into the footlocker. Every inch of every object there was laced with lifeblood.

"That's why he had the footlocker here," said Reena. "It served as a place of storage for his nasty little security system. He could put everything in there, move it aside, and dig out whatever he stashed on the Astral Plane. When he was done, he could stuff it all back."

"One thing I'm not getting," said Terrence. "Why didn't Laban use his little Astral compartment to, I don't know, get off The Plane with no Name?"

"I don't think it works like that," said Jonah. "The compartments, I mean. Physically living objects probably wouldn't even fit in it. Just things that are inert. Even lifeblood loses its life essence eventually."

Terrence nodded. "You are quite intelligent, man, bro. I'd have never made that connection if I saw Laban pulling things from thin air. I wouldn't have thought to prod the gap before putting my hands in there either."

"I think on my feet," said Jonah, flattered. "But even with all the booby traps out, I'm still not putting my bare hands in there."

He pulled out some gloves he'd brought along, pulled them on, and used his gloved hands to clamp his batons. He stuck the tip into the void and clamped on an object almost immediately.

"Got something. Hang on ..."

Terrence and Reena leaned in. From the void, Jonah extracted a rather old-looking booklet, bound in leather, lined with very dark piping. Jonah frowned.

"What the hell? It's a book with no pages—"

"My God," whispered Reena.

Jonah and Terrence looked at her. Jonah hated when Reena did that. "What, Reena?"

Reena actually looked afraid. Never a good sign. Not ever. "Jonathan told me about this, years ago. It's Essence Cognition."

Now it was Terrence's eyes that widened. "Oh, hell no. No fuckin' way!"

"What am I missing?" asked Jonah, impatient. "What is Essence Cognition?"

"It's a way to store intentions," answered Reena. "It's a practice where one isolates specific thoughts—the ones which contain the most ambitious and sinister of your intentions, I mean—and stores them in one place."

"Only Spirit Reapers could ever do it," added Terrence. "This is probably Creyton's! Laban must have stolen it. Screw that bullshit that he told you about his failsafe, Jonah. I bet that thing in your hand was enough for Laban to voluntarily turn himself in, so that he was out of Creyton's reach."

"So, what is it exactly?"

Reena pointed at the piping. "The dark stuff there? It's

essence. Dark essence. If that is Creyton's essence, then it prob-ably contains his plan, or whatever The Final Destination is."

"So how do—what do I do with it?"

Reena seemed reluctant to tell him. He looked at Terrence, who also seemed reluctant. He gave him the best evil eye he could muster. Terrence attempted defiance, but eventually cracked.

"Alright, alright. You ... puncture the piping. The essence supposedly enters your own consciousness, revealing its secrets."

Jonah looked down at the object. He'd taken a gamble on the answer he was looking for being provided by Laban, and it seemed that he was right. It could possibly be right here, in his grasp. But Terrence and Reena were terrified. More terrified than he'd ever seen them.

"What do you guys know?"

"Pop told me—us—a story some years back," replied Terrence. "A Spirit Reaper had kidnapped a woman and had used Essence Cognition to keep Spectral Law from finding her, something like that. Some S.P.G. practitioner found his little Spectral Recorder, which is what you call objects like that thing you're holding. He punctured the piping, took the Spirit Reaper's intentions into himself. But ... but he wasn't built for it."

Jonah considered Terrence. "It ran him crazy?"

"No, Jonah." Reena's eyes were on the ground. "It killed him."

Jonah's blood ran cold. Of course. Of damned course. It was the Mandy spirits all over again. A chance to assist every-body, only it hinged on a physical-life threatening risk.

But if it held any information on what he needed ...

"What would you guys have me do?"

Terrence and Reena looked at him, worried, confused, and scared.

"Jonah, Jonathan isn't here to reverse any ill effects that may happen," said Terrence.

"Jonah, I know you remember the thing with my dampener when the cleansing was undone," said Reena. "And I know you haven't forgotten the shit storm with that language of Spirit pages that I went through. Even with Jonathan's assistance and care, I was in a coma for days. What do you think would happen to you alone?"

Jonah was on the verge of deflating. On the verge of conceding and trying to figure things out via alternate means. But then, clear as a bell, an idea came into his mind. "Help me do it."

They both looked at him in surprise. "What?"

"Help me. Speak mentally to the spirits endowing you and ask them if they are willing to ... to merge their essences with the spirit endowing me. A triple-tiered front of protection, which will be fortified by my balancing ethereality. You asked what might happen to me alone. If we do this, then I won't be alone, will I?"

"Some of the apprehension in Reena's eyes faded. Terrence actually smirked.

"Pulled another one out your ass, man! That just might work!"

As he and Reena closed their eyes and gave their focus to internal conversations, Jonah couldn't help but wonder where that idea had come from. There was nothing whatsoever in his consciousness that resembled that plan. It just seemed to pop right into his head. It made him wonder about that internal advice he'd received back in Spirit Land. Was this the same source now?

He gave himself a mental shake. Task at hand.

Reena opened her eyes. Shortly thereafter, Terrence did as well.

"We're good," said Reena. "My spiritess is on board. She wants you to make it through this, after all."

"All systems go with my spirit, too, "said Terrence. "But Jonah, are you absolutely sure?"

Jonah looked down at the—what did Terrence call it? Spiritual recorder? It was a desperate time. Wartime. Therefore, it was desperate measure time. "I'm sure. High risk, high reward, right?"

Neither Terrence nor Reena looked to be onboard with that particular assessment, but even so, they clamped onto his arms, Reena on his left, Terrence on his right.

Suddenly, Jonah felt surges from both of their endowments. It was similar to how one felt after hunger had been sated. *Balance,* he said in his mind, and with a steeling breath, he pressed down hard on the piping. It cracked under the pressure.

Laban's shack instantly cooled. It was even cooler than Reena's cold spots. Jonah had his eyes closed, focusing on balancing his consciousness, but the strangest sensation in his hands forced them open.

The essence that had been contained in the piping was not dissipating. It was slowly inching its way up his hands and arms. The farther it reached, the clearer it became to Jonah that it was indeed Creyton's essence. The ambition, the self-righteousness, the ... *evil* of it ... functioned very much like an illness on Jonah.

How could a person go so far in the other direction? Jonathan had told Jonah that Creyton had had wonderful parents, a nice upbringing, and people who doted on him from an early age. But he'd also said that Creyton had been pampered like a damn deity because he was a Blue Aura. He had been reminded of his worth and significance from the cradle. The seed of entitlement was planted from the start. But that gave Creyton no right to do what he had to all the people he'd hurt and killed. All the lives, Tenth and Eleventh, that he had destroyed.

That, right there, was the primary difference between him and Creyton. One was an unassuming beacon of hope, the other was an unadulterated illustration of hell.

Strangely, that realization helped bolster Jonah's balancing and strength in that moment.

But not by much.

The dark essence migrated the entirety of his arms and quickly approached his mind. He closed his eyes once again as Creyton's darkness took residence in his own consciousness. Creyton was an evil man who reveled in the deleterious effect he had on everything. And his essence represented that in spades.

As his intentions became known to Jonah, he could barely pay attention to them. The solipsistic Messiah complex, the superiority, hatred, supremacy, disdain, and darkness were almost blinding. They almost blocked Jonah out of what he was trying to achieve. The man's inner substance, at its root, was tantamount to that of a monstrous beast. Pure, uncorrupted, and savage.

Balance, he said in his mind once more.

Slowly, he began to siphon through the evil. Creyton's plans were quite clear behind the emotions. One fueled the other. Jonah saw them now.

But wait—no. No, that couldn't be.

The horror-laden images Jonah saw in his mind were replaced by something else. A large obstruction, something that he'd hoped and prayed to never see in his mind again. Its sudden presence in his consciousness was enough to make him swear loudly and drop the spiritual recorder, thus breaking the connection. The abrupt expulsion of Creyton's stored essence was enough to knock him backward, as though he'd been drop-kicked.

Terrence and Reena crowded his personal space.

"Jonah!" cried Reena. "Are you alright?"

"I'm good. I'm here. Just ... just leave me be for a second."

Reena backed off, and Jonah lay there on the dirt for a few moments. It was so hard and unevenly packed that he didn't stay there long. He hoisted himself into a sitting position.

The connection was broken. His mind was his own again. The only thing in his consciousness was his own self.

None of those things gave him comfort. None at all.

"I saw Creyton's intentions. I saw what he's planning to do."

"You did?" said Terrence. "You understand what Laban meant?"

Jonah nodded, gazing at Terrence and Reena; the way he regarded them was perhaps more intense than he'd ever done so before since meeting them. "Creyton's plan is to exterminate every Eleventh that's ever been associated with me, the Light Blue Aura. Anyone who is a friend to me and a foe to him is on the list. That's what Omega is—the end of all things against him."

Terrence and Reena gaped, but Jonah waved a hand at them.

"I'm not done. In his mind, there is only one thing he needs to do to make a statement. One thing in his way."

"You?" asked Terrence.

"Not exactly," said Jonah. "He said that he wanted to kill me on his terms. I get that now. He wants to kill me at The Final Destination on his road to immortality."

"Where *is* The Final Destination?" demanded Reena.

Jonah looked her in the eyes. "The first place that he was ever spurned. He wants to make his biggest statement at the place where his transcendence began. The Final Destination is the Grannison-Morris estate. Before he sends out his extermination brigades, he wants to utterly destroy our home."

26

THE OFFER

"He wants to destroy the estate?" said Reena in a hollow voice.

"Yes. He wants to wipe it completely off of the map. But there is more to it, which I will explain later."

"Are you serious?" cried Reena. "Why can't we talk about it all now?"

Jonah gritted his teeth as fear and urgency warred inside of him. "Because we need to get off The Plane with No Name right now."

"Oh." Reena looked annoyed at herself. "Right."

"That's a wonderful idea," said Terrence, "but I don't think it'll be that easy."

"Why?"

Terrence had risen to his feet while Jonah revealed some things he'd seen from the recorder. Jonah saw perspiration on his face. "Prisoners. They must've glimpsed the ethereality in here."

Jonah swore and scrambled to his feet. Reena did the same. Upon following Terrence's line of sight, they saw them. Eight, maybe nine of them, bounding toward the shack like rabid dogs.

"Shit, shit, shit," spat Terrence. "We got to blaze, where are the Tallys—"

"No!" said Jonah. "We can't risk bringing one of those freaks into Amelia's house! We need to return to our origin point and use the *Astralimes* from the clearest space."

Reena looked over and scanned Laban's shack. "Not the most structurally sound place. Got an idea. Jonah, I know that you're still screwing your brains back on properly, so just stand there for a moment. Terrence, I need you."

Puzzled, Terrence moved nearer to Reena. She positioned him in front of her and then clamped tightly on his shoulders.

"Damn, Reena," he winced.

"Man up and be quiet. Hold up your hands, focus your endowments, and brace yourself."

The prisoners were gaining; Jonah didn't know what Reena was waiting for. Finally, when they were sure to breach the door, she roared and used her ethereal speed to propel Terrence forward. Since he'd braced himself and focused, Terrence's ethereal strength detached the front of the shack from the rest of it, and the portion collided with the prisoners, which stunned and threw them in disarray.

Jonah, completely recovered, sprang forward, tagging two of the prisoners who'd dodged the new projectile and ran for Terrence and Reena, who'd fallen to their knees. He yanked them up, gave their energies a quick balancing boost, and guided them in the opposite direction.

"That was awesome, Reena. Now, we have to run!"

They all ran, headed for the center area where they'd started. With prisoners at their heels, there wasn't much time to get bearings. Jonah was thankful that Reena ran at a normal speed to accommodate him and Terrence, because she could have easily outstripped them. When they passed the *pankration* spot, a prisoner grabbed his shoulder. Jonah swung blindly and heard a grunt. After twenty more yards of running, Jonah had a realization. He was aware of Creyton's plan. He knew about The Final Destination, which was his home. But he and his friends now experienced a hindrance from sharing that knowledge, because of psycho prisoners who were stupid enough to stay on this cesspit Plane because they didn't know any better ...

He stopped running. Terrence and Reena hurried five or ten more feet before they realized that it was just the two of them.

"Jonah!" hissed Terrence. "What in the name of God are you doing?"

Jonah ran his tongue across his teeth and yanked out his batons. "We don't have time for this shit."

He turned and whacked one pursuing prisoner so hard in the face with the baton that he did a backflip before slamming the ground, facedown. He briefly charged one baton and struck another prisoner with it, which sent the man flying back. One prisoner grabbed him from behind, but he threw his head back, reveling in the crunch he felt when the man's nose broke like a seashell. He flipped that guy over his back and then decked another in the face, right before using wind ethereality to knock out a fifth prisoner. The sixth and final prisoner, who hadn't expected Jonah's offense, lunged with a snarl. Jonah dropped his batons and stopped the guy with a kick to the gut. When he doubled over, Jonah clamped the guy's head and collapsed backward, which drove the man headfirst into the ground. He then stood up, willed the batons back into his hands, and faced Terrence and Reena. They stared at him, completely awestruck.

"Jonah," said Reena, "what the hell was that?"

"We don't have time to waste right now. And they were holding us up."

Terrence's eyes gleamed. "Did you have to give him a DDT?"

Jonah shrugged. "If you can Superman-Punch people, I can DDT people."

"Uh, guys," said Reena, "we're about to have more company!"

Jonah looked over and saw a dozen prisoners who'd noticed their activities and were rapidly heading their way. Swearing, he grabbed Terrence and Reena, pulled them through the *Astralimes* and back into Amelia's living room. The instant they stepped inside, both Amelia and Tempie shot up, relieved.

"Are you guys alright?" demanded Amelia.

"Yeah," said Jonah. "Things got hairy for a moment, but we're pretty much unscathed. And thank you, Amelia."

He dropped the Tally in her hand.

"Did you find what you were looking for?" asked Tempie.

"I did. But I'm not talking about it here."

"What?"

"I need you to do something," he told Amelia and Tempie. "Alert everyone that you know you can trust and tell them to go to the estate." He turned to Terrence and Reena. "Text, call—I don't care what you do—but I need you to tell everyone."

"Tell everyone what?"

Jonah took a deep breath. "That Jonah Rowe has made an executive decision as Overseer of the Grannison-Morris estate. Everyone is recalled, and their family and friends are welcome as well. The exodus is done."

Tempie and Amelia began to contact allies that very second, as did Terrence and Reena. Then, Tempie took a second to reverse the Spectral Illusions she'd placed on Jonah, Terrence, and Reena. Then, as a collective, they used the *Astralimes* to the estate.

Jonah had to pause for a moment to take it in. The place

was every bit as palatial and comforting as it was when Jonah first saw it. The land was plentiful, but not as colorful and vibrant as it usually was, on account of it being late winter. In spite of himself, Jonah thought of the mornings that he'd slept in, the times that he'd seen Liz with her straw hat, and other friends walking around with armloads of flowers and weeds. He thought of Thanksgiving and Christmas festivities. How many things did he take for granted? He spent the majority of the time enjoying that he had a family again, and simply wished the best for them all.

"Jonah," said Reena, "are we doing this outside, or in the family room?"

"Family room. Just seems like that would be more organized."

Reena removed her dampener for a few seconds, and Jonah was just about to ask her why when she froze.

"Jonah, you might want to move."

Jonah obliged, and not a second too soon.

With a sharp gust of wind, the floodgates opened. Liz, Nella, Sandrine, and their parents showed up. The entire Decessio family. Malcolm and his mother. Patience, Reverend Abbott, Spader, Douglas, Katarina, Magdalena, Themis, Akshara, Prodigal, Autumn Rose, Stella Marie, Obadiah, Xenia, Jada, R.J., and Sebastian. There was Jerry Bladen, another one of Amelia's colleagues that they'd rescued. A lot of them brought their families, as Jonah had requested.

Then, there were people whose presence surprised Jonah.

Ben-Israel. Sherman. Barry. Noah. Maxine. And Grayson.

"Grayson?"

"Yeah," said the burly guy. "It's me. I actually had Terrence's and Reena's phone numbers. So, I got their texts. I wasn't going to miss this, not for anything."

Jonah was about to question him further when another appearance shocked the hell out of him.

"*Rheadne?*"

"None other," said Rheadne with a grin.

"You came alone?"

Rheadne nodded, her grin fading. "Michael and Alicia, along with Gabe, of course, were trying to convince others to show up when your friends sent out the summons. "I didn't feel like waiting. I hope they'll come, but I wasn't staying back. I didn't need Gabe's permission to come here." She appraised him. "You look amazing, Jonah. Been doing Crossfit?"

"Nah. Juicing."

His face warmed as Reena snorted.

Then—as if the moment couldn't get any more awkward—the wind picked up again, and another person stepped out of nothingness. Jonah's eyes bulged.

"Vera!"

"Aw, shit," said Terrence.

Vera reddened somewhat when she saw Jonah but then her eyes fell on Rheadne. Her awkwardness faded completely, and her upper lip curled as the two women sized each other up.

"Rheadne."

"Vera," Rheadne responded. "Watched your play. It was pretty awesome."

"I know it is." Vera was neither moved nor flattered. "I wrote it."

Just then, Daniel appeared, a bow across his back, looking alert and wary as always. He saw the small collection and approached them.

"What's the deal, son? Surely, you didn't rescind the exodus to converse on the lawn? Let's head in here."

All weirdness was temporarily forgotten. Thank God for Daniel's timely arrival.

They joined the group heading inside the estate. Reena cut an eye at Terrence, who looked disappointed.

"Really, Terrence?"

He looked at her in surprise. "What?"

"Fess up. You're down in the dumps because Rheadne didn't speak to you."

Terrence frowned. "Not at all. I'm not thinking about that woman. I was hoping that the summons would have ... brought some support from Spirit Land."

Reena looked pleasantly surprised. Jonah wasn't. He got it now; what was strange to him before was strange no longer. Terrence had merely desired Rheadne; that was a fantasy. His feelings for Haniel, however, ran further than surface level. There was actually some substance there.

He hoped that Terrence would get to see her again when this was over. But he couldn't think about that. It depended on what happened here.

Right before they reached the door, the wind picked up again, and another unexpected face appeared out of thin air.

Felix.

Rheadne, Vera, Tempie, Amelia, and Daniel had already gone inside. It was just Jonah, Terrence, Reena, and Felix.

"You got room for another pair of hands in there?" the sazer asked.

"Depends." Jonah gave him a scrutinizing look. "Who are you?"

Felix drew himself up to full height. "I'm a sazer who has screwed up one time too many. I'm paying for those issues and walking that path gladly. I am also a man,"—he reached into his pocket—"who now carries a sobriety chip in his pocket instead of a Vintage bottle."

He pulled out a chip and showed it to them.

Jonah nodded. "It's good to see you again, Felix."

"It's good to be back. Lead the way."

Jonah walked into the family room, very happy to see such a gathering that was further augmented by their families. A number of spirits and spiritesses were there as well, and they seemed to be led by his old spirit friend, Graham, the Very Elect Spirit who used to work under the Phasmastis Curaie. Rounding out the group were the heralds, led by Bast. Jonah felt a mild pang not seeing Naphtali there, but he filed it away.

"It's a blessing to see you all here. I am aware that the last time most of you were here, the Deadfallen disciples took us by surprise. But now, we're all here to prevent something worse than that happening."

They all looked at one another, concerned and fearful.

"Creyton's goal is immortality. Didn't take a genius to figure that one out. But the way he plans to go about achieving it is another story. His plan is to make a big statement right here at the estate, which he has deemed the Final Destination. I now know that that was his plan when he did the Decimation in the 1940s."

"What is he going to do?" asked Liz.

Jonah sighed. "His plan is to completely and totally destroy the estate. And then he plans to send out extermination teams to hunt down anyone who opposes him. That is his goal with Omega—to end me, as well as the physical life of everyone who doesn't bow down."

There were gasps. Daniel gripped an arrow tightly. Reverend Abbott closed his eyes, as though he wanted to pray.

Jonah continued matter-of-factly. "For those of you who understand my next words, great. For those of you who don't, that's unfortunate, because I don't have time to explain. But the Final Destination was the largest crow from that dream I had years ago. Jonathan said that it was Omega, and we all believed him. He was partially right, but the large crow, the one that never landed, is the event that Creyton plans to lower now."

"Why does he feel the need to destroy the estate before he goes and unleashes extermination?" asked Spader.

"I learned that, too," said Jonah. "The estate is a living force in many ways. It's able to do things that a normal home does not. Was I alone in wondering why the estate has always had space for everyone? Like now, in this room? Why we are all comfortable in here, despite our huge numbers?"

There were murmurs of interest.

"It's the estate's life force," Jonah revealed. "It's called The Blessing of the House. All are welcome, and there is always room and comfort. It's also how the estate manages the Christmas trees each year, despite no one ever knowing how Jonathan did it. The estate and the land are tied to one another. Same life force, which makes it one big link. That link is a vital threat to Creyton's occupation. Always has been. Right up there with how he views me. He wants to destroy me, this estate, and the land. Raze it to the ground. Kill the plant at the roots."

"That's the part you left out on The Plane, Jonah," said Reena slowly.

"What Plane?" asked Bobby. "You guys went to The Plane with No Name?"

"You're right, Reena." Jonah didn't mean to ignore Bobby, but what happened on the Plane was a long story. "Creyton has known exactly what he was doing all along, from the Six up until now. I've been on his hit list since the minute he met me, and he's always viewed me as a monkey wrench. He made it so there was enough fear that people would contemplate an exodus. Creyton knew Jonathan would never go for that, and that's why the Cut happened, because a Splinter was sure to follow in some way, shape, or form.

"The exodus ambush was meant to solidify the fear that was already in place, as well as the belief that leaving here was the best thing after all. Why he wants to kill me first? And destroy the estate? It's psychological. If he destroys the last beacons of hope, me and the estate, who would oppose him? Who would have the will to fight? He wanted the estate to be wide open—"

"And yet," said a voice of winter, "here you all are."

There were screams all over the place. Those among Jonah's friends who'd brought their children gripped them tightly as they looked on in horror. Jonah shot around.

Creyton was there, right behind him.

"Don't be so surprised," said Creyton, but there was something odd.

The Creyton in front of Jonah hadn't said a thing, yet they'd all heard his voice.

Then Katarina let loose a scream that brought everyone's attention toward her. Jonah felt a surge of horror as he saw Creyton standing on the stairs ...

And behind him as well. There were *two* Creytons.

"Holy Christ," whispered Reverend Abbott, wide-eyed.

"Not quite, Preacher," said the Creyton nearest Jonah. "Though I can see the mistake. I did come back from the dead, after all."

Jonah noticed something. When the Creyton behind him spoke, the one on the stairs didn't move his mouth at all. It was as if the two of them were having independent interactions.

"Rowe, this is what a superior being is capable of doing," said the Creyton nearest to him. He'd noticed Jonah's shock. "But the best part is the fact that I'm not done just yet."

He pointed near the front door and there was yet another Creyton standing there. A great many people yelped and scrambled away from him.

The Creyton at the front door grinned. That brought a frown to Jonah's face. And this man accused Laban of being changeable?

The Creyton nearest Jonah cracked his neck muscles. "I believe that I have everyone's attention now. Good. Hear me and hear me well."

He glared at the doppelganger at the front door, and it vanished. He turned to the one on the stairs and it vanished as well. Then he regarded them all, much like a teacher would regard impertinent pupils.

"I had hoped to avoid this." He looked apologetic. Disappointed. "I expected Rowe to return alone, not with the rest of you infidels in tow. Had Rowe not run around hiding all these months, this could have been over and done with. He could have been dead, this place could have been in ruins, and Omega could have been over. But he had to string it out, hiding all over the place. I must admit though, your travels did lead me to the Tool of Omega—"

"Which you can't use," snapped Jonah.

Creyton glared at him. "I don't need a fancy toy to defeat you, boy." He then turned back to the crowd. "How very much like children all of you are. Then again, it has always been true that the ones in need of the most guidance are children and fools. That being said, I freely understand and accept that you do not know what you do. So I will grant you a generous option. The same option that I gave your acting Overseer, in fact."

Jonah's eyes narrowed. Creyton didn't even bother to look at him.

"Walk away. Walk away and accept that you had no chance against me. This estate and these lands will be obliterated. And the exterminations—the fulfillment of Omega—will commence afterward. There is nothing you can do to stop that. However, if you accept my offer, I will tell my forces to exercise restraint when my culling begins in earnest. I will tell them to pass by your homes, much like the avenging angel in your Bible."

Revered Abbott gritted his teeth. Even in a moment such as this, sacrilegious connotations pissed him off.

"You can either watch the inevitability safely from afar." Creyton made his voice provocative. "Or you can remain here, with the knowledge that despite my offer, you opted to die. Those are my terms, nonnegotiable. The choice is yours."

There was silence as Creyton laid his eyes on Jonah, as if he hadn't been standing there the entire time.

"Jonah Rowe, these next words are for you and you alone. I told you long ago what would happen if you remained in my path. You didn't listen, and therefore sealed your fate. Make no mistake; the fact that you are also a Blue Aura is merely an accident of birth. Your very life is an accident. I cannot stress that enough. You are a random detail who has flailed through life until the time was ripe for the wrong to be corrected. That time was not in Spirit Land...I granted you a reprieve. That reprieve is now over.

"This is *my* time now. Jonathan couldn't stop me. He couldn't get the job done in his physical life, nor his afterlife. Not even the grave could hold me, Rowe. How many signs do you need? My time is now and forever. Your time is at an end. If you have any decency, any at all, you will spend this time convincing your friends to save themselves and abandon you to your fate. Because I assure you, that is the only thing that you have power over now. Don't fail them. Do the right thing. You have four hours, thirty minutes."

He vanished, leaving a deafening silence in his wake. All eyes were on Jonah, and he stared back at every one of them as he steeled himself.

"I am the Overseer of the estate, but I am not your master. I am not leaving. I will fight until my very last breath if it comes to that. But I will not obligate you guys to do that, too."

Terrence looked at the family room's occupants, and then back at Jonah. "To hell with Creyton's offer. I already told you I've always got your back, Jonah."

Reena stepped forward. "I'll accept a blind date from a man before I abandon you, Jonah."

Some of the others began to mirror the same sentiments.

Jonah blinked. "No one's leaving?"

"No," said Patience. "We will get the children, non-fighters, and the elderly to safety, but the rest of us will remain here, no matter what."

Jonah closed his eyes. There was such a surge of gratitude in his heart that words couldn't convey it. He nodded and turned to Reverend Abbott.

"Reverend Abbott, as a man of faith, I would never ask you to take up arms again. But I would like to ask you to oversee a task that is equally as important. Could you personally lead the children, non-combatants, and elderly to safety."

Reverend Abbott was a conflicted man. He was a clergyman; his days of violence were long over. In his heart, however, some part of him remained a soldier and a pugilist. That part of him seemed to be giving him a very hard time about abandoning a fight. He swallowed. "I'll lead them to safety. The Abbott tunnel?"

"Not possible," said Daniel. "When the exodus was ambushed, the Deadfallen disciples caved it in."

Jonah was distracted for only a second. "Katarina, would you be so kind as to make a link to Reverend Abbott's faith haven?"

"Absolutely." Katarina headed to a closet door and grabbed it. It began to glow purple. "I'll even help with moving the kids and the elderly. You coming, Dougie?"

Douglas hadn't moved. "Katy, I can't." There was a silent apology in his eyes. "I'm not a non-combatant anymore. I can't leave here."

Katarina blinked slowly as fear and concern altered her face. She fought back frightened tears but nodded. "Please be careful, baby. I love you."

"I will," promised Douglas. "I love you too."

They kissed, and she opened the closet door to reveal the sanctuary of Reverend Abbott's faith haven. The movement of children and elderly began. Jonah looked Daniel's way, feeling puzzled.

"Four hours and thirty-something minutes? I did it in my head. When the time's up, it'll be 11:11 P.M. That time supposed to mean something?"

"Yes," said Daniel at once. "It is a highly spiritually significant time, 11:11. Tenths have gotten it in their minds that it's a time when they'll be able to see spirits. Cute, but untrue. In actuality, 11:11 signifies the emergence of a new prevailing spiritual consciousness. Creyton must be planning to use that time to attack, as though it will be a good omen for him."

Jonah let that sink in. Good omen, huh? He'd just have to make his own luck in all this.

He noticed Douglas, who seemed troubled. He instantly understood. He knew that he didn't want to abandon the fight, but he didn't really know where to go from there. Jonah had a thought and was suddenly struck with inspiration.

"Doug, you're a chess prodigy."

Douglas looked up. "Yeah, so?"

"So, you have tactical know-how. Tell me, if the estate grounds was a chessboard, how would you defend it?"

The concern and doubt in Douglas' eyes faded as a gleam entered them. Jonah could practically see the gears turning. "Get me a map of the grounds."

Daniel provided one. Jonah took it to a nearby table and flattened it for Douglas. He scratched his temple and looked it over.

"There are some solid places to set up lines of defense," he murmured after a while. "To the east, there are a bunch of places where the land inclines, so there is much higher ground. An ideal place to set up some archers."

Jonah nodded. "Daniel, are you up to setting up a contingent of archers in the eastern part of the grounds?"

"Of course." Daniel rose. "I will even have assistance."

He pointed to the window. Everyone looked. There were dozens of spirits and spiritesses out front, who all appeared to be tangible and strapped with bows and arrows like Daniel. Jonah looked at him in confusion.

"Nature spirits and spiritesses," Daniel explained before Jonah could ask.

"What?" said Reena. "I've been here for years, and I've never seen a single nature spirit or spiritess."

"That's the mark of a good nature spirit, Reena," Daniel told her. "But they've always been here. Who do you think keeps things tidy when Miss Manville and her revolving door of helpers aren't here to garden and do yard tasks? Who do you think replenished the deadened Christmas tree in winter for Jonathan, making it fresh and strong for your holidays? Who do you think kept critters from eating all of you alive with all the time you've spent in the Glade? Now, if you'll excuse me, we will go and fulfill your request to do sentry duty in the east."

He rose and the archers among them followed him outside to join the nature spirits. When Daniel reached the door, he paused, and turned back to Jonah.

"I very nearly forgot, Jonah. When you get the chance, gather all of the heralds outside and say, 'Commence Alter Ego'."

"Huh? Why?"

"You'll see. If you're a praying man, pray that I see Brore-amir. I have an arrow ready-made for his jugular."

He and the archers were gone.

"That was baffling, and scary," commented Douglas, who returned his focus to the map. "Jonah, I was thinking about wild cards among us. The people who might not function well with strategy, but can still play a charter role in defense—"

"That is so me right there, it ain't even funny." Spader hopped up and elevated his voice for the crowd. "Who in here doesn't have a problem stealing?"

Hands rose. Some were eager, others hesitant. Spader grinned.

"Cool beans. Y'all come with me. Jonah, we'll be back about an hour before the night games begin."

He and a collection of Elevenths left. Liz looked after them with disdain while Bobby laughed.

"Okay." Douglas was back at it. "Jonah, the next parts are on the front grounds. Where face-to-face and melee would happen." He narrowed his eyes, and then snapped his fingers. "The people with sharper weapons can take the north side. Southside can go to those with blunt-force trauma weapons. The clubs, the bats, the knucks—that sort of thing. They don't need strategy, not when the whole point is to just beat someone to a pulp."

Jonah looked at Douglas, very impressed. "Excellent, Doug! Who could lead the northern group?"

"I've got that," volunteered Tempie. "Amelia left with the archers; she can have that. But I'm good and sharp. Look."

She unveiled a vicious short sword, which gleamed with the silver of her aura. Reena looked at it, intrigued.

"I carried a javelin that I practiced with for years. But then, I found this." She lifted up the socket wrench.

Tempie grinned. "Savage and ruthless. Fits you somehow, sis."

"Take care out there," said Reena.

"Always," said Tempie. "Now, everyone with sharp weapons, follow me!"

She led a group of people outside, which included Sterling, Nella, Themis, and Magdalena.

"Raymond," said Jonah, "I have a feeling that the melee group might be the largest. Can you take a portion with you?"

"Thought you'd never ask." Raymond held a two-by-four with ethereal steel studs aloft. He beckoned to a group of people, and they rose and followed him out.

"That still leaves a few people." Jonah looked around. "Patience, Felix, you think you can man the rest of them?"

"I'd be honored," said Patience. "Felix? Ready to redeem yourself?"

Felix looked discomfited for only a second, then nodded. "Yeah. I'm on top of it."

Unexpectedly, Malcolm stood up. "I'm throwing my hat in with this group. Liz, Bobby, Alvin—can you join us, too?"

All the names he called rose with curiosity. Jonah asked the question.

"Why the preference, Malcolm?"

"One, Bobby can put some power behind a blunt weapon. Second, Liz has always had to rely on where to hit people, since she doesn't have much strength. Alvin doesn't possess a primary weapon. And I think I can outfit everyone."

"Really?" asked Terrence. "You've been building a weapons cache, independent of the armory?"

"For years now."

Liz's eyes widened. "You mean your discards?"

"Exactly."

"Seriously?" demanded Bobby. "I thought you threw them all away!"

Malcolm focused his attention on Bobby. "I'm a perfectionist, not a fool."

The big group left.

"You guys that are left can set up right here, inside the walls," directed Douglas. "You know the traps, the defenses, everything. Plus, you can grab armaments from the armory, whatever feels right for you. Mr. and Mrs. Decessio, could you coordinate that? And Mr. and Mrs. Manville?"

Mr. Decessio stood up. "You can count on us, son."

Mrs. Manville shook her head. "Never thought I'd see the day that Sandrine had a crowbar in one hand and a switchblade in the other," she remarked as they headed to the armory.

Jonah straightened from his bent over position on the table, grinning at Douglas. "I wouldn't have been able to organize the troops without you, man. I mean that."

Douglas shrugged but looked pleased. "I do what the leader says, friend."

"A good leader knows when to delegate," countered Jonah. "I've got something for you. You deserve it, especially after what you've just done."

He placed a chess piece in Douglas' hand. The knight piece.

"It's fitting, I think," said Jonah. "Now, go arm yourself, brother, and watch your back."

With a quick nod, Douglas headed to the armory. From outside, Jonah could hear a whole host of spirits and spiritesses teeling Elevenths, "You have been endowed."

"Did either of you see where Grayson went?" he asked Terrence and Reena.

Reena frowned. "Random, much?"

"I know," admitted Jonah, "but he's the only one who can help me with this next thing. Let's check outside."

They went out to the front, where all types of activities were going on. Jonah still looked here and there for Grayson, and glimpsed Vera conversing with Tempie. The moment he saw her, he was distracted by a sudden weight in his left pocket. He dug in his pocket, wondering what was there, and then his mouth dropped.

How in the hell did that get in his pocket?

"Time out, Terrence, Reena. Vera!"

He jogged her way.

Vera's eyes narrowed as he got closer. "Jonah, I hope you won't try to talk me into leaving this fight. You needn't even bother."

"No, no. I've, um, got something for you."

He lifted the object from his pocket. It was the ring that Jonathan had given Vera a couple of years prior with the Protector's Proximity on it, which kept her Time Item ethereality in check. Somehow, it was affixed to a necklace.

Veralooked at it for a few seconds, surprised. She glanced a few feet away, where Rheadne was practicing slashes with a cerise-gleaming dagger. Her activities fooled no one; her eyes darted at the two of them every couple of seconds. Something changed in Vera's eyes when she noticed Rheadne's glances. She walked into Jonah's personal space but didn't take the necklace. Still facing him, she hoisted up her hair, which gave him free rein of her neck.

"Go ahead. Put it on me."

Jonah reached around her neck and clasped the necklace. She grinned devilishly.

"Thank you, Jonah. You're a blessing."

She returned to Tempie. Jonah walked back to Terrence and Reena.

"Did you see that?"

"Saw it all," said Reena.

"Would you happen to have any idea what that was all about?"

"Not a clue," replied Terrence.

Reena rolled her eyes.

"What?" said Jonah.

"Jonah," said Reena, ignoring the question, "you forgot a certain portion of our group."

"Huh?"

She means us, Jonah.

Jonah turned around and saw Bast with all the heralds. "Oh, right. My apologies, my friends. Commence Alter Ego."

All the cats, every single one of them, closed their eyes. After several seconds, Jonah Terrence, and Reena bore witness to the most incredible phenomena they'd ever seen.

The heralds began to grow, transmogrifying and lengthening. Each one became lither, more muscular, and sleeker. The bodies weren't the only things growing, either; their teeth and claws took on vicious edges as well ...

And then, the house cats were no more. In front of them stood full-blown predators.

Lions, cougars, tigers, cheetahs, leopards, bobcats, marble cats, panthers, ocelots, and lynxes. It was a dangerous-looking group.

"Holy shit!" exclaimed Terrence. "I never knew they could do that! And what the hell is that thing that Laura turned into?"

"A jaguarondi," said Reena, mystified.

"Um, you mean a jaguar?"

"No, I mean a jaguarondi. South American. Another name for them is a leoncillo, or little lion."

"Oh." Terrence remained transfixed. "Cool. Badass, though."

Jonah approached Bast, now a graceful lioness. He had half a mind to flee, but Bast moved closer to him.

It's still me, Jonah, she verified. *Rest assured that I am not a danger. To you, anyway.*

"Good to know," said Jonah with relief. "Claw up some disciples for us, why don't you?"

Much obliged.

The predator heralds dispersed. One moment later, Jonah saw the guy he'd been looking for.

"Grayson! I need a favor."

"Sure, Jonah. What's up?"

Jonah hesitated. He needed to scrounge every ounce of resolve that he had in his body to choke out the next words. "I need you to get in contact with Trip. Tell him that we need to talk."

27

11:11 P. M

It was 10:35 P.M. now.

Thirty-six minutes remained until Creyton's deadline. Mostly everyone was in position, and a great many of the blunt-force brigade was now equipped with, among other things, ethereal steel bats from Malcolm, which Alvin had given the corny name of "base bombs." Bobby kept going around, trying to psych people up, saying, "This is for the championship, people! Nothing less than your A-game now!"

Spader and his little band of thieves, which had included Autumn Rose and Stella Marie, came back with over thirty cars, which they parked in a strategic half-ring at the front of the drive. Spader referred to it as an "Iron Semi-Circle". Then he and the others came to Jonah, all with wooden boxes.

"Come on, J," said Spader eagerly. "Do your Zeus, electro-man thing."

"Why?"

"The cars are only half the trap, see," Spader explained. "If those dumbasses try to get past them, they'll fry like chickens once you put some of your electric shtick in here."

Intrigued, Jonah willed his fingers to sting and touched each box. Each of them began to buzz, and Spader grinned.

"How exactly are you going to make the cars into electric traps?" asked Reena.

"Trade secret." Spader's trademark mischief all over his face. "Thank you kindly, Jonah!"

The brief levity was punctured almost immediately by Felix, who came to Jonah, looking grim.

"Jonah, something isn't right in town."

"Huh? What do you mean?"

"When Spader returned, he said stealing the cars was easy. Said the town was even quieter than usual. He took it as thieves' luck. But I have always been leery of things that were too good to be true."

"Meaning?"

"Meaning that I requested of the nature spirits to go into town and check things out," said Felix. "The townspeople are all ... asleep. But not like normal slumber. Like ... some type of comatose trance."

"What? What the hell is happening to them?"

"Think, Jonah." Some of Felix's old hardline demeanor was in his tone. "Take a wild guess."

Jonah looked at Terrence and Reena. A bone-chilling realization hit him like bricks. "Creyton is tugging at their essences right now?"

Felix nodded, his mouth curled into a sneer. "Looks as if he's powering up and making preparations as well."

"He's *that* powerful?" demanded Terrence. "To usurp people while they're still physically alive?"

"He can't usurp physically living people, not entirely," answered Felix. "It's more like leeching. And he is doing that to the town."

Jonah shook his head. "How the hell do we stop him?"

"By *winning*, Jonah!" Felix threw up hs hands like it was the most obvious thing in the world. "Kick his ass!"

Felix headed away. Reena appeared to file away her alarm with Felix's last words.

"It's nice to see him back to his former self, at the very least. But Creyton doing that—"

Jonah stiffened, prompting Reena to cease. He'd just gotten the strangest feeling.

"Jonah? Are you alright?"

"Trip's here. Grayson came through."

"Say what?" said Terrence. "How do you know?"

"I—I sensed him. I sensed the moment when he touched ground here at the estate. It's the damnedest thing."

"No," smirked Reena. "You're the Overseer of the Estate. You can sense when people appear inside there. How many times did Jonathan say that he knew when people showed up? It's an Overseer thing."

Jonah marveled at the ability for a but second; they just didn't have the time. He looked at his watch. 10:42 P.M. "Cutting it fine, isn't he?" he said, a little annoyed.

"You need to keep it in the box, Jonah," warned Reena.

"Yeah, dude," said Terrence. "Liz won't be there to choke you out this time."

Jonah rolled his eyes. "Thanks," was all he said to them.

He headed back inside. His friends, who had taken posts at the windows and set traps indoors as well, looked very apprehensive next to Trip's cronies: Karin, Markus, Ian, Jax, Indica, and the rest of them. They were all seated or standing near the kitchen door, where Jonah knew Trip to be. It was as though they were guarding it or poised to eavesdrop. Jonah took a deep breath and made a point to balance his emotions once more.

"Thank you, Gray," he said.

Grayson, who stood apart from Trip's group, simply

nodded. Jonah nodded at Terrence and Reena, who weren't willing to allow him to walk into the situation alone. He paid no further attention to Trip's clique as he pushed open the kitchen door and walked inside.

Trip sat at the table, staring straight ahead at the staircase that led to the upstairs bedrooms. Jonah couldn't help but realize that Trip was in the exact same place he'd been when they'd first met.

Full circle, in some weird way.

Jonah hadn't seen Trip since he'd bashed in his face, and he'd been bandaged up due to the work of the Greens assisting him afterward. Now, it looked as though nothing had occurred. But that was from a physical standpoint only. Trip didn't even look at him, but the hatred radiated off him. It was almost like it had an aura of its own.

"Gray said that you wanted to talk, Rowe," he said in a tone conveying controlled calm. "So, I suggest you do so."

Jonah gritted his teeth and measured his words. "I'll cut to the chase because we ain't got the time for anything else. Creyton wants to burn the estate to the ground, preferably with me in it."

Trip snorted. "Sucks for you."

Jonah closed his eyes. This was hard as hell. Almost harder than the essence cognition thing. "We need you and your friends' help with defending our home."

Trip raised and then lowered his eyebrows with such apathy, Jonah almost lost it right then and there.

"In case you forgot," he said, his voice a whisper because he didn't trust it otherwise, "this is your home, too."

Trip repositioned himself in the chair but said nothing. Jonah blinked.

"Trip, what is your deal? Where is your head at, huh?"

He was doing all he could to maintain his anger, which had

always been such a tumultuous thing concerning Trip, anyway. But he knew that he had to. Securing Trip's aid in this fight would be invaluable.

Trip remained silent for a while longer. He didn't even acknowledge Jonah's presence. His face remained inscrutable as he stared in the opposite direction. The silence steadily chipped away at Jonah's restraint and just when he was about to say something else, Trip spoke.

"I have no desire to deal with you, Rowe, because I refuse to be slighted a second longer."

"Slighted? Sorry, but you'll have to explain that."

Eerily, Trip hadn't changed position, nor had he changed his expression. He did, however, tighten his fists so his knuckles cracked. "You want an explanation? Here goes. I'm tired of dealing with your presence, Rowe. I tolerated your hotheaded, maverick, and irresponsible demeanor for far too long, and I will not do it anymore."

Jonah's anger did its damndest to erode his resolve but, miraculously, he maintained it. He could handle the insults and the jabs; Lord knew how many times he'd heard them from Trip. But they'd already had one fight, and Jonah had experienced rage so fierce that, in hindsight, it frightened him. At the same time, Trip had his beef with him. Jonah didn't care what Trip thought of him, but he needed his help. Maybe they could reach a thimbleful of understanding if Trip finally got his bullshit out of his system.

"So, this is about me, huh? Let it out, Trip. Why do you hate me? Forget that shit that you said in Family Court before you coaxed everybody into leaving. Just put all the cards on the table right now."

Trip shot out of his seat and was in Jonah's face. Like Jonah, he, too, seemed to have a paltry grasp on restraint. Jonah didn't want another fight; that could very well shatter morale.

But he was no fool, nor was he a bitch. If Trip swung, he'd swing back.

"You must *always* be the focal point, don't you? It's always about you! The estate was thriving. All was well. Jonathan did excellently, and no one had a need for a damned beacon. Then you came along, and, like I said before, you had this hold over Jonathan. You broke the cohesion that was in place. Suddenly, my every tactic was questioned. Second-guessed. You divided Jonathan. You fractured a good thing. And you reveled in being a savior! And suddenly, everybody wanted to affix their lips to your ass!"

Jonah's gaze vacillated between Trip's face and fists. He'd heard some of this before, but he was better prepared for an attack this time.

"Jonathan got vanquished, which was unthinkable. But he gave you the Vitasphera. You. For what reason, other than you being a Blue Aura, and not even the one who's the most power-ful? Jonathan is gone. His leadership, tutelage ... gone forever. And we, the ones that got left behind, are supposed to be led by you?"

Jonah's eyes widened. Was this man insane? "You're a few sides short of a full meal, Trip. You think that I wanted to be the Overseer? You think I'm happy to have succeeded Jonathan? That man was the closest thing to a father that I ever had! Are you so blind that you can't see that all I've ever wanted to do was help people here? I would do anything for my family here! I never wanted to be a damn beacon!"

"There you are again, needing to take control!" snapped Trip. "All of this could have been prevented if everyone had listened to me in the first goddamned place! I had the leader-ship skills! I had the tenure! I had the logical insight! I had everything, except that Vitasphera! It went to you, the glory hog, the saving grace of the Eleventh Percent, complete with his admirers, coattail riders, and Blue Groupies here, at Sanctum, and the chunky one that went to England. It's a surprise you weren't banging your little golden Hollywood friend who used to visit here all the time! But you got chosen to be the boss! Where was the sense in that? It's as deluded as fully grown adults believing in some fairy-tale god or children believing in Santa Claus."

Jonah stood there, numb with disbelief. All of his instincts screamed at him to hit Trip, but a modicum of rationality helped him back.

Unfortunately, Trip mistook Jonah's silence for regret. "What's this? Has Master and Ruler over all he surveys, Jonah Rowe, been rendered speechless? No wit? No histrionic comeback? Then again, you can't, can you? Because I know what you're thinking. After all of these years, you realize that I make perfect sense."

"Nope," responded Jonah. "I was actually thinking about how much you sound like Creyton right now."

Trip froze, stupefied. He hadn't seen that one coming, least of all from Jonah.

"Yep. You are so blinded with ire, so angry because you feel that you were stepped over. You are ignorant to the true enemy —the enemy that wants to destroy the home of the Protector Guide who took you in and told you that you could be a better man. Where is that better man now? People have been murdered, displaced, tormented, you name it. But all you've worried about is your imagined slights. While you sit here, stewing and brooding, the only thing *thriving* is Creyton's evil. Your inactivity makes you part of it, Trip."

Trip's eyes flashed in cold surprise, but Jonah wasn't done.

"You like lording your intelligence over people, Trip? Like profound sayings and all that? Try this one on for size: *He who does not punish evil commands it to be done.* Leonardo Da

Vinci said that. Speaks volumes, doesn't it? Well, you know what? I commend you, Trip. You are a better man than me. I would have never abandoned people I've known for years just because I felt stepped over ... and couldn't take my ego out of the equation. I couldn't ignore all the good things that a benevolent Protector Guide did for me, just because I got called out on my bullshit. It takes a strength that I cannot fathom. Kudos. A round of applause for commanding murder and torture to be done."

Mockingly, he brought his hands together a few times in fake applause. Then, he turned his back on Trip and exited the kitchen. In addition to Trip's sneering buddies, other people had been eavesdropping as well, including Grayson, Terrence, and Reena.

Jonah regarded them all. "I guess you all heard that. Whatever. It is what it is. We've got this."

He made to walk, but a hand blocked him.

It was Karin.

Jonah blinked, confused, but Karin didn't keep him waiting long.

"Rowe, we ain't friends, and we ain't ever gonna be. But you were right. Jonathan did save all of our lives. We'd all be in hell now were it not for all the things Jonathan did for us. I'll play ball, for *him*. Tell me where you want me."

Jonah blinked at her again. Did she just say what he thought she said? Her friends were just as dumbfounded, and Grayson looked at her as though she'd grown a second head. Jonah recovered faster than the rest of them. "Um, what weapon are you carrying, Karin?"

Karin opened her jacket to show him. "Slapjack."

"Head to the southern part of the grounds. You'll find the melee troop; they've all got blunt-force weapons like your own. Gray can show you the way, because he's with that group, too."

He looked at the rest of Trip's friends. "You'd best get your ringleader and blaze. Wouldn't want you to risk staying here too long and wind up helping us out by accident."

He, Terrence, and Reena walked back outside, where Gray and Karin left them, both heading south without another word. Terrence shook his head.

"Damn. Who would have thought that that bitch had a better nature to appeal to?"

"I know," said Reena. "Her head was so far up her ass, I thought it'd take an executive order to get it out."

Jonah fervently tried to corral the thoughts that teemed in his mind. He saw all these people: friends, allies, mentors, protégés, heralds, spirits, spiritesses, and the few sazers. All the Elevenths had their aura color on display; several were the same. And right there, on the front lines, he was the only blue.

The only one.

His mind was split in two. One half tried to ignore the grim truth that not all of them would make it through this. It wasn't reality to think otherwise. But the other half of his mind—which shocked him—was fully aware of the fact that there was no other place in the world that he would rather be than right here, on the front line, with his family.

People's watches began to go off simultaneously. Jonah wasn't surprised. He had set his own as well.

It was now 11:11 P.M.

People followed his lead and silenced their watches. The collective all waited in silence to see what would happen now.

There. At the head of the driveway, about fifty yards away from the two of the cars that made up Spader's iron semi-circle, was Creyton.

And he had Jessica with him.

Jonah looked at Terrence and Reena in surprise. What the

hell was this? Where were his Deadfallen disciples? His army of dark ethereal beings?

Creyton surveyed the whole landscape, and slowly shook his head. He then shoved Jessica forward. She took two steps, covered in sweat, clearly not happy about something.

"What's that skank doing?" whispered Terrence.

"You're asking me?" asked Jonah.

Jessica closed her eyes, as though she was concentrating. Then, over fifty or sixty spirits and spiritesses appeared, fettered with ethereal chains, looking terrified.

There were sounds of surprise from Jonah's friends. He was right there with them. What was going on?

Jessica swallowed, raised her right hand, and uttered one word. *"Regress."*

The petrified spirits and spiritesses became pearly mist, which lowered into the ground. With that done, Creyton grabbed Jessica's arm and roughly pulled her away. They faded from view, leaving puzzlement and confusion in their wake.

Silence. The most frightening silence.

Then the earth shifted and began to shake.

"What the—? What did she do—Reena?"

She stood next to Jonah. The socket wrench hung limply at her side. She had the purest terror on her face. "No. No fucking way—"

"Reena, what is it?" Jonah demanded. "What the hell did Jessica do?"

Seconds later, Jonah found out.

Corpses, ghastly, grisly-looking corpses, broke through the earth in multiple areas on the grounds and began to wrest themselves free of the dirt. Groups of them climbed back into the world. Everywhere, people lowered their weapons in horror.

"Jesus Christ!" shouted Terrence, gaping at the monstrosities.

"Are you serious?" cried Jonah, horrorstruck. "Zombies?"

"No, Jonah," said Reena, her tone matching the expression on her face. "Not zombies. Moortuses. Re-spirited remains. Jessica forced those spirits into deceased bodies!"

"Oh no," said Terrence "If those things break through the wine cellar ... there could be a whole bunch of them in there, because of that Blessing of the House thing! Dad, Mom, and everybody still in there won't have a clue or chance!"

He tore off without another word, running for the front door. Reena raced after him. After struggling with himself for several seconds, Jonah abandoned the front line and followed his friends.

28

THE STAND AT GRANNISON-MORRIS

Terrence reached the door first, with Jonah and Reena hot on his heels. Terrence practically knocked the door down, surprising defenders set up inside.

"What's going on out there?" demanded Mr. Decessio.

"Damn zombies, Pop!" cried Terrence. "Came straight up out of the ground!"

"*Moortuses?* Creyton took it there?"

"We're securing the basement!" said Terrence. "Watch your—"

One of the windows shattered as a crow bulleted through it. The deafening caw made its intention more than a little obvious. Without thought, Jonah snatched up a vase and lobbed it at the crow, hitting its head. The crow slammed into the wall, reverting to human form almost immediately as it hit the floor, where the disciple was then immediately overwhelmed by defenders.

Jonah about-faced and followed Terrence and Reena through the kitchen and to the stairs that led to the basement. Reena was still in utter disbelief.

"That was a heinous thing to do! It's almost unholy for spirits to take up the forms of corpses! They'll lose all sense of self being tied to those bodies!"

"Is it like in the movies?" Jonah had to ask. "If they bite you, you become one of them?"

"No, actually. If they bite you, your ass is gone. That's the end of your physical life."

"Good to know," Jonah muttered.

Terrence almost met with disaster once they got off the stairs; a Moortus made to grab him, decayed teeth bared. Terrence showed an unexpected presence of mind when he ducked out of reach and swung upward with one of his burnt-orange-gleaming steel knuckles. The thing's head flew clean off while the body collapsed. He'd decapitated it with an uppercut.

"Been bitten one time in my physical life by a freak monster," Terrence growled. "It isn't ever happening again."

Jonah stared down at the headless corpse. "Good one, Terrence."

"Thanks, bro. Now, I never believed that they could break through the floor, but there are loose areas down here that need tending to. If we take care of them, then the basement should be good."

"Okay, fine—"

Jonah was shoved—or more accurately, *steamrolled*—into the gym. The force was such that he actually rolled a few times when he hit the floor. The Moortus that had done it had dark hollow holes where its eyes should have been, but somehow it knew that it had prey.

What it didn't know, though, was that it had made a horrible mistake viewing Jonah as prey.

He was back on his feet in seconds and used the baton in his left hand to bat away the arms that attempted to grab him.

The other baton went to the Moortus' gut and groin, but Jonah wasn't aiming to hurt, because he knew a corpse wouldn't feel pain. The strike was for breathing room only. When he had that, he jabbed the batons into his belt, flung his hands up, and willed a vicious wind to catch the Moortus, and slam him into the opposite wall. He'd done the same thing months ago to a Deadfallen disciple and had grievously injured him. The Moortus, on the other hand, hit the wall, and broke apart on impact.

Jonah turned to see that Terrence and Reena were under attack as well. Reena slapped a corpse's head back and forth with her socket wrench; it looked as though the head couldn't take much more. Terrene put some space between himself and his Moortus by detaching a barbell and flinging it at its feet, shattering its shins. He then took an E-Z bar and bashed the thing. The ground underneath a gym tile began to shift and a few Moortuses reared, breaking the earth with their heads—

"Jonah! Help me!"

Jonah rushed forward and took an end of the weight rack that Terrence tried to upend. Together, they dumped the massive thing on top of the Moortuses before they'd gotten out of the ground. It was over with a brief series of guttural cries. Jonah looked at dismembered body parts with disgust.

"Reena, what happens to those poor spirits and spiritesses when the bodies are destroyed?"

"I don't know," said Reena, anguish in her voice. "I never knew. As I told you, they lose sense of self when they enter corpses. If they're lucky, maybe they experience a blissful oblivion."

Jonah felt troubled about that one. "I hope so. Where else, Terrence?"

"There's one more place: the wine cellar. There is a part of the floor that isn't stone. But if we knock some heavy things down on it, like we did here, we ought to be fine. As far as the undead rising out of the floors, anyway."

Jonah nodded. "I'll lead the way."

They left the gym, looking around warily. It was eerily quiet down here; they couldn't even hear the sounds from upstairs. A part of him wanted to get back up there to help with Creyton's army, but if they'd have to contend with Moortuses seeping out of the basement, this situation would be that much graver. He got over himself and led the way to the cellar.

He cracked the door and opened it fully when he didn't hear any guttural sounds. The cellar was largely foreign to Jonah; he wasn't a drinker, and this particular wine cellar was empty anyway. The only things on most of the racks these days were dust and cobwebs. There had never been any reason to be in here. Now that it was important, he wished that he'd bumbled in here every once in a while, just for familiarity purposes.

"So far, so good. Now, Terrence, where would the soft spots be?"

"Farthest corner there." Terrence pointed. "Never really knew why the entire floor wasn't stone."

Jonah nodded. "Think if we knock some shelves on the spot, they'll be heavy enough?"

"Shouldn't be an issue."

"Good," said Reena, "let's get this done. The real fight's up there, after all."

Jonah smirked. So, he wasn't alone in how he felt.

He walked to the end of the shelf nearest the spot that Terrence indicated and clamped onto the side, ready to shove it down. It was at that moment that a voice said, "Peek-a-boo, bitch."

Jonah started in shock, but a blade was at his throat within a second.

"Drop 'em," said the voice, flicking the blade down long enough to indicate Jonah's batons.

Jonah dropped his weapons and backed away. The wielder stepped out of the shadows, and Jonah's eyes narrowed.

It was Iuris Mason.

"Surprised to see me? Don't worry, this won't take too long. You probably thought you'd never see me again."

"Didn't think about it one way or the other, to be honest," Jonah murmured.

Iuris glared at him but composed himself and raised his voice. "Brock? Knoaxx? Bring his buddies."

Terrence and Reena rounded a corner of another tall shelf, arms raised, with Tenta and Cisor at their backs. The three of them looked haunted and grim, as if The Plane with No Name had robbed them of humanity. Then again, they might very well have lost that long beforehand, doing the deeds they'd done as a part of Gamaliel Kaine's Network.

Jonah scowled and snapped, "How did you get in here without being seen?"

"Twigs," said Mason. "Duh."

Terrence made a derisive noise. "Latched your lips onto Creyton's ass, huh?"

Mason bristled. "We took his offer to get off The Plane, yes. But we are not Deadfallen disciples."

"Bullshit," was Jonah's immediate response. "You really expect us to believe that?"

"Don't give a rat's ass what you believe," spat Cisor.

Reena laughed coldly. "I can see the bruise on your throat, Mason. No doubt, Tenta and Cisor have them, too. You sold out to get off The Plane. I imagine it wasn't that hard a choice; you'd already sold out with Kaine and that stupid Network. Tell me, did you lose your nuts the same day you lost your freedom?"

Tenta whipped around and punched Reena hard in her midsection. With a cough, she fell to her knees. Terrence bellowed in rage and attempted to come to her defense, but got rapped from behind, knocking him down. Jonah could do nothing as Mason pressed the knife so far into his skin that he felt a thin trickle of blood running down his neck.

"So, Muffy still hasn't learned her place," grunted Tenta. "Shame."

Iuris leered at Jonah. "You know the only thing that kept me going on that Hell Plane? What I was gonna do to you when I got off of it."

"Must have been depressing," commented Jonah. "Because I thought that it was all those *pankrations* you kept throwing."

Iuris blinked. Jonah wasn't supposed to know that. He might have smiled were the situation different and there weren't a blade at his throat.

"It doesn't matter how you know. In honor of Mr. Kaine and G.J., you die now."

"Death isn't real," Jonah shot back. "And to hell with them *and* you. You're all Creyton's bitches."

Iuris roared, but Jonah had been prepared for almost a full minute. He'd been balancing an empty Chateau bottle in the air with his raised hands. When Iuris attempted to cut his throat, Jonah relinquished his hold on the bottle. It crashed right on top of Iuris' head and he fell to a knee, dropping the blade. Reena whipped around on Tenta and attempted a chokehold, but Tenta elbowed her in her gut again. Terrence hopped up from his knees and head-butted Cisor, then kicked him in the groin before running to aid Reena.

Iuris was back on his feet, and punched Jonah twice in the chest before hitting him once in the face. Jonah made himself as oblivious to the pain as possible when he saw another punch aimed his way, knocking it aside, and kicking the man away from him. Mason leaped back up before Jonah could will his batons back into his hands and tackled him down to the floor. The bastard wasn't going down easy, but Jonah wasn't going down quietly either—

Then a loud scream and a guttural growl froze them in mid-action.

A Moortus had leapt from the shadows and grabbed Cisor. They'd never secured the soft part of the cellar floor.

"Whoa!" shouted Terrence, who grabbed Reena and distanced them from the monstrosity and his screaming victim.

But the problem was far from over.

Three more Moortuses freed themselves from the exposed, unsecured earth. Exclamations sailed forth, and Tenta even abandoned his attempts to attack Terrence and Reena. The distraction cost him, because Reena broke away from Terrence and swept Tenta's legs out from under him. He landed awkwardly and his ankle popped loud enough for them all to hear. He howled, and Reena spat at him.

"Oops," she muttered.

More Moortuses broke through, prompting them to move. Jonah attempted to put distance between himself and Iuris, but the former Sanctum member tripped him.

"You're not goin' anywhere, Rowe!" he bellowed. "This ends now!"

"Are you blind, dumbass?" Jonah cried. "Get off me!"

Iuris didn't take the hint. He must have been too far gone to see reason.

He tried to pin Jonah down so that he couldn't escape. Tenta fought to force himself upright on his damaged ankle, and grabbed an empty bottle of his own, having long since lost his weapon. When Terrence and Reena tried to get past him to help Jonah, he broke the bottle and swung the sharp-edged neck of it at them, waving it this way and that like a drunken man.

"Everything is wrong!" he shouted. "We were supposed to kill you meddling idiots and then—no!"

He was so focused on Terrence and Reena that he hadn't noticed the Moortus behind him. It grabbed him by the leg, forcing him to lose his already shaky balance. Cisor was no longer in view.

Jonah and Iuris continued to wrestle; the man wouldn't be ignored. Unfortunately for him, Jonah didn't have time to stay down in Zombieland.

Or Moortusland. Whatever.

He encased his fist in fog for a touch of ethereal strength and gut-punched Iuris. Iuris clutched the point of impact and rolled, and Jonah used the time to scramble away. Two other Moortuses had climbed through the earth, greedily seeking prey. One of the shelves had fallen over and empty bottles smashed everywhere. Jonah managed to dodge the hazardous mess, but Iuris tripped and fell. Jonah was sure that he'd heard bones crack, though the locations of the breaks were a mystery to him.

"Jonah, come on!" screamed Reena from the stairs.

Jonah was nearly there, but a clamp on his foot brought him to his knees. He immediately thought that it was a Moortus, but when he turned, he saw that it was Iuris yet again. It that broken leg, he must have done a desperation lunge.

"I came to kill you," he grumbled. "You ain't getting' away."

"Dammit," snarled Jonah, "get off of me—"

Jonah worked free a baton and bashed Iuris' wrist. It crunched like hard candy. Iuris gritted his teeth but didn't have much time to do anything else, as the Moortuses had over-whelmed him. His snarls of rage became screams of terror as the things began to disembowel him.

"Shit!" yelled Terrence wildly when Jonah reached them. "We didn't secure the spot!"

"Quick, Terrence!" urged Jonah. "Destroy the stairs!"

It took maybe a half-second for Terrence to catch on. He focused his ethereality until his hands gleamed burnt orange, like the steel knuckles he was wearing. Then he began to batter the steps, throwing punch after punch on the aged wood. The stairs didn't hold much longer, collapsing within moments. A Moortus who'd been crawling up the stairs grunted in surprise as he crashed to the cellar floor. Terrence then slammed the door and broke off the knob.

"They can't get out of there now," he said. "The door has no knob, and there are no stairs to climb up. We'll have to come back and deal with it later."

Jonah grimaced, thinking about Mason, Tenta, and Cisor. "Stupid idiots. Guess they weren't aware of Creyton's plan to use the corpses, huh?"

"It was what it was, Jonah, just like you always say," said Terrence. "It's really, really hard to pity someone who brings the downfall on themselves."

"And who knows," said Reena in a wintry tone, "maybe they will finally see their beloved Gamaliel and G.J. again. The whole carton full of dumbasses will be back together again in the afterlife."

Jonah felt the scowl still on his face due to Mason and Company's actions, but he was cognizant of the fact that there were larger matters to attend to. "We need to get back."

They hurried back into the kitchen in time to see Felix slamming a vampire through the kitchen table, where he then staked it. He didn't wait to see it wither—he'd already retrieved his mace and dagger from the floor and was heading out the back door.

"Watch your asses!" he threw over his shoulder as he

exited. "They brought sazers that seem to be locked in Red Rage, and I suspect that Creyton didn't allow the vampires on their side to feed before the battle. This is going to be a *long* night!"

Upon hearing that, Jonah asked, "Terrence, will the vampires be an issue for you?"

"Not anymore."

Jonah nodded, and they ran into the family room.

Where everyone was in mortal battle.

There was brutal fighting going on everywhere. Themis was on a Deadfallen disciple's back, clutching him around the throat while she beat him on the top of his head with the edge of her class ring. Sterling was in a dogfight with Asa Brooks. Further away, a herald in the shape of a panther swung bloody, nasty claws at an equally feral sazer. There were countless others and, due to the Blessing of the House, there was plenty of room for every one of them.

Jonah glanced out of a window to see that there were far more Moortuses than there were before. And it was clear that Creyton and Jessica used the Moortuses to soften the defenses. After that had occurred, the Deadfallen disciples swooped in. Some ran on foot while others had been too impatient for that, having shape-shifted into crows and taken flight.

Jonah's inattention cost him. Someone grabbed him through the window and yanked him out. Terrence roared, but he could do nothing as another Deadfallen disciple jumped him. Reena was apprehended by a disciple who seemed deadset on decapitating her.

Jonah had his own problems at the moment.

The heavily scarred disciple who'd grabbed had just about knocked him senseless with two punches and was drawing back for a third. Instinctively, Jonah mentally said the word *"shield"* and the disciple slammed his fist into a fog shield hard enough to break two of his fingers. When the man cried out, Jonah angrily rose, grabbed him by the shirt collar, and slammed him four times into one of the pillars before pitching him off the porch.

"Jonah!"

Vera had come out of nowhere and knocked aside a spike headed for Jonah's head. The disciple who'd thrown it, a hard-featured woman, shouted in rage.

"You stupid bitch!" the disciple called. "Stop *this* one!"

She pitched a stainless-steel knife, which still looked black with her darkened aura, at Vera. Jonah made to push her aside, but Vera gritted her teeth and her fingers gleamed white. The flying knife paused inches from her face, and she snatched it from the air and pitched it back at the woman. It hit the disciple square in the chest. She bleated like a sheep as she collapsed.

Jonah stared at Vera. "Vera ... what the hell?"

"Surely, you didn't think all Jonathan and those other spirit tutors taught me was to just *manage* my Time Item powers. I can use time as a weapon, should I wish to. Now, watch your back, Jonah!"

She pulled out her knife, which immediately gleamed the same color as her fingers, and left the porch to rejoin the fight on the grounds. Moments later, the disciple who'd attacked Terrence flew out of what was left of the window, shapeshifting into crow form, and bulleted into the outside fighting. Clearly the contest hadn't gone the way he'd hoped.

Jonah ran back into the family room—which was easy, because the front door was gone—and rejoined his friends. Terrence was still glaring at the window.

"That's right!" he yelled. "You better run, bitch!"

"Terrence!" hissed Reena. "Focus!"

A phantasm caught Terrence about the waist, toppling both

of them. Reena got caught up in a socket wrench-on-shank fight with Sean Tooles. Jonah looked here and there, searching for the source of the Phantasm to assist Terrence. He got bashed from behind and collapsed against an end table.

"My wife is the one doing that there Phantasm, see," said the voice of Lance Harkness. "And I can't very well have you stopping her, can I?"

He grabbed Jonah by the throat. Jonah attempted to counter the move by clutching Harkness' wrist with a stinging hold. Harkness clenched his teeth but didn't let up.

"Stimulating!" he cried. "But is that the best that you can do?"

Jonah gasped for air but steeled himself. "Not quite."

He used his leg to upset Lance's footing. A baton blow to the sternum later, and Jonah was free. He scrambled to his feet, careful to avoid the crowbar that Lance had grabbed when he hit the floor. Lance slashed at him with the sharp end, but Jonah knocked it away. Harkness barely even blinked and went across Jonah's face with a haymaker. Jonah staggered. *Damn* that hurt. Lance hadn't given him much of a breather and swung at him again.

Jonah wanted nothing more to do with Harkness' fists and purposely moved at him from a lower base. His plan worked; he screwed up Harkness's stance and wrecked his balance by colliding with him. When he lost his footing, the momentum carried him over Jonah's back, resulting in a perfect back-body drop. Harkness landed painfully on his back, baring his teeth, and writhing once he hit the floor. Jonah complicated the bastard's situation even further by flipping the end table on top of him, just to give himself some breathing room.

He'd just gotten a lucky break.

When he'd been in the fight with Lance, he'd seen his wife, Athena. She was cunningly hidden indeed. She had the same gift that Trip had—the ability to will herself not to be seen. It had been pure luck that Jonah glimpsed her through peripheral vision. She was in an alcove near the stairs, mere feet from a fight between Magdalena and Wyndam O'Shea.

Jonah couldn't throw a baton because it might get lost in all the ruckus. Plan B was necessary. He willed the winds to levitate an encyclopedia that was on the floor. It was a pretty heavy volume. He willed it to a level position and carried it on the winds to hit her square in the face. Athena became completely visible as her head swung to one side. She was unconscious before she hit the floor. The Phantasm Terrence was battling dematerialized on the spot.

"You cold-cocked that bitch? Thanks, man!"

With a roar of frustration, Reena shoved, then kicked Sean Tooles away from her. He tripped over a fallen object, swearing the whole way down. At that moment, Jonah heard a scream of terror and saw Liz on the second landing, fleeing two Deadfallen disciples.

He raced up the stairs, knowing that Terrence and Reena were right behind him. He didn't know if they would get there in time, and then he saw a sazer take a fall from the higher landing, taking a nasty spill on the floor.

"Bobby's on the third landing," said Terrence. "He was fighting that sazer. Must have gone well!"

Jonah grinned. Liz knew what she was doing. She was outmatched, but she was leading the freaks to her own equalizer, Bobby. *That a girl, Lizzie.*

He, Terrence, and Reena reached the landing the same time that the two disciples realized their mistake. They were blocked on both sides with Liz and Bobby on one side, and Jonah, Terrence, and Reena on the other. Jonah distinctly saw alarm and then defiance on one of their faces. Just like Iuris Mason.

That reckless man tightened his eyes and what looked like shards of glass made from pure shadow came flying at Jonah. He easily willed the winds to blow them aside. Reena pushed past him and speed-shoved the disciple down to the ground, rendering him instantly unconscious. The other disciple foolishly charged Bobby, who stopped him cold with a forearm. When he tried to retaliate, Liz poked his neck with three fingers, tweaking a nerve. He collapsed, as though paralyzed. Bobby kicked the incapacitated disciple across the face.

"If you come near Elizabeth again, I will kill you."

"Always the white knight," grinned Liz.

"Of course, baby," said Bobby with humility. "Would you have it any other way?"

The remark elicited chuckles. Jonah shook his head, glancing to the floor in the process.

Something was wrong. The light above them shone on the floor, so why was it so dark?

Then Jonah remembered. The grin faded and his eyes bulged. "Move! We have to—"

The darkened portion of the third landing lurched violently and then began to disintegrate. Jonah caught a glimpse of Bobby instinctively wrapping Liz in a protective embrace as the floor collapsed.

It was a petrifying experience. The last vestiges of stability faded, then ... the fall.

Just like in the Jeep back in Dexter City, there was the initial feeling of weightlessness, followed by the horrid realization that gravity was not on their side. There was nothing available to catch, grab—nothing. Jonah thought for a moment that the fall was over, but the fall continued seconds, minutes, or hours more—

Then it came to a halt. He was on stable ground but felt pain in his back and left wrist. His equilibrium was utterly shot, and the location of his batons was anybody's guess. As he was already prone, he could see above; it was no trouble seeing what had happened.

It had been the same dark ethereality that Creyton had used back in Blood Oaths a couple years back, where he used a sweeping shadowy substance to disintegrate objects. It was dynamite without the explosion. The last Jonah had seen it, Jonathan had been there to intercept. This time, though ...

A large portion of the third landing was gone, and all of them fell with it. Jonah didn't know whether it was due to the weight of the third one or whatever else, but a portion of the second landing had collapsed when they'd fallen on it. It had come to an abrupt, painful culmination on the first landing. When Jonah realized that his body was still working despite the pain, he immediately wondered about the welfare of his friends.

Somewhere to his left, he heard a sickening popping noise, and then heard Reena cry out in anguish. He hoisted himself up with a grunt of pain and saw her. She had just popped her shoulder back in place and pulled herself to a standing as well.

"You—you alright?" he coughed her way.

"I'm breathing. A trickle of blood oozed down from her hairline. "Terrence?"

"I'm good," grumbled Terrence. "But that hurt like a bitch ..."

Jonah helped pull him to his feet. "Liz? Bobby?"

They were both some feet away, with Liz coughing like the rest of them. Bobby still held her tightly.

"God only knows what would've happened if you hadn't been protecting me, baby," she said. "Come on, let's get up."

But Bobby didn't let her go.

"Bobby? Let me up, we've got to—"

Liz paused. Something wasn't right. It was at that second

that Jonah realized what. Bobby wasn't embracing Liz. His arms were just around her, but limp.

"Bobby!"

Liz screamed and tried to wrest herself free. Terrence helped her and then rolled Bobby over. Bobby's eyes were rolled back in his head.

"What's wrong with him?"

Liz ignored Terrence completely and splayed green-tipped fingers over Bobby. She paled to the point that she resembled a spiritess ... she was that bloodless.

"Liz, what is it?" demanded Jonah, terror numbing his injuries.

"Please God, no. Cervical fracture. Bobby, don't you leave me! I can fix it, just hold on baby, please!"

The jade that gleamed on Liz's fingers faded. She stared at her fingers, and then at Bobby, the horror on her face absolute.

"No. No!"

The green at her fingers had faded because there was no longer any physical life to read. Bobby had passed into Spirit. This amazing machine of a young man had forever ceased with his final act: sacrificing himself for the woman he loved.

29

THE LOOSE END

Jonah lost all the feeling in his feet. They simply wouldn't carry his weight. He didn't fight his body as it lowered back down to the ground.

Bobby was gone. Robert Decessio, the football impresario who'd made the mature decision to fine-tune his skills before trying for the pros. He'd planned to propose to Liz.

None of that would happen now.

God, if Liz ever saw that ring ...

Terrence bellowed a string of swear words and punched a hole in the wall up to his elbow. Reena lowered her head, crying her tears in silence.

None of that compared to Liz.

She was buried in Bobby's chest, sobbing bitterly, and trembling so hard that it appeared she was having convulsions. Jonah banged his feet to get feeling back into them, to no avail. So, he crawled to Liz and placed a hand on her back. He hoped that the support would suffice because there wasn't a damned thing he could say.

Then Liz's sobs abruptly ceased. She went silent. Jonah was so alarmed by it that he tensed.

"Liz?"

She raised her head, and Jonah's blood ran cold.

Liz looked ... inhuman. Beyond reason. There was rage in her jade eyes that made her appear as though some foreign entity had overtaken her body. The only word that seemed to aptly cover the situation was what Jonah had already thought: inhuman.

And it frightened the hell out of him. "Liz—"

"I'll kill them all." Even Liz's voice sounded like someone else had taken over.

"Liz, no, you need to—"

Liz ignored Jonah completely as she reached over Bobby's body and picked up the steel bat he'd had. "I swear to God," she growled, "I'll kill them all!"

"Liz, no!"

She barreled past him. The bat gleamed a green that soon would have nothing to do with healing. Jonah scrambled up; his feet were working again.

"Reena, she'll get herself killed!" he cried. "We've got to do something!"

Before Reena could respond, there was a feeble groan. She and Jonah followed the sound. One of the Deadfallen disciples, the one whom Bobby and Liz had taken down together, had survived all the falls. Slowly, he rose to his feet. Terrence, whose eyes hadn't left his brother's body, glared at the disciple murderously before charging him and pummeling his ribcage.

The disciple burbled and spat blood out of his mouth as they crashed back down to the floor; Terrence hadn't even ceased his punches. It took Jonah a fraction of a second to realize that Terrence had no plans to stop. Reena realized it first and tried to intercept.

"Terrence, no!"

Terrence shoved her away and then drew back a punch that would surely send a chunk of rib into the disciple's lung. Jonah willed ethereality to encase his hands in the mist that increased his strength and grabbed Terrence's fist. His steel knuckle apparatus was so bloody that the burnt orange gleam could barely be seen.

"Terrence, you've got to stop!" he declared.

"Let me loose!" snarled Terrence. "My brother saved Liz's physical life and gets a goddamned broken neck. This piece of shit tries to kill us, and he gets to survive the fall? Fuck that! He deserves it!"

"You're right!" Jonah shot back. "He deserves it! A great deal! But I will not sit here and let you murder him in cold blood! Save your anger!"

Terrence rose to double down on his resistance, but Jonah held him fast.

"Save it!" Jonah snapped. "This bastard is already down. There are plenty of Deadfallen disciples who need to feel it."

Terrence's expression barely changed, but Jonah saw humanity creep back into his eyes. He stopped fighting Jonah. "Fine," he ground out through clenched teeth. "I'll play it your way. But I'm dropping bodies tonight, Jonah. Believe that."

"Nothing wrong with that," said Jonah. "So am I."

"Guys, we really need to find Liz," said Reena. "She's got a kamikaze complex, and I'm afraid how far she'll go for revenge."

"You're right," said Jonah.

He closed his eyes, manipulated the wind, and thought, *Back.*

The batons detached themselves from the rubble and flew into his hands. Before they left, he looked at Bobby's body, had a brief and intense conversation with God, and then headed outside with Terrence and Reena.

Something in Jonah's mind had changed. He hadn't gone Mr. Hyde like Liz or ribcage-bashing like Terrence. But Bobby being killed had changed something. It was as though he were much more aware of the warzone that his home had become.

The situation had gone downhill since they'd secured the basement. People fought for their physical lives all around them, and the damages of war were visible even in the dead of night. Then flames caught Jonah's eye. The gazebo was on fire. His and Vera's favorite place was going down in flames.

It took the sight of that for Jonah to become acutely aware of another fact. Something that had occurred at the beginning of the fight.

After Creyton had Jessica re-animate the Moortuses, he had turned his back on him and walked away. He *walked away* like Jonah was no threat at all.

What was the deal with that?

"Rowe!" someone roared.

Jonah turned. It was Abimelech, the turncoat sazer. He spat on the ground as he regarded the three of them.

"I bet you're sorry about the side you're on now, ain't you?"

There was the anger again. Jonah didn't have the time, nor was he in the mood for this shit right now. He readied his batons, but someone grabbed his shoulder.

"This ain't your fight, friend."

It was Prodigal. He had pulled his hair out of his face, and his hurt and hatred were evident in every inch of it. Abimelech hissed.

"It wasn't personal, bro. Just saving my ass, which is what we always did."

Apparently, Prodigal was in no mood for talking. With a snarl, he propelled himself at his former best friend with the velocity of a small vehicle. Abimilech growled and responded with equal furor. Jonah, Terrence, and Reena hurried off, desiring to get as far away from the potential Red Rage fest as possible.

Then, they saw Phantasms. But this time, they weren't in human shape. Jonah saw bulls, serpents, bears—there were even some in the form of mastodons. They were all over the place amongst the fighting. Jonah, Terrence, and Reena ran past Patience, who was in a fight with Broreamir. A Deadfallen disciple had attempted to sneak attack Tempie, but his plan flopped when a herald in the form of a mountain lion pounced on him, and raked claws across his body. Jonah didn't pity the bastard at all.

Maxine and Nella both took on Matt Harrill, who slashed and swiped with that hooked weapon he'd had before Jonathan sent him to the Plane with No Name. Terrence sprinted over to help, while Reena raced away to help Themis and Autumn Rose. Jonah, who was distracted by a fire, slammed into a sazer. She was nearly seven feet and easily three-hundred pounds. She was also in Red Rage and sounded more akin to an animal that had seen too many 'roids than a woman. She swung an actual tree limb at Jonah, who instinctively conjured ethereal fog to shield himself. Even so, the force knocked him to the side. He swiped at her with a baton, but the sazer shook it off. When Jonah swung with the opposite baton, the sazer swatted it aside, and swept him into a bear hug, squeezing his already injured back. Jonah growled in pain. It was like being wrapped in iron.

"You're nothin', Light Blue Aura. You're weaker than a child."

Painstakingly, Jonah willed his batons back to him and began to bash the crazed sazer in her face. It had no effect whatsoever. Then his vision began to darken.

To hell with that. He was not tapping out here.

He focused his ethereality and used the trick he learned a while back to charge his batons with electrical current. Then, he jabbed the baton ends against both sides of the woman's head.

The jolts made the sazer finally release him, and she staggered away, clutching her skull. She looked mightily disoriented, and Jonah soon saw why.

The voltage had knocked her out of Red Rage.

Jonah smirked. That meant that she was really feeling those earlier head shots now. Her head was probably in so much pain that she didn't even notice Jonah. All it took was for Jonah to give her a light shove, and she keeled over. Jonah left her there.

And locked eyes with a Moortus.

Jonah's reaction time wasn't what it should have been after that bear-hug but then a very loud dramatic scream distracted him.

Spader was running as if someone pursued him, which turned out to be true. He had no less than fifteen Moortuses behind him; what he'd done to rile them, Jonah had no idea. Spader caught his eye and saw his concern but shook his head vigorously.

"I got this!" he cried before he threw words at the Moortuses. "Come and get me, bitches!"

The Moortus near Jonah made a guttural sound and joined its fellows. Whatever Spader's plan was needed to be implemented, and soon.

Spader ran into the shed, of all places.

"No, fool!" screamed Jonah, running that way. "You'll be trapped in there!"

All the Moortuses followed Spader inside the shed. Jonah would never reach it in time—

But then, Spader forced himself out of a window and

scrambled to the nearest car part of the Iron Semicircle. He started it and accelerated, shouting at Jonah over the noise.

"I'll be needing your help in a sec, Jonah!"

Luckily for him, Jonah understood. Spader jumped out of the car, and Jonah willed the winds to assist him as he hit the ground. As such, Spader's landing resulted in less impact, and he landed painlessly on the ground. The car crashed into the shed, resulting in a spectacular explosion. None of those Moortuses would be getting out of that.

"Appreciate that, Jonah! I set a trap to thin out some of those things! Wish I could have gotten some Deadfallen disciples mixed in there, too!"

"You are the bravest person on Earthplane, Spader...or the dumbest."

"Whatever," shrugged Spader. "If only Lizzie could have seen that! But she's probably still inside somewhere, being wowed by Bobby's musclehead stunts. Lucky bastard."

A sharp pang stung Jonah's insides when he heard Bobby's name, but Spader didn't notice. He'd already yanked some red-gleaming blades from his black camo pants and dashed off.

A growl yanked Jonah out of his reverie.

A Haunt raced his way. The thing was murder and chaos enveloped in a shadowy black form. Jonah had been trying to stuff down the pain of Bobby's killing, but Spader had inadvertently brought it back into fresh relief. Consequently, he didn't notice that the thing wasn't alone. There were three of them.

The thing at the forefront of his mind was Bobby, so he didn't really have the mental focus for a Mind Cage. And he had no doubts that the three Haunts sensed that.

A white-gleaming grappling hook came from out of nowhere and lodged into one Haunt's neck. Magdalena was responsible. She yanked the demon canine to her and decapitated it with a similarly white-gleaming machete. The second

Haunt was downed and clawed to nothing by a panther, whom Jonah knew to be the herald Anakaris. Jonah was so relieved to be aided that he didn't factor in the fact that there was one left. He got blindsided by the third Haunt. Instinctively, he raised a baton to prevent his throat from being ripped out. But the fear that he had for the safety of his remaining friends made it impossible to contend with ...

Then the Haunt's body shuddered, and it yelped. Despite Jonah's blurred vision, he'd seen a silver gleam. The silver arced again, shuddering the Haunt's form once more. But it still hadn't freed Jonah, who gritted his teeth in frustration.

"Hit him again, Tempie!" Jonah cried, remembering her silver aura.

"Who?" said a voice that was clearly not Tempie's, but was another silver aura he knew quite well. The voice was so shocking that it cleared Jonah's vision.

"*Doug?*"

Sure enough, it was Douglas. He'd been trying to aid Jonah by bashing the Haunt with a silver-gleaming golf club.

"Yeah, it's Doug! No fear, Jonah! No fear! Now, let's drop this thing!"

Jonah was in shock. Douglas had been mortally afraid of Haunts at one time. He'd actually fainted after being Haunted once. But somewhere along the line, he'd moved past his fear.

And that was a boon for Jonah himself.

Timing it just right, he jabbed the Haunt through one of its red eyes. There was a shrill yelp, which was followed by a burst and dissipation of dark essence. The thing was no more. Jonah rose to his feet, seeing Magdalena nearby.

"Thank you, Magdalena, Doug—"

"Don't thank us, Jonah!" cried Magdalena. "Help us! *Mira!*"

Jonah saw more than a dozen Haunts barreling toward

them. Inspired by his friends, Jonah visualized the cage locking in his mind. The ground began to boil, and then gave way to the dazzling blue cage, which was the weapon of his expression. The Haunts whimpered and squealed, and Jonah took savage pleasure in disintegrating them.

When they faded, there was a roar of frustration nearby. It was Broreamir, liaison to Creyton's sazers, and current handler of the Haunts.

"Impressive, Rowe, I grant you that." The man shook dreadlocks from his pale, ashen face. "But unlike you, I have a cavalry."

He waved his hand, and more Haunts than Jonah had ever seen in his physical life appeared. There were over a hundred, maybe more, resembling dogs, wolves, coyotes, foxes, and jackals.

Their sudden appearance didn't go unnoticed, and more than a few fighters screamed. Terrence and Reena, who'd finished assisting friends, rejoined Jonah as he stood in stunned silence with Douglas and Magdalena.

"Did he empty out the Astral Plane?" demanded Terrence.

'Don't know," said Jonah. "But I can't cage all of those things. Not right after I've done one already."

"What's our play then?" asked Reena.

"Divine intervention?" suggested Douglas.

Broreamir roared, and the pack charged. Jonah braced himself, having no idea how this was going to go.

What resembled a metallic green river flooded the entire area. It completely ignored Jonah and his friends, as well as the other people alarmed by the Haunt's arrival. The Haunts, on the other hand, were literally caught up in some Eleventh's Mind Cage's weapon of expression. All were disintegrated; not a single one escaped. Broreamir ran off, bellowing in shock and anger.

"Who did that?" Reena was grateful and stunned at the same time. "Whose weapon of expression was that?"

Jonah turned. Divine Intervention, indeed.

"Reverend Abbott? Really?"

The reverend stood there, looking pleased with himself. He also held one of Malcolm's steel sluggers at his side, and the green gleam on it matched the green river they'd seen. "I didn't kill anything. Haunts weren't ever alive in the first place."

Jonah shook his head. "Thank you, sir."

Reverend Abbott nodded. "I'm here to incapacitate only. But Jonah, you might want to figure out what Vera is up to."

"Huh?" said Jonah, distracted.

"That woman you're sweet on. You didn't just see her pause that vampire in her tracks long enough to run up the drive about five minutes ago—"

A disciple engaged Reverend Abbott in a fight. Three more attempted to gang up on him, but Douglas, Magdalena, and a nearby Rheadne ran over to him to support him. Jonah, Terrence, and Reena were left to themselves.

"I would have never imagined that Vera would tuck tail and run," grumbled Terrence, "'specially after all that crap she said about you not talking her out of fighting."

Jonah looked at Reena, but Reena shook her head.

"I will not attempt essence reading. There is entirely too much interference."

Jonah was puzzled, but only for a second. Vera had come a mighty long way from when she'd first discovered that she was an Eleventh who also happened to be the Time Item. She was now more confident, surer of herself, more adventurous, more forthright and brave—

"Damn," muttered Jonah.

Reena and Terrence looked at him.

"Vera isn't abandoning the fight. She didn't run away."

"Then what's she up to?" questioned Terrence.

"She's going to go confront her big sister," Jonah answered.

Reena choked. "Has she lost her fucking mind? That's suicide! Jessica is too far gone. Plus, where Inimicus is, Creyton will be too!"

"Wait, what?" said Terrence. "You don't think Creyton is out here somewhere?"

"Hell no. Creyton is an Oscar-night, red-carpet, attention-seeking whore. Being in the thick of the battle isn't his shtick. I think I know where he and Jessica are, though. And I think Vera knows where to go."

"Ballowiness," said Terrence instantly. "It's close enough to here to keep tabs on his people. That's where we're going."

"And what about saving Liz from herself?" asked Reena.

Jonah took a deep breath, making himself as oblivious to the battle around them as possible. "We just have to have some faith."

"And Jonah," said Reena with inscrutable eyes, "are you still going to kill Jessica?"

Jonah felt the dagger apparatus in his pocket. It suddenly seemed to weigh more, as if it were reminding him that it was always there and ready to be used. He released a slow breath as he pulled it free and affixed it to his baton. "We've already had that conversation, Reena."

* * *

Jonah, Terrence, and Reena used the *Astralimes* to go into Historic Rome, where the Ballowiness Rec Center was located. After all the noise and chaos, the quiet here on the opposite side of Rome was jarring. Then Jonah remembered: all the citizens of Rome were in some type of coma-like sleep, courtesy of Creyton. They depended on Jonah and his friends as much as everyone else. Jonah rolled his eyes as that sandbag of responsibility resettled onto his back.

He thought that it would be a wise idea to walk into Ballowiness rather than use the *Astralimes* into it. He didn't know what the situation might be. But he was worried about Vera. What was she hoping to accomplish? Did she think that she could talk Jessica down? Surely not? Surely, she didn't believe that she could reason with the sister who once threw her through a glass coffee table?

"How long do you think Vera has been in there?" asked Terrence.

"Hard to say. She could have altered time. But I don't know if she's—"

"Vera's in there," said Reena. "Jessica, too."

Jonah looked at her. "Creyton?"

Reena shook her head. "Creyton is not the most complex of essences. Hatred, ambition, thirst for power, and self-righteousness pretty much cover him. And none of those are present in the rec center at this time."

"Good to know," said Jonah.

He picked the lock to the back door, knowing that Creyton, Vera, nor Jessica wouldn't have used it. The minute that they stepped in, however, Reena grabbed Jonah's arm.

"Jonah, listen to me. We do not know what Vera's angle is, and I know you are ready to shank Jessica into the next world, but the sight of you might make her homicidal. And, despite your hatred of that bitch, I know that you don't want to put Vera at risk. Brinksmanship is a very delicate thing; we don't want to provoke Jessica, nor do we want to undermine Vera. Let's assess before you ... intervene, alright?"

Jonah wasn't on board with that; he knew Jessica better than Reena did after all. And being this close to Jessica, the opportunity was too good to pass up. Still, Reena's words made sense. "Fine. But if Jessica tries anything to hurt Vera, all bets are off."

When they stopped speaking, Vera's and Jessica's elevated voices reached their ears. Surreptitiously, they walked up the hall and came out to the largest part of Ballowiness, which the local kids referred to as the Main Zone. It housed all the arcade games, the kid slots, trivia corner, and the ping-pong tables. Jonah, Terrence, and Reena ducked behind the slots, where they had clear view of the sisters. Jonah held aloft the baton with the dagger apparatus. All he needed was the right opportunity.

"You had some fuckin' nerve finding me, Altie," snapped Jessica. "If you had any sense, you'd be on a tour van somewhere, chasing your fucking dream."

"My dream is peace, Jess!" Vera shot back. "My friends are being massacred by those psychopaths you run with, and they're being helped by an army of zombies *you* brought to life. Meanwhile, you're sitting here, comfortably docile—"

"The Transcendent ordered me to stay back—"

"There was a time when you didn't listen to anyone in authority. You were always the defiant bitch and proud to be so! What's so different now?"

"The Transcendent is the one who truly made me come alive," drawled Jessica. "Because of the life he has given me, I am whole."

"Says the woman mind-controlling zombies," remarked Vera.

"They are named—"

"Do I look like I give a shit what they're named?"

"You would never understand, Altie. The Transcendent—"

"Will you hang that Transcendent bullshit?" interrupted Vera angrily. "The man's name is Creyton! I know him well; he *did* try to burn my spirit from my body!"

"You're a dilettante if you think you know a thing about him!" snarled Jessica.

"And you're a fool if you think he gives a damn about you!" countered Vera.

"Something's wrong," whispered Jonah. "Jessica has never allowed people to talk to her like that. She has murdered people for less than what Vera's saying."

Reena smacked his arm, prompting him to focus on the conversation once more.

Jessica's eyes had flashed after Vera's last words, and her hand went to her pocket. Jonah almost shot up, dagger ready, but Terrence and Reena stopped him.

Vera noticed Jessica's action but didn't back down in the slightest.

"Can you do it, Jess? You shamed our father, broke our mother's heart, and threw me through a coffee table. But can you kill me now? Like you've killed so many others?"

Jonah frowned. He actually lowered the baton with the knife apparatus. He was right: something *was* wrong. Something was off about Jessica. Was that doubt in her eyes? Uncertainty?

"You want to know something, Jess?" Vera went on. "Let me tell you some things you wouldn't know, seeing as how you were nowhere in sight, flashing your ass on the Dark Side. Before Mom passed into Spirit, I was her caregiver. I dropped everything in Seattle and came back to take care of her. I was with her until the end. In those last days, she prayed for you. More than she prayed for me."

Jessica looked as though she was trying to sneer, but her face couldn't quite manage it. She looked very distracted and a light layer of sweat covered her face, arms, and upper chest. Vera pushed aside her hair, revealing her facial scar. She then removed her top, leaving only her sports bra. None of her scars were concealed. Jonah had already seen them before, but Terrence and Reena, who hadn't, winced.

"Even after you did this to me, she prayed for you. I won't lie to you, Jess ... I lost my faith after what you did. I kept people at arm's length because of you. Mom, though? She never wavered. And do you want to know the words she said, on that very last day?"

"No fucks to give," said Jessica coolly.

"Your heart is so full of strength, Altie," Vera recited, undeterred. *"You were the strong one, always were. Promise me that that strength will be enough for you to one day tell Jessica that I still love her."*

Jessica's face was inscrutable. Jonah wondered if Vera had ever shared that with anyone. A tear slid down her face.

"She had every reason to hate you, just like I did. But she loved you until the end. Now, bearing that in mind, tell me—to my face—that you're not strong enough to stop what you're doing."

Jessica took slow, deliberate breaths. Jonah didn't know what would happen next. Vera was all but defenseless; her knife was no use to her at all, lodged in the back of her belt. Jessica opened her mouth, and Jonah would have paid money to hear what she had to say at this point.

The area suddenly got at least twenty degrees cooler. Jessica's eyes widened.

"Get out!" she hissed at Vera. "Go!"

"I will not. Some part of you is decent, Jess! You are better than this! Mom never gave up on you—"

"Damn it, Altie!" Jessica batted a hand at her. "Hide behind the slots and stay there."

There was that thing in her voice. She'd used C.P.V. on her own sister.

"Oh, shit," hissed Terrence. "Vera's going to come back here and see us!"

Jonah hadn't thought of that, but he kept his eyes on Vera. She glared at Jessica as her body moved, void of her control.

"Damn you, Jessica!" she growled as she fought her sister's ethereality.

Her efforts were useless, and she walked behind the slots. She started when she saw Jonah, Terrence, and Reena, but Jonah placed a finger to his lips. When he looked back at Jessica, he also saw Creyton. He had only turned his head for two seconds to look at Vera, the bastard had appeared that quickly.

Creyton had dispensed with the duster he'd always worn. He was simply attired in a dark blue shirt, black creased pants, and boots. In his left hand was the crow-tipped staff; in his right was the puzzle box that contained the Tool of Omega. It brought Jonah comfort to see that he still hadn't figured out how to open it. But that was a small comfort. Very small.

"To whom were you speaking, Inimicus?"

"No one, Transcendent."

Creyton looked her over. "You look disheveled," he observed. "Is the single, solitary task you are performing right now of puppeteering the Moortuses taxing your abilities?"

It didn't take a brain surgeon to notice the condescension in Creyton's voice as he asked the question. Jessica blinked and swallowed.

"Of—of course not."

Creyton placed the puzzle box on a table. Then he gave Jessica his undivided attention. "I would beat around the bush, as they say, but it is not my way. I'm concerned about you, Inimicus. I do not think that you are the treasure you once were."

Jonah looked at his friends. They mirrored his expression. Vera's eyes were deadlocked on the two conversing.

"H-how so, Transcendent?" asked Jessica.

"You used to be the heart and soul of my disciples. Now, you are unsure of yourself. Insecurity, second-guesses, and your C.P.V. is now halfhearted, at best. It seems as though the bloom is off the rose, Inimicus."

Jessica looked angry. "Who's been talking about me? Charlotte? Sam? Tell me!"

Creyton's eyes flashed. "Mind your tone, girl."

Jessica blinked. "Yes, Transcendent. I am merely stating that you are aware that Charlotte's feelings for me are less than savory, and Sam can't even *spell* savory, let alone accuse me of being subpar. Who are they?"

"Who are *you?*" asked Creyton quietly.

Unless Jonah was mistaken, Creyton had elevated the end of the staff Jessica's way. He'd done the same thing when he'd killed Laban. Jessica noticed this as well, and her fingers curled into fists.

"I'm Inimicus." The haughty, iron note of old was back in her tone. "I'm the embedded enemy, the one they never saw coming. I found your remaining essence, secured a spirit and body for you while Charlotte was at LTSU, printing off syllabi. I'm the one whom you re-activated into the fold when the 49er decided to take over your plans for Praeterletum. I'm the one who did all those things, did them perfectly, and assisted you in returning to an even higher prominence than you had before. I'm the woman who pledged herself to you, and always said that I would do anything for you. I meant it then, and I mean it now. *That* is who I am, Transcendent."

Jessica had regained some of her old flair. She'd even gotten a little worked up. But was it enough for Creyton to lower the staff?

His face was set. The staff dipped to the floor.

Son of a bitch. Jessica had actually saved her own ass. She stood there, pleased with herself, daring to believe in the reprieve she'd just earned herself.

But Creyton hadn't moved. He hadn't said anything. The half-smile on Jessica's face slightly faltered. Creyton still didn't move or speak.

Jessica frowned. Then, she gasped.

"Tr-Transcendent," she choked. "Please ... *please—*"

Jonah was dumbfounded. What was happening? Vera's eyes widened with horror. She tried to move, but Jessica's ethereality held her fast.

Blood spilled from Jessica's nose and mouth. She clutched at her gut like the issue originated there. Only then did Creyton move. He walked forward and shoved Jessica to the ground. She landed hard on her back.

"Oh, my dear Inimicus," he said quietly. "I did not mean your current failures. I meant when you failed in making Jonah Rowe murder you that night in the tattoo establishment. For what it's worth, you've been dead to me since that evening. Now, it is just official."

He looked at a clock over the vending machine and, for some reason, smiled. He then grabbed the puzzle box and backed into thin air.

Jessica's power over Vera must have faded, because Vera wasted no time in going to her sister's side. Jonah, Terrence, and Reena followed, but Jonah walked further than they, kneeling on Jessica's other side.

"Oh, Jess." Vera in a voice sounding equal parts saddened and disappointed. "Why didn't you listen to me? Why didn't you take control?"

Jessica coughed and cast teary eyes on Vera, then Jonah. "I'm ..." she attempted before her voice caught. "I'm scared."

Jonah simply regarded her. It was the first time in who knew how long, that Jessica had told the truth. The purest terror was in her eyes. She knew that her physical life was fading, and the things at the forefront of her mind had to be all the terrible, heinous, and unspeakable acts that she'd committed. She didn't know what awaited her on the Other Side.

Vera clutched Jessica's hand. "Save your strength, sister. You don't have to be afraid anymore. You're free from Creyton now. You'll be even freer soon."

Jessica still wasn't pleased. Her pale fingers tightened on Vera's hand and then, surprisingly, she grabbed Jonah's fingers with her free hand. Jonah hadn't expected it, but something motivated him to clutch her hand.

"I ... I ..." It was taking Jessica a great deal of effort to get out what she was trying to say. But with another painstaking swallow, she managed it. "I'm so sorry."

The most unanticipated thing happened. Jonah's hatred of Jessica ceased. It completely fell away. He dropped the baton with the knife apparatus from his other hand. He responded, noticing that his voice wasn't the only one. Vera did as well. Two different voices, two levels of pain, yet the phrase they said in unison had the same meaning.

"I forgive you."

Jessica's eyes gleamed. Gratitude and satisfaction were in them now, and she managed a hint of a smile.

That smile was the last expression that Jessica Hale would ever have.

Vera knew exactly what would happen from the second Jessica was attacked, but that didn't stop her from lowering her head and letting tears fall. Jonah's jaw was tightly set as he freed his hand from Jessica's and laid it across her chest. Out of Vera's view, he removed the knife apparatus from the baton and tossed it away. He never imagined that he'd ever feel sorry for

Jessica. But life was strange like that. Complex like that. He didn't know about the Other Side. No human being had those answers. He wasn't a religious man by any means, but maybe, just maybe God would have mercy on Jessica's spirit. He hoped so, anyway.

Reena saw what Jonah had done and though her expression hadn't changed, he saw relief in her eyes. Just then, Terrence's cell phone rang. It was a random sound that took everyone by surprise.

"What the hell?" frowned Terrence and answered it. "Hello?"

He listened intently to whomever it was on the other end. The frown grew larger and larger on his face with each passing second. He ended the call, looking beyond flabbergasted.

"That was Malcolm. Creyton has called a respite."

"What?" said Reena, surprised.

"Yeah." Terrence still looked confused. "The Deadfallen disciples are temporarily withdrawing. That's suspiciously generous. Why would he perform a kindness?"

"It's not a kindness," said Jonah, low-level heat in his voice. "It's a game. A game that is actually one of the most *un*kind gestures imaginable."

"What are you talking about, Jonah?"

Jonah rose from his knees. "Creyton wants us to assess our damage and losses, just so we will be more disillusioned. Crush the prey when they are at their weakest. He doesn't want to simply destroy us. He wants to destroy us at our absolute lowest."

30

THE EXECUTIVE DECISION

Jonah grabbed his batons and put them in his pocket. If it was truly a respite, then he wouldn't need them at the moment.

"We need to get back to the estate. The assessment of damage has probably already begun."

Neither Terrence nor Reena seemed keen on that. God only knew what they'd find when they returned home. But it had to be done.

"Alright," was all that Reena said.

Jonah looked down at Vera, who was still on her knees next to her sister's body. "Come with us, Vera."

"No."

"Vera, there isn't anything you can do for her now."

"No, Jonah—"

"Vera, please." Jonah extended his right hand, the hand that Vera had always wound up holding in some way, shape, or form in times past. "I don't want you to be alone here."

Vera raised her head but didn't take Jonah's hand. "My sister was brave at the end. It took balls to seek atonement for all the shit she did. In my book, that makes her a hero."

Jonah looked into her stubborn hazel eyes, working the idea into his mind. If he readily agreed, Vera would write it off as bullshit and accuse him of trying to placate her. So, he gave it some serious thought. "Yeah, Vera. I suppose she is."

The stubbornness—most of it, anyway—faded from Vera's eyes, and she took Jonah's hand. "Favor. Can we use the *Astralimes* to a certain point, and walk instead of going directly in? I need to ... put up some walls first."

You aren't the only one, thought Jonah. He glanced at Terrence and Reena, who both looked as though they thought that idea to be a wise one. "Sure thing."

Once Vera was on her feet, Jonah slackened his grip to release her. Almost by reflex, she tightened it again.

"No. Don't let me go."

"Gotcha."

The four of them took two steps through to an area five minutes away from the estate path. It turned out to be a welcome thing not to walk through town—the last thing that Jonah needed to see were all the townsfolk in their coma-like trances due to Creyton. However, Jonah didn't want to do this. It made sense to suggest heading back, but those were just words.

Actions were another matter.

Man up, Jonah, he thought to himself.

The path to the estate had never seemed so long. So tedious.

Why, then, was it over so soon?

The first thing that Jonah paid attention to was the estate. It had sustained significant damage—oh, who the hell was he kidding? The damage was catastrophic. Jonah supposed that he could be optimistic and say that at least it was still standing ... at least Creyton hadn't razed it to the ground yet.

But he didn't have much use for optimism just then.

"Where is everyone?" asked Vera.

"The Glade." Jonah's voice was void of emotion. "Nowhere else would make any sense."

They followed the Glade path, and it didn't take long for Jonah to see that he'd been right. Everyone was there.

Now, the real test of strength began.

There was a makeshift medic area overseen by Nella and Akshara. Nella looked a bit overwhelmed, but that could have been attributed the things she'd seen in the night. Still, she did her level best. Reverend Abbott assisted them, as did Sandrine, Katarina, Noah, and Themis. Jonah wasn't surprised that Liz, the estate's best medic, was not there with her sisters.

He knew that she would only be focused on the one person she wasn't able to heal.

That was what inevitably brought his attention to the bodies of the people who'd been cut down in the night—they were lined before the trees.

Terrence looked at Jonah to signify that he was leaving and walked into a tight embrace with Raymond. Vera walked up to Liz, who was kneeling next to Bobby's body and embracing an equally distraught Mrs. Decessio. Sterling wasn't crying, but the devastation was all over his face. Alvin sat on the ground near his family, repeating over and over, "Death's not real. He's still living somewhere, right? Right?"

Jonah saw Mr. Decessio rise from his wife's side and pocket something. He knew instantly that it was the engagement ring Bobby had planned to give Liz. She'd never see it. He, like Jonah, thought that that was best. Spader stood nearby, regarding the Decessio family rather awkwardly. Bobby had been the first person to befriend Spader when all everyone else saw was nothing more than a creepy, ratty goth. That in itself was ironic because Spader had always had a massive crush on Liz. Jonah knew beyond a shadow of a doubt that Spader was thinking about the remark he'd made earlier about Bobby wowing Liz and felt horrible for it. As he didn't know what else to do, he lowered himself to the ground and placed his head between his knees.

Jonah didn't care. He was Overseer of their home. He had to see who had made the ultimate sacrifice for the estate.

No. No need to gloss it over. He needed to see who had made the ultimate sacrifice for *him*.

"Do you want my dampener?" asked Reena. "It would only take a second for me to tweak it."

"No. We got to feel it all, right? But don't worry about me. Thanks, though."

Reena nodded and went to aid in the medics' area. Jonah was alone now.

Something that caught his attention was Vera, who had left Liz for a moment and demanded that some of the residents positioning bodies go to Ballowiness and collect Jessica's body. She felt that Jessica deserved to be lain with the others. He looked at the medic area, wondering why Ben-Israel and Barry weren't there helping Nella and Akshara with the injured.

It was because they were under white sheets near Bobby.

Jonah closed his eyes tightly. He'd never quite bonded with either man, but it didn't change the fact that it was a blow to see their bodies.

"Ben-Israel," he whispered, "I know you were an atheist, but for your sake, I hope that you're in the presence of God, in whatever form that would take. And Barry, thank you, man. Peace and blessings to your spirit."

He didn't know what else to say, so he gritted his teeth and moved on.

He passed by several other sheets, not bothering to lift them but saying, "Peace and blessings to your spirit" because it felt right to say. While walking, he noticed Autumn Rose near a white sheet with Obadiah. Both of them looked woebegone ...

No, not Prodigal ... He ran to them, not pausing to speak. He lifted the sheet and saw that it was not Prodigal. It was Stella Marie.

Autumn Rose walked over to him and uncharacteristically placed a hand on his shoulder.

"All those years we were moving around, runnin' from the vampires and the Curaie. We always knew that loss could happen. Made us view everyday as a gift. Still didn't prepare us for if and when it did happen."

Jonah nodded. "Where is Prodigal?"

"Gone," said Autumn Rose. "He wouldn't say where. He just promised that he wasn't abandoning us."

A little ways away Jonah saw Karin, nursing several broken fingers but appearing to have no desire to be tended to. She was red-eyed and staring unblinkingly at a sheet. Jonah felt a hot boiling sensation in his gut. Grayson.

"Karin," he said when he reached her. "I'm so sorry—"

"Yeah, Rowe," said Karin without looking at him. "I know you are."

Jonah didn't want to linger there. He knew that Karin was pissed on top of her sadness, but when Trip found out that Grayson had fought with them and gotten killed, *he'd* kill Jonah.

And Jonah didn't care.

"Jonah," gasped someone behind him.

He turned. It was Douglas.

"You need to come with me."

Jonah didn't question it and hurried with Douglas to a place nearer to the medic setup. They went past cots and seated individuals, and Douglas stopped at the last one.

Bast.

Douglas wiped his eyes. "There wasn't anything that could be done. She wouldn't let Nella, or anyone else, waste time on her. Her words, not mine. She only wanted to see you."

Cold and numb, Jonah knelt near the battered lioness, trying to ignore her injuries. She must have sensed the movement because she opened her eyes.

Jonah. Bast's eyes gleamed faintly. *Thank goodness you survived the night.*

The emotion that Jonah was trying to balance fought for the upper hand. And it was winning, too. "Yeah, Bast, I did," he said. He felt no pride, nor any sense of achievement for it though. "You told Doug that you wanted to see me?"

Bast blinked. *I never thanked you for saving me from that minion that night at your apartment. Thank you.*

Jonah's attempts at balancing his emotions were about to fail. "I ..."

But he looked into Bast's eyes. There was only one thing that would please her now. Nothing else, and no other words.

"You're more than welcome, my friend," he said.

Bast smiled with her eyes, and closed them for the last time.

Jonah broke down in earnest with that. He couldn't help it. Bast was gone, too.

He felt Douglas patting his back. He allowed himself to sob until his emotions reached a level that he could handle. At that point, he rose to his feet and wiped his face with a sleeve.

"I'm good, Doug. Thanks, man."

"Of course, friend." Douglas and returned to aiding the injured.

Jonah began to walk again, taking in sights. He looked over at Magdalena, who was tending to a gash on her calf while Maxine wrapped an Ace bandage around her ankle. He saw Felix clutching his arm, but when Themis offered him a tonic, he shot her down. It was as if he would not allow substances of any kind into his body, not even ethereal ones. He saw Reena in conversation with Tempie and Amelia, whose left arm was wrapped snugly. Terrence was still with his family. Reverend Abbot walked past bodies, no doubt praying over them. Patience and Daniel were nearby, solemnly looking on. But Jonah merely passed them all.

His mind was in another place.

After seeing Bobby, Ben-Israel, Stella Marie, Grayson, Bast, and all the others who had fallen, he couldn't help but wonder: why did he have to be a good person? Why did he have to feel? Would it have been better to be callous and indifferent, like Trip? Or like the psychos they were fighting?

He no longer wanted to feel guilt. Or grief. Or anger. Or self-loathing.

But he knew what he had to do to fix it all.

As the decision came into his mind, he didn't know what was stranger: the fact that it came so willingly to his mind or the fact that he wasn't afraid. The words that Creyton said about Jonah needing to do the right thing haunted him more and more with each passing step. He should have requested a one-on-one duel or something. Something that might have saved his friends. And now, because he hadn't had the foresight to do that, so many members of his estate family were now in Spirit.

Jessica had become null and void after Jonah hadn't murdered her back at Blood Oaths a couple years back. That had stuck in Creyton's craw from the second it happened. He had actually banked on Jonah's killing Jessica. When he hadn't, Creyton went forward with Omega.

Jonah caught himself wondering if he *had* killed Jessica back then, how many people would still be physically alive right now?

But the murder would have tainted his spirit. He would

have been a Dark Blue Aura as well. Both he and Creyton would be public enemies.

Jonah almost found that funny. He hadn't given his soul over to vengeance and remained a Light Blue Aura. Yet he still became public enemy in some people's eyes.

And then there'd been another opportunity to drop Jessica. He even had a weapon especially for it. But then fate, or whatever, prevented him from doing so. Creyton got there first and Jonah wound up forgiving her for all she had done. Score one for the decency column. Fat lot of good it did him. And Jessica for that matter.

But that wasn't the issue here.

Bobby had had his whole life ahead of him. Accolades were sure to come in droves. He would have been an invaluable commodity to any football team that would have him. He and Liz would have been married, with bliss around every corner. Grayson had finally grown a brain and made friends in spite of Trip. He'd trusted Jonah, respected him. Stella Marie, Ben-Israel, Bast—oh, it didn't matter. The point was, what did *Jonah* have? What was he worth?

He had a Master's degree that he hadn't used in forever and probably never would again. The best job he ever had wasn't even in his field and that job ended when his boss and dear friend Bernard Steverson was murdered by Jessica. Yeah, he'd forgiven her, and that had been sincere. But it didn't take away from Mr. Steverson being another casket on his conscience.

This was his time to atone. This is what his life, his purpose as the Light Blue Aura, would be: to atone for the people he'd failed, and save the people who were left.

He thought of what would become of his friends, but easily stamped it down. They were strong people; they'd recover. It wasn't like he'd been in their lives for decades or anything; in time, they'd move on. Terrence could very well be on Food

Network one day. Reena could find Kendall in Tullamore—hell, she could even stay there with her. Malcolm never showed emotion anyway, so he'd be fine. Liz, bless her, would have her work cut out for her moving past Bobby. Jonah was content in the knowledge that Liz missing *him* would be a distant second.

Then, another thought crept into his mind ...

What about Vera?

Strangely, that gave him pause.

Vera.

She was not on the hook with him, and she probably wasn't over East breaking her heart. But it hurt Jonah to think that she would miss him.

Could he eschew crossing on? Could he be a Protector Guide like Jonathan? Perhaps even take Jonathan's place? He was unaware of that process, obviously. Jonathan had never told him about it, and he had never asked. There were a great many things he'd never asked Jonathan.

He suddenly thought of being at some bright, eerie tunnel, where he'd be discussing his options with a hooded figure, like a morbid afterlife version of *Let's Make a Deal*. If he became a Guide, would it hurt to be near Vera? Of course, he wouldn't want her to be like Francine Mott and never marry. That was totally unfair, and he didn't want her denying herself. But would he have the strength to see her in another man's embrace?

A herald in the form of a snow leopard bounded up to him and delivered a message. With a deep breath and a grimace, he elevated his voice for everyone to hear.

"Creyton and the Deadfallen are returning," he announced. "The respite is over!"

The weary and fearful group looked around at one another. Spader broke out of his contemplative stupor and looked at Jonah, aghast.

"That was quick! It wasn't even a full day!"

"I highly doubt that we were going to get a full day, Spader," Jonah muttered. "But the fight is about to recommence."

He turned his back on Spader and began to walk up the Glade path. And all the while, he had his hands in his pockets, charging his batons.

"Straight is the path, and narrow is the way," he whispered to himself, going back to the words that Mr. Steverson once told him.

He heard all his family following him up the path, but he didn't wait for Terrence and Reena. He would give them the gift of not having to say goodbye. Yeah, they'd cry and grieve, but they'd move on. Terrence would see the world, one cuisine at a time. Reena had Kendall, and had a reforged bond with her favorite sister, Tempie. There were so many veritable options for them both when he'd be gone.

Now, onto his plan. Most likely, Creyton would want to start out with a crowd-control maneuver, which made Jonah think immediately of Creyton's trademark Timebomb, where he'd forcibly freeze time and then allow it to resume in such a way that it caused a concussive blast.

If Jonah's plan worked, then the Timebomb would be the last thing Creyton ever did. The unusable Tool of Omega be damned. He continued charging his batons with current as he began to speak under his breath once more.

"God," he mumbled, "I haven't really spoken to you since Nana, but that is what it is. I'm talking to you now because I'm about to end Omega for my family and my home. Why am I praying about that, exactly? Simple ... because this is my last act as a physically living being. So, kindly see to it that it works properly, would you? Thanks."

Yes, the prayer was terse and a little testy. But that didn't matter to Jonah. He didn't have the time for florid dramatics.

He was ahead of everyone as the Glade path gave way to the estate grounds. Creyton and the Deadfallen disciples were already there. Jonah couldn't help but notice the absolute bliss on Charlotte's face as she stood at Creyton's side in Jessica's stead. The rogue sazers were there. The vampire contingent, heavily cloaked against the coming sunrise, were there. Jonah even saw a small group of suuvi. Deluded fools. There weren't any Haunts; Reverend Abbott had wiped them all out. There weren't any Moortuses, either. They'd fallen to dust when Creyton murdered Jessica. But even with those "losses", Creyton's army was still substantial.

But that would be immaterial soon. The wolves would have no Alpha.

Creyton caught sight of the weary band of estate defenders and raised his staff. Jonah could have smiled. A Timebomb. Predictable as hell.

"God? You're up," said Jonah as he tore off toward Creyton.

"Jonah!" Reena shrieked. "What are you doing?"

Jonah ignored her. *Goodbye, big sis.*

Creyton locked eyes with Jonah, and Jonah was ready. His hope was that the combination of their endowments would be enough to take out the both of them. He'd been charging current into his batons, hoping for a type of critical mass. He'd figured out whether he'd been successful soon enough ...

Jonah was maybe thirty feet away from Creyton, and Creyton smiled. *Smiled.*

What the hell was with that?

Then Creyton did something Jonah had never seen him do.

He twirled the staff like some type of drum major.

Instantly, Jonah knew something was horribly wrong.

The estate and its grounds vanished, and his body felt lighter. He fell to the ground, but there was no ground. It was fog ...

Creyton's laughter jarred Jonah even further. He looked up.

"Congratulations, fool. You thought that I was going to do a Time Attack, didn't you? Hoped to cancel out our physical lives by overcharging?"

Jonah, despite the vast sense of weakness, was confused.

"Oh now, don't be surprised," said Creyton. "I know everything that you could possibly do. You could never stop me, Rowe. Never."

Jonah was very weak. Even getting to his knees was a struggle. "Wh-what did you d-do?"

Creyton shook his head. "When you attempted to sacrifice yourself, I didn't even bother combating you. I detached your spirit from your body. We are now on the Astral Plane."

Jonah's eyes widened. *No.* "You're lying," he managed to whisper.

"That so? Feast your eyes, boy."

He raised his hand and a portion of the Astral Plane seemed to erase. It was like a moving picture of real life.

Jonah was on the ground, batons still clutched in his hands. His eyes were wide open, seemingly frozen in shock. He looked completely lifeless.

He stared. Creyton laughed.

"That's right, Jonah. You're dead. And I didn't even need to figure out how to open that cursed box that contained the Tool of Omega."

Horrified, Jonah raised his hands. They were wispy, transparent. "What the hell is going on?"

"Allow me to explain," said Creyton with mock helpfulness. "I am in no need to rush because I'm there, standing over your body. I have already proven to you my ability to be in many places at one time."

Indeed, Creyton's words were true. In whatever that image was, he stood over Jonah's form.

"Now, then, as Jonathan would have said, life has to flow. Has to have a synchronous balance of flesh and spirit. One helps the other for the entirety of your days, and when the flesh ceases to operate, the spirit removes itself, and carries on. But in your case, I yanked you away from your physical body before it had ceased operating, which violates the process. It fades both your physical and spiritual forms. Turns out I didn't need the Tool, after all. I mastered how to destroy a spirit."

Jonah couldn't fight, nor could he disagree. He was getting weaker by the second.

"Before you fade, Rowe, I want you to understand something." Creyton walked up to him slowly. The mirth was gone from his face, replaced by the trademark coldness. "You were always going to fail. I was always going to raze the estate. I quite possibly would have shown your little friends mercy, but you made them follow in your defiance. For that, I am going to cremate you, right in front of them. Then, the estate will be razed. And finally, when they are at their lowest, I will kill every living thing that survived my first strike. And, oh yes, all the sleeping people in the town of Rome will die. So much, death ... so many glorious spirits to take."

Jonah barely had the strength to gaze into Creyton's face; Creyton looked into his without hesitation.

"It has been interesting, Rowe. You have had your miracles. But by definition alone, miracles are brief. Fade into oblivion knowing that every single drop of blood that will be spilled is on *your* hands. Goodbye, Light Blue Aura."

Creyton vanished. Jonah was still on his knees.

He'd failed. He'd been ready and willing to sacrifice his physical life for the estate and for his family, but all he'd done was get himself taken out of the game. Creyton had won, and he was going to exterminate all of Jonah's friends, plus drain all the spirits and spiritesses in Rome.

All to stick it to Jonah, one final time.

With the distinct feeling that he was dissolving, Jonah collapsed facedown. His position was very nearly identical to that of his physical body on Earthplane. His sensations began to dull, one right behind the other.

First, all sound went out. There wasn't even a ringing in his ears. Then the lights began to dim. He could almost time the drop in his senses. Fifteen seconds and the Lifeblood in his mouth, once coppery and bitter, was now bland and tasteless. Ten seconds and all the pains in his spectral form numbed at once. Seven seconds and his vision extinguished. Jonah exhaled. There was nothing to do but wait.

Six ... five ... four... three ... two ...

One.

31

REDEEMER

Jonah was so angry and sad, he didn't know what to do.

The stupid school bus wouldn't get him home fast enough.

Shane Mack had stolen his lunch money per usual, and when Jonah showed enough bravery to confront him, he got tagged in the face, and then laughed at by a girl he'd had a crush on. Until today, anyway. But even with the black eye, Mr. Butcher had told him that he couldn't punish Shane because he didn't actually see him punch him. Shane and his buddies laughed about that and made sure that Jonah didn't forget all day long.

The bus was no better. He sat two seats behind the driver, but that didn't mean anything. How many times had he been hit in the back of the head with something, heard immediate snickers, and told the driver about it, only to be frowned upon for being a "tattletale"?

Jonah hated it all. His school, his useless teachers, this stupid bus, the stupid ... everything.

Finally, the bus stopped at his refuge: 1310 Blackrock Way.

Nana was inside, waiting for him. Man, if she wouldn't be a sight for sore eyes, especially since one of his eyes actually *was* sore.

The white house with the greenish roof and shutters was the only home he's known since his mother had dumped him off some ten years before and had never returned.

Most of the time, though, he didn't even wonder about his mother. Nana was all he needed. As long as this house was here, with Nana in it, all was right with the world. No matter what happened at school, all was right with the world when he got home.

But, as he walked past the old station wagon, something in the back of his mind told him that something was wrong ... something was odd ...

He ignored it. He was called odd on an almost daily basis; maybe that belief had simply taken hold at long last.

He walked in the front door. *Guiding Light* was going off, which meant Nana was already making dinner. He hurried to the kitchen, flinging his backpack on the floor as he did so. The resulting thudding sound brought his grandmother out of the kitchen.

She was ready for cooking, wearing her big flowery dress and cooking apron that had once belonged to Jonah's grandfather. She looked at Jonah sternly.

"Jonah, is that the place for your backpack?"

Jonah rolled his eyes but stopped himself. This was Nana he was with now, not those stupid idiots at school. "No, ma'am. Sorry, Nana. I'll pick it up."

He grabbed it and put it in a chair, next to him. Nana smiled.

"Thank you. Now, what happened to your face?"

Jonah lowered himself at the kitchen table and wiped angry

tears from his eyes. "Shane took my money again. I tried to get it back, but he punched me. I told Mr. Butcher, and he didn't do anything. Shane bought snacks at lunch with *my* money, Nana."

His grandmother looked ticked off about that one. It was a rare sight to see her mad. "I'll go to that school tomorrow. I'll straighten that teacher out."

Jonah's eyes widened. "Nana, Mr. Butcher is taller than you. He coaches football, and lifts weights every day."

Jonah's grandmother turned off the stove, pleased with the progress of her food. She then turned to Jonah. "Good thing he does all that," she told him, "because he'll need those muscles now that I've found out he's letting those little boys bother you."

Jonah felt a smile spread across his aching face. That's all there was to it. Nana would set his stupid teacher right. She was the best.

Nana smiled back when she saw his grin. "That make you feel better?" she asked him knowingly.

Jonah nodded enthusiastically. "Yes, ma'am!"

"Then don't worry about it anymore, alrighty? Get ready for dinner, and afterward—well, I'm surprised you haven't noticed anything yet!"

That was when Jonah smelled it. His anger had made him oblivious to it. "Gingerbread!"

Mrs. Rowe smiled. "Sure is. Now, go get ready! The sooner you eat dinner, the sooner you can have some! I may even put vanilla frosting on it!"

That was all Jonah needed to hear. He stood up, ready to hurry to his room to wash up for dinner ... when he noticed something odd.

"Nana, where is your cane?"

His grandmother eyed him closely. "Very good, darling."

"I thought you—wait." Jonah stopped his own words. That sense of oddness was there again, but this time it was more of a challenge to file away.

When did he ever say *file away*? And why did it seem foreign and familiar at the same time?

Mrs. Rowe looked at him with concern. "Relax, Jonah. Don't think too hard."

"You're right, Nana ..." Jonah paused again.

There was something odd about his voice. It was much lower ... did he do something to his throat in that fight at school?

Then it hit him: none of this was right. At all.

"Nana," Jonah looked her in the face, "you're ... you're gone."

The instant he said it, the confusion vanished. He was an adult again and felt the pains from all the fighting at the estate. But those pains were fading. Jonah actually felt quite well.

His grandmother didn't seem the slightest bit alarmed by his metamorphosis from boy to man. In fact, she looked quite pleased. "That was wonderful, Jonah. I thought you would catch on quickly, and you did."

Jonah disregarded the praise, staring in disbelief. "*Nana?* Is it really you?"

"Very much me," said Mrs. Rowe. "You've grown into such a wonderful man, Jonah."

Jonah's eyes narrowed. He had encountered a ghost from his past before, and it had turned out to be a Phantasm. But Doreen Rowe shook her head.

"You think that I'm a trick, like that night in Rome." It wasn't a question. "I can understand that. But tell me something, Jonah: would a Deadfallen disciple have known your childhood address? Known to use an incident that had Shane

Mack in it? Would they have bothered to include nuances as simple as having *Guiding Light* on television?"

Jonah's doubts faded on the spot. "My God ... Nana ..."

He wrapped her in the biggest hug, which she returned with a laugh. His last memory of her had been her frail form in that damned white casket, but she was far from that now.

"How are you here?"

"I didn't come to you," she clarified. "You came to me."

That gave Jonah pause. He backed away from her slightly. "Am I dead?" he asked, remembering Creyton's words and the feeling of dissolution.

"Life never ends, Jonah."

Jonah blinked slowly. "You know what I mean, Nana," he said with enough respect to keep the impatience out of his voice.

Doreen looked up at him. "You're right. I do know what you mean. Doesn't change my answer to your question, though."

Jonah merely nodded. He felt that that was about all he could do. "What was that whole thing about me being a kid, and all that?"

"The revisiting of the childhood memory was necessary," Doreen explained. "You were fading, and I had to choose a time before you believed in limits. A time when any problem you might have had could be solved by kind words, grandparent insight, and, of course, gingerbread with vanilla frosting."

"You had to choose—?" Jonah shook his head. "But I thought you said that I came to you, or something."

"You did. I had to make it a simpler process. That's all I can say." She smiled so big. "I have missed you, my boy."

Jonah hung his head, tears falling from his eyes. Nana had always been so kind, so understanding. So helpful. Now, he could tell her. "Nana, I want to tell you—*need* to tell you—that I am so sorry."

"For what?"

Jonah managed to stem the tears. "For failing you."

"Failing me?" Jonah's grandmother frowned. "Jonah, let me show you something."

She walked around the kitchen. Her stride matched Jonah's.

"I'm not sorry that my arthritis is gone." She then took a huge, protracted breath. "I'm not sorry that my respiratory issues are gone. I'm not sorry that the congestive heart failure is gone. I'm not sorry that I don't need a cane, and I don't need glasses. Darling, I'm happy. So happy, and free. It was not your fault. It was my time."

"I wished that it hadn't been," said Jonah. "I've missed you, Nana. I've needed your help so many times—"

"I know." Doreen clutched Jonah's shoulder. "But had I been around, you wouldn't have grown into the man you are now. I was never meant to be in your life forever, Jonah. Not physically, anyway. But I have helped you. Through my words, teachings, and memories you have of me. And recently, I've helped you beyond that."

Jonah looked at her, curious. "How do you mean?"

Doreen smiled. "When you got to Spirit Land, the advice that you saw in your mind. *Tell the truth, volunteer nothing.* That was me."

Jonah's eyes widened.

"When you were on The Plane with No Name and got the idea for the three-tiered protection with Terrence and Reena? Also me."

Jonah chuckled in disbelief. But his grandmother wasn't done.

"When you felt that weight in your pocket before you started fighting, the necklace for Vera ... that was me, too."

Jonah shook his head slowly. "Nana ... how—"

"How is not important. Life and Spirit are interesting things. But I need you to understand that you couldn't have done anything for me when you were eighteen. It was my time. Something that is *not* true for you right now."

Jonah looked at her, as stunned as he was when she revealed she'd helped him.

"Jonah, it was brave of you to want to sacrifice your physical life for your loved ones," she told him. "But that is not what your life was meant for. It is not yours to give; it is yours to *live*."

Jonah looked away. "It's not fair, Nana. Bobby, Ben-Israel, Stella, Bast, all of those people—"

"Did not pass into Spirit because you failed them," interrupted Doreen. "They were fighting for something they believed in, just like yourself. None of it was your fault, Jonah. There are no coffins on your conscience."

That made Jonah raise his head. "You knew about that?"

"I've been with you all this time, Jonah. Haven't I proven that already with your insights from nowhere? The three-pronged ethereality idea? The necklace in your pocket for Vera?"

Jonah could only smile.

"When you went and decided to throw your physical life away, though, my aid couldn't be so subtle. So, when you were dissolving, I saved you. Directed you to this experience. And before you ask,"—Doreen overrode him when he opened his mouth—"I've already said that how it happened is not important. Things that can't be explained happen to all people. Just be thankful that you are one of them. But there is no place on the Other Side for you, son. It's not your time. Simple as that."

Jonah felt so conflicted that it wasn't funny. He had been willing to give up his physical life. But listening to Nana now, he realized that that plan was not a smart one. To call it rash was an insult to rash decisions. "I don't know what to do, Nana."

"Son, there is no concrete list of laws for you to follow," his grandmother told him. "Being the Blue Aura gave you all sorts of powers, but knowing everything isn't one of them."

That was lighthearted, and Jonah managed a laugh. Nana laughed along with him but sobered sooner.

"Jonah, listen to me. I want there to be no doubt in your mind. You are needed. The reasons why you are a great leader are because of your falters, because of your setbacks, because of your perceived mistakes. That is the difference between you and Creyton. You have experimented with life and found ways to be better. You've pruned what wasn't useful and, as a result, improved yourself with each advancement. Creyton thinks that to be powerful means that you must rule over people, snuff out opinions and views that are different. He believes that if you aren't apart of unified thoughts, you are a problem. That was never true, Jonah!

"The people that deserve to be in charge welcome challenges. They aren't put off by different opinions. How do you grow as a person if everyone around you has views that mirror your own? Creyton believes that he has the perfect system, enforcing fear and worry in every facet of people's lives. His disciples are not to be feared. They are to be pitied. Who knows how far they could have gone if they weren't stunted by servitude and intimidation? This is why your friends love and respect you, Jonah. They'd follow you to whatever outcome because you trust them to make their own choices, not force them to agree with you. True leadership has a foundation of cooperation, not domination."

Jonah listened to his grandmother. Her words helped him in ways she couldn't possibly imagine. Or maybe she could.

"You said at my grave that you hadn't made good on the promises you made me because you were coming into your own as a man. Jonah, you are hearing this directly from me: Coming into your own is proof that you *did* keep your promises."

Jonah looked at her, dumbfounded. She nodded.

"All I ever wanted you to do was never believe that you couldn't do, or be, anything you wanted. That ten-year-old boy that was just sitting at my kitchen table believed that his grandmother could fix anything. Wasn't that a great feeling? Believing in possibilities?"

"That little boy is long gone, Nana."

"Not true," countered Doreen. "He still pops up from time to time in you. Why do you think that you've never been able to give up writing? Where do you think your enjoyment for life and laughter stems from? Where do you think that your desire for belonging and unity comes from? Those are the things that make you who you are, Jonah. You didn't spring fully formed from the ground. You had to grow into who you are. But those elements that shaped you from childhood never left you. That boy, *my* boy, simply became a man."

She placed her hands on Jonah's shoulders like she always had when he needed words of reassurance as a kid. Jonah hadn't realized how much he'd missed that until this moment. It was always the little things.

"Jonah, I am so proud of you. Don't you ever believe differently. You are my son. Family titles don't matter—you have always been my son. I always knew that you would be noteworthy in some way. If you were wondering if I knew about The Eleventh Percent, the answer is no. I did not. But I knew that you would be somebody someday. In what way, I didn't know, but that was fine. I was proud of the boy you were, and I am proud of the man you are. I always have been, and I always will be."

Jonah needed to hear that. It was one of the primary things he'd needed since he'd lost Nana. He hugged her tightly. The words were like a balm. No, screw that ... they were validation. Almost like new life. The blade of grief and regret seemed to weaken within him. It would probably never be gone because he didn't think he'd ever get over her passing. But this conversation, this miracle, made it significantly more manageable.

When they parted, Jonah nodded vigorously.

"I'm ready, Nana. I'm going back. Can you show me the way?"

"Yes, son," said Doreen with an approving smile. "I will. Couple more things, though. First, you have been endowed."

Jonah felt like his body had been fortified in iron. He looked at his grandmother with wide eyes.

"An endowment from you, Nana? You're giving me your strength?"

Doreen chuckled. "I'm giving you my support, Jonah. The strength is and always has been yours. Answers always reveal themselves, after all."

She returned to the stove. Jonah couldn't help but smile. There was no time for sadness because the reminder of his best childhood times just had that effect.

"Last thing. Remember when you told me to say hi to Jonathan and Mr. Steverson? Well, they say hi back. They love you and are proud of you, too."

Jonah nodded, feeling a comfort that he couldn't really put into words. "Will I see you again?"

"Someday, yes." Doreen smiled again. "But know that I am always with you, my boy. Life is always, forever, and eternal."

Without warning, she threw something at him. He caught it by reflex.

It was her wooden cane.

"Like I said, answers always reveal themselves. I love you, son."

"I love you too, Nana." Jonah was forced to blink rapidly a few times. "Bye for now."

He closed his eyes as his childhood faded into a swirl of wind and mist.

3 2

A. F. E

Jonah was back on the Astral Plane. He felt invigorated—he surely wasn't dissolving or wasting away now. Seeing Nana again, being relieved of guilt, and receiving a new spiritual endowment ... it had changed something in him.

No. It had changed everything in him.

And that thing that Nana said, "Answers always reveal themselves." She'd said it twice. There was some significance to it. That much he understood.

When it would become relevant was another matter.

He looked down at his grandmother's wooden cane. She hadn't actually specified why she gave it to him, but—

Wait.

He was in spirit form. He needed to return to his physical body. Nana had promised to show him the way. She then threw him the wooden cane and said that the answers always revealed themselves.

The wood was an ethereal thing. It had come from his grandmother, a person who was on the Other Side, yet he'd seen her and spoken to her. The wood was the answer.

One answer, anyway.

It was to function as a twig portal; a spectral piece of wood for a spectral being to return to a physical body.

Now, the question was *how?*

He wished that he could do that video-like thing that Creyton had done to show Earthplane.

The instant he wished that, it happened. A portion of the Astral Plane dissolved once more, and he had a view of the estate once more. He saw his physical body there, still in the same position.

But some things were different.

The Deadfallen disciples, heartless bastards, were all doubled over in laughter and joviality. Some were howling with glee.

At what, exactly?

Some unseen force obliged him. The scene shifted to his friends. Jonah winced, wishing he couldn't see what he now saw.

It was utter despair. Many people were in tears, others were dejected as hell. Terrence had his hands on his face, trembling at intervals. Reena was on her knees, head lowered, with a teary-eyed Tempie attempting to console her. And Liz didn't view him as secondary, it seemed. She was sobbing as hard as she had when Bobby was killed, Nella right along with her.

Then he made the mistake of looking at Vera. The woman was bawling. She hadn't shown that much emotion when her own sister was murdered. Both Patience and Daniel attempted consoling her, but she shoved them away. He even glanced at Spader. He wasn't crying, but he stared at Jonah's body like he couldn't take any further misfortune.

Creyton, Jonah saw, had left his disciples to their levity, and the locked box that contained the Tool of Omega was on the ground near him. Why would he still have that thing if he knew he was victorious?

"It is a rapturous pleasure to see the effect that the inevitable is having on you," he said in a honeyed tone. "At the same time, common sense should have told you fools that this would happen. Jonah Rowe, like his mentor before him, failed at a task that he simply couldn't achieve. He is dead. And if any of you are clinging to some desperate hope that *he* might achieve Praeterletum like me, you needn't worry. It is an impossibility. That fact will be even truer soon."

Creyton snapped his fingers and two of his disciples moved forward, the spring in their steps not unlike children on Christmas morning. They had an assortment of twigs, but they were not to be portals.

They were meant to be kindling.

They placed the twigs around Jonah's body. It was at that point that Jonah looked down at his grandmother's cane again, wondering how to use it as a portal. He wanted to do it as quickly as possible, even though he knew that Creyton would not rush. He was going to milk this for all it was worth. It was to be expected.

Like Jonah had said before, a red-carpet-attention whore.

What Jonah hadn't expected to see was one of his friends break away from the group, stunning everyone who witnessed it, especially Creyton.

It was Doug. His Dockers were irreparable, and his polo was so slashed and ripped that you could see his bare chest. He held his golf club, which still gleamed with the silver of his aura, but he paid it no mind.

"Douglas!" said Katarina, terrified. "Get back here!"

"Dude, have you lost your natural mind?" demanded Terrence.

Douglas ignored them both. Looking woebegone and

solemn, he walked right past an unpleasantly surprised Crey-ton. He was dumbfounded by this defiance and made no attempt to hide it.

Douglas lowered to his knees, crunching some of the twigs underneath him. Deadfallen disciples exclaimed in cold shock. To Jonah's surprise as he watched from the Astral Plane, Douglas placed the knight's chess piece into his lifeless hand.

"I never ever got to tell you how sorry I was that I made you join my stupid chess club, Jonah."

Jonah needed to get this spirit portal to work. Douglas was going to need some help very soon. He knew that when he saw a livid Creyton walk over to him.

"And what exactly do you think you're doing, boy?" he whispered. "Unless it is your heart's desire to burn along with Jonah Rowe's corpse, you need to get back to your little friends over there."

Douglas didn't move. Jonah clutched his grandmother's cane tightly. He needed to sync his spirit back with his physical body. He didn't like the look on Creyton's face.

"I said, get away from him," Creyton repeated. His voice was quiet, but the undercurrent of rage was undeniable.

Douglas still didn't move. Jonah pointed Nana's cane at the scene, willing the portal to succeed and sync him back up, but it needed to happen before Douglas got demolished. He was doing something right; he began to feel an inexplicable pull.

Meanwhile, the scene on Earthplane continued to play out.

"What is wrong with you, boy? Do you wish to die before the rest of your comrades?"

"You're nothing, Creyton," said Douglas softly.

Incredulity rang from both camps. Creyton stared.

"Excuse me?" he whispered with the air of an adult speaking to a defiant child. "What did you say to me?"

Douglas pulled his eyes from Jonah's physical body and

looked up at Creyton. He didn't show one iota of fear. "You could never, ever beat Jonah in a straight-up fight." His voice was loud and clear. "You are supposed to be so almighty, yet you had to dupe Jonah to get the better of him. You are not superior, Creyton. You are a punk-ass bitch."

The entire grounds went quiet. Katarina brought her hands to her mouth, eyes bulging. On the Astral Plane, Jonah was almost distracted from his activity. He would bet everything he had that Douglas had never spoken like that to anyone. He put even more focus on the portal.

"Hurry up!" he pleaded to the cane. "Douglas has grown a set and, if I'm not there to help him, that set's going to get cut off! Hurry up! *Come on!*"

Creyton whacked Douglas hard near his left ear. He toppled near Jonah's physical form, and something strange happened.

Douglas started *laughing.*

Everyone, even a few Deadfallen disciples, looked alarmed. What had gotten into Douglas that prompted him to test Creyton like this?

Jonah noticed that his spiritual form began to blink out. The pull got more and more intense with each passing second. He could almost feel his spiritual and physical selves as one again ... almost ...

Creyton stood over Douglas' laughing form, looking almost irradiated with rage. "What could possibly be funny?"

Douglas hoisted his weight on his arms, still cackling. "I don't agree with my grandmother much. Don't agree with her on anything, actually. But, seeing you get so angry, and then punching me in the head after I called you a punk-ass bitch? It made think of one of Grandma Dine's favorite phrases. The things that make you the maddest are the things that are true. I'm guessing it's true even for you, Creyton!"

With a bestial roar, Creyton raised his staff, aiming squarely at Douglas' face. Katarina screamed in terror. Creyton's fatalistic weapon began its descent, rapidly on its way to claim another physical life—

And Jonah shot up from the prone position and blocked Creyton's strike with both batons, shielding Douglas from harm.

Yeah. He was back.

"You will not hurt Douglas. You will not hurt anybody else, you solipsistic son of a bitch."

He used his batons to swipe away the staff and rose to his feet, then helped Douglas up as well. Douglas looked gleeful as a madman as he rejoined his friends, whose exclamations of joy heavily contrasted with the screams of fear from the Deadfallen disciples. Several of them, including the group of suuvi, tried to flee.

Jonah extended a hand, manipulating the winds, and yanked every single one of them back. Even the ones who'd attempted the *Astralimes* were pulled back. He didn't even have to have eye contact with them to do it. He only had eyes for Creyton.

For a second—just one second—Jonah saw fear in Creyton's eyes. There was no mistaking it.

"You were dead!" he shouted.

"How many times do you have to hear it, Creyton?" Jonah shot back. "Death isn't real."

Creyton shook his head rigorously. "This is not what is supposed to be happening!" he snarled.

"You were never the final say on that, man!"

"I am the ultimate!" roared Creyton.

"That is your eternal problem, right there!" said Jonah. "This has always been about you being the best! You think that you made yourself superior by breaking all the natural rules, blocking the paths to the afterlife, usurping spirits, and killing anyone in your way. You thought that being separate would make you better. *You* are far more deluded than you claimed *I* ever was! Look there!"

He indicated his friends and the plethora of colors that made up their auras.

"Not a single one of them is the same. Even the people who share the same aura colors bring different attributes to the table. But the thing that defines us is not our powers. It's our goal. Different paths, but we're chasing the same star. Beating your ass. Your being separate isn't your strength because the goal is harmony. That's why you hated Jonathan, and it's why you want me gone so badly. Never in a million lifetimes would I compare myself to Jonathan, but I can honestly say that he and I were alike in understanding that harmony far outweighs superiority. You have always been ignorant of that, and guess what? That makes you the vulnerable one, not me."

Jonah's friends looked inspired; all their weariness was gone. The Deadfallen disciples (the ones who weren't terrified anyway) looked enraged.

"Poetic, Rowe. I'm touched," said Creyton. "But are you done?"

"Yeah, actually." Jonah cracked his neck muscles, as he'd done a thousand time before. "The time for talking is past. Time to end this."

Creyton's smile was the most pronounced thing in existence. "Noble. But as you can see Rowe, your people have sustained heavy losses. Even without our Haunts and the Moortuses, you're outnumbered two to one, and that assessment is a generous one."

"I beg to differ," said a deep voice.

Surprised, Jonah turned, along with everyone else.

It was Gabriel Kaine, along with what looked like the entire contingent of Sanctum Arcist. Even that bitch Penelope Pulchrum was there. Michael and Aloisa were there as well.

"I think you need to reconsider that generous assessment," said another familiar yet welcome voice. "And I'm a teacher, so I'm willing to help you with that."

Jonah could have laughed. It was Haniel Rainey, along with Mayce, Josephine, Horace, Maurice, Abner, and a hefty group of citizens of Spirit Land.

"Um," said Spader with a frown, "who are those people?"

"Long story," Jonah heard Terrence say. "They're on our side, that's all that matters."

"You stole from our home, Creyton," said Haniel, her tone cold. "You think we'd let that go?"

Creyton looked angry beyond all reason. Jonah regarded him.

"You were right, Creyton. Miracles are brief. But their effects? Much more long-lasting."

Creyton raised his staff. "Kill them all! Send them to hell!"

Creyton's disciples charged, with the vampires advancing first. Suddenly, what felt like a gale-force wind swept over them all.

A bus, a damn Greyhound bus, barreled through the *Astralimes* and plowed over many of the vampires. Everyone looked at the bus in amazement, but the occupants wasted no time spilling out of it.

They were sazers, a great many of them. They looked as ragged as could be, but they were clearly ready for a fight. The person driving the bus, Prodigal, had kept his promise to Autumn Rose. He'd come back with reinforcements.

"Drop these crazy bastards!" he shrieked to his friends. "I've seen Creyton's plan for us sazers, and it sucks! Fight with Jonah!"

The scene dissolved into chaos after that. The battle recommenced, but the infusion of reinforcements and inspiration from Jonah's continued existence had greatly altered things. The vehicular attack wasn't enough to kill the vampires obviously, but many of Prodigal's sazer friends received some cheap victories by going up to the incapacitated ones and snatching off their hoods or ripping off their cloaks. Their explosions under the morning sun were almost instant.

Haniel turned to Terrence with a question in her eyes. With a shrug Terrence said, "Go ahead!"

She flicked the band on her wrist and suddenly began to barrel through Deadfallen disciples with strength that she was not in possession of seconds prior.

Jonah allowed himself to be so distracted by the upsurge in support that he didn't notice a Deadfallen disciple's hand gesture, which mimicked slamming a door. He found himself on the ground, sprawled and disoriented. It was a serious error to not be watchful. The disciple hurried at him but was whipped across the face by something Jonah didn't see. The disciple spat blood in a wide arc and collapsed. Someone had killed him. Jonah looked around for the source of the assistance and was dumbfounded. Standing there, with a length of chain like a snake around his neck, was Trip.

Jonah noticed that the chain Trip wielded was Grayson's. So, he knew what happened to him and wasn't trying to kill Jonah for it. That was a plus.

Trip extended a hand. Jonah frowned at it. Had hell frozen over?

"Get your ass off the ground, Rowe!"

Jonah grabbed Trip's hand and was on his feet instantly.

"Is Karin alive?" Trip asked.

Jonah didn't answer. All the activity around them, and he was still just surprised to see Titus Rivers III and his cronies, who'd all joined the fight.

"I asked you a question, Rowe. Is Karin still physically alive?"

"Yeah man."

Trip nodded once. "That was a stupid error in judgment. Watch your ass and maybe, just maybe, it won't happen anymore."

Trip stepped on the Deadfallen disciple's corpse and used it to propel himself onto another enemy. Jonah paid no attention as he sensed another attack.

He grabbed the arm before it hit him, and blindly elbowed backward, hearing a satisfying crack. When he turned, he saw that he'd dropped a suuvus, one of the ones who'd tried to flee when he'd realized that Jonah hadn't been killed. Stupid bastard had chosen the wrong team.

After the vampires were handled, Felix and Prodigal led their fellow sazers to the rogue sazers. The sazers in Creyton's employ hadn't expected a cavalry and, consequently were no longer in Red Rage. Abimelech attempted to confront Prodigal, but Prodigal didn't hesitate in snapping his neck. When the other rogue sazers saw that, they were all but putty in the hands of Felix's and Prodigal's forces.

A blade came Jonah's way and he blocked it easily.

"I owe you, Rowe!" the disciple snarled. "You cracked my skull!"

"Cry me a river," retorted Jonah. "My spirit was just detached from my physical body. See me whining?"

The disciple growled and charged. Jonah struck him in the shin with his foot, hit him in the gut with his right baton and, when he doubled over, used his left baton to sweep out his legs from under him.

Mayce mounted the Greyhound and did a quadruple somersault off it, taking down seven disciples when he landed. Haniel, who hadn't yet dispensed with Terrence's strength, had no interest in putting her body through that. She simply blinked and knocked out several enemies as a result. Spader and Douglas tag-teamed Deadfallen disciples left and right. Nella and Themis tossed some type of black liquid on their enemies, which instantly made them violently sick. Jonah didn't know what was in that liquid and didn't want to.

Patience and Reverend Abbott were putting on a clinic, dropping enemies all around them. Amelia and Tempie certainly didn't look like charity cases right now with the way they accounted for themselves. Raymond, Sterling, Terrence, and Alvin did their fallen brother proud, cleaning out pockets of vampires that their sazer friends missed.

The remaining heralds' predatory attacks were something to behold. Even the spirits and spiritesses assisted them. Jonah glimpsed Graham, Samantha Lockman, Ruthie, and his favorite World War II veteran guiding archer's arrows to make impossible shots among the Deadfallen ranks. With great satisfaction, he saw Daniel's specially made arrow go straight Broreamir's throat. The turncoat bastard didn't get the cinematic downfall. It was simply boom and done. After all that he had done, it was almost poetic.

Josephine had a very neat trick and she soon had Magdalena, Maxine, and Mrs. Decessio performing as well; when the Deadfallen disciples cast various Phantasms, the women somehow made the shadow beasts turn and attack their casters. What was left of the suuvi fled for their physical lives from bloody-clawed heralds. Karin and Mr. Decessio leveled a behemoth sazer and—Jonah did a double-take and still couldn't believe his eyes—Vera and Rheadne worked in flawless cohesion, with Vera slowing people to a crawl and Rheadne cutting them down. And Reena and Penelope knocked several disciples on their backs with neat, concerted attacks.

War made for strange bedfellows. Strange ones indeed.

Eventually, though, a glaring fact pulled Jonah's attention from the shifting tide.

Deadfallen disciples were falling all over the place, but there were several that he didn't see.

And where had Creyton gotten off to?

One of those questions was answered almost as soon as he'd wondered about it.

"Looking for us, sugar?" asked a familiar southern belle.

Jonah turned. It was Charlotte Daynard, the murderous debutante. Matt Harrill, who orchestrated the murder of G.J. Kaine. Wyndham O'Shea, the lunatic. The disgraced 49er, wrapped thickly against the sun and the only vampire left. And finally, India Drew, whose star-white hair was a flyaway mess due to the fighting.

Creyton's inner circle. They were completely unscathed. How?

"We avoided the ruckus, sugar," said Charlotte, who for once wasn't sporting her sweet smile. "This is far more important than expending energy on these non-believers."

Wyndham O'Shea brandished the serrated-edged knife. "Rowe, the devil himself wouldn't even want no part of this," he rasped. "How you gonna 'take out' the Transcendent when you won't even be able to get past us?"

"Dropping you fools isn't Jonah's job," said Reena. "It's ours."

Jonah smiled. Another miracle.

The odds were now equal. Reena was the one who had spoken but she was joined by Terrence, Malcolm, Liz, and Trip. Jonah assumed that Trip hated Creyton and his followers more than he hated Jonah himself.

Fair enough.

But Jonah couldn't help but notice something else. These were the original people he'd met at the estate. His first friends, plus Trip. Bobby wasn't there. And on the Deadfallen side, Jessica was missing. With all that had happened, this almost felt full circle.

"Terrence?" Jonah glanced at his brother. "Remember the anger I advised you to save? Well, it's time to spend what you've been saving."

Terrence punched his steel knuckles together. "Obliged."

Jonah stepped aside. Terrence went for Matt Harrill. Malcolm engaged Wyndham O'Shea. Reena rushed Charlotte. While Trip circled India, she raised some razor-sharp twin blades while remaining leery of the chain. The 49er tapped that bonesword of his, which made it malleable ... and then headed straight for Jonah.

Jonah was surprised only for a second. The 49er was a deceitful bastard, after all. He readied his batons when—

"No!"

Jonah felt weight on his back and yelped in surprise.

It was Liz. She had used Jonah as a springboard, leapt at the 49er, and bashed him in the face with Bobby's baseball bat. Jonah heard horrible crunching; when Liz's strike met the vampire's face, it sounded like eggs had cracked. The 49er crashed to the ground, which brought attention to the incident.

Liz had tucked and rolled and was back on her feet in seconds. She looked over the 49er with venom in her eyes.

"You just disregarded me? You just ignored me like I'm no threat? You'll pay for that, I swear to God ..."

Jonah knew that Liz was full of high-octane rage, but the 49er was still a vampire and damn near a foot and a half taller than she was. "Liz, let me—"

"No, Jonah! Stay out of this! I'll kill this lifeblood-sucking bastard myself!"

Spectators had visible doubts about this, too, but it was Spader who walked forward, switchblades at the ready.

"Back off, Lizzie, I'll help Jonah—"

"Royal Cornelius Spader!" Liz roared. "I said no! *You* back off!"

Spader froze. "You ... you know my full name?"

Jonah, who'd gotten the hint by this point, grabbed Spader and pulled him back.

"Don't flatter yourself man. Liz's memory is stellar."

The 49er stood, looking at Liz with equal parts surprise and rage. The grisly damage to his face was already repairing itself, bones only, as the flesh had been rendered irreparable long before. "You little human bitch. I'll cleave your skull in two ... send you in parts to whatever hole they dumped your dead boyfriend into—"

The jade in Liz's eyes looked as though it'd burst into flames. "Mother—"

She didn't finish as she swung the bat, but the 49er dodged it with unearthly grace. He swung the bonesword at her, still in its malleable state. Liz's eyes widened for a moment as she danced out of the way. Jonah didn't know what to think. They'd already lost Bobby, and now Jonah could lose Liz, too. Had he made the right choice in letting her have this fight?

The 49er came at Liz, fangs bared, at which point Liz tossed the bat into the air, distracting the vampire. She capitalized on the distraction by upsetting his cowl, which had the double purpose of obscuring his burned visage and to cover him from the sunlight. The minute he raised his hands to his steaming face, Liz dropped to her knees and stabbed him in the groin with a silver nail.

The 49er dropped to his own knees, nearly gagging from pain. The nail continued to gleam green with Liz's aura, and Jonah understood why. Incomplete spirits were vulnerable to Green Auras. He'd learned that from Reverend Abbott some years back. And the 49er, like all vampires, was in what was called a life limbo, not quite physically alive, and not quite in Spirit. As such, he was an incomplete being.

Suddenly, he wasn't so worried about Liz's chances.

"Elizabeth!" called Felix.

He tossed something at her, and she grabbed it from the air. It was a customized stake, wooden on the outside with ethereal steel at its tip. The 49er could only be vanquished if both his natures were purged simultaneously. He looked at the stake in horror.

Liz flipped the stake in her hand so that the tip was in line with his heart. "Goodbye, *bitch.*"

She staked him. With a terrible cry, the 49er fell facedown, withering to a husk before everyone's eyes.

That elicited shock and awe. Most everyone looked at Liz, astounded. She paid them no mind; she neither gloated nor preened. She had never looked more dangerous the entire time Jonah had known her.

The other fights wound down as well. Terrence, from the sound of it, ended his fight with Matt Harrill when he cracked his sternum with his steel knuckles and then put a cherry on top with a Superman-punch. Malcolm brought his fight with Wyndham O'Shea to an end by countering his insanity with sheer brutality, using his weight as a type of battering ram, laying him out. The resulting crack Jonah heard made it clear that if O'Shea survived that hit, he'd probably never walk again. Charlotte Daynard held her own for a long while with Reena, but then Reena resorted to vintage tactics: speed and cold spots. When she got hold of Charlotte's throat with some type of choke, there wasn't enough dark ethereality in the world to help her. As she faded, Reena snapped her neck and let her drop.

"Servitude to a man." Reena glared at the corpse. "I did you a favor, skank."

The final fight between India and Trip was a grueling affair, but not for too long. Eventually, Jonah heard Trip say, "Fuck this bitch."

Then India dropped her weapons, brought her hands to her ears, and began screaming the shrillest, most dreadful scream conceivable. By the time India fell to the ground, blood flowed from her ears into her white hair. She didn't look lucid or capable of rational thought.

Jonah looked at Trip in confusion. "What the hell did you do?"

Trip spat on India's prone form. "I finished it."

That was all Jonah needed. Creyton's inner circle was finished.

That left the man himself.

He stood some feet away, the anger on his face absolute as a result of his army now being in shambles.

Jonah neared him, batons at the ready. "Just you and me, Creyton. Roll the dice and take your chances."

Creyton's eyes smoldered. He then surprised Jonah by shifting into a crow and taking flight. Without thought, Jonah tore after him.

"Oh, *hell* no!"

Jonah leapt. Where he got the hang time was anyone's guess. But he grabbed hold of the crow's left wing. With an anguished caw, the crow changed trajectory and headed for the estate. Jonah couldn't believe that the damn bird still had the strength of a man. But when he saw the new path Creyton took, all he could do was utter, "*Shield.*"

The air solidified in front of him not a moment too soon. They crashed through a wall into one of the upstairs bathrooms. Jonah slammed into a tub. It instantly knocked the breath from him. Creyton's transformation back to a man was instantaneous, and he sneered at Jonah.

"You thought I was fleeing, did you? My promise is far from fulfilled! And it will be a cold day in hell before I ever flee from you, boy!"

Creyton yanked Jonah to a standing position and struck him with near concussive force, which caused him to slam into the toilet so hard that it cracked and became disjointed from the connecting pipes in the floor below. Despite his thinness and gaunt state, Creyton's strength was still a frightening thing.

Jonah managed to escape the unpleasant, gritty water from getting into his mouth, but it did temporarily blind him. Creyton took advantage of his disorientation by slamming him into a bathroom wall. Jonah, without conscious thought, tucked his chin so that the back of his head wouldn't hit the wall. When Creyton grabbed Jonah's shirt but didn't move back, Jonah realized what this was: Creyton wanted to take advantage of this infernally tight space. It wasn't about efficiency; it was about dirty fighting, plain and simple. Creyton didn't even have his crow-tipped staff; it, like Jonah's batons, was on the ground outside. Creyton's plan was to simply batter him with his bare hands.

Jonah allowed instinct to take over in his body, shrouded his fists with ethereal fog, and tagged Creyton in the gut a few times. The punches put a small amount of space between the two of them. He widened the gap further by kicking Creyton in his chest and then pressed that advantage by grabbing Creyton's head and slamming it downward into his knee. Creyton growled and staggered back, clutching his bleeding nose.

Wait. Creyton was bleeding? The monster himself was surprised by it, too.

Jonah was dumbfounded. He remembered that night when Creyton returned from the grave. He couldn't even touch him that night. What was different now?

Then it came to him. It was the endowment from Nana.

Jonah had a spiritual endowment from a spiritess who had crossed over. He and Creyton were on equal footing.

Nice. Nana still had his back, even on the Other Side. He loved that woman.

Seemingly shaken by the reminder of his vulnerability, Creyton impatiently wiped aside the blood and lunged again. It was clear that he didn't want to lose this enclosed advantage. But Jonah readied himself and charged the both of them out of there, into the door of a room across the hall. He'd be damned if the final fight in this ethereal war would end in a bathroom.

Unsurprisingly, their combined weights splintered the door, but it gave Jonah the window he needed. Placing his weight upon the remains of the barely hinged thing, he turned his head downward and to the left—a tactic to protect his eyes— and muscled Creyton full strength into the wider room. With a jolt, Jonah realized that this had been Bobby's room. The realization was like paint and colored his already riled emotions with a fresh coat of rage. His friend was gone because of *this* bastard, not him ... he understood that now.

He threw a punch at Creyton, but Creyton blocked it with a wall of pure black shadow and struck Jonah in the chest, knocking him back. Jonah shook that off with relative ease, but the next part wasn't so simple.

His lungs constricted. He couldn't breathe.

When he doubled over, Creyton smirked. "See what happens when you think, boy? It's my understanding that you were warned in the past not to think so hard—"

In a desperate maneuver, Jonah grabbed Bobby's weight belt and lashed out. The buckle slapped Creyton in the neck, distracting him. Just like that, Jonah could breathe once more, but he lost his balance on the rug and fell to the floor in a heap.

Creyton raised his hand to do the lung constriction once more, and Jonah punted him in the knee—an unabashed cheap shot—which caused something to pop. Creyton roared, and Jonah jumped to his feet. If Creyton performed the move again, Jonah might not be so lucky.

He extended his right hand to the lightbulb but focused beyond that. It wasn't the bulb he needed, after all, but the wires were another matter.

Jonah yanked a sufficient amount of current from the wires —it wouldn't take much—and flung it at Creyton's face.

Creyton immediately abandoned his attempts to restrict Jonah's oxygen. His hands shot up to his face, muffling his exclamation. Jonah went on the offensive with a flurry of endowment-powered rights, lefts, and kicks. Creyton slammed him in the gut with his knee, but Jonah ignored the pain as best he could as he pressed a forearm across Creyton's jaw and staggered him back. Blood trickled from a cut on Creyton's forehead, and an electrical burn had seared the left side of his face. Jonah moved slightly to his left, a reckless idea in his mind ... a dangerous idea in his mind ...

This whole fight started with crashing into the estate. It would only be fitting to give Creyton his receipt.

Jonah ran at Creyton full speed. Mere inches away, he lowered his head, clamped the dark Eleventh at his midsection, and they slammed through Bobby's window. It was a rushed haze and Jonah heard the cries of surprise from the people still outside, but he paid no attention. He didn't bother with shielding or cushioning either.

Creyton would break their fall just fine.

The force of their landing was jarring as hell. The wind got knocked out of Jonah once again. Though he'd expected it this time around, it hampered him nonetheless. He rolled away slowly from Creyton and attempted to clear cobwebs. Creyton was dazed himself—he was trying to get back to center too.

Jonah was glad to be in one piece and pleased that he'd managed to get the upper hand.

High risk, high reward indeed.

Creyton looked at some point past Jonah's head and froze, seemingly stunned. It was almost as if he'd forgotten that he'd just been thrown out of a window. Jonah looked around. His eyes bulged.

Some feet away, Charis Rayburn's box was open.

The Tool of Omega jutted from within, visible for everyone to see.

Jonah was confused but then again remembered his grandmother's words. *Answers always reveal themselves.*

Charis Rayburn had not taken the lock combination into Spirit with her. There had never been a lock combination. It couldn't be opened by jimmying the lock.

It was opened by Omega.

More specifically, the *end* of Omega.

The weapon was available when Omega neared its end—to put a stamp on the matter, so to speak.

Jonah didn't know if Charis Rayburn had had the foresight to know that a Dark Blue Aura would enact the ethereal endgame. But, in the grand scheme of things, it didn't really matter.

What mattered was what happened next.

Unencumbered, into Jonah's mind came Mayce's words. "What do you think this is, Thor? Worthiness, good and evil, they don't play a part in it. I'm pretty sure that the first Blue Aura who touches it wins."

Jonah had filed that away. At the time, it seemed a million years off. Now it was back.

He pulled himself to his feet and was instantly overtaken by Creyton, who clamped a vicelike grip on his throat. Jonah jostled his grip, and the chokehold became a wrestling struggle.

"Not while I breathe, boy!" snarled Creyton. "It is mine! You are dead!"

"Life is always, forever, and eternal, Creyton! Besides, I thought you didn't need it!"

Creyton didn't respond. Once he got one of his hands back to Jonah's throat, he extended the other hand, and willed the winds to do his dirty work. The Tool began to move, to align with Creyton's pull, and zipped his way. It would reach his hand any second.

In a rage, Jonah broke Creyton's grip—and damn if Creyton didn't play dirty and constrict his oxygen again.

Mentally cursing, Jonah clutched his throat. This could not be happening *now*!

Creyton snatched the Tool of Omega from the air. He'd gotten to it first.

He looked at Jonah, who still clutched his neck, and smiled.

"*Per mortem, vitam,*" he whispered.

Creyton drew back and slashed. Terrence, Reena, and Haniel screamed.

But in Jonah's mind, agonized though it was due to the constriction of his lungs, one word appeared.

No.

When Creyton's slash reached Jonah, something crazy happened.

Jonah's body took non-corporeal form, like true spirit. Creyton swung the Tool right through him, hitting nothing. Creyton's eyes widened in shock. Jonah's body reverted to its natural form, and he took advantage of Creyton's unbalanced stance. While Creyton's equilibrium was still off from the failed attack, Jonah disarmed him, flipped the Tool in his grasp, and stabbed the Dark Blue Aura directly in the heart, shoving the ethereal weapon to its hilt.

"Always, forever, and eternal," whispered Jonah.

Creyton stumbled back, dumbstruck at what had occurred. He fell to his knees and lost all interest in Jonah, undoubtedly caught up in his own diminishing thoughts. Then his eyes rolled backward, and he collapsed on the ground. His already pale skin faded, followed by muscles and sinew, which was followed by the liquefying of internal organs. The effect that had rejoined Creyton's form when he achieved Praeterletum was now unraveled, going in the opposite direction.

Very soon, all that was left were the bones that had once been Tony Noble's. The Tool of Omega then faded, its purpose served. In what had to be the most poetic irony ever, Roger Thaine Cyril Creyton was himself the first and only true death in history. Jonah stood over his remains, the victorious Light Blue Aura.

Within a nanosecond, the stunned silence was replaced by deafening screams of euphoria. Jonah raised his hand a few seconds before he got swarmed. He allowed it to happen, but the truth was he hadn't raised his hand in victory.

It was in honor of everyone who had sacrificed themselves in contribution to this moment. Jonathan, Mr. Steverson, Barisford Charles, Elijah Norris, Bast, Bobby, Ben-Israel, Stella Marie, Barry, Grayson, the forty-eight people that lay side-by-side in the Glade, the fallen citizens of Spirit Land, the exiled people forced through the Gates ... all of them. He prayed that their celestial journeys were blessed ones. They would be in his heart forever, and he'd have love and gratitude for every single one of them for the rest of his days.

His consciousness was pulled back by the cheerful noises. Sazers laughed with Elevenths. Heralds returned to their original forms and playfully pounced people. Douglas was on Malcolm's and Raymond's shoulders, with Katarina, Themis, and Magdalena jokingly screeching: "Oh Douglas, you're so fine, you're so fine you blow my mind, *hey Douglas!*"

Trip's cronies were interacting awkwardly with people around them. Those interactions seemed far from warm, but whatever. The spirits and spiritesses chatted happily with people all around them. People's spiritual endowments left them, but there was no fatigue to be had anywhere. The elation was real and present as ever. Jonah felt his own spiritual endowment leave him; all he could do was smile and ignore the tears stinging his eyes.

"Thanks, Nana," was all he said.

He turned and by pure accident locked eyes with Trip. They looked at each other for a few seconds, and Jonah nodded. Trip nodded back, then returned to Karin, Ian, and Markus. Jonah understood it perfectly.

There would be no Hollywood-style cliché friendship after all the enmity. There could be no reconciliation, as they'd not been friends in the first place. But the respect was there. Finally. It had been earned through fire on both sides. That was that.

Jonah saw Felix conversing animatedly, not looking as haunted. Nice. Not too far away, he saw Liz, Akshara, Nella, and others helping the injured. Spader awkwardly approached them, not backing off this time. Liz caught his sheepish demeanor and with heavy impatience, asked, "What do you want, man?"

Spader dispensed with his ripped flannel and straightened. "I'm here to help. Need another pair of hands?"

Liz contemplated him for a second. "Yeah. Come on."

Jonah grinned at that. Seconds later, Benjamin and Prodigal came running down the drive, looking giddy.

"Whatever Creyton did in town is over!" they screamed for all of them to hear. "Everyone is awake again! They don't have a clue what happened!"

There were cheers, with Jonah cheering the loudest. More lives freed of Creyton's nightmarish reign.

Reena was on her phone, and it was clear by her expression who was on the other end. Terrence was in conversation with Mayce and Haniel. Jonah would reach the both of them in a second. There were a couple of things he had to do first.

He sought out Vera, who seemed to have tired of all the socializing and needed a few moments to collect her own thoughts. Jonah could relate. Steeling himself, he approached her. She smiled when she saw him.

"Congratulations, Mr. Rowe," she said. "You went and saved us all."

Jonah snorted. "Thank you, Miss Haliday."

Vera shook her head. "It's Hale. Vera Hale."

Jonah nodded and took a deep breath.

"Vera, I love you."

Vera's eyebrows knitted ever so slightly.

Jonah had already started, so he continued. "I do. I think it's been that way for a while now. I'm ... I'm tired of beating around the bush and playing these games. You said once that we had been 'more than friends, but less than lovers' for a while. I want to change that. I don't want to be away from you anymore."

Vera still said nothing. Her silence might as well have been blaring. Jonah took the opportunity to get out another concern that he had.

"I know that you can choose some stage actor, or whatever. You would probably be a lot happier with someone else—"

"There is no one else."

Vera's interruption took Jonah by surprise. "What?"

"You heard me, Jonah."

"How long has that been the case?"

"Since ... since forever, Jonah," answered Vera. "I'm not even joking."

Jonah frowned. "Then what the hell was your deal with East?"

Vera sighed. "That was me trying to convince myself that I was the master of my own fate. That I was in control. You know I didn't have a lot of control over anything when I was younger, so I became a bit obsessive about it. I won't lie. Me being a bitch and being so difficult? It was because you were the one thing I couldn't stamp down. The one thing that I couldn't control. And I fought it hard, but that was a mistake. I was afraid to lose control, and my fear just made me come across as a stupid, shallow asshole."

She sighed again. "When we don't listen to what's inside us —what we know to be true—we've lost ourselves. Being with East was one of those lost times for me. From the bottom of my heart, Jonah, I apologize for my behaviors in the past. I hope you can forgive me because I love you too. I have always loved you."

Those words were about the most wonderful ones Jonah had ever heard. And the beautiful thing about him and Vera? They had been through too much shit together to have to deal with the gushy preliminaries of it all. Words couldn't describe what a relief that was. "If I could forgive your sister after all the wrongs she did, I can forgive you too," he said. "But there is one thing we can do here and now that requires zero discussion."

He kissed her right then and there. Vera responded with more fervor than he expected from an exhausted person, but it was welcome just the same. When they parted, Vera gave him a sinful look.

"There is one other thing we can do that won't require much of a wait time," she told Jonah. "Meet me tonight, when it's quieter around here."

Jonah looked at Vera. "With everything going on? A war just ended—"

"Shit's always going on in the world, Jonah," Vera reminded him. "Besides, the end of war is cause for celebration, wouldn't you say?"

"No arguments there." Jonah snorted once more. "See you later tonight, baby."

"Damn straight you will."

They kissed again, joined hands for a second, and then Jonah walked away.

One thing down.

He looked here and there, and then found who he sought.

Daniel sat alone. The former Protector Guide looked aimless. Wistful. He had embraced life as an ethereal human to aid Jonathan and deal with Broreamir. He'd fulfilled both of those purposes and was now a man in need of a new one. Jonah approached him, adopting a slightly pleading look. "Way with words," he reminded himself.

"Daniel, I'm Overseer of the Grannison-Morris Estate, as you're aware. I'm grateful that Jonathan passed it to me, and I mean that from the bottom of my heart. That said, I do not feel that I am sufficiently equipped to fulfill the role as efficiently as is necessary. But I do know someone who is better suited."

He removed the Vitasphera from his pocket, and both he and Daniel were temporarily dazzled by it. It was restored to its beautiful amber state. The golden infinity symbol was once again visible for all to see. Daniel pulled his eyes away from the sight and gave Jonah a curious gaze.

"Why would you abdicate such an honor, Jonah?" he inquired. "You were, after all, Jonathan's handpicked successor. And, while you were shaky at first, you've evolved into a real leader."

That was high praise from Daniel, but Jonah merely

adopted a respectful expression. "Jonathan did indeed choose me, and I'm honored by that. But I cannot live my life in Jonathan's role. No disrespect to Jonathan at all, but I have to be the man I want to be. Thank you for saying that I have evolved into a real leader, because that means that you will respect it when I say that a true leader understands when someone else is better equipped for a role."

He extended the Vitasphera.

"Become the Overseer of the estate, Daniel. Restore it to glory; shepherd in a new era. Consider it a new life's purpose since you've fulfilled the other ones."

Daniel took the Vitasphera. The listlessness began to fade from his eyes as he did so. "I would be honored, Jonah. I will take Jonathan's teaching methods and incorporate my own. Each day will be a challenge and a blessing."

Jonah smiled. That was a huge weight off him, for sure! "What will you do first?"

"Not all of Creyton's miscreants were killed. They need to be detained, and The Plane with No Name is in shambles. I will personally oversee its reconstruction."

Jonah frowned. "That's great and everything, but on whose authority will these things be done?"

Daniel's face warmed to an almost smile. "The new Phasmastis Curaie, of course. Graham, the former Very Elect Spirit, is heading it. Your friends among the spirits and spiritesses will aid him in rounding out the new Thirteen. So far, it is himself, Ruthie Carey, Samantha Lockman, and Richard Stemple."

"Who?" asked Jonah.

"That is the name of your World War II veteran spirit friend," Daniel revealed. "I also thought you would be pleased to know that Patience will be replacing Evelyn Tribby as head of the Networkers, effective immediately."

"Wait, hold up." Jonah stepped back, head spinning. "All of this has already happened? So fast?"

"Spiritual beings don't have to have snail-pace deliberations the way physically living beings do, Jonah," Daniel reminded him. "Time doesn't exist where they are."

"Gotcha." Jonah nodded, awestruck. "Well, Daniel, you get to handling things. I look forward to seeing what you do from here on out."

"And I you, Jonah," said Daniel. "Again, excellent job, boy."

And then Daniel shocked him. He actually smiled.

Jonah had to get away. He couldn't take too many more miracles, or he'd explode.

Finally, he made it back to Terrence and Reena. The older brother and sister he never had but had now. He wrapped them both in the tightest group hug conceivable, like the family that they were. Together, they left the celebrations and found refuge on the Greyhound bus, which had been moved nearer to the three cars that remained of Spader's Iron Semicircle. Jonah sprawled across two seats, Terrence seated himself, and Reena got on her knees on another seat.

"Felix is making arrangements for Kendall to come back from Tullamore," she said excitedly. "I have half a mind to take her to the mountains and hide out for about two months."

Terrence and Jonah laughed. Reena didn't.

"You think I'm playing?"

"Nope," said Terrence. "That's the funny part. And check this out: I asked Haniel what made her change her mind about coming to help us. She looked me right in the eye and said, 'When I realized I didn't want anything to happen to you'. How 'bout them apples!"

Jonah could tell them about the changes in the Curaie. He could tell them about Patience's promotion. He could tell them about how he had passed the role of Overseer of the Estate to

Daniel. He could even tell them that he and Vera were finally a couple. All the wonderful things.

But there was only one thing in his mind salient enough to share first.

"I saw Nana again."

Terrence and Reena stared. He recounted the entire story, from the childhood memory setup to the wooden cane functioning as a portal. Reena laughed in amazement. Terrence shook his head and said, "Wow."

Reena regarded Jonah with interest. "So, what are you going to do now?"

"Great question," said Terrence. "What's next for the Blue Aura? The *only* Blue Aura?"

Jonah laid his head on the bus seat. "I don't know. For once, I can say that I don't know what the future holds and be just fine with it. So, I have no idea. But I am very interested in finding out."

SEVERAL NOVELS, SEVERAL PAINTINGS, AND MANY MEALS LATER

Ω

Jonah was stationary, with his eyes on the Grannison-Morris Estate. The place was as grand and majestic as always. It never got old. With all the places he'd been around the world, the estate always took precedence. He could never understand why this beautiful place, tucked away from everything in this little North Carolina town, was the most important place on the entire earth to him.

"You act like we weren't just here six months ago," said Vera, who rolled her eyes. "And yet, you still have that wonder about you, like you've never seen it before."

"Guilty," replied Jonah. "Place just doesn't get tired. As for my sense of wonder, I get to be like that. Writer, after all. It isn't like you would have it any other way."

Vera chuckled. "You got me there. I'm just messing with you. It never gets old to me, either."

"Besides, we have the privilege of just standing idly by. One of the perks of getting places early all the time."

He glanced at Vera, who meekly raised her hands.

"Time Item. It's what you love about me."

With a grin, Jonah placed a hand on her thigh. "It's *one* of the things I love about you."

He kissed her. She wrapped her arms around his neck and responded in kind. When they parted, she took a slow breath.

"Damn it, Jonah." She gritted her teeth. "You can't kiss me like that knowing that we can't do anything about it!"

"Sorry, darling." Jonah gave her a devilish grin, and reveled in the sight of her swallowing, attempting to stamp down her arousal. "You're going to have to wait. Now is not the time to be the goddess of sex. It's time to put on the smiles."

Vera seemed to compose herself, but still narrowed her eyes at him. "I'm going to punish you later. Just so you know."

"Look forward to it," said Jonah. "Now, it's Showtime."

Jonah didn't say it a second too soon.

A car pulled up right behind theirs. They knew who it was.

"What's up, people?" said Terrence jovially as Haniel got out of the passenger side, followed by Baxter, their black lab. The dog bounced excitedly around Jonah and Vera while Haniel freed Starbright, their Abyssinian cat, from her traveling crate. "You two were always going to be here first, but that's alright. I'm not ashamed of being a close second!"

Vera grinned as she hugged Haniel, and Jonah did the same before the two women walked further along the grounds with the pets. Jonah and Terrence began to walk to the estate.

"It really was nice of Daniel to set up that spot for the animals," said Terrence.

"He had to," snorted Jonah. "How else was he going to keep unwanted company away from the Glade when everyone visited?"

"Vera can do her time tricks, like always," said Terrence. "I love it when she acts like being around Baxter and Starbright is a hassle."

"She enjoys it more than she lets on," conceded Jonah. "But I know for a fact she loves doing those tricks. Being everybody's favorite aunt and uncle has its benefits."

"I'm sure," said Terrence, laughing to himself. "But you two ought to get a dog of your own. Grab a nice pit bull buddy for Bastie."

"You know Bastie is the most territorial cat on Earthplane," said Jonah with the same grin he always had when the subject was breached. "Plus, she is so low-maintenance. She's the perfect pet for the cool author who writes in the loft and the awesome actress who is on Broadway."

"Hey, now," said Terrence with mock offense, "the guy who's also a chef has its cool points, too!"

Jonah laughed. "I will take your word for it, big brother!"

They shared a laugh before Reena walked out of the front door. Her eyes gleamed when she saw them.

"Hey, Jonah! Terrence!" she said as she wrapped them both in a hug. "So great to see you! How are the fur babies, Terrence?"

"Fine," Terrence said. "They're running around with Vera and Haniel."

"I'll see them in a few, then," said Reena, turning to Jonah. "And how are *your* babies, Jonah?"

"Bastie is precious as ever, claws and all. As for my other babies, two books are still on the *New York Times* bestseller list. My newest project is within thirty, forty pages of being done. How are the new works of art going?"

"Phenomenally," answered Reena. "The Known Gallery in L.A. actually wants to put some of my pieces there!"

"Wow, really? That's awesome news! Is that why you asked us all to convene here?"

Reena shook her head. "That was one reason. But not the only reason."

"Seriously?" said Terrence. "Of all the art galleries your stuff is in, that particular art gallery must be a huge deal. It's got to be, because you're amenable to them putting up your work without your usual amount of due diligence. And when you called us, you made it sound mightily important."

"The Known Gallery *is* mightily important," Reena replied, "but this is just as important, if not more so. I had to call all you guys, and it had to be now. This is the only time Daniel managed to get all the residents out of the estate for me. But hang on ..."

The air picked up and Malcolm stepped out of thin air, followed closely by Liz.

"Malcolm! Hey!" Reena hugged him. "How is Franchesca?"

"Fine, just fine," said Malcolm. "You know I can't argue about a wife who is nearly my equal in carpentry."

"Or a tad bit better," murmured Jonah to Terrence, who snorted.

"So good to see you all!" Liz flashed her dazzling grin at everyone and gave hugs all around. She reached for Jonah, who regarded her with the same consideration he always had for his little sister.

"Hey, Lizzie! How is Spader?"

Liz chortled. "Always on his Ps and Qs."

Jonah eyed her shrewdly. "Always?"

"Of course!" scoffed Liz. "You know I wouldn't have it any other way."

Jonah raised an eyebrow. Liz blushed.

"Okay, mostly," she conceded. "But he handles his business, so I make allowances here and there."

Everyone laughed. Jonah wrapped Liz around the arms.

"I got to say, I'm proud of old Spader. From working in the MGM Grand to actually running his own casino and hotel on the North End of the Strip. Even with his acumen, that had to be hard."

Liz grinned. "Nothing's hard for my Spader. He's always ambitious nowadays. And speaking of ambition ... *bam.*"

She lifted her hand and revealed a gorgeous ring. This elicited more exuberant remarks, but Jonah smiled in contemplative silence. He was happy that Liz finally got to have an engagement ring on her finger. It was a blessing to see, and if anyone deserved it, it was Liz.

Terrence hadn't noticed Jonah's solemn expression and simply beamed.

"Man! You and Spader are gonna get hitched. Let's not forget that Doug and Katarina are expecting their second, and Felix is off vampire hunting to his heart's delight—what is this, his third European vampire-hunt trek?"

"Fourth," Jonah chimed in.

"Right," said Terrence without skipping a beat. "Seems like our family is where it's at!"

Reena nodded. "True, Terrence. A lot of awesomeness. A lot of new beginnings. Which brings us to why I called all you guys here. Follow me."

Reena led them through the family room and kitchen, down the basement steps, and to the area that was formerly her studio. It had been some years since Reena had had paintings down here. Some younger Elevenths had drums down in that space now, but that was fine. Her paintings didn't have to be in this basement anymore. Not when they were across the globe.

Reena stood in front of Malcolm, Liz, Terrence, and Jonah.

"I know that all of us, and I'm including the ones of our family that aren't here right now, have moved on to bigger and better things. I love all of our family. But when I think about my core? My tightest bonds? My mind always goes back to one group. No matter what, it's always one group."

Jonah was interested to see where Reena was headed. When she called them, she made it sound like a dire need. He found himself hanging on to every word.

"I'm an artist to the core, as you all know. I prefer my art speak for me. Therefore, I started something. About seven years ago. It's taken that long for obvious reasons, but I've been steadily working on it. No matter where Kendall and I are in the world, even when we're home, I've used the *Astralimes* to sneak down here and work on it, only for an hour or two. I am a very busy woman, after all."

They all laughed.

"I called you guys to share this with you. It was important to me that you all were the first to put eyes on it."

She walked to the far wall, and splayed her fingers, which gleamed yellow. She then pressed them against the wall, which gleamed in its entirety, dazzling their eyes. Then Reena's aura dimmed and faded away, revealing her goal.

Everyone's jaws dropped.

It was a painting, but unlike anything Reena had ever done before. It showed the six people that were at the estate when Jonah showed up there for the first time. There was Liz, her girlish smile bright enough to light up a room. Malcolm, stoic and studious, but one of the most loyal friends you'd ever meet. Terrence, holding a greasy bag of fill-in-the-blank breakfast. Reena herself, paintbrush in one hand and a celery stick in the other. Even Trip was there, with his usual inscrutable expression, headphones around his neck.

But the centerpiece, clutching an unwritten novel and blue batons, was Jonah.

He walked to the painting, open-mouthed. It was like

looking at his younger self from a window that revealed another time. But to be at the center?

"Really, Reena?" he said quietly.

Reena nodded. "You were the one who'd brought us together, Jonah. We were here and already friends, sure. But *your* arrival was what bonded us. Glued us."

"She's right man," Terrence told him. "She ain't ever lied."

"And I've always called you the biggest blessing, Jonah," Liz grinned. "You made everything come together perfectly, whether you own up to it or not."

"There you go, Jonah, no disputing it," Reena told him with a snicker. "And I think they would agree, too."

Reena pointed upward, and Jonah lifted his gaze to the top of the painting. Atop a beautiful collection of clouds stood Jonathan, Bobby, and golden Bast. They looked to be smiling down.

Liz wiped her eyes but smiled. Terrence looked on respectfully, as did Malcolm. Reena had a hand on Jonah's shoulder. He turned around and took her hand, as well as Liz's. Terrence took Reena's other hand, and Malcolm finished the link with Liz's hand that Jonah hadn't grasped.

"Next to my wife," Jonah said, his voice cracking somewhat, "you guys are the greatest family anyone could have. I mean that."

And it was sincere. It was also in that moment that he realized why this estate would always be special. When Doreen passed into Spirit, Jonah was alone. He had no one. Nothing. The Grannison-Morris estate gave him a new family. The Eleventh Percent had given him new self-worth and a purpose. Hell, by extension, this estate and the Eleventh Percent had even led him to his wife Vera, who had joined him in an amazing life with just the two of them. Although they'd all moved on, branched out, and had separate lives of their own, this estate was what brought them all together as family.

In other words, it gave Jonah a new life.

And with everything that had happened past and present, and whatever might come along in the future, Jonah could truly say, beyond a shadow of a doubt, that he loved his life.

ABOUT THE AUTHOR

 T.H. Morris is an unabashed bibliophile who has been as such his entire life. From an early age, he ate up works from all genres, ranging from Greek and Norse mythology to suspense and paranormal. At times, it was nothing strange for him to read every day, all day.

He was born and raised in North Carolina, and now resides in Denver, Colorado. He has a background in social work and inventory. When he is not writing, he can be found in the gym, hanging with his wife, sitting in a corner with his Kindle in hand, looking up the next tattoo he wants, or exploring the beautiful city of Denver.

* * *

To learn more about T.H. Morris and discover more Next Chapter authors, visit our website at www.nextchapter.pub.

Omega
ISBN: 978-4-82415-407-1

Published by
Next Chapter
2-5-6 SANNO
SANNO BRIDGE
143-0023 Ota-Ku, Tokyo
+818035793528

18th October 2022

CPSIA information can be obtained
at www.ICGtesting.com
Printed in the USA
LVHW110439201122
733290LV00003B/145